Riot Act

Also by Zoë Sharp

Killer Instinct

Riot Act

Zoë Sharp

PIATKUS

⌘ **Visit the Piatkus website!** ⌘

Piatkus publishes a wide range of exciting fiction and non-fiction, including books on health, mind, body & spirit, sex, self-help, cookery, biography and the paranormal. If you want to:

- read descriptions of our popular titles
- buy our books over the Internet
- take advantage of our special offers
- enter our monthly competition
- learn more about your favourite Piatkus authors

visit our website at:

www.piatkus.co.uk

Copyright © 2002 by Zoë Sharp

First published in Great Britain in 2002 by
Judy Piatkus (Publishers) Ltd of
5 Windmill Street, London W1P 1HF
e-mail: info@piatkus.co.uk

The moral right of the author has been asserted

A catalogue record for this book is available from the British Library

ISBN 0 7499 0607 3

Set in Bembo by
Phoenix Photosetting, Chatham, Kent

Printed and bound in Great Britain by
Mackays of Chatham plc, Chatham, Kent

Acknowledgements

First of all, there are people to thank who patiently provided technical information, particularly Ian Cottam and Lee Watkin for their self-defence expertise; Glynn Jones for his in-depth practical knowledge of body armour and ballistics; all the staff at the DFW Gun Club & Training Center in Dallas, Texas for letting me brush up my handgun skills; John Robinson at Safety Services Agency in Northern Ireland; Dr Andrew Parkes MB, BS, for invaluable inside information on gunshot wounds; Jonathan Lodge and Tim Winfield for the low-down on shotguns; former magistrate Sue Pickles; and Peter Gilmore, for introducing me to the right people. I take full credit for any errors.

Once again, many people were kind enough to offer their opinions during the early stages, including everyone at the Lune Valley Writers' Group. My grateful thanks for particularly critical reading go to Peter Doleman, Claire Duplock, Sarah Harrison, Clive Hopwood, Glynn Jones, Iris Rogers, and Tim Winfield.

The biggest thank yous of all belong to my husband, Andy, who has suffered with me through every twist and turn; to my editor Gillian Green; my publisher Judy Piatkus; and my copy editor Sarah Abel, who also did such sterling work on the first Charlie Fox book, *Killer Instinct*.

As always, my most heartfelt gratitude goes to Steve Calcutt and Maggie Heavey at the Anubis Literary Agency, for patience, faith, and dedication.

For Andy, who encouraged me to write in the first place.
See, this is all your fault...

One

Phone calls that come out of nowhere, in the middle of the night, rarely herald good news as far as I'm concerned. This one arrived somewhere between midnight and one am. It yanked me forcibly out of the warm leisures of sleep, and proved no exception to the rule.

Right from the outset, in that fraction between dreaming and waking, I was overwhelmed by an instinctive dread.

By the second ring, I'd jerked upright in bed, fumbling for the bedside light and swinging my legs out from under the blankets before I'd really kicked my brain into gear.

It took a moment or two to work out that I wasn't safe in my own bed. Instead, I recognised a small, oppressively-wall-papered room, made smaller still by the pair of dark oak wardrobes that loomed over me from both sides.

Pauline's place.

I'd been house-sitting for Pauline Jamieson for three weeks at that point. Ever since she'd flown to Canada to visit her son. Waking up in her bed still brought a feeling of disorientation.

The phone noise ran on, shrill and imperious. I groped for the receiver and tried to rub the grittiness out of my eyes.

'Yeah, hello?' It was a relief to stop the damned phone ringing at last, but that feeling didn't hold.

'Oh, Charlie, please come quickly, and bring the dog!' A woman's voice, scratchy with alarm and close to weeping. 'They are in the garden and Fariman has gone out after them. I am afraid they will kill him!'

The last vestiges of sleep evaporated. 'Shahida?' I said, suddenly recognising one of Pauline's neighbours. One of *my* neighbours for the moment. 'Calm down. Now tell me who? Who has Fariman gone after in the garden?'

'The thieves!' she cried, as though it was obvious, the pitch of her voice rising like a banshee spirit. 'They are trying to steal his equipment. Please, come now.'

I started to ask if she'd called the police, but the phone was already dead in my hand.

With a muttered curse, I dialled the local cop shop myself, giving them the bare bones and demanding that they come at once. While I was speaking, I clambered into my clothes. By the time I hit the narrow staircase I was dressed and fully alert.

Well, almost alert. In the darkened hallway I nearly went sprawling over Pauline's Rhodesian Ridgeback, Friday. The dog had been sleeping with his back against the bottom riser, and he bounced up with a startled yelp.

I grabbed his lead from the hall table and snapped it onto the thick leather collar. Just for a second I hesitated over the wisdom of taking him with me, then dismissed my doubts. He might be a handful, but there were times when a big dog like Friday comes in very useful.

Now, he barely gave me time to lock the front door before he was towing me along the short driveway to the road. Fariman and Shahida's house was on the other side of Kirby Street from Pauline's, and further down the row of mainly dilapidated semis. I headed quickly in that direction.

I'd only met the elderly couple a few times, but I knew Fariman had been a cabinetmaker. Since he'd retired recently he'd kitted out the shed in his back garden with enough tools to keep his hand in. Trouble was, he'd turned it into your average burglar's car boot sale gold mine. By the sound of it, it hadn't taken them long to cotton on to the fact.

I was surprised now to see one or two other figures emerging from doorways, pulling on coats over their pyjamas. Some carried torches.

It startled me, the reaction. Lavender Gardens was a notoriously crime-ridden estate and I would have expected a far more apathetic response to any cry for help. Maybe there was hope for the area after all.

My sense of complacency lasted until I reached the far crumbling kerb and we threaded our way through the line of close-packed empty vehicles.

Friday lurched to a halt so abruptly that I ran into his rump and nearly stumbled. It only took a second before I realised the reason for his sudden check. For me to register a bulky figure rising behind a parked van.

Shock made me gasp, sent me reeling backwards. Fear convulsed my hands, so that I tightened my grip on Friday's lead.

A harsh laugh greeted my recoil, as though that was the effect its owner always hoped his appearance would have, and had yet to be disappointed. 'A tad late to be walking the dog, isn't it, Fox?'

The man swaggered forwards into the glow of a streetlight, sending a spent cigarette butt sizzling carelessly into the gloom. Three other shadows solidified behind him, keeping station. All of them were dressed in military surplus urban cam fatigues, and carrying an assortment of makeshift weaponry that would have been laughable if it hadn't been so deadly serious.

Friday settled for giving out a low growl. It was difficult to tell if his hackles were up, because Ridgebacks have a line of opposite-growing hair down their spines anyway, but the sight and sound of him was enough to stop the men in their tracks.

I unwound slowly, trying to steady my heartbeat. 'What are you doing here, Langford?' I asked sharply. 'Bit outside your territory, isn't it?'

With one eye on the dog, he treated me to a humourless smile, glancing round at the men behind him for back-up. 'We go where we're needed,' he said piously.

'Well, you're not needed here.'

'No?'

'No,' I snapped. 'These people have got enough problems with law and order without your bunch of bloody vigilantes joining in. Get back to Copthorne. There's plenty for you to do over there.'

'Oh, don't you worry,' he said, voice sly, 'we've got Copthorne all sewn up.'

'Well, that'll be a first,' I threw back at him, starting forwards again. The one nearest to Friday moved back quickly, but the other two made sure I had to shift course to step round them. The cheap little power play brought grins to their faces.

Langford, self-styled leader of the local vigilante group, shared the same basic mental genotype with playground bullies and third world secret policemen. I'd recognised it the first time I'd met him and his cronies, and I'd gone out of my way to avoid contact ever since.

Commotion broke out further up the street. I turned and started to run again, Friday loping alongside me, ignoring the heavy footsteps pounding along behind.

Shahida was standing in her nightdress in the middle of her driveway, wailing. She had nothing on her feet, and her normally neatly-plaited greying hair was a wild halo around her head.

Several of her neighbours clustered round, trying to soothe her. Their efforts only served to enrage her further. 'Of course everything is not *all right!*' she shrieked at them, half demented.

I skidded to a halt and pushed my way through. 'Shahida,' I said urgently. 'Where are they?'

'In the garden.' She waved towards a gate that led round to the side of the house. Then, having passed on the baton of responsibility, her face crumpled into tears. 'Please, Charlie, don't let him do anything stupid.'

Langford's men shoved past me, making it to the gloomy back garden first. Where the lawn had once been was now a square of gravel and artistically-placed rocks, leading down to the box hedge at the bottom.

The shed where Fariman kept his tools was a squat wooden building that stood over by the hedge on a raft of concrete slabs. It was a dingy corner, despite the orange glare of street-lights reflected by the low cloud overhead, and the light spilling out from the open kitchen doorway.

Even so, I could see that the lock that had once secured the shed had been ripped out, leaving a jagged scar, pale against the dark wood that surrounded it. It should have left the shed totally exposed, but the door was firmly closed, all the same.

Shahida's husband was thrusting his not inconsiderable bodyweight against the timber frame to wedge it shut as though his life depended on it. His bare feet were digging in to the edge of the gravel to give him extra purchase. Fariman wasn't a tall man, but what he lacked in height, he made up for in girth.

He looked up, proud and sweating, as the group of us burst into view round the corner of the house.

'I have them! I have them!' he shouted.

Something hit the inside of the door with tremendous force. It bucked outwards, opening by maybe three or four inches, before Fariman's sheer bulk slammed it shut again. His

5

thick, black-framed glasses bounced down his nose, and almost fell.

The fear leapt in my throat. 'Fariman, for God's sake come away from there,' I called. 'They can't take anything now. Let them go.'

Langford treated me to a look of utter disgust and strode forwards. On the way past, he swung a provocative fist at Friday's head.

The dog made a solid attempt at dislocating my shoulder as he leapt for the bait and the lead brought him up short. Goaded, he let out half a dozen rapid, raucous barks before I could quieten him. The deep-chested sound of a big dog with its blood up, raising the stakes for whoever was sweating inside the shed.

Langford flashed me an evilly triumphant grin. 'Keep the little bastards pinned down,' he bellowed, breaking into a run. 'We'll take care of them. Come on lads!'

The trapped thieves must have heard Langford's voice, and if they didn't know the man himself, they could recognise the violent intent. Behind the small barred shed window, I could see movement against torchlight. It grew more frantic, and the hammering on the door increased in ferocity.

'Don't worry, Charlie,' Fariman cried, the old man's voice squeaky with excitement. 'I have them. I ha—'

There was another assault on the shed door. This time, though, it wasn't the dull thud of a shoulder or boot hitting the inside of the panel. It was the ominous crack of metal slicing straight through the flimsy softwood.

Fariman's body seemed to give a giant juddering twitch. His eyes grew bulbous behind the lenses of his glasses, and he looked down towards his torso with a breathless giggle. Then his legs folded under him and he slowly toppled sideways onto the gravel.

Behind him, sticking out a full six inches through the shed

door he'd been leaning into so heavily, were the four vicious stiletto prongs of a garden fork. Where the exposed steel should have glinted brightly under the glare of the lights, instead it gleamed dark with blood.

For a moment, the wicked tines paused there, then were withdrawn with a sharp tug, like a stiffly re-setting trap. Even Langford's brigade hesitated at the sight. The blood lust that had lit their initial charge faltering in the face of an enemy that hit back.

Before they had time to assimilate this new threat, the shed door was kicked open. Three figures emerged, furtive, moving fast. They were dressed in loose dark clothes, with woolly hats pulled down hard and scarves tied over the lower half of their faces like cattle rustlers from the Old West. Despite the disguises, it was clear at once that they were just boys.

Langford and his men had a renewed spasm of bravery. Then they wavered for a second time, coming to a full stop halfway across the back garden. When I realised what the boys were holding, I understood the vigilantes' sudden reluctance to continue the attack.

Fariman's shed was crammed with odds and ends, like any other. Old pop bottles that he'd never quite got round to returning; a bag of rags for cleaning brushes and mopping up; and plastic cans of stale fuel for some long-discarded petrol-driven mower.

All the ingredients, in fact, for the perfect Molotov cocktail.

The leader of the boys edged forwards. He was holding a disposable cigarette lighter ready under the wick. His hand shook perilously.

'Get back or I'll do it!' he screamed, voice muffled by the scarf. He sounded as though he was about to burst into tears. 'All of you, get right back!'

'Give it up,' Langford warned, teeth bared. 'This doesn't have to happen.' He held up both hands as though to placate, but he didn't retreat as ordered, wouldn't concede ground.

The two sides faced off, tension crackling between them like an overhead power line in the rain. They yelled the same words at each other, over and over, the pitch gradually rising to a frenzied level.

Behind the boys, close up to the shed doorway, Fariman's body lay still and bleeding on the ground.

Finally, Langford broke the cycle. 'Give it up,' he snarled, 'or I'll send the dog in.'

I knew I should have left Friday at home.

Before I could react to contradict this outrageous bluff, Shahida and a group of her neighbours appeared *en masse* round the corner of the house. They had the air of a mob, racking the boys' nerves another notch towards breaking point.

Then Shahida caught sight of Fariman's inert body and she started screaming. It was the kind of scream that nightmares are made of. A full-blooded howling roar with the sort of breath-control an opera singer would have killed for. It didn't do me much good, so it must have struck utter terror into her husband's attackers.

And, having accomplished that, Shahida broke free of her supporters, and bolted across the garden to avenge him.

'Shahida, no!' I'd failed Fariman, I couldn't let her down as well.

As she rushed past me I let go of Friday's straining leash and grabbed hold of her with both hands. Such was her momentum that she swung me round before I could stop her. She struggled briefly, then collapsed in my arms, weeping.

Suddenly unrestricted, Friday leapt forwards, eager to be in the thick of it. He bounded through the ranks of Langford's men and into plain view on the gravel, moving at speed. With the idea of an attack from the dog firmly planted in his mind, the boy with the cigarette lighter must have thought he could already feel the jaws around his throat.

He panicked.

The tiny flame expanded at an exponential rate as it raced up the rag wick towards the neck of the bottle. He threw the Molotov in a raging arc across the garden, onto the stony ground. The glass shattered on impact, and sent an explosive flare of burning petrol reaching for the night sky with a whoosh like a fast-approaching subway train.

Langford and his men ducked back, cursing. I dragged Shahida's incoherent form to safety, yelling for Friday as I did so.

He appeared almost at once through the smoke and confusion, ears and tail tucked down, looking sheepish.

Voices were shouting all around us. Langford's crew had skirted the flames and redoubled their efforts to get to the boys. Christ, would they never give up?

Another Molotov was lit, but it was thrown in the other direction. Away from the vigilantes.

And into the shed.

This time, there was more than the contents of the bottle to fuel the fire. With bitumen sheeting on the roof, and years of creosote on the walls, they couldn't have asked for a more promising point of ignition.

The flames caught immediately, sparkling behind the window, washing at the doorway. The speed with which they took hold, and the heat they generated, was astounding.

Fariman!

'Get the fire brigade,' I yelled, jerking one of the neighbours out of their stupor. 'And an ambulance.' Where the hell were the police when you needed them?

I shouted to the dog to stay with Shahida, but didn't wait around to find out if he obeyed me. I ran forwards, shielding my eyes with my hand against the intensity of the fire. The old man was still lying where he'd fallen by the shed door. The flames were already licking at the framework nearest to him. I grabbed hold of a handful of his paisley dressing-gown and heaved.

For all the difference it made, I might as well have been trying to roll a whale back into the sea.

I shouted for help, but nobody heard in the brawl that was fast developing all around me. The smoke hit in gusts, roasting my lungs, making my eyes stream. I tugged at Fariman's stocky shoulders again, with little result.

In the mêlée, somebody tripped over my legs and went head-first onto the gravel, landing heavily. I lunged for the back of their jacket, keeping them on the ground.

'Wait,' I said sharply as they began to struggle. 'Help me get him out of here.'

The boy stared back at me with wide, terrified eyes over the scarf that had slipped down to his chin. He tried again to rise, but desperation lent me an iron grip.

Something exploded inside the shed, and shards of glass came bursting out of the doorway. I spun my head away, but still I kept hold of the boy. I turned back to him.

'If you don't help me, he'll burn to death,' I said, going for the emotional jugular. 'Is that what you want?'

There was a moment's hesitation, then he shook his head. Taking a leap of faith, I let go of his jacket and fisted my hands into Fariman's dressing-gown again. To my utter relief, the boy did the same at the other shoulder.

He was little more than a kid, but between us, a few feet at a time, we managed to drag the old man clear.

We got him onto the crazy paving by the back door of the house. It wasn't as far away from the inferno as I would have liked, but it was better than nothing. The effort exhausted the pair of us.

I searched for the pulse at the base of Fariman's neck. It

throbbed erratically under my fingers. I heaved him over onto his stomach and pulled up the dressing-gown. Underneath, he wore pale blue pyjamas. The back of the jacket was now covered with blood, which was pumping jerkily out of the row of small holes in the cloth.

I glanced up at the boy, found him transfixed.

'Give me your scarf.' My words twitched him out of his trance. For a moment he looked ready to argue, then he unwound the scarf from his neck and handed it over without a word.

I balled the thin material and padded it against the back of Fariman's ribcage. 'Hold it there,' I ordered. When he didn't move I grabbed one of his hands and forced it to the substitute dressing.

The boy tried to pull back, didn't want to touch the old man. *If you didn't want his blood on your hands, sonny, you should have thought of that earlier.* With my forefinger and thumb I circled his skinny wrist, and dug cruelly deep into the pressure points on the inside of his arm, ignoring his yelp of pain. 'Press hard until I tell you to let go.' My voice was cold.

He did as he was ordered.

I checked down Fariman's body. When I got to his legs I found the skin on one shin bubbled and blistered where it had been against the burning shed door. It looked evil. I carefully peeled the charred pieces of his clothing away from the worst of it, and left it well alone.

Burns were nasty, but unless they were serious they were low on the priority list when it came to first aid. Besides, without even a basic field medical kit, there was little else I could do.

'Where the hell's that ambulance?' I growled.

Shahida reappeared at that point, with Friday trotting anxiously by her side. I braced myself for another bout of hysterics, but she seemed to have run out of steam. She slumped by her husband's side and clutched at his limp hand, with silent tears running down her face.

I put my hand on her shoulder and shot a hard glance to the boy, but he wouldn't meet my eyes.

The neighbours had swelled in number and organised themselves with buckets of water and a hosepipe. Where the first petrol bomb had landed there was now a soggy, blackened patch on the sandy-coloured stones.

Then the whole of the roof of the shed went up. A rejuvenated blast of flame kept the people back to a respectful distance. Burning embers came drifting down on the still night air like glitter, dying as they fell.

'Well, we lost the little bastards.' Langford's voice was thick with anger as he came stamping up. He lit a cigarette, cupping his hands round the match and dropping it on the paving. His cold gaze lingered briefly on Shahida, but he made no moves to try and help. The boy kept his head down.

The first wail of sirens started up in the distance. We all paused, trying to work out if the sound was growing louder.

When it became clear that it was, the boy's nerve finally broke. He jumped to his feet, abandoning his nursing duties, and ran like a rabbit. Langford suddenly realised that he'd had his prey right under his nose. He gave a bellow of outrage and took off after him.

The kid might have been built for lightness and speed, but gravel is murder to sprint on, and he didn't get the opportunity to open out much of a lead. Before they hit the hedge at the bottom of the garden, Langford had brought him down.

And once the boy was on the ground, the vigilante waded in with his feet and his fists. His methods were unrefined, but brutally effective, for all that.

I was up and running before I'd worked out quite what I intended to do. I only knew I had to stop Langford before he killed the kid. No matter what he'd done.

'Langford, for God's sake leave him alone,' I said. 'Let the police deal with him.'

Langford whirled round. In the light from the blazing shed, his eyes seemed to flash with excitement. This was what took him and his men out patrolling the streets night after night. Not some altruistic vision. It all came down to the age-old thrill of the chase, the heat of the kill.

'Get lost, Fox,' he snarled. 'I'm sick to death of all this passive resistance crap. Take a look around you. It doesn't work.' He held up a bloodied fist. 'This is all these bastards understand.'

'Leave him,' I said again, my voice quiet and flat.

He laughed derisively. 'Or what?' he said, turning his back on me. The boy had half-risen in the lull, and Langford punched him viciously in the ribs, watched with grim delight as he dropped again.

Though I tried to hold it back, I felt my temper rise up at me like a slap in the face. My eyes locked on to a target. I didn't need to concentrate on the mechanics. All the right moves unfurled automatically inside my head.

'Langford!' I called sharply.

And as he twisted to face me again, I hit him.

I'd like to think it was simply a clinically positioned and delivered blow, carefully weighted to disable, calculated to take him quickly and cleanly out of the fight.

The reality was dirtier than that. I hit him in a flash of pure anger, harder and faster than was strictly necessary, not caring for the consequences. It was stupid, and it could have been deadly.

For a moment I thought he was going to keep coming, then he swayed, and I realised that his legs had gone. He just didn't know it yet.

There was a mildly puzzled expression on his face as he struggled to focus on me. Then his knees gave out, his eyes rolled back, and he flopped gracelessly backwards onto the stony ground.

I started forwards on a reflex, but he didn't move. I stood there for a moment or two, breathing hard, my fists still clenched ready for a second blow I never had to launch. Then I slumped, defeated by my own anger. It slipped away quietly, leaving me with a fading madness, and a roaring in my ears.

I turned slowly, and found what seemed to be half the population of Kirby Street standing and watching me in shocked and silent condemnation.

Oh God, I thought, *not again* . . .

Somewhere beyond them, the first of the night's procession of police cars braked to a fast halt in the road outside.

TWO

It wasn't until the following morning that reaction to the whole thing set in. On a number of fronts, and none of them good.

The first hit me when I stepped out of the shower in Pauline's nice centrally-heated bathroom. I reached for a towel from the equally warm radiator and my hand stilled abruptly.

Pauline had gone in for mirrors in a big way in her bathroom. I found this strange considering, much as I liked her, she was a woman for whom the battle with rapidly encroaching cellulite was already a lost cause. I don't think, in her position, I would have wanted to be constantly reminded of the fact from almost every angle. And certainly not first thing in the morning, that's for sure.

I didn't seem to have too much of the wobbly stuff myself, but instead all I saw were the scars.

I was putting together quite a collection of them, it seemed, on my arms and torso. They'd been caused by sharp blades of varying descriptions, all wielded with deadly intent. None of them, I'm sorry to say, were gained during the course of routine surgical procedure.

The most serious stretched round the base of my throat

from a point just under my right ear, to my Adam's apple. A thin pale line, crossed by fading stitch marks, like you'd find on an old cartoon drawing of a Frankenstein monster.

Not exactly the prettiest bit of needlework you ever did see, but it wasn't the appearance of the thing that worried me. I never considered myself much to look at to begin with. I don't go for a great deal in the way of make-up, and my hair-style is one that has to survive being constantly squashed under a motorbike helmet.

No, the thing that bothered me most was what those scars represented. How close I'd come to dying, and the depths I'd had to sink to in order to survive. I'd sworn that I'd never put myself in that position again, and had carefully reorganised my life in an attempt to ensure it.

But, when the necessity – or the opportunity, anyway – had presented itself, I'd jumped straight back into the fray without pause for reflection.

The memory of my actions in Fariman and Shahida's garden came back to me. The way I'd so easily abandoned reasoned argument in favour of violence. I'd sunk straight back down to Langford's level. What the hell had I been thinking?

I hadn't – been thinking, I mean – that was the trouble. I'd been acting on an instinctively triggered response to a perceived threat. No doubt my old army instructors would have been delighted that all those months of training had paid off in such an aggressively Pavlovian style, even when I'd been out of a uniform now for longer than I'd been in one.

As for me, I was terrified.

Eventually, I shook myself out of it for long enough to go and get dressed, venturing downstairs to be greeted by an anxious Friday, who went through his usual performance of trying to convince me that he'd wasted half away during the night. I scooped up the post as I passed the front door, then carried on through to the kitchen with the dog trampling on my heels.

Just to get some peace I dumped a double handful of dog biscuits into an aluminium bowl which the Ridgeback was soon shunting enthusiastically round the lino with his snout. I filled the kettle and glanced at the mail while I waited for it to boil.

Besides the usual junk was a reminder notice for a Residents' Committee meeting to discuss the rising tide of crime on the estate. The meeting was to take place in the back room of the pub just down the road, at seven-thirty that evening.

Whoever had delivered it must have known my aversion to becoming even peripherally involved in anything that has to be run by committee. They had added a personal persuader to my copy, scrawled in red biro across the top and down one margin.

'Miss Fox,' it said, 'we'd all be v grateful (underlined twice) if you'd come to meeting, espec in light of events of last eve. Many thanks.' There was a signature to follow, but it could have been anything.

I read the rest of the leaflet again, but it didn't tell me much beyond the time and the place. I shrugged. Technically, I wasn't a resident, so I didn't think it was a wise move to go along to their meeting and stick my oar in, personal invites notwithstanding.

In the end, I tacked it to Pauline's kitchen cork board, alongside the slightly blurry photographs of Friday. The pictures had been taken indoors with a flash and either the poor dog was secretly the spawn of Satan, or he'd been badly affected by red-eye.

Also pinned up there were money-off vouchers for tubs of low-fat frozen yoghurt, pages of calorie values from Pauline's slimming club, and a card giving the date of her next hair appointment. No doubt somebody, more talented than I at the art, could have studied that board and told you everything there was to know about Pauline's lifestyle and character.

I'd known her for just over a year, but she was one of those people you instantly warm to, full of energy and an enthusiasm for collecting new experiences. I expect that Pauline's life would have worked out quite differently, had her husband of twenty-five years not run off with a nineteen-year-old telesales manageress some time before.

Where most women of forty-eight would never have recovered from this devastating occurrence, for Pauline it offered up a whole new lease of life. She started going to her slimming group, and dyeing the grey out of her hair. She'd even taken up with a boyfriend who rode a Harley Davidson, and signed up for self-defence lessons.

That was where I came in, because at that time I was teaching regular classes to groups of women all around the area. She wasn't quite at the end of her first course when the events of last winter overtook me, and my teaching career had come to a rather abrupt end.

She'd kept in touch while I was out of action, even held my hand at the inquest. I wasn't always glad to see her, I must admit, but it was difficult to be depressed for long with Pauline around. Afterwards, I felt I owed her one, and house-sitting for her was the least I could do. Even if it did mean braving the little horrors of Kirby Street.

When Pauline had moved in to number forty-one, Kirby Street hadn't yet started on its downward course. It was one of a maze of streets of ugly brick and pebbledashed semis built in the fifties on reclaimed marshland, down near the River Lune. As far as anyone knew, the area had never been remotely cultivated, despite the picturesque name.

For the past twenty years, Lavender Gardens had been slowly taken over by the local Asian population. Mainly

Pakistani, they'd moved into the streets one house at a time as they came up vacant. And, as is so often the way of these things, the more the Asian numbers swelled, the faster the other houses seemed to come up for grabs, and the lower the prices fell.

For as long as I'd lived in Lancaster, the place had been known as Lavindra Gardens. At least, that was one of its more repeatable nicknames.

Pauline wasn't remotely Pakistani, but she'd stayed put. 'I get on all right with them,' she'd informed me stoutly. 'I just don't stick my nose in where it's not wanted, particularly with the kids, and they leave me well alone.'

She didn't appear to make any connection between this wide berth and the presence of Friday, who had the run of the house when she was at work. The dog had arrived as an abused puppy not long after Mr Jamieson had departed and, in the long run, Pauline reckoned she'd got the better end of the deal. If nothing else, he was the best home security system you could wish for.

The Ridgeback was big, and totally aware of his own strength. Besides, he had the much-envied local reputation of once having chased an imprudent dustbin man up onto the roof of the shed in the back garden, and kept him up there all morning. Part of the reason I was staying at Pauline's was so that Friday could stay in residence, and on guard.

So, I'd moved in to make sure his food came in tins rather than in trousers. I'd agreed to keep lights on in the evening, and the curtains opening and closing at the appropriate hours.

I'd also promised not to interfere in local problems. Not to take sides. Not to get involved. After all, I was only going to be there for a relatively short period. The last thing I'd wanted to do was draw attention to myself.

But it looked like I'd managed it, just the same.

★

After I'd let Friday tow me round the block on the end of his lead, my conscience got the better of me. I bundled him back into the house and crossed over the road to go and bang on the faded varnish of Fariman and Shahida's front door.

It took a long time for anyone to answer. When the door was finally opened, it wasn't Shahida who stood there, but an Asian teenager. He was one of those beautiful Indian boys with almost androgynous features, flawless skin and a slender body. It was emphasised by the tight, but grubby white T-shirt he wore, along with dusty jeans, ripped at the knees.

I vaguely recognised him, but seeing him out of context, it took me a moment to put a name to the face. Nasir, that was it. His widowed mother, Mrs Gadatra, actually lived next door to Pauline. Although I'd seen and talked to her two younger children, the elder boy was rarely home, and remained aloof when he was.

I realised that he hadn't spoken, and was eyeing me with apparent disfavour, as though something with a faintly unpleasant smell had crawled onto his upper lip.

'Yes?' he said at last, sharply, and totally without the grace his appearance would have suggested.

'Hello Nasir. I'm here to see Shahida,' I said, somewhat uncertainly, and when that didn't seem to impress him, I added, 'to find out how Fariman is.'

The boy glowered a little more. 'Wait,' he said. 'I'll ask.'

He turned and stalked away up the hall, not quite shutting the door in my face, but making sure I knew I wasn't invited over the threshold. I hovered, uncomfortable, and almost regretted the impulse that had made me come over.

I glanced around and noticed, with a knot in my stomach, the net curtains twitching in the houses opposite.

After less than a minute another figure appeared round the door, almost completely filling the narrow hallway. He was unusually large for an Asian man, with huge callused hands, but he was squeezed into a suit that, if I was any judge, hadn't come off a market stall.

'Yes?' he said, too, but with less aggression than Nasir had injected. His voice was oddly high-pitched.

I repeated my inquiry about Fariman and he eyed me bleakly for a second.

'You heard about what happened, then?'

'I was there,' I said.

'You are Charlie?' he asked.

When I nodded he paused for a moment, considering, then swung the door open and gestured me in, but laid a heavy restraining hand on my arm before I could advance much further. 'Fariman's condition is not good,' he said quietly. 'One lung collapsed and his leg is badly burned, and there is some talk of infection in the wounds. Please do not upset Shahida with your questions.'

I nodded again, and the weight was lifted from my arm.

We went through into the small, neat front sitting room. Nasir was slouched by the netted window, scowling at life in general, and me in particular.

Shahida was sitting on the sofa, looking utterly dejected. She barely glanced up as we came in. Nasir's mother was sitting next to her. She was holding both Shahida's hands in her own as though she could impart inner strength that way.

'Shahida,' I said gently, after a few moments of silence, 'I'm so sorry.'

She looked up slowly, as though only just registering my presence. 'I begged him not to do anything stupid, Charlie,' she whispered.

The sense of guilt rose quickly, had to be swallowed back down. It stuck like dust in my throat. 'I tried,' I said, 'but when Langford and his bunch joined in, it all got out of hand so fast.' As excuses went, it sounded pretty lame to my own ears.

'So, why did you stop them beating the boy?' Mrs Gadatra

demanded suddenly, her normally placid face fierce. 'Look what he did to my sister's husband. He needed to be taught a lesson, or where will it all end?'

Nasir pushed himself away from the window ledge abruptly, as though he couldn't maintain his silence any longer, and agitatedly raked his hands through his hair. 'You think that, but there are others who deserve to be beaten more,' he said with quiet feeling, starting to pace jerkily. 'He's not the one who was behind this attack.'

'Nasir!' protested the big man, his voice more squeaky than it had been before. 'Just remember, boy, it wasn't so long ago when that could have been you.'

Mrs Gadatra paled visibly at the man's words, but Nasir twisted to face him. 'I know who's behind this,' he said, vehement, 'and I'm going to see they get what's coming to them.'

'Nasir!' It was his mother who broke in this time, her voice hushed with outrage. 'Show some respect to your employer. Mr Ali has kindly brought you away from work to see your aunt, and this rudeness is how you repay him? You should be ashamed.'

I vaguely remembered an over-the-fence conversation with Mrs Gadatra when she mentioned that Nasir was training to be an electrician, and had a good job with a local builder. Mr Ali had built up his business from nothing and Nasir much admired him. You certainly saw enough of Mr Ali's green and purple painted vans driving round to vouch for his success.

The man himself dredged up a weak smile for Mrs Gadatra, fluttering a hand to show that it really didn't matter. There was only a slight tightening round the corners of his mouth, a stiffness to his neck, that called him a liar.

I didn't get the chance to express my doubts. He pointedly checked his gold wristwatch and glanced at Nasir. 'We have to go now,' he said, smiling at the women to belie the hint of steel in his thready voice. 'I have a meeting, and you are needed back on site, Nasir,' he said.

Nasir nodded sullenly, head bowed. The fight seemed to have gone out of him.

Mrs Gadatra got up to see them out, the soft folds of her bright silk sari rustling as she moved. 'I'm sorry about my boy,' she said to Mr Ali, flashing Nasir a speaking look, but unable to stop defending him, even so. 'He is upset about his uncle.'

'I'm sure the police will do everything they can to bring those responsible to justice,' Mr Ali said, but his voice held little conviction.

'I'm sure they will,' Mrs Gadatra agreed, but she sounded less convinced, or convincing, than he had. She turned to her son as he moved past her. 'I want to hear no more talk of retribution, Nasir,' she said sharply. 'Let the police take care of things.'

Just for a moment, the fire was back in Nasir's eyes. 'They don't know what's going on, and they don't care,' he muttered. He brought his head up, oddly seemed to look me straight in the face, as he added, 'Maybe you should be asking who really profits from trying to rob an old man?'

Mr Ali shot a quick, nervous glance to Shahida to see what effect the boy's inflammatory words were having, but she was still sitting frozen on the sofa, and seemed oblivious. He grabbed hold of Nasir's shoulder and practically hauled him out of the room. The front door banged shut behind them a few moments later.

I would have turned and gone back to Shahida, but Mrs Gadatra laid a hand on my arm. It was half the size of Mr Ali's, but it had the same detaining effect, nevertheless.

'I think you should go now, too, Charlie,' she said to me, more softly than the tone she'd used on her son. 'My sister has been through a lot. I'm sure she appreciates your calling, but she needs some peace.'

There wasn't an easy way to argue with her and, I must admit, I didn't even try.

Nasir's words troubled me as I walked back over the road to Pauline's. Surely there wasn't anything more sinister behind the attack on Fariman than a group of frightened kids who'd panicked when they'd been cornered, and who had lashed out blindly.

So, what did he mean about working out who'd profit from robbing an old man?

I shrugged. It was rubbing me up the wrong way, but part of me just wanted to hope that Fariman recovered from his ordeal without any lasting side-effects, and to forget about it. Besides, I'd promised Pauline I wouldn't do anything rash and, at that point, I really did fully intend to keep my word.

Ah well.

Three

As I approached Pauline's place, I dug in my pocket for my keys, noticing out of habit the man leaning on a sleek-looking sports car by the kerb next to the house.

He was middle-aged, balding, shortish and rather rotund, wearing a grey anorak that had three lots of carefully knotted drawstrings and a hood. As I drew nearer I could see that the skin of his face was pale and clammy. He mopped at it with a wilted blue cotton handkerchief.

He certainly didn't look the kind of bloke who'd own a Mercedes of any description, unless he was just cheekily using this one as a perch. Not that it was a new car, but a classic square-shaped SL convertible. The shine on the dark green metallic paint was so deep you felt you could reach into it right up to the elbow.

As I drew nearer he straightened up, leaning down to pick up a battered briefcase that had been resting against his grey-slacked legs. I had time to weigh him up before we got within hailing distance. Social worker, or council official, probably. Only the Merc didn't quite fit the bill.

'Miss Fox, is it?'

I nodded, hesitating on the pavement by Pauline's driveway. He fumbled in his anorak pocket and produced a

25

slightly dog-eared business card, which he handed over to me. Eric O'Bryan, it said, with Community Juvenile Officer in smaller print underneath, and an official-looking crest.

'You're with the police?' I said. I wouldn't have pegged him as that.

'Not quite,' he said. 'Associated with, but not part of, if you see what I mean. I work with them on occasion, in a sort of mediatory capacity. Do you mind if I have a word?'

I shrugged, and leaned on the lichen-encrusted concrete gatepost. 'Feel free.'

He looked uncomfortable, as though aware of the net curtains fluttering at the windows across the road. 'Er, no, I meant somewhere – less public.'

I eyed him for a moment, but he didn't strike me as the axe-murdering type, so I nodded and led him up the short driveway. I got the outside door open, then stopped him going in to the porch. 'You'd better let me go and get the dog out of the way first,' I said. 'He's big, and he's mean, and he's not mine, so I wouldn't like to guarantee that he'll do as I tell him. Especially not when he's hungry.'

O'Bryan swallowed and nodded quickly, clutching his briefcase like that was going to save him from Friday's savage jaws. By this time, the animal in question had gone into what sounded like a slathering barking frenzy on the other side of the door.

I shouted to him through the panelling, and gradually the din subsided into woeful whining. Only then did I risk pushing the door open, getting my knee through first so that Friday couldn't ram his powerful snout into the gap.

Once I'd actually got into the hallway, the dog decided that he did remember me after all. He went through a big show of sucking up, standing on my feet and butting against my legs.

'Come on, you,' I said when he'd calmed down enough, grabbing hold of his collar. 'Kitchen.'

I dragged his unwilling bulk into the other room in a scrabble of claws on the lino, pulling the door shut behind him, then went to let O'Bryan into the house. He checked me over dubiously when I opened the door, anxiously looking past me, as though I should have been losing blood through numerous bite holes and gashes.

'So, Mr O'Bryan,' I said once he was ensconced on the sofa in Pauline's living room, 'what is it you feel the need to talk to me about in private?'

'Well, bit of a sticky subject this, no doubt,' he said. He put his head on one side, rubbing absently at his chin as if trying to gauge in advance my response to his next words. 'Not to put too fine a point on it, well, it's about young Roger.'

I stared at him blankly for a moment. 'Roger?' I repeated.

Whatever reaction he'd been expecting, that clearly wasn't it. He looked at me in surprise. 'Roger Mayor,' he prompted. 'The young lad who was arrested last night. I have got it right, haven't I? You were there?'

'Oh, right,' I said, feeling foolish. 'Sorry, I didn't know his name. When they put him into the back of a police car last night he was doing his best impersonation of a deaf mute.'

O'Bryan snorted. 'Yes, well, they soon learn that keeping their mouth shut is their best option, I'm afraid. Keep quiet, say nothing, and wait for their parents or social services to come and get them out.'

'So that's all that happened to him, is it?' I demanded, aware of a spurt of anger. 'Fariman's half dead in the hospital, and this kid is sitting at home watching TV?'

O'Bryan looked wary. He pushed his glasses up to his fore-head so that he could try and squeeze the stress out of the bridge of his nose with a finger and thumb. When he finished the glasses dropped back into place as though on elastic.

'It's not quite as simple as that,' he said, speaking quickly as though afraid I'd cut him off in mid-sentence. 'We've found that keeping these wayward youngsters out of the justice system for as long as possible seems to stop them re-offending, and the feeling is that it might work in this case. Roger's basically not a bad lad, but he's had problems at home.'

I rolled my eyes. What teenager didn't?

O'Bryan missed the gesture, too busy snapping open the briefcase on his knees and rifling through the contents. 'It's all here,' he said, tapping the manila folder he brought out. 'He's only fourteen. The youngest of three kids, two boys and a girl. Violent father who died in a drunken road accident. Older brother got involved with a pretty rough crowd before he left home. Sister's one step up from prostitution, if the rumours are to be believed. She's got a bit of form for shoplifting, and she's just got herself knocked up, too.'

'Where's he from?'

O'Bryan's hesitation was only fractional, but there, all the same. 'Copthorne,' he said.

I nodded. It figured. Living in Lancaster for a few years, I thought I knew all about Copthorne. Living on Kirby Street for a few weeks, I'd found out a whole lot more. None of it good.

The Copthorne estate had the undesirable local reputation of being an open remand centre. If O'Bryan wanted to take his Mercedes through that particular battle zone, he'd have to keep the wheels spinning to stop them undoing his wheelnuts as he went past.

Copthorne and Lavender Gardens faced each other with sinister normality across a derelict piece of wasteland that had once been three more streets of houses. When they'd been built in the late fifties, there'd been a waiting list to move in. By the time the council engineers sent in the bulldozers, the rush to leave had become something of a stampede.

It was an area long scheduled for redevelopment, but so far

the only thing that had developed there among the crumbling brickwork were the weeds. They hadn't even finished knocking the houses down properly, and half of them were still clinging on, boarded up and vandalised.

'So,' O'Bryan said hopefully now, pushing his glasses up his nose with his forefinger. 'Do you think you might be able to put a good word in for the lad, help him get off with just another caution?'

I glanced at him sharply. 'Another one?' I said. 'Why, how many has he had already?'

O'Bryan looked momentarily frustrated, though whether at himself or me, it was hard to tell. He checked the file again, stalling for time. 'One or two,' he admitted. 'Breach of the peace, vandalism, that sort of thing. Minor stuff, you know how it is.'

No, I didn't. 'And how long did each of those keep him out of trouble for?'

'Oh, well,' he cleared his throat and gave a sort of nervous laugh, 'not long enough, I suppose. I see your point, but—'

'No, Mr O'Bryan,' I cut across him, 'to be quite honest with you, if the first caution didn't stop him, he's not going to be stopped, is he? Maybe he needs something like this to bring him up short.'

Besides, I'd been on the receiving end of an official caution myself. A stern lecture of sorts delivered by a senior police officer, telling me in no uncertain terms why I couldn't go around clouting WPCs just because I didn't agree with them. True, I hadn't hit a police officer since, but then, the need for doing so hadn't really arisen.

When O'Bryan didn't answer, I added, 'Don't you think it's time Roger paid the price for this one?'

'He's only young,' he tried again. 'I hardly think he was the brains behind this particular escapade.'

Nasir's words came back to me again, brought me up short.

'So you think there's something more to this as well, do you?' I asked slowly.

O'Bryan looked puzzled. 'What do you mean?'

I told him briefly what Nasir had said, that he seemed certain there were others behind the recent spate of robberies than the kids who'd apparently been responsible. 'Nasir was fairly positive about it,' I confirmed, 'and he seemed determined to make sure something was done.'

'Ah, well,' O'Bryan said, 'Nasir and I have crossed paths before. His father died when he was about fourteen, and he went off at the deep end. Got himself into a lot of trouble, but I managed to keep him out of prison, and he came round in the end.' He half-smiled. 'Had quite a temper on him, as I recall. A few years ago last night's little adventure would have been much more up Nasir's street.'

'I must admit, Roger didn't seem quite the ruthless type,' I said, 'otherwise he wouldn't have helped me drag the old man clear of the fire. He probably saved his life.'

'He did that?' O'Bryan sounded surprised. He shook his head and tut-tutted a few times. 'He didn't tell me.'

'Your biggest problem,' I said, wanting to help in spite of myself, 'is that the people round here need a scapegoat for Fariman's injuries, and right now, Roger is it. I don't think they'll be happy to see him get off in any way that's thought of as lightly.'

'But surely, if he helped rescue this chap, they won't object?'

'If Roger and his mates hadn't tried to rob Fariman, he wouldn't have needed rescuing in the first place,' I said. 'Look, I'm sorry, Mr O'Bryan, but feelings are running a bit high at the moment, and I don't know what you think I can do about it.'

'Well,' he said, clearing his throat as though his collar was suddenly too tight for him, 'I was hoping that you might be able to persuade the people involved to go easier on him—'

'You're joking,' I cut in. 'Right now I'm not flavour of the month for stopping the vigilantes beating him up, never mind trying to get him off altogether.'

'Well, maybe if it comes to court you could speak up for him. Tell them how he helped save the old man.'

I'd be well out of Kirby Street by the time those particular bureaucratic wheels ground into slo-mo action, but I still didn't relish the prospect of having to look Shahida in the face across a courtroom as I spoke up for one of the boys who'd tried to murder her husband.

I shook my head. 'I don't think I can help you,' I said, standing up. This interview was over.

O'Bryan rose, also. 'Well, if your mind's made up, it's made up.' There was a faint snap to his words, which he tried to soften by smiling at me. 'I must say I think you're taking a very brave stand.'

'Brave?'

He cast me a calculating look, the lenses of his glasses blanking out his eyes. 'Well, if you're not for the defence, you'll be one of the main witnesses for the prosecution, and Roger knows where to find you. So, no doubt, do his mates,' he said carefully. 'And the older brother's known to be a bit of a hard-case, too.' He watched me while he imparted this information, but I didn't show him what he wanted to see.

'And then there's the court case itself,' he went on. He pursed his lips, considering. 'Never a nice experience, having to stand up in court, is it, Charlie?'

I felt the colour draining away from my face like someone had just pulled the plug out of a bath. It was the first time he'd used my first name, and the sly familiarity of it brought the hairs up on the back of my neck.

The last time I'd been in court it was to testify against a group of my erstwhile brothers-in-arms. I tried not to think

31

about it much these days, but their names still ran through my head like a chant.

Donalson, Hackett, Morton, and Clay.

There was a rhythm and a flow to them that chilled my skin and cramped my muscles. When the barrister had read them out in a different order, I had almost failed to recognise them as the same group.

Almost. The memory fades, but I don't think I'll ever forget them entirely. I was claiming rape. They were claiming it was all some happy drunken orgy that had got out of hand.

I'd already been through the agonies of a military court martial, and been found guilty of gross misconduct. Foolishly, as it turned out, I'd sought justice in the civil arena.

I might have got it, too. Then the whispers started. Whispers about the affair I'd stupidly indulged in with one of my training instructors. It was against the rules, and soon got blown up out of all proportion.

My main witness defected, and the inevitable happened.

I lost.

It cost me my career in the army, one I'd spent four years carefully constructing. It also cost me my self-respect, and the repercussions blew a hole in my relationship with my parents so big you could have driven a Boeing 777 through it, sideways on.

Still, I'd walked across that burning bridge. It had taken me a while, but eventually I'd picked up most of the pieces. I didn't know if I could do it all again.

I looked up at O'Bryan, found him watching me intently. I led the way to the door without speaking.

'Look,' he said as I pulled it open for him to leave, 'juvenile detention would break a lad like Roger. Perhaps turn him to crime permanently. It could ruin his whole life. Just say you'll think about it, eh?'

I found myself nodding reluctantly as I stood to one side to let O'Bryan out.

'OK,' he said, 'I'll give you a few days to – *Oy! Get away from it you little bastards!*'

I jumped as O'Bryan's voice rose from softly persuasive to a full-blown roar. He leapt out of the front door and went dashing towards the pavement, the briefcase swinging against his legs as he ran.

I stuck my head round the door and saw a group of kids scrambling away from the ruin that was now O'Bryan's Mercedes, like malicious monkeys in a safari park when the game warden with the tranquilliser darts appears.

The kids scattered with a precision that spoke of long practice, all disappearing over garden hedges and through gates in different directions. O'Bryan got as far as the pavement before it dawned on him that trying to catch any of them was an utter waste of time.

He faltered and then stopped dead, putting his case down slowly on the cracked paving next to his feet. His full attention was taken by the beautiful example of the German sports car maker's art. Or what had been, when he'd set out that morning.

I saw him lift his hands to his chubby face in horror. As he shook his head the sunlight glinted off the lenses of his little wire-rimmed glasses, as though his eyes themselves had flashed fire.

Almost against my will, I found myself following him out, stopping just behind his shoulder as he surveyed the damage.

The Merc was wrecked. The hood was in tatters, the chrome windscreen wipers had been twisted into loops, and all four tyres had been comprehensively slashed. Something heavy and sharp had been dragged along the bodywork, leaving deep gouges right down to the bare steel from head-light to tail-light.

'The little bastards,' O'Bryan whispered. 'Three years I've spent rebuilding this car. Bought it for peanuts as a right basketcase.' He turned and favoured me with a sad, lopsided smile. 'I only brought it today because the clutch has gone on my Cavalier. *Three bloody years.*'

I didn't speak. There wasn't anything I could say. I've never owned a car, just an elderly Suzuki RGV 250 motorbike. Still, I could understand his distress. If anything happened to the bike it would be like losing a limb.

Suddenly, O'Bryan jerked round to the back of the car, and was staring at the boot lid. The lock had been punched out of it, and the lid itself was partly ajar. He yanked it open fully, looked inside with an anger that turned his already pale features ashen.

'I don't believe it,' he muttered.

'What?'

'They've taken—' he broke off, scrabbling through the debris in the boot with the air of somebody who knows he isn't going to find what he's searching for. Finally, he slumped, defeated.

'What is it, Mr O'Bryan?' I asked again, gently. 'What's been taken?'

'What?' He focused on me, distracted. 'Oh, my case notes,' he said weakly. 'Private stuff, you know, important documents.'

'Would you like me to call the police?'

'No.' He gave a sigh that was almost a snort. 'I don't suppose it would do much good, would it?'

I thought of the kids I'd seen disappearing from the scene of the crime. None of them looked in double figures, let alone old enough to prosecute. 'Not if you're going to spend all your professional time trying to get them off with a caution, no,' I agreed.

O'Bryan's face dropped suddenly, and I felt ashamed of my unworthy dig.

We went back into the house and I fed him a cup of tea with plenty of sugar in it to help deal with the shock. He recovered enough to borrow the phone to ring his garage to come and cart the remains away. Once that was done, he called himself a taxi, and departed. A sad, harassed little figure, with the weight of the world sitting heavy on his rounded shoulders.

After he'd gone, I rang my mother. Quite a momentous occasion in itself, if truth be told. There was a time when I would have cheerfully chewed off my own hand rather than use it to pick up the receiver and phone home. My, how things change.

I suppose, to be fair, I was never any great shakes as a daughter, even before the disgrace of my court martial, and the endless horrors of my trial.

I lost my father's interest very early on by dint of surviving my birth when my twin brother failed to do so. My father had fiercely wanted a son to follow him into the medical profession, but the complications that followed my arrival meant that, after me, there were no more children.

I think my mother secretly hoped that I'd turn into one of those girlie girls. It wasn't her fault that I firmly resisted any attempts to mould me into an ideal daughter. You can take a girl to ballet lessons as much as you like, but you can't necessarily *make* her into a ballerina.

It was an accidental discovery on a team-building outward bound course in my late teens that led to my choice of a military career. I found I was physically tougher than I'd realised, and had the natural ability to shoot straight with a consistency that amazed the instructors.

Finally, I'd found something that earned me approval and respect. I'd gone home in triumphant defiance and dropped the news that I was joining up onto my parents with a fearful sense of excitement.

If I was expecting an emotional explosion of atomic proportions I was sadly disappointed.

Now, my mother answered the telephone herself, which saved me having to make polite, if brief, conversation with my father.

'Hi,' I said. 'It's me.'

For a moment there was a silence brought on by surprise. Although I'd made an effort since the winter before to get back on speaking terms with my parents, we were still at the stage where contact from either party brought about a profound discomfiture, just in case either of us said the wrong thing.

'Oh, Charlotte, how lovely to hear from you,' she cried, her voice jerky and bright almost to the point of manic. 'How *are* you, darling?'

'I'm fine,' I said.

She heard the mental step back and toned down her manner. 'So, tell me all your news,' she said, still heartily. 'How are you keeping? What have you been up to?'

'I'm fine,' I said again. 'I'm house-sitting for a friend. Well, dog-sitting actually.' The dog in question, who'd been spark out on the rug in the middle of the living room, sat up long enough to scratch behind his ear with one hind foot, then flopped back down again.

That launched us into a conversation about her dogs, two elderly Labradors. She seemed relieved to be on neutral ground and had nearly started to relax by the time I got round to the real reason for my call.

'I need to pick your brains,' I said.

'About dogs?'

'No, not really, although I suppose that comes into it,' I replied, thinking of the part Friday had unwittingly played in last night's events. 'I need to pick your professional brains.'

There was silence again, and this time it went on for a while. My father's lucrative job as a consultant surgeon has meant my mother never needed to work after she married, but to pass the time she'd become a local magistrate.

That had turned out not to be as much use as you'd imagine when it came to my own trial, but sordid little cases like mine didn't crop up too regularly in the stockbroker belt of Cheshire. Burglary, however, was another thing.

'Of-of course I'll help, Charlotte, if I can,' she said now, wary, but still amenable.

Before she could change her mind, I jumped right in and explained about the botched burglary by Roger and his mates, including the injury to Fariman, but glossing over any active part I'd played in the proceedings.

I finished by telling her about my feeling that Roger should end up in court, and O'Bryan's opinion that a caution would better keep him on the straight and narrow. 'But, he's already had cautions before,' I said. 'I don't know what to do for the best and I was hoping for some advice.'

'Not exactly the sort of advice mothers are usually called upon to dispense,' she said wryly, and for the first time there was a trace of humour in her voice.

'No, I suppose not,' I agreed.

'I'll do a little research, if that's all right. I never applied to sit on the juvenile bench, but one of my colleagues deals with that type of case and I'd like to check my facts absolutely before I speak. Can you wait a few days. Maybe a week?'

I thought of O'Bryan and wasn't sure how long I could stall him without making a decision.

My mother heard the hesitation and mistook the reason for it. 'He's not threatening you is he, Charlotte?' she demanded. 'Are you quite sure you're safe where you are?'

'Oh yes,' I said, glibly. 'I don't think anything's going to happen for a while on this one.'

Honestly. There are days when I only open my mouth to change feet.

Four

It may have been a coincidence, but the trashing of Eric O'Bryan's Mercedes seemed to mark the beginning of a step-up in the usual level of crime on the Lavender Gardens estate. The next day all the cars which were left parked overnight on Kirby Street had been vandalised.

I made a mental inventory of the damage when Friday took me out for his regular morning walk. I had to keep him on a short lead to stop him from paddling about in the debris with a blatant disregard for vet's bills.

By the sounds of the shouting going on, the kids of the street were getting it in the neck for the damage. I supposed it was difficult for them to convince anyone they were blameless in this exercise, when just about everyone with a net curtain to lurk behind had seen them pulling the Merc apart the previous day.

As I waited for Friday to finish his minute nasal examination of a tree trunk, it struck me abruptly that, unless they were very, very stupid, that was precisely why the kids on the road hadn't had anything to do with it.

It was a train of thought that kept me occupied almost right back to Pauline's front door. I discovered when I got there that two pairs of brown eyes were anxiously watching my return through a gap in the hedge.

Aqueel and Gin were Nasir's younger brother and sister, of around eight and six. I discovered very soon after my arrival that they regarded Friday with a kind of horrified fascination. They were particularly intrigued by the fact that I could get so close to him, when Pauline was away, without getting bitten. I didn't enlighten them as to how suddenly tolerant the dog became of the person who controlled the can opener. When Pauline returned, she would want to find Friday's good name savagely intact.

I waved to them through the hedge and, having been spotted, they waved back. Or at least, Aqueel did, being the braver of the two. Gin merely ducked behind her brother's back, chewing her hair.

'Is Friday being very fierce today, Charlie?' Aqueel asked me gravely.

'Yes Aqueel, I've struggled to keep him from attacking several people,' I told him, with equal seriousness, adding with a hard stare, 'He is very annoyed about all this broken glass all over the pavements where he has to walk. It hurts his feet and makes him especially bad tempered.'

Aqueel swallowed and, over his shoulder, his sister's eyes grew round as coffee cups.

I knew I was trying that one on for size, but I was pretty sure that one of the Mercedes vandals had been Aqueel. Despite his angelic face and general air of butter-wouldn't-melt.

'Please tell Friday that it wasn't me, Charlie,' he begged now. 'It wasn't. Honest!'

I glanced at the dog, who had given up waiting for me to open the front door and had sat down heavily on the drive. He stared up at my face with his head on one side, as though considering.

I shrugged. 'I'm not sure he believes you, Aqueel,' I said sadly. 'You see, he thinks he saw you out there yesterday, and—'

'That was yesterday,' Aqueel protested. 'All these cars, that was not us. It was white people, like you.'

'Aqueel! Gin! Get inside immediately, and get ready for school.' It was Nasir who rebuked them, stepping out of the front porch to favour me with a contemptuous glare. He cuffed them both round the head as they dodged under his arm and through the doorway.

Nasir wasn't dressed for work today. No ripped jeans and T-shirt, but designer labels were in abundance and he had the right build to show them off.

'Morning Nasir,' I said now, as cheerfully as I could, but he didn't answer. Before I could find a way of bringing the conversation round to his outburst at Shahida's house, he'd ducked back indoors without speaking further, letting the front door close firmly behind him. I shrugged. There'd be another time. Then I finally let a patiently yawning Friday into his own home for breakfast.

It wasn't until later that afternoon that I was treated to the next instalment. I'd decided to wheel the Suzuki onto the concrete flagged patio in the back garden to give it a good clean, having only worked a half day at the gym.

If you're into serious body-building, and you live anywhere round Lancaster, then the chances are that you do your training at Attila's place. Not that Attila was the muscular and athletic owner's real name, but his German parentage and almost stereotypical Aryan good looks made the misnomer inevitable.

I'd been going to the gym on and off for practically as long as I'd lived in Lancaster, and I'd been working there for around three months.

I'd fallen into the job by accident, really, having spent a good deal of my time rehabilitating there during the early part of the summer. I might have technically emerged as the victor from my encounter with a vicious killer the winter before, but it was a points decision at best. The knife wounds had healed a lot quicker than the broken bones, and it had taken me quite a while to get back to something approaching full fitness.

By that time, Attila had grown used to seeing me as part of the furniture.

'I think I need to encourage more women to come and train here,' he told me. 'Having you around to show them we are not all macho apes with bulging muscles has been very useful, Charlie, and you know what you're doing. We'll see how it goes, yes?'

And, having nothing better to occupy me at the time, I'd agreed.

Working a regular number of set hours a week had taken a bit of getting used to after several years of working for myself, but I was just about getting into the swing of it.

It had meant that I'd neglected the bike a bit, which was not something I could afford to do when the council were throwing salt around the roads like it was going out of fashion. The aluminium box frame was pitting with corrosion faster than I could keep up with it.

I washed the worst of the salt away thoroughly, then leathered it off and gave the whole of the bodywork and the exposed bits of frame a coat of wax. While I waited for the wax to glaze over, I sat back on my heels and just looked at the bike.

It wasn't in its first flush of youth, but it was still my pride and joy. Lightweight and compact, the two-stroke RGV was frighteningly quick for a quarter-litre machine, with straight-line performance that bikes more than twice its size struggled to match. Not to mention the cornering agility of a cheetah.

They were out of production now, and when the time eventually came to replace it, I struggled to know what to go for instead. Which made keeping it in good condition even more important.

'Oh, there you are, Charlie,' Mrs Gadatra's head appeared over the fence. She seemed to have recovered her good humour. 'Did you see all the mess on the street this morning? Wasn't it terrible?'

I agreed that it was and enquired after Fariman's condition.

'They are still worried about the infection, but his breathing is much easier,' Mrs Gadatra replied. She stared at the Suzuki. 'However do you ride such a machine?' she asked. 'Whatever does your mother think?'

'She thinks it's better than walking,' I said, which was nearly the truth.

'These days, I can understand her thinking,' Mrs Gadatra said, nodding wisely so that her earrings jangled. 'Still, at least this street should be safer soon, don't you think?'

'Safer soon? What do you mean? Have the police caught the vandals?'

'The police? Ha.' Mrs Gadatra pulled a face and flapped her hand languidly from the wrist at the very suggestion, setting a dozen gold bangles jingling. 'I don't think they have even looked,' she said. 'No, last night the Residents' Committee asked Mr Garton-Jones to come and take over. I think they were going to telephone him this afternoon. There is another Committee meeting next week. You should come along perhaps. But isn't that good news?'

'I'm sorry,' I said, shaking my head, 'I think I missed an episode somewhere. Who is Garton-Jones and what is he taking over?'

Mrs Gadatra laughed. 'Oh, of course. I think this is before

43

Zoë Sharp
Zoë Sharp

Zoë Sharp
him, though. He and his men have been patrolling the streets
on some of the other estates. Of course he is not cheap, but
the crime there was awful before he came, and now they say
it has almost disappeared completely because of him. He
sounds wonderful.'

'Mother!' Nasir's voice from the back doorway as he came
out into the garden was sharp enough to cut through his
mother's chatter. 'The children will be home from school
soon and they will be hungry.'

'Oh yes, of course, Nasir, I was just coming now,' his mother
replied serenely, and hurried inside, giving me a cheery wave
as she went.

I turned my attention back to the bike. The polish had set
to a fine white mist and I began rubbing it off briskly with a
soft dry cloth.

'It's a bit of a waste, isn't it?' Nasir's voice made me jump. I
hadn't realised he was still in the garden, regarding me over
the fence with that brooding stare.

'What's a waste?'

He looked me up and down with a slow thoroughness that
was as insulting as it was intended to be. 'A bike like that
belonging to a girl.'

It was the way he said the word 'girl' that really got my back
up. The same way some people would say 'whore'.

'I hate to break this to you, Nasir,' I returned sweetly, 'but
we've just hit the twenty-first century, not the nineteenth.
Women have the vote and everything now. Much as I'm sure
you'd approve, we can't all be kept permanently chained to
the kitchen sink, barefoot and pregnant.'

His head came up, eyes flashing as his mouth set into a line
of fury.

'You want to watch your step,' he hissed, raising his finger.
'You are an outsider here, and you are not welcome.' With that

44

friendly thought he stepped back from the fence, his body rigid. I heard the back door slam behind him.

Ah well, I thought, so much for maintaining cordial relations with the neighbours. Sorry Pauline.

The day after, my morning walk with Friday revealed that the police were back on Lavender Gardens. It was half a dozen or so burglaries this time, which had brought them out. That and, I suspect, a growing realisation that if they didn't at least make a show of force round the estate, the public's trust in them was going to break down completely.

As it was, the local families advanced beyond their net curtains and their front doors. Now they came out into their untidy gardens to stand taciturn in their reproof at how little positive action had been taken before.

It wasn't just the older generation who stood and muttered, and eyed the squad cars suspiciously. There seemed to be more teenage boys in the mix than I'd noticed hanging around before. Angry, cocky, eager to prove themselves in the face of authority.

For the moment they contented themselves with silent posturing, but I wondered how long it would be before one of them crossed the line. For their part, once they'd come back out into the street, the police stayed close to their cars, tense. I know most of them wear body armour as a matter of course these days, but in this instance it seemed like provocation.

To keep out of the way, I took Friday by the long route, out onto the main road via the cycle way that ran alongside the river. As I popped up onto the main road by Carlisle Bridge I spotted another of Mr Ali's green and purple vans. You generally saw them all over the place, but this one made me sit up and take notice.

For a start, it had pulled up just where the two lanes from over Greyhound Bridge narrow into one under the railway line, and was causing quite a major constriction in the traffic flow. The second thing that turned my head was the man leaning in through the passenger-side window to talk to the driver.

It was unmistakably Langford.

As I watched, he took his last cigarette out, stuck it between his lips, and tossed the crumpled empty pack onto the pavement behind him. Then he opened the door and climbed in, ignoring the annoyed hooting of horns. The van driver pulled straight out into traffic with enough disdain for the Highway Code to have earned him an instant re-test.

I wondered vaguely if Mr Ali knew that the head of the Copthorne vigilante brigade was cadging lifts at his expense.

Several hours later, I wheeled the bike out and headed for work. Within fifteen minutes of relatively easy town traffic I'd pulled up outside the gym.

Attila's place used to be an auto salvage yard with such a dodgy reputation that some wag had once painted 'reserved for police vehicle only' on a section of the rusting iron fencing just inside the gate. It was still there, despite the change of use and ownership, and I ran the bike into the space underneath the faded lettering.

Against every advice, Attila had snapped the whole property up for a song when it finally closed down for good a few years ago. He'd turned the tatty workshop and storage area into a spacious fitness room, complete with a sauna. It wasn't snazzy, but it had the workmanlike atmosphere that suggests real people who are seriously into the job, rather than a poseurs' palace.

Usually, it was bustling, but today of all days, it was dead. I spent the first hour as the only inhabitant, and took the opportunity to get my own workout in, just in case things hotted up later.

I used to train a lot, starting when I was in the army and needed to build up both my strength and my stamina. After I was kicked out, it became a method of relaxation of sorts. A way to shut my brain down through sheer physical exhaustion. To rid myself of my frustration and anger, taking it out on the machines.

I was halfway through a tough set of bench presses when I finally got some company. The two blokes who came in were regulars, and they were into it enough to wave me on with the set. Conscious of them watching, I rushed through the last five reps before moving over to the counter to sign them in.

They were a friendly enough pair, giving me the usual cheery amount of stick as they hefted their sports bags and went to get changed. It was only when they reappeared that a sudden thought occurred to me.

'Wayne,' I said to one of them, while they were still doing their warm-up exercises, 'don't you work for Mr Ali, the builder?'

Wayne gave a grunt, but whether that was at my question, or because he was attempting to touch his toes, I couldn't be sure. He was a well-built black man, with hands like shovels. He was currently struggling to ward off a beer gut and only just keeping pace with it. 'Used to, girl,' he said. 'Got laid off couple of weeks back.'

'Really? I thought he was doing well.'

'Yeah, so did I.' He gave me a wry smile. 'Half a dozen of us got the punt at the same time. Last in, first out. That's the way it goes. He reckons he's got a big contract coming off soon, and we'll be back in there but, tell you the truth, I'm not bothered. I'm working for that mob who are converting the old asylum now. Pay's better.'

I digested the information, then decided a hunch was worth a try. 'D'you know a guy called Langford?'

He frowned. 'Oh yeah,' he said, suddenly guarded, 'we all know him.'

If I'd been a horse, my ears would have pricked straight up at his tone. 'Why's that?'

For a moment Wayne looked as though he'd said too much, then he shrugged. His loyalties lay elsewhere these days. 'He and the boss, well, there's something going on there, and I'm damned if I know what, girl,' he said. 'That Langford used to flag us down like we was bloody taxis. Take me here, take me there. I tried to complain to the boss about it once, but he said don't ask questions.' He shrugged. 'I got rent to pay, so I didn't ask.'

'And you've no idea what was going on?'

He shook his head, plonking one foot up on a bench and reaching over it to stretch his hamstrings. When he came upright again, he said darkly, 'All I *do* know is, he always turned up on a site, convenient like, on a Thursday afternoon, and the boss used to hand him a pay packet just like the rest of us. If Langford wasn't such a bloody racist, I'd say they must be related or something. Know what I mean?'

The door went again as more of the evening lads came in. I smiled my thanks to Wayne, and went to deal with them. Langford and Mr Ali? As unlikely combinations went, it was right up there at the top of the list.

Attila came in around six-thirty, and that's when the place really started to busy up. Once people knew his schedule they tended to time their visits to coincide with his presence. I didn't take it personally. It was his place, after all.

I finished around nine, changed into my leathers and stuffed my gear into my tank bag. It was dark outside, cold and drizzly. I didn't wait too long for the Suzuki to warm up before I was on my way.

Traffic was starting to bulk up through town. As I filtered

down the outside of it going past the bus station, a taxi stuck its nose out from the rank into traffic, blocking my path. I sighed and braked to a halt with the rain tenaciously drilling its way down the back of my neck.

I tried to leave as much room as I could between my front wheel and the taxi's exhaust pipe while I reflected morosely that it didn't seem to be my day for clean air.

There were times when riding a bike all year round was a real pain. I really was going to have to splash out on a decent pair of gloves. My fingers were already wet and before I got back to Pauline's I knew the tips of them would have gone numb.

We were alongside a little café and I glanced idly through the window into the brightly-lit interior with something like envy. There were two people sitting at the table by the window, drinking coffee. Their hands were wrapped round the mugs and I could just imagine the warmth of the hot liquid seeping through the china.

As I watched, one of them lifted the mug to his mouth and drank, and as my gaze followed its progress I realised I was looking at a face I knew. It was the boy from Fariman's garden.

Roger put the mug back on the table, keeping one hand round it, using the other to illustrate his speech as he talked earnestly to his companion. It was with some sense of shock that I recognised the other boy, too.

He was probably the last person I would have expected to find relaxing in the company of a teenage thug on the fast track to a long stretch inside. Yet there they were, chatting away like old friends.

Nasir.

Five

The driver of the car behind me blew his horn, making me jump, and I realised that the taxi was long gone. I hastily booted the bike into gear and flung the clutch out with all the finesse of a first-day learner. The Suzuki made its displeasure plain by bounding forwards, and then refusing to drop cleanly into second.

Cursing under my breath at the fluffed change, I brought my mind back onto the job in hand. The last thing I could afford to do was try and ride through darkened rush-hour traffic preoccupied. I like my legs just the shape they are, thanks all the same.

With an effort I pushed the significance of what I'd just seen way into the background. Roger was from Copthorne. Nasir was from Lavender Gardens. They should have been at each other's throats. Race almost didn't come into it.

I swung across Greyhound Bridge and onto the road to Morecambe, filtering down the outside of the cars when they shuffled to a standstill. It didn't take long before I was turning in to Lavender Gardens and weaving through the gloomy back streets.

I'd let my brain wander by this point, churning it over and

over to try and make some sense of it. What on earth was the connection between Roger and Nasir? I knew Nasir had been in trouble, too, but I also remembered the way he'd flown off the handle over the attack on his uncle.

At the time, I'd thought his anger was aimed at Roger and his mates, but it wasn't. He knew far more than he was telling about all this. I needed to talk to him about it. Try and get something more out of him. Perhaps O'Bryan might have a better idea of what was going on. As I turned in to Kirby Street, I made a mental note to give him a call.

Then a big man carrying what looked like a baseball bat stepped out of the shadows into the road in front of me.

My first thought as I grabbed for the front brake was that Roger had somehow already got wind of my intention to go the distance, and had sent the boys round. Timing and logic didn't come into it. This was straight gut-reaction fear.

The Suzuki's tyres slithered on the wet greasy tarmac as I locked the wheels up tight, stepping the back end out. Somehow, I managed to bring the bike to an untidy halt within about six feet of him, slanted across the road. I put my feet down, shaky, heart bouncing against my ribs.

The man had made no move to get out of my path. Arrogance made him confident that I would stop in time. That I wouldn't dare run him down. I wondered if he tried the same tactic with buses and trucks.

For a couple of beats, nothing happened. Then he swaggered forwards to meet me, and I saw that the baseball bat was actually one of those oversize torches. The type so favoured by jumped-up security guards without the authority to carry a weapon for real.

He came right up to the fairing, crowding me, tall enough for me to have to crick my neck up to make eye-contact with him through my visor. His was a face that had seen some action, the bridge of the nose lumped with scar tissue. There was the line of an old knife wound cutting through his moustache stubble from nostril to upper lip.

He was a sizeable bloke, wearing the black bomber jacket and dark cargo trousers of the professional bruiser. I've come across enough of them in my time to recognise the type without needing a diagram. I was reminded strongly of Langford.

It was only when he spoke that my preconceptions took a knock. 'OK, sonny, where do you think you're going?' he demanded, surprising me with the genuine cut-glass accent that came out of his thuggish mouth.

I didn't bother to correct his mistake. Even in these enlightened times nobody expects a girl to be riding a motor-bike. 'Home,' I said shortly, my voice muffled by my scarf. 'What's it to do with you?'

'You'd be wise not to take that tone with me, my lad,' he warned with a grim smile. He thrust his chin forwards, showing me his teeth and the whites of his eyes all the way round the irises. The skin of his face was stretched over wide cheekbones that protruded through it, revealing the shape of his skull.

Close up, he was older than I'd first thought. Even under the streetlighting, I could see that the hair cropped short to his scalp was silver, not blond. The lines were etched deep into his face like penknife graffiti in an old school desk.

'Come on,' he said, roughly now. 'Let's have that helmet off and have a look at you.'

'*What?* You've got to be kidding?' I managed, appalled. 'Who the hell d'you think you are?'

At that moment another figure appeared from a ginnel between two houses and joined the first. He was younger, shorter, not so broad in the shoulder, but the haircut and the uniform was the same. This was starting to get creepy.

'You got trouble, boss?' he asked, not taking his eyes off

me. His voice wasn't nearly so far upmarket, but he was trying hard to match it, and his tone was hopeful, spoiling for a fight.

I pride myself on being a pretty good judge of sticky situations, but I didn't have to be to work out that now was a good time to back down.

With a sigh I yanked my gloves off and undid the chinstrap holding my battered old Arai helmet in place, pulling that off over my head.

For a moment, surprise held them still, then the big bloke laughed.

'Well, well,' he said softly. 'I'd no idea that I was in the presence of a lady.'

'You're not,' I said, my voice icy. 'I don't suppose you'd like to tell me who you are and what the hell is going on?'

'My apologies,' he said, mocking. 'My name is Ian Garton-Jones. Myself – and Mr West here – and my colleagues, have been contracted in a clean-up capacity on this estate.'

I suddenly remembered my last conversation with Mrs Gadatra over the garden fence. She'd mentioned a Mr Garton-Jones, but I feigned ignorance. 'Clean-up?' I queried, frowning.

'That's correct.' He showed his teeth again. Friday would have made the gesture look more friendly. 'We're here to gather up all the rubbish, the crap, the dregs, and the trash, and keep it off the streets,' he said with deliberate emphasis. The inference was clear.

'Animal, vegetable, or mineral?' I asked flippantly.

He shrugged. It was of no importance to him. 'Whatever it takes.'

'And that involves doing a "stand and deliver" routine on every passing motorist coming into the estate, does it?'

'Oh that's just a temporary measure, Miss–?' He left the question hanging.

'Fox,' I supplied, unable to find a reason other than pure pigheadedness not to tell him who I was. Even so, it was tempting. 'My name is Charlie Fox.'

'There, you see, it's not so bad, is it, Miss Fox?' Garton-Jones said. His tone was supposed to be soothing. It only succeeded in winding my irritation up a notch higher. West stood slightly back and to his left, keeping quiet, but missing nothing. 'Once we've identified everyone with a right to be here, you won't be troubled again.'

When I gave my name, West pulled out a hardbacked notebook from his inside pocket and flicked on his own torch as he studied the pages. 'I don't seem to have you listed as a resident here, Miss Fox,' he said politely, his voice deceptively mild. 'Would you mind telling me the purpose of your visit tonight?'

'I'm house-sitting for a friend,' I bit out. I knew I was going to have to tell them more than that, but they were going to have to work for it.

'House-sitting?' Garton-Jones repeated, his interest quickening. 'For whom? Which house?' He rapped out the questions. Despite his upper-class accent, the civility was little more than a cigarette-paper thin veneer covering the savagery underneath. I knew that if I was clever I'd stop being obstructive now, and tell them what they wanted to know.

So, I gave them Pauline's name and address, told them how long she was going to be away. West jotted it all down in his notebook, which he shut with a snap when he was finished.

'OK, Miss Fox,' Garton-Jones said. 'You can go now. We'll be having a word with Mrs Jamieson when she returns, though. Just to let her know that there's no need to trouble any of her friends in the future. Streetwise Securities are in control of this area now. Next time she's away, we'll be looking after her property.'

I bridled silently at his smug tone. Pauline would probably have something to say about that, but it wasn't up to me to put words into her mouth. 'I'm sure she'll be thrilled,' I told him sweetly.

Garton-Jones either didn't hear the sarcasm or chose to rise above my low wit. 'It's all part of the service,' he said neutrally, standing back and waving me on with a slight bow.

I tugged my helmet back on, trying not to mutter under my breath. But, as I toed the bike into gear, I was blinded by the sudden flare of main-beam headlights from the other end of the street.

'What the——?' Garton-Jones spun round, jerking a hand up to protect his eyes.

I heard the roar of a big V8 engine, being caned straight down the middle of the road. The sound seemed to leap towards me, increasing in size with such speed and ferocity that for a moment I was paralysed.

At the last minute, I grabbed a handful of throttle and banged the clutch out. The bike jumped forwards like a racehorse leaving the starting gate and shot across the road.

I just about managed to slot into a gap between two parked cars, and jolted clumsily up the low kerb onto the pavement, stalling the motor.

I twisted round to see Garton-Jones and West dive out of the way with an undignified haste that was grimly pleasing. It was difficult to make out much more than the basic shape of the vehicle that came barrelling through the space we'd so recently vacated. One of these new four-by-fours, with a set of industrial bull-bars on the front. Other than that, I couldn't even have given you the colour.

It reached the corner of the street and slithered round it in a near-perfect sideways drift, engine howling as the tyres skittered over the wet road surface. I couldn't suppress a certain amount of admiration for the driver. Whoever was behind the wheel obviously knew his stuff.

Before the tail-lights had even disappeared, Garton-Jones had grabbed a walkie-talkie from his belt and was snarling into it. 'Gary! What the fuck's going on at your end?' he demanded. 'That damned Grand Cherokee with the Dutch plates on it has just been through here again like it's a fucking racetrack. Either keep that end of the estate locked down, or I'll put someone in charge who can.'

He shoved the walkie-talkie into his jacket pocket without waiting for a reply. He glared first at West, and then across at me, as though daring either of us to comment. Neither of us fancied the prospects of that move overmuch.

I busied myself with flicking the gear lever back into neutral so I could kick-start the bike again. I rode it carefully ten metres along the uneven pavement until there was a gap between the parked cars, and dropped back into the road.

As I rode the short distance to Pauline's place, I reflected that the arrival of Garton-Jones and his mob on Lavender Gardens should have meant things had just got better. So why couldn't I shake the feeling they'd just taken a downward turn? And one so steep it was more like a nose-dive.

That evening, unable to put it off any longer, I rang Pauline in Canada.

I'd been avoiding making the call, in the hope that things were going to get better. The likelihood of that one was far away, and growing dimmer all the time.

I couldn't lie to her when she asked what had been going on, and even though I severely edited down the truth, she was still horrified by news of the attack on Fariman, and the arrival of Garton-Jones and his boys.

'The Committee were talking about calling his lot in before I left, but I didn't think they'd be stupid enough to actually go ahead with it. They'll bleed us dry,' she said bluntly, her voice coming across the transatlantic line as clear as a local call. 'Oh, why did this have to happen now, when I can't do a damned thing about it?'

'There's another Committee meeting next week. I'll go,' I heard myself saying. 'I'll try and stall them. He's just totally the wrong man for the job.'

'OK, Charlie,' she said, still sounding worried, 'just don't do anything rash, will you?'

I said of course not in what I hoped was a convincing tone, and Pauline rang off, slightly more reassured.

I didn't want to go walking into that meeting completely blind, but it still took me a few moments of staring at the telephone to make the decision to call Jacob and Clare for help.

If you'd asked me at the beginning of last winter if they were my friends I would have said yes without hesitation. Then I'd put Clare in a position of danger from which she'd been lucky to escape alive. It wasn't that they hadn't forgiven me over it, you understand.

I hadn't forgiven myself.

I picked the receiver up quickly, and dialled before I had chance to change my mind. Jacob answered almost straight away.

'Oh, hi Charlie,' he said. Was it me, or did he sound a little cool in his greeting? 'Long time, no hear.'

I could picture the long rangy figure, his dark wavy hair flashed through with grey. He would be sitting at the scrubbed pine table in the kitchen of their big, comfortably untidy old house just outside Caton village.

In theory, Jacob had a study from which to run his classic motorbike spares and antiques business, but I'd never seen him do any work there. He always preferred to use the kitchen, where he could listen to the radio and be company for the dogs.

Even now, once Clare was home from work in the evening, he tended to stay put, still making or waiting for phone calls from other dealers in the States. He always complained that they had no idea which way time zones operated.

'Sorry, I've been a bit up to my neck,' I said, feeling even more guilty that I was only ringing now because I needed a favour.

'So, girl, when are we going to see you round here for some supper?' he said, and I realised I'd been being over-sensitive. 'I've got this great new way of roasting lamb that'll have you drooling.'

'Sounds great. I'll try and get up there soon,' I promised. 'I'm house-sitting at the moment. A friend's place on Lavender Gardens.'

'Yeah? Well, I hope you've got your bike alarm set fine, then, because from what Clare tells me all things both red hot, *and* nailed down have been disappearing from round that neck of the woods lately.'

Clare works for the local paper, the *Lancaster & District Defender*, so she gets all the news and gossip before it filters down to us proles. Not that she's a journalist, but even working in the accounts department she still hears plenty.

'I was hoping she might be able to give me a bit of gen about that, actually,' I said, wincing in case Jacob saw through my obvious ploy. If he did, he was too much of a gentleman to comment on it.

'Hang on,' he said. 'I'll give her a shout. She climbed straight into the bath when she got home and I think she might still be there, the wrinkled old prune.' I heard him cover the mouthpiece to yell for Clare up the stairs. 'No, you're in luck,' he said after a moment, 'she's surfaced and she's on her way.

You take care now, Charlie,' he added softly, 'and don't leave it so long next time, hey?'

'I won't,' I told him, unable to suppress a warm, gooey kind of feeling at the rich sincerity in his voice. Jacob has that persuasive way of talking that makes even the most casual of conventional remarks seem like it's been said just for you. The best thing is, he hasn't the faintest idea he's doing it. If he wasn't just about double my age − not to mention well and truly spoken for − I'd be in there like a shot.

Still, the age thing has never worried Clare much. She's twenty-six, like me, but there the similarity ends. I'm afraid I can't lay claim to blonde supermodel good looks, nor her ability to ride her Ducati 851 Strada like the local B-roads are her own personal racetrack.

She and Jacob have been together for as long as I've known them. They might seem an unlikely couple, particularly as he's partly crocked up from too many youthful motorbike racing accidents, but I couldn't honestly imagine either of them with anybody else.

I heard Clare come into the kitchen and take over the receiver. 'Hello stranger,' she said brightly.

We exchanged idle chit-chat for a few minutes, then I steered the conversation back round to the recent happenings on Lavender Gardens, with particular reference to Ian Garton-Jones's presence on the estate. 'I understand his company, Streetwise Securities, have been working on a couple of other estates locally, and he's had quite an effect,' I said. 'Your mate on the crime desk wouldn't be able to fill in any gaps for me, would he?'

'Probably,' Clare said. 'The name rings a bell, and I seem to remember us running some stories on him. I got the impression that we took a slightly disapproving stance − you know, the vigilante angle − but the residents all thought he was wonderful. I'll find out what I can and give you a shout.'

After we'd finished our conversation I spent some time thinking over the decision to intervene more than I had done already in the affairs of Lavender Gardens. I wondered if it was a poor choice.

I came to the conclusion that it probably was.

Six

By the time Streetwise Securities had been on guard for three days, my vague impression of unease had hardened into certainty.

Garton-Jones was efficient all right, but he achieved his results with a ruthless disregard for personal freedom. Nobody got in without their say-so, which was irritating, but OK. But, nobody got out either. In the space of a few short days, Lavender Gardens had been ghetto-ised. I doubt the Gestapo could have done it better.

The kids in particular were running scared of him. Before, they'd played football in the road, or sat around on the corner of the next street along, by the little late-night convenience store, furtively smoking cigarettes. Now they were conspicuous by their absence. It was like they were under curfew.

For myself, I remembered my promise to Pauline, and kept my head down. After my initial run in, Garton-Jones's men didn't stop me again, but they always seemed to be around, lurking in the background to note my movements. I wondered if they were compiling a dossier.

They popped up out of nowhere the first few times I took Friday for his twice-daily constitutional. The way they suddenly materialised was too constant ever to be coincidence.

It was at this point I discovered that, either by good luck or good training, the Ridgeback regarded any approaches on the street by strange men as a hostile act. Afterwards, they steered well clear of us.

As the dog's senses were infinitely more acute than my own, he provided me with a superb early warning system. If I was on foot, I took him nearly everywhere with me and remained totally unmolested.

Sod's law, then, that the one time when I could have really used the services of a big fierce dog was also the one time I'd left him at home.

It was another miserable evening. A thick stifling blanket of fog had coasted up from the River Lune and was hanging over Lavender Gardens like doom. Friday had been singularly unimpressed by it during his walk. When I rattled his lead to suggest another outing just before nine o'clock, he slunk onto his beanbag in the kitchen and studiously pretended to be asleep.

It was only a short distance to the shop. I set out alone in search of something as mundane as a pint of milk, and didn't think I was risking my neck by doing so.

As it was, I cut through another of the little ginnels that dissected all the streets on Lavender Gardens, keeping my head down against the mist that clung to my face like a cobweb. The illumination from the streetlights was reduced to an eerie cone-shaped glow round their bases. I began to wish I'd been a little more insistent with Friday.

The fog muffled sound as well as sight, so that I was almost on top of the men before I realised they were there.

Looking at it clinically, it was a good quiet spot for an ambush. A secluded area tucked away behind the shop, little more than an alleyway, colonised on one side by a row of lock-up garages. There were no overlooking windows, and plenty of space to put the boot in.

And somebody was doing that with gusto. Putting the boot in, I mean. I heard the sickening sounds of fists and feet being applied with enthusiasm. Grunts of exertion, and corresponding gasps of pain. So much for Garton-Jones and his boys stopping this sort of thing happening, I thought bitterly.

Without really knowing what I was going to do, I edged closer, staying close to the garages. Gradually the scene unfolded out of the murk. On balance, I think I preferred it when it was out of focus.

There were two men standing with a boy lying buckled at their feet. They were part of Garton-Jones's merry brigade if looks were anything to go by. I wondered if he made all new staff have the same company haircut.

I moved forwards, keeping slow and careful, although it was difficult to be stealthy with so much loose gravel under my feet. The two men had their full attention riveted on their fallen prey. Their faces told me that's all he was to them. Blood lust is never pretty, and this was about as ugly as it gets.

The boy was down, but he wasn't out yet, I'll give him that. I don't know how long they'd been working him over, but as I watched, he dragged himself up onto his elbows and tried to escape. To crawl away on his belly, oblivious to how hopeless a cause it was.

The man nearest to the boy let him move a couple of feet, then kicked him brutally in the ribs, hard enough to flip him over. He put all his strength into it, arms splayed for balance, like a pro footballer aiming to blast the ball right through the back of the net.

'You Paki-loving little bastard,' he spat. 'You've had your warnings, and your chances, but you were too fucking stupid to listen, weren't you, sunshine? And if this doesn't teach you a lesson, you know who we're going to come after next time, don't you?'

I reckoned I'd let things go about as far as I could stand.

Abandoning my cover, I stepped out into open ground, and walked towards them. I aimed for calm, but the rage was bubbling away dangerously under the surface.

As I closed the gap between us, the boy lay mewling quietly on his back, exposed. His clothes were caked with dirt, his face an unrecognisable slab of blood and swelling. He wasn't Asian, but that was about as far towards identifying him as I could get. Right now, his own mother would have struggled.

The second man moved forwards eagerly for his turn, pulling back his fist to land another grinding blow to his victim's head.

'I think he's had enough, don't you?' I said coldly, pitching my voice just loud enough to be heard.

The men wheeled round in sync, shifting to stand between me and the boy, as if to hide what they'd been up to. Only their faces weren't ashamed.

'Fuck off if you know what's good for you,' one of them growled.

'And let you kill him?' I demanded. 'What's the matter – don't you have the balls to pick on someone your own size?'

The would-be footballer gave me a vicious grin. 'Nah,' he said. 'And I don't mind hitting women, neither.'

Just to prove it, he launched himself at me. It was clumsy and obvious, but then, he wasn't expecting opposition. I made sure I hit him hard enough for his legs to fold under him. Caught the dull surprise on his face as he went down.

Astounded, his partner watched him fall. He came on then with a ferocity laced with guile, feinting me out. I nearly didn't make it out of the way at all, and thought myself lucky to dodge back, smarting, with just a split lip to show for the exchange.

You should have run, I told myself bitterly, riding another punch. *You should have run screaming for the police. They would have left him alone then. Ah well, too late for that now.*

When the first man got to his feet and joined in, I knew I was in big trouble. They were brawling without restraint, but I couldn't free my mind of the last time I'd truly let go. I'd unleashed a demon I couldn't control, and daren't try to again.

It was like trying to fight with my hands tied, and eventually it was what overpowered me.

A stunning blow to the side of my head took me off my feet. Once I was on the floor they started in with their boots, as they had done on the boy. It wasn't exactly what I'd choose to do for fun.

Then, as suddenly as it had started, it stopped. I rolled over onto my side and was aware of a band of brilliant light cutting through the mist. There was no mistaking the bellow of the V8 that accompanied it, rumbling through the concrete under us.

The Dutch-registered Grand Cherokee that had run me off the road only a few days before roared into the mouth of the garage area. The headlights leapt and shuddered as the wheels smacked through the potholes. It slammed to a halt twenty metres away, nodding on its suspension.

For a moment the Cherokee just sat there, and my attackers stilled with it, wary. Then the engine note rose sharply, and the tyres scrabbled for grip on the loose surface. The two men jumped for safety as a couple of tons of off-road vehicle came bowling down the alleyway, with myself and the boy directly in its path.

Just when I was expecting to be turned into pavement pizza, the driver stood on the brake pedal hard enough to trip the ABS. As it kicked in, the anti-lock system let out a terrible graunching noise, like a wounded cow, but slewed the vehicle to an effective standstill. I covered my face against the shrapnel burst of small stones scattered in its path.

Garton-Jones's men didn't hang around to see if the boy and I were going to be squashed flat. They legged it as soon as the four-by-four started its run. Sprinting away down the alley, vaulting over a rotting fence at the bottom.

They needn't have worried about being run down. The jeep stopped within a dozen feet of me, but I found I didn't have the energy to get up. My head was splitting and my back burned. I swallowed, and found the inky tang of blood in my mouth.

The fog swirled like dust in the beam of the lights, blocking my vision of anything much past the big slatted grille. Where the moisture hit the hot radiator, it raised breaths of steam. I vaguely saw both doors opening. Two pairs of booted feet jumped down onto the concrete, moving quickly. One set went straight past me, heading for the boy.

I lifted my head and saw a big dark-coated figure bending next to him. He pulled off his gloves and searched for a pulse under the boy's jawline. There was something familiar about him, the size, the shape, but placing it defeated me.

I couldn't see the man's face, but I read anger in the sudden tensing of his body. Very gently, he worked his arms under the boy's shoulders and legs, and lifted him clear off the ground easily, as though he were a child. The boy cried out as he was picked up, and the man muttered darkly under his breath.

The second figure approached me, rolling me gingerly onto my back and peering into my face. I was surprised to see a very attractive girl, with long dark hair. She looked startled.

The man stepped round me, intent on getting his burden into the vehicle. The girl jumped up, laying a hand on his arm.

'Wait!' she said sharply. 'What about her?'

'Her?' The man hardly paused, dipping his head to flick a single, indifferent glance at my crumpled form. 'We don't have time for complications,' he snapped. 'Leave her,' and his voice was cold.

'We can't just leave her,' the girl argued quietly. 'By the

looks of it she's taken a hammering as well. If they come back and find her, you know what they'll do.'

The man let out his breath in a controlled hiss. 'OK, Madeleine, get her in, but hurry up. This place will be crawling any minute.'

Madeleine, bless her, didn't need telling twice. She hauled me to my feet, draping my arm across her slender shoulders to half-drag me to the jeep and bundle me into the back seat. She slammed the door behind me, and hopped nimbly into the front.

The man loaded the boy in from the other side, lying him sideways across the plush leather bench seat. I ended up with his battered head on my lap.

'Hold tight,' he ordered briefly over his shoulder as he regained the driver's seat. It threw me for a moment until I realised that the Cherokee was left-hand drive.

He thrust the gear lever into reverse and the four-by-four did its best to pebbledash anything within ten feet of the front end as the tyres bit, firing us backwards. I clutched at the boy to stop him going crashing into the footwell.

The man rocketed through the estate, shooting junctions with a blatant disregard for possible other traffic. A couple of times I saw running figures as Garton-Jones's men tried once more, in vain, to close off our escape route.

Finally, wrestling with the wheel, he broadsided out onto the main road, causing an oncoming BMW driver to dive for the brakes and the horn. Then we were barrelling along in the direction of Morecambe.

I glanced down at the boy's face. His eyes were closed, one of them forced shut by the swelling, and the other not far behind. The bruising was already starting to show, great blotches of discoloration. His nose was bleeding, but probably not broken. I reckoned the cuts and grazes that covered the left side of his face would mostly heal without scarring.

It was only then, as I studied him in the intermittent waves of illumination from the streetlights, that I recognised the boy as Roger.

It was odd, the emotion that filled me at that moment. Mrs Gadatra had been so emphatic when she'd said he deserved a beating. I wondered if she'd still be so vehement if she could see him now. The idea was one thing, the reality quite another.

I looked up at my rescuers sharply. Who the hell were these two? I remembered O'Bryan saying Roger was one of three, with a brother and a sister. The brother, he'd remarked, was known to be a bit of a hard-case. Hell, I could believe that of this guy.

I wasn't so sure about his appraisal of the sister, though. The girl in the front seat had that ex-private school look about her. All long bones and good breeding. She didn't act like a trainee hooker, however you squared it.

'So, where are we going?' It was Madeleine who asked, but if she hadn't, I probably would have done.

'We need to get him home, get him cleaned up,' the man said, not taking his eyes off the road.

'You want your mum to see him in this state?' she demanded, blowing my sister theory right out of the water. 'He needs a doctor.'

'Don't worry about Mum. Between me and my dear departed Dad, she's seen plenty of trouble in her time. We'll get him home, check him out,' he insisted. 'The first sign that he's got internal, I'll take him straight to the hospital, OK?' He risked a glance across at her then, and for the first time I saw his profile clearly against the lights.

It stopped my breath.

When O'Bryan had told me Roger's surname, I thought he'd said Mayor, but I'd been wrong. It was Meyer. And he had an older brother, all right, who'd fallen in with a rough crowd, and had moved away.

He'd joined the army, for which he'd been perfectly psychologically and physically suited. He'd excelled as a soldier, quickly making sergeant. Eventually he'd become a training instructor on one of the toughest courses devised by the military.

I know, because I was there.

I'd loved him, and he'd betrayed me. Dropped me to the wolves and left me to be ripped to pieces by them alone. Once the news of our affair had broken, and the press had turned on me, that love had withered, died, and rotted into hatred.

Sean Meyer was a name from my past that I'd hoped never to hear again in this lifetime, let alone come face-to-face with its owner. . .

Had he recognised me? He'd certainly been watching the estate, keeping tabs on his younger brother. I thought he'd been aiming for Garton-Jones that night when he'd nearly run us down, but it could just as easily have been me.

Leave her. With a shudder I remembered his words back there in the alleyway. If it wasn't for Madeleine, whoever she was, I'd still be there, with the hard-liners from Streetwise Securities using me as a surrogate punchbag. Venting their frustration that their real victim had got away.

Still, Sean was damned good at abandoning people when they needed him.

Now, he veered the Cherokee off the main road, ducking through half a dozen dark and empty back streets, veiled by the fog. I watched his eyes keep flicking to the rear-view mirror, constantly checking for any sign of pursuit. I suppose it was inevitable that eventually he'd have the chance to take a proper look at me.

And as soon as he did, he knew.

How could he not?

I saw the eyes widen. He jumped like he'd been shot, and stamped on the brakes, twisting round in his seat to stare at me directly, as though the mirror might have lied. Madeleine gasped as she was thrown forwards and the inertia jammed her seatbelt. I nearly lost hold of Roger's still-unconscious body.

Then I took one look at the angry disbelief in Sean's face, and totally bottled it. Before the vehicle had even stopped, I'd flung open the door, and catapulted out onto the road.

We can't have been doing more than ten miles an hour or so by that time, and decelerating hard, but it was enough to unbalance me. I rolled through the fall, and came up on my feet, already running.

I heard Sean shout to Madeleine, 'Stay with the boy!' and then he was out of the vehicle too, and pounding hard on my tail.

I was never a fast runner, but adrenalin is a powerful stimulant, and fear gave me a turn of speed I didn't know I possessed. I reached a junction and dipped round it. Unless I was out of his sight, I knew I stood no chance of evading him. Sean was predatory and relentless. It was in his nature.

I ran with everything I'd got, not lifting my head, not looking back. I made another couple of frantic turns, found myself outside a short row of closed-up shops. There was a yard alongside one of them, barred by a mesh gate about ten feet high.

It was an instant decision. I took a flyer at it, sheer momentum carrying me far enough up to grab the top rail and swing my body over in one fluid movement. By the time Sean appeared, I was fifteen feet further back, down behind a stack of pallets. Breathless and terrified.

For such a big man, Sean moved smooth and quiet, with a deadly purpose. Even in army boots his ability to creep up undetected on the unwary had bordered on the supernatural. In the intervening years it seemed he hadn't lost the knack.

I peeped through the slats in the pallet and saw him stop by the gate, staring up at it. Judging the height, and the probability of my having fled this way. He was still as heavily muscled across the shoulder as he had been when I'd known him. Built like a boxer, exuding menace.

I squeezed my eyes shut as if I was a kid. As if my being unable to see him would also work in reverse.

I heard his footsteps and risked another look. He'd moved back from the gate, turning a slow circle. Alert, as if trying to sense where I'd gone to ground. I fought to keep my breathing steady.

Headlights swept across the gateway then. Sean rounded sharply, and I shrank back. I saw the Cherokee pull up at the kerb next to him. Madeleine had moved over to take the wheel. She leaned out of the window.

'Have you found her?'

'No.'

'What on earth made her take off like that?'

Sean didn't answer that one. Prowling back over to the gate, he reached up suddenly to smack the mesh with both hands. Making it clatter and jangle. Making me gasp.

'Charlie,' he called out, 'I know you're in there somewhere.'

I kept silent, but my heartrate took off.

'You can't hide forever, Charlie,' he said, more quietly. 'We've unfinished business, you and I.'

The words were left hanging. Sinister. Malign.

'Sean, I hate to hurry you, but we really need to get your brother fixed up,' Madeleine broke in. 'Judging by the way she did a runner, the girl's not so badly hurt, and she obviously doesn't want to be found. Come on. We've got enough problems of our own to worry about.'

Sean let out a pinched breath through his nose, shoulders hunched, then he turned without a second glance and stalked back to the jeep. I squirmed round, seeing him climb into the passenger seat and slam the door.

'OK,' I heard him say tightly, 'let's go.'

For a good quarter of an hour after the heavy exhaust note had faded into the night, I remained in my hiding place, not moving. It was only when a thin drizzle of rain started to fall out of the mist that I forced my frozen limbs to stir.

It took willpower to do it. I had an evil headache and the metallic bitterness of the blood I kept swallowing left my stomach raw.

Without the primitive flight reflex boosting me, I found I couldn't get back over the gate. My hands were grazed and starting to throb, and my bruised body protested more at every failed attempt. Eventually I had to drag one of the pallets over to the base and use that to gain initial purchase on the mesh. Even so, it was an undignified scramble.

On the other side, I realised I had no real idea where I was. I turned in the opposite direction to the way the Cherokee had gone, and started walking. Finally, I reached the main road. I plodded on, one step after another into fog that hung like smoke under the streetlights.

Partly by luck, and partly by keeping a very low profile, I managed to get back to Pauline's without encountering either Sean, or Garton-Jones's mob. The way I was feeling, I don't know which would have been the less preferable option.

Seven

The next morning I dragged myself out of bed with enough aches and pains to send me groaning for the bathroom. My flat only has a shower, and the prospect of access to a long soak whenever I wanted one had in no way helped persuade me to house-sit for Pauline in the first place.

By the time I'd soaked my way through three chin-deep refills of hot water, it was time to get sorted and head for the gym.

I briefly took stock of my reflection in the mirror in the hall on the way out, and found the split lip much less noticeable than it had felt the night before. I reckoned I could probably claim a bit of boisterous behaviour on Friday's part to explain it away if I had to.

The day was uneventful apart from a phone call from Eric O'Bryan, asking if I'd had chance to reconsider my decision to support Roger. I took the opportunity to pick his brains about the relationship between Roger and Nasir.

'If they're mates, it just doesn't fit in with Nasir's threats against whoever's behind the robbery,' I said. 'But, on the other hand I suppose if he's so friendly with one of the lads who was involved, he might have an inside track, know there's something deeper going on. What do you think?'

'Hm,' O'Bryan said. 'You may be right. There certainly seems to be more to this than meets the eye. Tell you what, leave it with me and let me nose around for a few days, and I'll get back to you. It gives you chance to think a bit more about that caution as well, eh?'

I made noncommittal noises, which obviously failed to reassure him about my change of heart, but when he probed further, I stalled him.

He wasn't happy being fobbed off, but knew pushing me wouldn't get him anywhere. He took my continued indecision on the best of his chins, and promised to call again.

I trundled home again in the early evening, running the gauntlet of Garton-Jones's boys. They stood and watched the Suzuki pass as I rode into Lavender Gardens, but made no move to intercept me. A glance over my shoulder found they'd moved out into the road behind me and were speaking into their walkie-talkies. I couldn't shake the smothering feeling that I'd just stepped into the closing jaws of a trap.

Back at Pauline's, I wheeled the bike through the back gate quickly, and into the shed. When I came back out, snapping the padlock firmly shut, I stilled, listening. It was only the faintest suggestion of a noise from over the garden fence, but it sounded very much like a sob.

I sneaked up to the fence and peered over it. The Gadatras weren't big on gardening and the place had been allowed to run wild. Uncut dead winter grass lay brown and matted over most of the area.

Halfway down, past the looping washing line, the garden had been abandoned entirely to the children. The main feature was a half-deflated paddling pool that didn't look as though it had been capable of holding water for years, the sides mouldy and creased.

And there at the bottom, on a lopsided rickety swing, sat Nasir. He was wearing jeans and just a T-shirt with no thought to the sting of cold, rocking himself gently backwards and forwards, as though in a trance.

He had a cigarette held with the lit end shielded in the cup of his hand, like a seasoned outdoor smoker. Every few seconds his hand went jerkily to his mouth, and he dragged air through the filter in quick, nervous puffs. When the cigarette was dead he looked at it in surprise, as though he didn't remember smoking.

For a moment he stared at nothing, eyes blank and stony. Then something seemed to break inside him. His face crumpled in on itself, and he brought his hands up to cover it, body beginning to shake.

'Nasir?' It was little Aqueel who spoke as he came trotting down the path past the washing line with its swaying string bag of pegs. He faltered about a dozen feet from his brother. 'Nasir?' he said again, less sure this time.

Nasir's head snapped up, and he waved Aqueel away sternly, rapping out rough commands that obviously told him to go, to leave him alone.

Confused, upset, Aqueel hesitated. Nasir leapt to his feet, arms flailing, and repeated his order. His voice rose until it was almost a scream.

Aqueel fled without looking back.

Once his brother had vanished into the house, Nasir sank back onto the swing, as though the burst of action had exhausted him.

Ah well, I thought. *In for a penny...*

'Hello Nasir,' I said quietly.

He turned to look at me, his expression shrouded, then glanced away, head bent. 'What do you want?' he asked sullenly.

I knew his tolerance to me was low, so I might as well start at the top. 'I want to know about you and Roger Meyer,' I said.

Nasir's head came back up at that. For a second or two the fire was back in his eyes, then it fluttered weakly, and went out.

He shrugged. 'I don't know who you mean,' he said, sounding tired.

'Come on, Nasir,' I said sharply. 'I've seen the two of you together. It's not exactly a secret. Was he on his way round here to see you last night? Is that what he was doing on the estate?'

Nasir jumped to his feet, looked about to crack, then thought better of it. He reached for another cigarette, stuck it between his lips and lighted the end.

I paused, watching his edgy fingers, then went out on a limb of guesswork. 'What happens when your aunt finds out you're best buddies with one of the boys who stabbed your uncle?' I asked gently. 'Don't you think coming clean now is going to save you a load of trouble in the long run?'

'*Trouble?*' Nasir threw his cigarette away untasted and whirled to face me, stabbing the air with an accusatory finger. 'Violence – that's all you people understand!' he spat. 'Well, I hope you're happy now with the trouble *you've* caused, spying on us. You and your fascist bully boys! But you make the most of it while it lasts, because I swear to you that we won't lie down and be beaten for much longer!'

With that he marched up the garden towards the house, ignoring my attempts to call him back, and slammed the door heavily behind him.

I was still puzzling over my run-in with Nasir when I set out with Friday for his evening walk a couple of hours later.

The dog was going loopy at the prospect. He tore round the living room making incongruous squeaking noises while

I pulled on my coat, and then kept trying to bite the lead when I attached it to his collar. My rebukes were met with a cheerfully blatant disregard.

I stopped to pull on my bike gloves as we left the house. My hands were still feeling delicate and Friday tended to haul me along with more gusto than a pair of plough horses. It was a good job it was so cold that it didn't look suspicious.

Yesterday's fog had dissipated, but the air was bleak, grainy with a damp that knifed its way straight through to your bones. I shivered as the chill of the evening bit, and made yet another mental note to treat myself to a warmer pair of gloves.

We'd only got as far as the next street before Friday suddenly started acting nervous. Things happened quickly after that, but it gave me the few seconds I needed to ready a game face.

So, when Garton-Jones and West stepped out from behind a parked van onto the pavement in front of me, I raised an enquiring eyebrow, but otherwise kept my cool. They'd been going for shock value, and West looked vaguely disappointed when I didn't react. His boss, on the other hand, was too composed for any show of emotion, one way or another.

A slither of sound behind made me half-turn. Two more of Garton-Jones's boys had come round to block off my retreat, staying back in the shadows. With the van on one side, and a high privet hedge on the other, I was well and truly boxed in.

I knew I should have been frightened. It would have been the logical response, but all I felt was a kind of deadly calm. I couldn't take on four of them, not without getting the rest of the kicking they'd started on the night before. Still, I hadn't had Friday with me then.

The Ridgeback didn't know which pair to snarl at first, but he did his best to dole out bile in equal measure. He set up a low warning growl in the base of his throat and left it ticking over there, just in case.

I glanced at the dog to reassure him, then turned back, pulling a quizzical face. 'Well, Mr Garton-Jones,' I said, allowing a faintly sardonic note to creep into my voice, 'it would appear you have my undivided attention.'

Garton-Jones took a step forward, the streetlight overhead shifting on the shiny material of his bomber jacket, emphasising the solid bulk of him. He inclined his head, apparently unconcerned by Friday's display. 'Miss Fox,' he drawled by way of greeting.

They were simple, innocuous words, but my scalp twitched at the intonation. Surely he wouldn't do anything stupid, anything vicious? Not right here, in the middle of the street? *Why not?* asked the devil on my shoulder. *Look what happened to Roger . . .*

I knew he was just trying to fluster me, playing on my nerves. But I didn't like the rules of the game, and I wasn't going to play.

'I assume this isn't a social call, so what can I do for you?'

'Oh, just a little exchange of information, Miss Fox,' Garton-Jones said smoothly. 'A little mutual co-operation, if you like.'

'What — I scratch your back and you don't send the boys round with baseball bats to scratch mine?' I said, aiming for flippancy.

His face was mostly hidden, but even in the gloom I saw his lips pull back to crack a smile. 'Ah, yes, very droll,' he said, then he turned off the smile like he'd pulled a plug on it. 'I think you're aware that we've been having a bit of trouble with a certain blue Grand Cherokee, Dutch registered, which keeps refusing to stop at our checkpoints,' he went on. 'I don't suppose you'd be able to tell us anything about the driver, by any chance?'

I should have known that was coming, but it still jolted me. Some part of me didn't want to betray Sean, but it had more to do with my dislike of Garton-Jones than to any particular old loyalties.

I kept my head up, steady. 'He's tried to run me down – twice – but apart from that, I can't help you,' I shrugged.

'Are you sure about that, Miss Fox?' His voice should have warned me, but I stood my ground.

'Yes.'

He studied me quietly for a few moments, then clicked his tongue in mock self-reproof, as though he'd been remiss in some way. 'Oh, I'm sorry, I'm forgetting my manners,' he said, gesturing politely like we were at an ambassador's reception, 'I believe you've met Mr Drummond and Mr Harlow, but I don't think you were properly introduced.'

I turned fully then. On cue, the men behind me moved forwards into the light. I recognised the faces of the two men who'd been laying into Roger, and then turned their focus onto me.

I was gratified to notice that the one indicated as Drummond had a noticeably bruised and swollen lump on the side of his chin. I always did have quite a mean left.

'I don't believe so,' I agreed, matching his formal tone with my own.

'You're denying that you've met?' It was West who broke in, harsh, his voice rising disbelievingly on the last words.

'Oh no, we've met all right,' I said, matter-of-fact. 'But Mr Garton-Jones is quite correct – we weren't introduced.' I nodded to Drummond, added recklessly, 'You should put some ice on that jaw.'

His brows came together like they'd just been jerked on a wire. He took a step closer. Friday leapt to block his path, teeth bared. For a moment man and dog faced each other off, then the man backed down. It was where I would have put my money, had there been time to place a bet.

Garton-Jones scratched the stubble behind his ear with laboured perplexity. 'Well, Miss Fox,' he said, 'this puts me in a bit of an awkward situation, because my men here – fine men, who've worked for me for years without a blemish on their records – swear they saw you get into that Cherokee last night and take off.'

'I'm amazed they had time to see anything of the sort,' I said with cold deliberation, 'when they were so busy running away.'

Garton-Jones glared at the pair of them, which gave me hope that they hadn't quite told their boss the full story.

'After these two had done a runner I managed to get out of the Cherokee's way before it flattened me, and then I made my own way home. There didn't seem to be any point in hanging around,' I lied. 'So, is it part of your "clean-up" brief to go round beating up children?' I asked, hoping to widen the crack. 'Or were they just having fun on their own time?'

'Children?' Garton-Jones dismissed with contempt. 'They're vandals by the time they're five years old. House breakers at seven. They're dealing drugs before they're into double figures, and they know the law can't touch them. That "child" as you call him, was a thief. A dangerous thief. I thought you would have known that. He doesn't belong on this estate, but he was being persistent, and we had to persuade him that he wasn't wanted here. Word that we mean business will soon get around. The only thing that gets their respect is violence.'

'Which you're quite happy to dish out.' It was a statement, not a question.

'I am a violent man, Miss Fox,' he said, without bravado or inflection. 'I can – and will – do whatever is necessary to control this estate. Remember that.'

He took another step closer and Friday nearly yanked my arm out in his fervour to take on this new threat. Garton-Jones's arrogance was such that he didn't even bother to glance at the dog.

'You can pass on a message to whoever is in that Cherokee,' the man added, looming over me so the sockets of his eyes and the lower half of his face fell into shadow, like a skull. 'You can tell him that we *own* this estate. It's *our* area.' For the first time his voice hardened, became gritted. 'If you have half an idea about what's at stake here, you'll know we're not about to let any other two-bit operation muscle in on our deal. And if *he* knows what's good for his health, he'll keep his nose well out of it.'

I didn't react to any of this diatribe, just watched them make to leave, keeping my face blank. It took all my self-control to maintain it when Garton-Jones turned to give me his final parting shot.

'Oh yes, one more thing, Miss Fox,' he said. He'd slipped the polite disinterest back into his cultured voice. 'If you ever let that dog loose on me or any of my men, I'll personally break its spine. Good night.'

They melted back into the night, leaving me standing there with Friday rigid by my side. Once we were alone he shuffled his feet, whining, confused. I put a comforting hand down to stroke the back of his neck, finding the fur there upraised and stiff.

Funny how things change isn't it? Yesterday I would have sworn that the dog was my protector.

Now, it seemed, I was his.

Eight

The Residents' Committee meeting that evening was held in a pub called the Black Lion on the edge of the estate, where they had a cavernous room upstairs that the management let out for next to nothing.

The Black Lion wasn't exactly the sort of establishment I would have taken my mother to for Sunday lunch. Not that I think the curling sandwiches and waxy pies they served from a hatch behind the bar quite warranted such a grand title.

Not, also, that I had the sort of relationship with my mother where cosy lunchtime chats were much on the cards. Things were getting better between us, but it was taking time. Inviting her anywhere like the Black Lion would have been a retrograde step in more ways than one.

When I walked in to the lounge bar, having chained the Suzuki up securely outside, the regulars stopped talking and regarded me with dark suspicion over the pint rims of their flat, watery beer. It was that kind of a place.

I did a quick visual sweep of the occupants, and was jolted to see Langford sitting in a corner, looking very much at home, with a pint in his hand. He was watching me, and when he caught my eye he raised his drink to me with a twisted smile, the promise of patient retribution. With a shiver of foreboding, I turned my back on him. I could feel his eyes digging in all the way across the room.

I ordered a soft drink from the resigned-looking barman, and asked about the meeting. He jerked his head towards the stairs to the room they were using. I picked up my three-quarter filled glass of tepid Coke, and followed his directions with an unacknowledged murmur of thanks.

There was already somebody speaking when I slipped in to the packed room. The local Crime Prevention Officer, if memory served me correctly, trying to get the crowd enthused about window locks, deadbolts, and security chains. I stood quietly at the back of the room and took the opportunity to scan the audience while he talked.

Apart from Mrs Gadatra there were very few people I recognised, let alone had even a nodding acquaintance with. My neighbour was rocking Gin on her lap, the little girl's eyes drooping progressively into sleep. Aqueel was sitting on the chair next to his mother, straight-backed and gravely aware of the importance of being invited to such an adult occasion. He was trying his hardest to stay awake. There was no sign of his elder brother.

In fact, there were hardly any younger males there at all. It seemed to be a mainly middle-aged Indian and Pakistani audience, bordering on elderly. The white faces stood out, probably mine included. There weren't many of them.

I noticed Eric O'Bryan was in attendance, sporting his habitual grey anorak, although as a concession to indoor wear, he had at least unzipped it. Even from a distance, I could see the perspiration glistening on the top of his shiny pate. He sat over to one side of the room, listening with an engrossed air that must have been very gratifying for the speaker.

Sitting at a small round table to one side of where the CPO was standing, were Garton-Jones and West. I began to wonder if those two were joined at the hip.

They were making no pretence of interest in the lecture on the prudence of asking for ID from visiting tradesmen. Their eyes moved slowly over the inhabitants of the room in a constant sift, as though mentally isolating the troublemakers, and committing everyone's details to memory. As a lesson in delicate intimidation, it couldn't have been bettered if they'd tried.

Still, if the information I'd got from Clare earlier that day had been right, they were experts at that sort of thing. She rang to say that her contact on the crime desk at the *Defender* hadn't been able to come up with anything concrete on Streetwise Securities, but there were plenty of whispers.

Garton-Jones's life had been following a more privileged course until he'd left his expensive boarding school and hit university. There his darker side had come to the fore. He'd started out working club doors and patrolling building sites, before branching out on his own. Streetwise had the reputation of being efficient, but brutally so. They left behind a gloss of satisfaction laid thinly over grumblings of heavy-handed tactics.

Watching them now, upstairs at the Black Lion, it wasn't hard to understand why.

To my left, someone fidgeted in their seat, leaning forwards to reveal the person sitting behind them. In profile, I saw long straight dark hair surrounding a memorable long pale face.

I certainly wouldn't forget her in a hurry. Not when she'd refused to leave me to have my head kicked in by Messrs Harlow and Drummond.

It was Madeleine.

For a moment the shock of the encounter felt almost tangible. I had taken only one step in her direction when I saw her finish polishing the lenses of a set of glasses and slide them back onto her face.

It was a small thing, but something about the action struck me as odd. It didn't gel. She didn't handle the glasses like someone who wore them regularly, and she certainly hadn't been using them that night when she and Sean had rescued Roger.

No, the glasses didn't fit. Things were missing, like the unfocused squint when she'd taken them off, and the little marks from the pads on the sides of her nose. The glasses, I realised quickly enough to still my feet from taking me any closer, were just a disguise.

Which brought an even more intriguing question. What was Sean's accomplice doing sneaking in to the Residents' Committee meeting, and from whom was she hiding?

I glanced back towards Garton-Jones, just as his gaze swept back over me, like the blaze of a searchlight. I forced my face into relaxed boredom, and stayed put. If I made any moves to contact Madeleine now, to speak to her, I stood the chance of exposing both of us to who knew what dangers. I'd just have to try and catch her as she left the meeting. In the meantime, I was minutely aware of her, like she was putting out heat.

The CPO wound up his talk and received a desultory round of applause for his pains. Someone from the Residents' Committee thanked him on their behalf for coming. He packed up his case, made his excuses, and left.

Then it was Garton-Jones's turn. The Residents' Committee man introduced him without undue enthusiasm, and sat down hurriedly, looking nervous in case he was blamed for heralding the bearer of bad news.

I could understand his reasoning once Garton-Jones got under way. The big man started innocuously enough, pointing out that the crime rate on the estate was already dropping. He'd even conjured up some figures from somewhere, which West parroted out when called upon to do so. Percentages and statistics that could have been twisted to mean anything, and probably had been. It was all very slick. Very pro. But then, that's exactly what they were.

The good times weren't designed to last long, and they didn't. Garton-Jones checked his notes, schooled his face into well-mannered contrition, and carried on.

'Unfortunately, these swift results have not been without their price,' he said. 'Streetwise Securities' original estimate did not take into account the particularly unruly behaviour we've had to deal with. Aware that you deserved a quick initial return to order, to public safety, we've had to allocate more manpower to the estate than we originally envisaged,' he reported. 'Of course, the results speak for themselves, and therefore we feel sure that you won't begrudge the slightly increased cost.'

For a truly modest fee, he told us, he and his firm would undertake to continue to patrol the streets and keep Lavender Gardens crime-free, round the clock, twenty-four seven. And then, per household, per day, he named his price.

I'm always much more suspicious when health clubs, insurance schemes and the like break down their annual fee into a daily amount. If the only way you can stomach a meal is to cut it into tiny pieces, you're eating the wrong food.

It took a few moments for the more arithmetically agile among the group to work out the cost per year, and the gasps they gave spoke for themselves.

The man from the Residents' Committee read the faces around him and didn't need to put it to the vote. He stood up and told Garton-Jones stoutly that the people were already paying as much as they could afford. He mentioned the number of young families on the estate, who were living on a restricted budget.

Garton-Jones listened with an apparently sympathetic frown, nodding seriously. 'Oh I quite understand,' he said soothingly when the man's speech stumbled to a halt.

'Unfortunately, much as we feel those families have a right to our protection, we also have a duty to the men who work for us, to pay them a reasonable living wage. We would very much regret having to withdraw from the estate at this stage, just when we feel we're making such progress . . . '

He tailed off the sentence artfully and stacked his papers on the table in front of him, preparing to clear them into his briefcase. West took his cue and stood, also.

The Residents' Committee man realised they were about to leave and started to panic. Surely, he said, his voice shaky, there must be some room for negotiation, some scope to talk about this?

'I'm so sorry, but myself and my colleague here have been over and over these figures to see if there was any way at all we could reduce them, but they're pared to the bone, I'm afraid,' Garton-Jones shrugged regretfully, then put a forced brave face on. 'Still, never mind, hey? I'm sure you people will manage without us somehow.'

The way he allowed just a fraction of doubt to cloud his voice at the end there was a masterful touch. All the passion he'd shown when he cornered me and made his threats to Friday might have never existed.

Without haste, the two Streetwise men finished packing away their papers, leaving the Residents' Committee stuttering.

'Look, obviously you need to think things over and let us know one way or the other,' Garton-Jones said smoothly to the spokesman, as though the whole thing was of no real importance to him. 'Why don't you make your minds up and let us know – say before the end of the week? We'll stay until then, anyhow.' He smiled, friendly for all the world. 'Least we can do.'

And with that, they strolled out, leaving turmoil behind them.

The Residents' Committee man, who'd looked so sure of his ground when he objected to the price hike, now looked doubtful and bewildered. His eyes darted quickly about him, checking to see if he was going to be generally blamed for this sudden turnaround in fortunes.

Somebody else spoke up, asking for suggestions.

I waited a few seconds to see if anyone was going to be brave. When it became obvious they weren't I took a deep breath, and waved my hand.

'I know that strictly speaking I'm not really entitled to stick my oar in,' I said. 'I'm only on the estate temporarily, but from what I've seen your problems are being caused by a small, but active minority, yes?'

I looked around me, and received one or two cautious nods. Madeleine was watching me with a sudden stillness. Mind you, so was everybody else. Perhaps calling attention to myself like this wasn't such a hot idea. Ah well, too late now.

'All I'm saying is,' I went on, 'that there's nothing to stop you taking the responsibility for your own security yourselves.'

The Residents' Committee man snorted his derision, glad to be back on safe ground again. 'We have tried Neighbourhood Watch before. It isn't enough,' he argued.

Cautiously, I agreed that Neighbourhood Watch schemes were a start, but the difference they actually made to crime figures wasn't that great. 'On the other hand, recruiting what amounts to a gang of mercenaries to garrison your streets is inviting disaster. I'm sorry.' I shrugged. 'But it is.'

'So what do you propose? That we do nothing?'

I took a deep breath, and launched into the details of a plan they could put into action themselves. It wasn't so much Neighbourhood Watch, more Neighbourhood React. The idea was not that they hid behind their net curtains and watched the crime happening outside, they needed to react to it.

So, if kids were vandalising cars in the street, the entire population of that street had to come outside and tackle them about it. It was a straightforward safety-in-numbers tactic. Even the bravest vandal will think twice about taking on a crowd of fifty, or a hundred, no matter what their age and ability.

There was a chain system they could easily put into operation, where the first person to spot a crime taking place would ring two neighbours, who would each ring another two, and so on. The whole street could be mobilised in minutes. Far quicker than any police response. Far cheaper than Garton-Jones and his men.

'All you need to do is get to know each other, keep in contact, and keep an eye out for each other,' I said at last. 'If you don't learn to look after each other, you're going to have to pay someone else to do it for you forever.'

I glanced round the faces. Some looked enthusiastic, others dubious, but the majority showed little emotion. I really had no idea whether I'd got through to them or not.

'So, Mr O'Bryan,' said the Residents' Committee man, 'what is your opinion of this scheme?' In the absence of anyone better, I suppose he was the nearest thing to a professional there.

O'Bryan's features were noncommittal as he slowly pulled a cigarette out of a new pack, and put a struck match to the end of it. For a moment, as he regarded me narrowly through the fresh smoke, I thought he was going to rubbish the idea.

'I'm always reluctant to advise anybody to confront criminals,' he said eventually, almost diffidently, 'but this sounds like it's got legs. I think you should get some detailed proposals from Miss Fox and give them some serious consideration.'

The meeting broke up about then. I found myself agreeing to put something together for the Residents' Committee before Garton-Jones's deadline ran out, and joined the throng as they headed out.

I looked round for Madeleine and saw that she'd managed to get to the exit ahead of me. Trying to push through to get to her proved difficult, and by the time I reached the car park she was just about to climb into a black cab that had pulled up in front of the pub. I started forwards, intent on speaking to her.

'Miss Fox.' It was O'Bryan's voice that stopped me. He came jogging out of the doorway of the Black Lion, car keys in his hand. 'Ah, I'm glad I caught you,' he said, panting slightly. 'Can I offer you a lift?'

I eyed Madeleine's back disappearing into the taxi with a certain amount of resignation, then turned back to O'Bryan and lifted my bike helmet. 'I have my own transport,' I told him.

'Ah, yes, of course you do,' he said, pausing awkwardly for a moment. 'I'm parked just at the back there. Can I walk with you?'

I thought it an odd request, but shrugged my compliance. If nothing else, it was a bit of insurance just in case Langford had decided that tonight was the night he wanted his revenge.

We moved round to where I'd parked the Suzuki, and I noticed a dark green MGB roadster, with wire wheels and plenty of chrome about the grille, parked a couple of spaces away from the bike.

'I like to leave it well out of harm's way,' O'Bryan confided unexpectedly. 'Some people are very careless of your paint-work when they open their car doors.'

'Don't I know it,' I said, bending to unlock the chain from round the bike's back wheel. I stood and nodded to the MG. 'It seems you've got quite a classic car collection.'

'Oh,' O'Bryan looked both embarrassed and pleased. 'Another one I restored myself,' he said, pride uppermost. 'I enjoy picking them up for a song and doing them up. That old thing was laid up for years. It was in a pretty sorry state when it came to me. Still, the thrill of getting them back out on the open road makes all the hard work worth while.'

'How's the Merc?' I asked.

He blinked and the smile went out. 'It's going to take a bit of effort to get that back up to scratch,' he said, and the steely glint was back in his eyes again. 'That was one of the reasons I wanted to speak to you, actually.' He hesitated before going on, occupying his hands with the business of lighting another cigarette.

I shifted from one foot to the other, trying not to shiver in the cold, and said oh yes, in a manner that I hoped was designed to prompt him on.

'Well,' O'Bryan said carefully, 'I wouldn't like you to find yourself in the same position, Charlie. Where they pick you out, I mean, make you a target. And if you take these kids on, set yourself up as some sort of leader in the fight against them, they will mark you out, believe me.'

He paused again, drawing on his cigarette. Took it out of his mouth and expelled smoke upwards into the chilled evening air like an industrial chimney. He glanced at me, his gaze calculating. 'They'll make it personal.'

Personal. I was on familiar territory there. The thing was, did I have to watch out for the kids who were causing the crime, or Garton-Jones's thugs who were supposed to be preventing it? Was I supposed to be guarding against the likes of Roger, or protecting him? And where the hell did Sean fit in to all this?

I swung my leg over the bike, then looked back at O'Bryan levelly. 'Thanks for the warning,' I said, 'but I know all about things getting personal, and I rather think they already have.'

★

My words to O'Bryan might have had the ring of bravado to them, but for days afterwards I lived with my nerves on a knife-edge.

Particularly after I'd put together some proposals for the Residents' Committee on how they could take over from Streetwise Securities and do the job themselves. It was a simple basic idea, that just involved people finding out a little about their neighbours. Their names and phone numbers for a start, their daily routines.

After that, if someone noticed anything out of the ordinary, they would have a network of neighbours to call upon for help. It was a system designed to build up, street by street, until the whole of the estate could be brought together into a proper community scheme.

Well, that was the theory, but whether it would work in practice or not was something else. In my experience, neighbourly disputes and personality clashes could drive wedges deep enough to bring the whole thing down round their ears. Still, trying it had to be better than leaving matters up to Garton-Jones on an indefinite basis.

The Residents' Committee must have thought so, too. According to Mrs Gadatra, who seemed to have an inside hotline, when his end-of-the-week deadline hit, they told him they'd decided to try another way, and had regretfully dispensed with his services.

'And how did he take that?' I'd asked with some trepidation over the garden fence.

'Very well,' Mrs Gadatra reported. 'If anything, he seemed enthusiastic about the whole idea.'

'You're joking,' I said, unable to believe he hadn't gone ballistic.

'No, no,' she assured me. 'He just offered to renew his company's services at some later date, if required, and left it at that. He was really quite gracious in defeat.'

I began to think I must have imagined his vehemence that night in the street, but I knew I hadn't. There was some wider game at stake here. I only hoped it wasn't part of Garton-Jones's plan to bring about his return in the wake of a sudden, violent return to disorder. It was a worrying thought.

With that and O'Bryan's warning in mind, I stayed away from Kirby Street as much as I could during the following week, without actually breaking my promise to Pauline. The gym became a sort of sanctuary, away from the dark corners of Lavender Gardens.

I went back to my martial arts training, tried to find calm and focus in the balletic smoothness of the moves, the intellectual control. And when that didn't work, I beat seven bells out of Attila's punchbag.

Even the big German noticed something was wrong. He had the knack of spotting physical problems developing at a very early stage by the way someone held themselves as they hauled on the rowing machine, or lifted a set of weights, but mental and emotional trauma usually passed him by.

'You're looking tense, Charlie,' he said, watching me send the punchbag swinging wildly in a flurry of fists and feet, elbows and knees. He folded his massive forearms across his sculpted chest, head on one side as he regarded me with a frown cutting deep between his eyebrows. He nodded towards the canvas bag. 'Want to tell me who you'd rather was hanging there?'

I turned, surprised, and wiped the sweat out of my eyes. 'I could just be doing this for exercise, you know,' I said, ruffled, trying not to gasp for breath. And I thought I was getting fitter.

'Oh, yeah, for sure,' Attila dismissed. 'But to me this does not look like exercise. This looks like training. So, who are you training to fight, because he looks like one tough customer, yes?'

'I'm not training to fight anyone,' I denied, straight away, but even as I said it, I wasn't sure if it was true. 'At least, I don't think so,' I added.

Attila sighed, and came to sit on the bench nearest to me, a doleful expression on his square face. 'You have a lot of scars, Charlie,' he said gently. 'And not all of them, I think, are on the outside.'

For a moment I said nothing. The only sound was a slight squeaking as the punchbag rocked to and fro. Instinctively, I reached out and stilled it. It gave me something to do with my hands.

'So,' Attila went on when I didn't speak, 'I think maybe you are training to fight your own demons. You are trying to come to terms with whatever has gone before, and maybe you think that by being strong, by being quick, by being ready, you can beat them next time, yes?'

'Oh, I've already beaten them. It's not the memory of what's happened in the past that I'm frightened of, Attila,' I said, giving him a twisted smile, 'but I tell you, the prospect of what I might do in the future scares the shit out of me . . .'

Nine

I don't know if I'd worried Attila unduly, but out of the blue he decided that I could go early that afternoon, and I left around half three.

'We're quiet, and the weekend's coming up,' he said, when I protested. 'Go home, Charlie. Relax. Try and unwind a little, yes?'

'OK,' I agreed eventually, even though I knew I wouldn't.

The life was already starting to fade out of the day as I rode through town and across Greyhound Bridge. Lancaster sits on the tidal estuary of the Lune, and that afternoon the tide was well out, leaving great expanses of stony sludge exposed to the greying light. There was a bitter wind sizzling in from Morecambe Bay, too. It whipped up over the exposed bridge, and the bike shied away from each gust.

Still, at least there wasn't much traffic to dice with, and I was soon winding my way through the streets of Lavender Gardens towards Kirby Street. Perhaps it was my imagination, but without Garton-Jones's paramilitaries lurking round every corner, the estate looked less grim, somehow.

At least the kids felt unharassed enough to be back playing out, despite the cold and the rapidly gathering gloom. They practised their guerrilla tactics among the parked cars, making me slow to a crawl as I threaded my way among them.

I was almost at Pauline's when a Transit van turned into the other end of the street and came speeding down the middle like the TV reconstruction of a hit-and-run. The driver held it in a low gear, the transmission whining in protest.

I pulled over into a gap, put my feet down, and waited for him to go past. It was one of Mr Ali's green and purple vans, and I made a mental note to ask him to have a quiet word with his drivers when I saw him again.

What I saw next pushed that thought right out of my mind. Instead of shooting past me the van pulled over right outside Pauline's house, and the passenger door swung open. I could see there were the obligatory three men in the front. For some reason there are *always* three men in the front of a Transit van. As I watched, the one on the furthest left hopped down to let the middle passenger climb out.

I was getting used to seeing Nasir in unexpected company, but this time it wasn't the Asian boy who was out of place. He reached back into the van for his flask and sandwich box, and nodded to the driver.

It was the other passenger who caught my eye. He seemed reluctant to move out of Nasir's way, standing close up to the open van door, deliberately obstructive. I wondered what it was that was lacking about Langford's psychological make-up that made him particularly enjoy that kind of game. Nasir had to go out of his way to step round him carefully.

The vigilante broke into a big smile as he recognised the boy's submission. It was like something out of a wildlife documentary about the pecking order of baboons.

He waited until Nasir had walked about halfway down the drive towards the house, then called after him, 'Hey, Nas!' The boy refused to give any sign of having heard him, so Langford added, 'Give my regards to the ladies, won't you?'

He laughed at the way Nasir's stride faltered, and climbed back into the van. 'OK, drive on,' he said to the other man, who'd stayed morosely silent during the brief exchange. 'Take me to your leader.'

The driver rammed the van into gear with a crunch and gunned it away down the street. The sense of realisation settled over me slowly. Wayne had told me that Langford used to turn up and collect a pay packet from Mr Ali every Thursday.

Today was Thursday.

With only a moment's hesitation, I paddled the Suzuki round in a half circle, and followed the van.

There was only one logical way out of the estate, so I didn't have to try and look too casual until we reached the main road. The van turned left, and headed towards Morecambe. I purposely allowed a few other vehicles to go by before I pulled out after it.

The Transit was easy to keep track of among the cars, particularly as the streetlights started to come on. If the driver's reckless lane changing was anything to go by, he wasn't using his mirrors much, in any case.

At the roundabout just past the college, the van veered off to the left and started to head towards Heysham. The manoeuvre was so abrupt that for a moment I thought he'd spotted me, although logically, I didn't see how he could have done. I kept up the pursuit.

I nearly lost him as he turned off the escape road they put in just in case anything goes seriously pear-shaped – or should that be mushroom-shaped – at the nuclear power station. I got pushed out of lane by an Irish trucker who was obviously late for his ferry, and had to do another quick circuit of the roundabout to take the right exit.

By this time, though, I'd a fair idea of where they were heading. There was a new three-storey office block going up on the edge of one of the industrial estates. Construction problems had ensured that it had made the local news a few times. I seemed to recall that Mr Ali's firm had the contract.

I dropped back further, letting the van rocket ahead along the narrowing road. There wasn't so much traffic to hide behind now, and as we reached the site entrance, the tarmac was clodded with earth from the construction machinery. It wasn't the sort of surface I wanted to approach at a gallop.

As the van turned in and bounced over the rough ground, I rode past carefully, and nipped into the old industrial estate next door. Half the ramshackle units were empty. The weathered shabbiness of the letting agents' signs was a clear giveaway that these weren't recent vacancies.

I slid the bike into a narrow gap between two of the boarded-up units that backed onto the new development, and killed the lights and the engine. For a few moments I sat there in the rapidly encroaching darkness, listening to the Suzuki's aluminium engine ticking and pinging as it cooled down, and chewing over my options.

I *could* just turn round and go back to Pauline's, but if I did that I'd have achieved little more than partial confirmation of Wayne's story.

Equally, I could go marching in through the front gate, demand to speak to Mr Ali, and then confront him about his connection with Langford's vigilante group.

Forthright, yes, but stupid, also.

On the other hand, the third alternative was possibly the least attractive. I could squeeze my way through the six foot fence in front of me. Then I could go sneaking around the building site on the other side to see what I could find out that way.

I had the darkness on my side, coupled with the fact that my everyday leathers are black anyway. They might be a bit bulky to be absolutely perfect for a bit of surreptitious B&E, but at least they were the right colour.

I left my helmet hanging over one of the bar-ends, but kept my gloves on. It was a good job, too. The planked wooden fence was made from cheap rough timber, and I would have come away with half of it bedded in as splinters.

I pushed my way through, stepping into the mud on the other side with a disconcerting squelch, and took a quick look around me. There wasn't much sign of activity, and no-one seemed to have noticed my arrival.

After a moment to get my bearings, I turned and walked openly in the direction of the site entrance, where I could see several of Mr Ali's Transit vans parked up. There were numerous big lighting rigs set up and as I moved I threw out multiple shadows from them like a floodlit football player.

I didn't see any point in scurrying from one shadow to the next like I was doing a prison breakout. If anyone did spot me, behaving furtively was going to look far more suspicious.

Still, when I saw Langford picking his way across the mud to one of the stacked Portakabins, I couldn't help but duck out of sight behind a parked digger. Peering out carefully, I watched him go over to the nearest one, push open the door, and walk straight in without knocking.

Once he'd disappeared, I came out of cover and hurried over to the Portakabin. Light was flooding out of a barred window in the side opposite the door, and I sidled up close to it.

Inside, the Portakabin was split into two, with a partition wall and a door down the centre. This turned the half I could see into a smallish square room containing a cheap veneered desk, a brown filing cabinet, and a swivel typist's chair with a torn tweed cover and the foam stuffing coming out of the seat.

The room was harshly lit with an unshaded fluorescent tube slung across the ceiling. There was a mess of what looked like architect's plans spread across the desk. But no occupants.

I could only assume that Langford had gone into the second room, for which there was no window. If I wanted to find out what was going on in there, I was going to have to get closer. Damn.

Still, I'd come far enough to be in deep trouble if I got caught, so what was another few feet between friends? As quickly as I could, but trying not to look as though I was hurrying, I moved round to the door on the other side of the Portakabin, and turned the handle. There was enough ambient noise from the diggers to mask any squeaks the hinges gave out, but I put the door to very carefully behind me once I was inside. The latch seemed to make an incredibly loud click as it engaged.

I tiptoed across the bare plywood floor to the closed door that separated the outer and inner office, and put my ear against the panelling.

'It's going to have to stop, Mr Langford,' came the unmistakable high note of Mr Ali's voice, tinged with bluster. 'Things are going too far. You've been doing a good job for me up until now, but this is too much.'

Langford's voice, when it came, was so close it nearly made me flinch back. He could almost have been leaning against the frame on the other side of the door. 'Don't back out now, Ali, just when things are starting to get interesting,' he said, insolent. 'As you've said, I've been doing a good job for you, and the wheels are turning. We both know it.'

Mr Ali had begun to pace, I could feel his footsteps through the wooden floor, making the Portakabin rock. 'That is beside the point,' he said, agitated. 'People are beginning to suspect something, and I can't afford for our arrangement to come to light, particularly not after what has just happened.'

'You mean the Gadatra boy?' Langford demanded lazily. 'Don't worry about him. He's got too many areas of weakness to be a threat, and I know just where to apply the right pressure so he'll fold.'

'And what about the girl, Miss Fox?' Mr Ali's mention of my own name made me draw in a breath more sharply than prudence called for.

'Her?' I could hear the note of disbelief, turning to discomfort. 'I know she managed to blind-side me, but you really feel she's a problem?' His inflection made it a question.

'She could be. From what I hear she was instrumental in getting Mr Garton-Jones thrown off the estate. If she finds out about us...'

'You worry too much, Ali. If anything, she's done us a favour. After all, we were just doubling up on the same job, weren't we? Anyway, I wouldn't bank on Streetwise being gone long. Garton-Jones knows when he's on to a good thing, and these community schemes are never up to much.'

There were more footsteps, the sound of chair legs scraping back. I tensed like a deer, ready to flee, but unable to resist the temptation to stay. 'So, what happens if they come back?'

'Well, the way things are hotting up, they could be just what we need. Besides, everyone has their price, and I'm sure with the right "financial inducements" shall we say, certain people could come round to our way of thinking, if you know what I mean.'

Mr Ali's voice became resigned. 'How much do you need?'

I could feel rather than see Langford's artfully casual shrug. 'I don't know,' he said, almost sly. 'Let me make some approaches, and I'll get back to you. Speaking of cash, though,' he went on, and the insolent tone was back again in full force, 'where's my pay packet for this week?'

Other voices approaching outside stripped my attention away from the conversation in the inner office. I looked around wildly and realised there was absolutely nowhere to hide. I scuttled away from that door and headed for the outside one, managing to open it, slip through the gap, and have it closed again in a flash.

'Can I help you?' It was a man's voice, flat with suspicion, and right by my shoulder. It made me jump.

I turned to see a middle-aged bloke in a dirty green fluoro jacket and a yellow hard hat standing only a couple of feet away.

'Er, no thanks, mate, I'm all sorted,' I said, smiling at him, but getting no similar response.

'What are you doing here? I didn't see you come in.'

God, did nobody have any trust in humanity any more? 'Bike courier, mate,' I said, keeping my voice cheery. I patted the top pocket of my leather jacket as though to indicate safely secured paperwork. 'I've just dropped off a package with the bloke in the office there,' I jerked a thumb to indicate the Portakabin I'd just left. 'Big Asian bloke. He signed for it.'

He was starting to run with me on this one, but the last vestiges of wariness remained. 'What was it, then?' he asked.

I shrugged, trying to stay casual, even though any minute now Langford and Mr Ali could emerge from the Portakabin behind me and expose me for the liar I was. I wondered if people really did end up buried in concrete footings.

'No idea, mate. They don't tell me, and I don't ask,' I said blithely. 'I just had to get the thing here from Manchester before close of play, and that's what I've done.' I checked my watch, just to prove it. 'Anything else is not my problem.'

He nodded, still mistrustful, but unable to put his finger on anything concrete. Until I'd taken two or three steps away from him, that was.

'So where's your bike?' he called after me.

I froze, painted on a smile and turned, indicating the gloopy mud underfoot with a grimace. 'I left it out on the road,' I said. 'You think I'm bringing my nice Suzuki through shit like this?'

He gave me the first sign of warmth as he nodded. 'No, s'pose not,' he said and waved his hand, dismissing me. 'All right then. Off you go. In future, just make sure you check in with the foreman before you go wandering around on site, will you? It's against the regs.'

'No problem, mate. See you.' I tried my best not to run the rest of the way to the road, but it was a close thing. Once I was out of the site I had to stamp my feet to get rid of the mud galoshes. Then I jogged back round to the trading estate and retrieved the bike.

All the time I was waiting for the sounds of pursuit. I didn't know how soon the man I'd bumped into would mention my presence to Mr Ali. If he mentioned it at all.

I wished I'd pretended to own a different make of motorbike. At least then if they decided to come looking for me, they'd have been on the wrong track to start with. Damn. Why couldn't I have said Kawasaki, or Honda? Even a lowly MZ would have been better than admitting to a Suzuki. Mind you, then I'd have had less reason for not wanting to trail it through the mud.

I rode back to Lavender Gardens by a circuitous route, and arrived with a headache from constantly squinting in the Suzuki's vibrating mirrors for any sign of stalking Transit vans.

There weren't any.

I had to assume, for the moment at least, that I'd got away with it.

Once I'd locked the bike away and recovered from Friday's usual clamorous greeting I had chance to think about the conversation I'd eavesdropped on. What was Mr Ali paying Langford to do? What wheels were turning? And what was it that people were beginning to suspect?

I cast my mind back to Nasir's outburst in Shahida's living room. He obviously knew more than he was telling, but about what?

And why did Langford think he and Garton-Jones's men were doubling up. Doubling up in what way? Streetwise were being paid to clean up the estate. I hadn't liked their methods, and neither had anyone else, so they'd gone. How had that left the way clear for Langford's mob? Unless he was doing the same thing . . .

It occurred to me, slowly, that maybe Mr Ali was paying the vigilantes to keep Lavender Gardens clear. The only thing was, their actions had misfired badly when Fariman had been stabbed. Maybe Mr Ali wanted to be seen as the public-spirited hero, but only after Langford had successfully done his job. When he'd cocked up, the builder was suddenly understandably keen to put as much distance between them as he could.

It wasn't unreasonable to assume that as Nasir worked for Mr Ali, he'd got wind of the plan somehow. But what was his connection with Roger? And why was Mr Ali taking it upon himself to clean up the estate in the first place?

I shook my head. I needed more information before I could even begin to draw any watertight conclusions. Much as I thought I was pushing my luck, I rang Jacob and Clare again.

By the time I put the phone down ten minutes later, I felt easier in my mind. Intrigued, Clare had suggested that she have a rummage through the *Defender's* archives first thing in the morning, and photocopy anything on Mr Ali or Langford that seemed relevant. I could collect what she'd got, she told me with a grin in her voice, when I went round for supper at the weekend.

With the promise of Jacob's cooking to lure me, that wasn't a difficult offer to accept.

Ten

The next day, which was Friday, I was due to work a late shift at the gym. I rode out of Kirby Street around four in the afternoon, and got my first inkling that maybe getting rid of Garton-Jones hadn't been such a good idea, after all.

It was fortunate I wasn't caning the bike, because as I stooged round a corner I found the gap between the cars parked down either side of the street was blocked by a group of teenage Asian lads. Some were leaning on the cars, while the others were just milling about.

I pulled the clutch lever in, tucked two fingers round the front brake, and coasted slowly to a halt about twenty feet away, eyeing them guardedly through my visor. A few of them saw me coming and shifted to one side, but there were half a dozen who stayed put, hands on hips, heads tilted. You didn't need a master's degree in body languages to be able to read their stance.

For a few moments, we faced each other off, while I did a furious mental search for alternative routes out of the estate. There weren't any. Even if I could have turned the bike round quickly in the space available, which wasn't easy with a steering lock that relied on speed to make it viable.

One of the boys took a couple of swaggering steps

forwards, beckoning me forwards exaggeratedly with both hands. He was mid-teens, difficult to put an age on accurately, with peroxide blond hair that was startling against his olive complexion, and orange wraparound sunglasses.

I knocked the gear lever down into first, but didn't let the clutch out. There was no way I wanted to just ride at them. There was no guarantee they'd shift. In fact, I stood more chance of hitting one of them and dropping the bike, and that wasn't likely to turn into a healthy scenario, particularly for me.

I got out of it by sheer luck. A police Astra turned into the other end of the road and came cruising towards the boys. They dispersed quickly, not ready quite yet for an all-out rebellion against authority. The two burly coppers inside glared at all of us suspiciously as they crawled past, but obviously didn't feel inclined to leave the safety of their vehicle to investigate further.

I took the opportunity when it was offered, letting the clutch out with a handful of revs and shooting through the empty space left by the Astra, before the boys had chance to close ranks behind it.

I glanced in my mirrors as I accelerated away down the street. With the police car safely round the next corner, I expected to see the boys moving out into the road again. Instead, there was no sign of them. I even stopped, turning to scan the area behind me, but it was eerily deserted. Had the police car spooked them? Or was there more to it than that?

They'll mark you out, O'Bryan had said. *They'll make it personal.* Yeah, well, I thought, trying to shrug off the itch that had suddenly developed between my shoulder-blades, maybe he was right.

As I was early for work, I did a quick detour through Lancaster and down onto St George's Quay to drop in at the flat. I left the bike next to the kerb outside and bounced up the wooden staircase to the place I called home.

The flat is on part of the first floor of an old warehouse. Before I moved in it had been a gym, which I suppose could be considered ironic, given my current means of employment.

I'd been there since I first moved to the city. My landlord had ripped the machines out when the place had closed down, but that was as far as he'd gone by way of refurbishment. I'd been the one who'd organised putting a kitchen of sorts into what had been the gents' changing room, and converted the office into my bedroom.

The area might have moved upmarket over the last couple of years, but the flat itself was pretty basic. The whitewash on the walls peeled with the damp, and few of the windows closed without gaps. The only heating came through overhead pipes and was erratic at best. There was rumoured to be a central boiler somewhere in the basement that was so decrepit it made Stephenson's Rocket look as modern as a nuclear fusion reactor.

Despite the fact the heating system operated regardless of my presence, the flat felt cold inside, unlived in. I pushed open the front door against a pile of mostly junk mail, and slid through the gap.

I picked up a few more clothes to stuff into my rucksack, having very much discovered the luxury of Pauline's washing machine. I sifted through the post quickly, but found nothing of any note apart from an irate card from my landlord, complaining because I'd changed the lock without telling him and had omitted to give him a key. In fact, I'd been forced to fit new locks over a year ago, when the place got turned over, and I wondered briefly why he'd wanted to gain access now.

I moved to the telephone. I'd given Pauline's phone number to most people who needed to know it, but even so the answering machine light was flashing to tell me I'd one message. I hit the button idly, while I tossed invitations to visit discount sofa factories and take out gold credit cards unopened into the waste paper basket.

When the tape rewound and started to play, however, it brought me to an abrupt standstill.

'Charlie, we need to talk.' Sean's voice, unmistakable, abrupt. He paused, as though I'd been there when he'd rang, and he was waiting for me to pick up.

When I hadn't done so, he sighed audibly, and went on in a quiet tone that was somehow more ominous than any shouted threat could have been. 'Don't even think about running again, Charlie. I meant what I said last night. You can't hide forever, and we've unfinished business. So call me.' He reeled off a mobile phone number which I didn't bother to write down, then rang off.

My legs folded me gently onto the sofa of their own volition. For a few minutes after the answering machine had clicked off, I just sat there, staring at it stupidly. How on earth had Sean got my number? Did he know where I lived? If he knew I was at Pauline's why hadn't he rung me there? Or was he just being cunning?

Suddenly, I needed to get out of there. I turned the lights off and yanked the door shut behind me, turning the key in the lock with hands that fumbled. I almost ran down to the bike, kicking it into life with clumsiness born of haste.

All afternoon at the gym, I was jumpy, and nervous. Attila wasn't in, and being on my own made things worse. I suppose I was expecting something to happen, but it wasn't until ten o'clock, when the last punter had cleared out, that things started going seriously awry.

I was just contemplating the usual untidiness of the stacks of dumbbells and the careless scattering of the heavy leather lifting belts when, in the best horror film tradition, all the lights went out.

For a moment I was totally unsighted by the darkness. The memory of the network of fluorescent tubes strung across the ceiling was flashed in to my retinas. I panicked at my own blindness, instinctively recoiling. I reached for the counter behind me, and ducked down.

I squeezed my eyes shut, willing them to adapt. They did so with frustrating slowness, like waiting for an old Polaroid picture to surface out of the emulsion.

After a few moments that felt like hours, I opened my eyes again and, blinking, I discovered I could make out the outlines of the nearest weights machines. I crabbed along until I found the opening to behind the counter, and edged through it, not stopping until my back hit the office wall.

All the time, I was waiting for the sounds of rapid entry. If this was just a blown circuit breaker, or a power cut, boy was I going to feel a right prat.

Then, muffled by the dividing walls, came the faint noise of glass shattering as someone smashed one of the windows in the changing rooms.

For a second I tensed, then the realisation hit. There were steel bars fitted on the inside of all the windows in the gym, clearly visible from the outside. No way was anybody going to get in that way.

But, a little voice in the back of my head piped up, the gap between the metal bars was plenty wide enough for them to toss an old vodka bottle full of Unleaded through, now wasn't it?

I carefully got to my feet, groping for the fire extinguisher Attila kept on a wall bracket just behind the counter. It was dry powder, I remembered. You could use it on just about any type of fire.

I yanked the plastic safety tab out of the squeeze lever handle, and hefted the nine kilo cylinder onto my shoulder, staggering out cautiously from my place of comparative safety.

I got as far as the start of the corridor that leads to the changing rooms, when the main door behind me lurched open. There was no attempt at stealth, it just slammed back against the frame.

The shock of it made me wheel round, gasping. I caught the briefest glimpse of two figures in the doorway, silhouetted by the sodium light from the car park behind them, casting eerie elongated shadows onto the gym floor.

It was impossible to tell an identity, but as one of them started to bring his right hand up, I recognised the shape of the object he was gripping in his fist.

A gun.

Before he'd got chance to take a bead on me, I'd twisted on the balls of my feet and started to dive for cover. The people who'd trained me had drummed it in from the start that to move will save your life, when to freeze will get you killed. So, it was a reflex reaction, elevated by the surge of adrenalin that rushed through my system like a flash flood.

Even as I started to shift, I knew I wasn't going to be quick enough. Instinctively, I shut my eyes and flinched my head, as though that was going to make a difference.

The sharp crack the gun made as it was fired was terrifyingly loud inside the confines of the building. At the same instant, the noise exploded into a reverberating clang like a giant struck bell. The fire extinguisher bucked in my hands. Something thumped me hard on the side of my neck, and I went down.

I lost my grip on the extinguisher as I fell. It landed with the valve downwards, bouncing hard enough on the handle to puncture the CO_2 cartridge inside and pressurise the contents. Suddenly, my view to the doorway disappeared in a hissing cloud of powder.

The extinguisher toppled over onto its side, but the discharge valve must have snapped off, because the powder kept billowing out of it even when there must have been no more force on the handle. I was enveloped in a choking layer of talcum-like dust.

My neck was stinging and my head felt dazed, but I knew the powder wasn't going to keep my assailants occupied for long. It takes under thirty seconds to empty a cylinder that size, and the clock was ticking. I had to move – now. Anyone who comes calling armed with a gun has to be pretty damned serious about killing you.

The thought chilled me, but I pushed it to the back of my mind as I scuttled across the carpet on my hands and knees. I cannoned into a stack of weights as I brushed past, and sent them crashing to the floor. Immediately, another shot fractured the air, pinging off the frame of the machine directly above my head. Shit! Too close for comfort.

I heard the men stumbling and swearing as they moved further into the room. In the dark the gym equipment was even more of a hindrance to them than it was to me.

Unless they were very experienced and knew to shut their eyes, every time the gunman pulled the trigger, the flare of the muzzle flash from the un-silenced weapon was obliterating whatever night vision they'd managed to build up. I hoped.

I eased my head up over the bench behind which I'd been hiding. I could just make out the shape of them, about ten feet apart, with the gunman in front, making a sweep of the place. They were moving gingerly through the swirling clouds of powder from the still-discharging extinguisher. Was it really less than half a minute since the first shot had been fired?

I ducked down again. Who was trying to kill me? And, more importantly, why? Maybe the man at the building site had told Langford and Mr Ali about this mysterious bike courier. The thought seemed so outrageous, I dismissed it almost straight away.

Or, maybe, despite his apparent nonchalance Garton-Jones had taken his dismissal a lot more personally than had been thought. I could follow the reasoning that, with me out of the way, the residents of Lavender Gardens might suddenly decide his services were cheap at any price. . .

Surely there were easier ways of dealing with me than sending a pair of thugs to shoot me dead? Or was it Garton-Jones himself out there in the darkness?

I knew that I was going to have to come up with something fast if I wanted to get out of this alive. I reached out carefully to the stack of weights I'd knocked over and quietly picked up a couple of two-and-a-half kilo ones.

With a final furtive check on the position of the two men, I quickly lobbed one of the weights into the gap between them, ducking back down fast.

I saw them both react to the noise the weight made when it crash-landed into the gloom beyond them. Trigger-happy wasted another couple of rounds firing rapidly in that direction. Having their backs turned gave me the chance to half-rise up from cover, take a bit more time over my aim with the second weight.

I flung it at the gunman with as much power as I could put behind it. I nearly missed. Something must have alerted him at the last moment and he began to turn. The weight clouted the shoulder of his gun arm hard as he came round, and I heard him cry out.

In a flash I was on my feet. This was my only chance, and I couldn't afford to bungle it. I jumped onto one of the benches, and used that as a springboard to launch myself at the second man.

I body-slammed him hard enough to smack the breath out of my lungs. I hit him at around mid-chest height, my momentum carrying him off his feet and hurling him skidding onto the floor. The air was punched out of his body in an explosive grunt as we landed, with me still on top. I jabbed a short blow to his head, then scrambled to my feet and sprinted for the open doorway.

As I reached the aperture, it became obvious that Trigger-happy had regained use of his gun arm. Another two rounds came whistling out after me. One of them clipped the door frame as I ran through it, splintering the wood and peppering the back of my shoulder-blades with shards as I ran through.

I dodged sideways out of sight, flattening against the outside wall of the building. I could see my breath in clouds against the bitter night air.

I bit down on my fear and anger as I waited for them to show themselves. I was past caring about how stupid it was to stand and fight. I wanted blood over this. Preferably not mine.

I didn't have time for second thoughts. It was only moments before the thud of running footsteps grew louder from the doorway. As the first figure burst through it I pivoted sideways and swung my leg hard into his stomach like I was doing a high-kick aerobics routine.

The impact jarred right through me, but he dropped instantly, the gun clattering away from him as he fell. My body was already spinning to continue the attack when my mind registered the face of my enemy, now visible under the lights, and put the brakes on. I stumbled to a halt, my movements suddenly jerky and uncoordinated.

'*Nasir?*' my voice came out incredulous.

The boy on the floor gave me a look of such intense and vicious hatred that I staggered back from it. I entirely forgot to take the other assailant into account. He rammed into me and sent the pair of us sprawling. I managed to get an elbow to his face, but it was no more than a superficial blow.

Still, it was enough to send him reeling, and when I glanced at him, I knew why. Harlow and Drummond were professionals. They'd obviously been told to make an example of

Roger, and when they'd worked him over they'd made sure they marked him where it would show.

His face was still a mass of tender bruises, and the left side seemed to be one big scab. The swelling was pulling his lip down, showing his teeth. Both eyes were open now, but the white of one was flecked with blood.

I took the opportunity to roll away from him fast, hearing him screaming to Nasir, 'Get the gun! Shoot her, for fuck's sake!'

If I'd known Roger was going to be so damned unfriendly, I would have left him to get what was coming to him in that alley.

Ah well, too late for regrets now.

I got to my feet to find that Nasir had indeed regained his grip on the gun, and had it pointing firmly at me. Closer, and in better light, I could see it was a nine millimetre semi-automatic pistol. A Browning Hi-Power design, made by FN in Belgium. I'd fired enough of them on the army ranges for the weapon to be familiar.

This one hadn't had the benefit of military upkeep, though. It was battered and abused, with traces of rust along the barrel. It didn't look like the sort of thing the FN Herstal company would want to use pictures of in their latest brochure. A workmanlike killing tool, no trophy piece.

Slowly, and without any sudden moves, I brought my hands up to shoulder height, and kept them there.

It was a strange tableau. We were all of us covered in the pinkish powder from the fire extinguisher. I'd been closest and come off worst in the exchange. I looked like a slightly effeminate ghost.

Roger's face had opened up again where I'd caught him, the blood leaving red trails through the powder and dripping down onto his T-shirt. He was holding himself stiffly, like an arthritic old man.

I just couldn't believe that he'd risen from his sick bed with the express purpose of coming down here with his mate to slaughter me. It seemed ludicrous overkill. In more ways than one.

'So, Nasir,' I said conversationally, 'are we going to stand around all night, or are you just going to shoot me?'

'Shut up!' he yelled, seeming close to tears. The gun was wavering alarmingly. 'Just shut up!'

Roger glanced at him, worry creasing his face. 'Come on, Nas, get it over with!' he urged nervously.

Ungrateful little bastard.

For a moment Nasir looked as though he was going to comply. I tensed, then he let out a tortured groan.

'I can't!' he wailed, letting the muzzle of the gun drop.

Roger jumped to his side, grabbing his arm and almost seeming to forget about my presence. 'You've got to,' he said sharply. 'She's got to die, tonight.'

I knew I should be asking questions, but for the life of me I couldn't utter a word. It was like watching the actors on a film set. This wasn't real. This couldn't be my own cold-blooded execution they were talking about . . .

Nasir gave out a sob. 'I can't,' he said again. He brought his hands up to cover his face. 'Oh, God help her.'

'You bastard!' Roger screamed at him. 'Don't you know what's going to happen? Don't you care?'

Before Nasir could respond, there was the roar of an engine turning off the road into the gym entrance, and the blaze of headlights as they cut a swathe across the car park.

Nasir took a horrified look at the Dutch-plated Grand Cherokee that was leaping over the loose surface towards us, and panicked completely.

By this time his gun hand was shaking so much he could barely take aim, but he loosed off three quick, startled shots in the general direction of the jeep. I was standing so close to him when he fired that my eardrums seemed to explode.

More by luck than by skill, his first shot hit the windscreen. It bloomed instantly into an opaque mesh of fracture lines, radiating out from the point of impact like ripples.

The second two shots cracked harmlessly overhead, way high.

As soon as the first round struck, the Cherokee's wheel was wrenched over, with the driver's side furthest away from us. It skated to a halt and I saw the door fly open.

Sean came out hard and fast, moving straight into cover. Even if Nasir had his nerve intact, he would have to have been at marksman standard to have stood half a chance of hitting him.

I took the opportunity presented by this new distraction to dodge forwards, stepping quickly in to Nasir's body and wrapping my arms round his right hand. I locked on to his wrist with a tenacity that Friday would have been proud of, and dug steely fingers into the nearest available pressure points.

With hindsight, it was a damned stupid move. Tackling someone who's pointing a loaded gun at you, I mean, but the whole thing had a surreal quality about it. Any moment the unseen director was going to shout, 'Cut!' and we'd all go off to grab a coffee together before the next take.

As I twisted my fingers, Nasir's grip on the weapon started to loosen, which would have worked out just fine, had Roger not realised what was happening. He gave a kind of strangled scream and jumped me, landing a vicious punch in my kidneys.

My legs buckled. I let go of Nasir's hand, and went down on my hands and knees. He jumped away from me and I looked up to stare straight into the muzzle of the FN, only a few feet away.

I could see Nasir's face beyond the wobbling barrel, watched as he screwed up the courage to pull the trigger while he still had the time to do it. At that range, there was no way he could possibly miss.

'*Roger!*' Sean's voice suddenly yelled out from somewhere behind the Cherokee, making all of us jump. 'What the fuck d'you think you're doing?'

'Just stay out of this,' Roger shouted back desperately. His voice gave way, close to tears, as he flicked his gaze back to Nasir, and then to me. 'You don't understand,' he cried. 'Why can't you leave me alone?'

'Leave you alone to become an accessory to murder, you mean?' Sean gave a harsh laugh. 'Oh yeah, *sure.*' He paused, then added more gently, 'Whatever she's done, Rog, it's not worth killing her for.'

'You don't know what you're talking about,' Roger told him bitterly. 'You don't know what's going on round here.'

Nasir glanced to Roger, agitated, and while his attention was off line I brought my hands up sharply, scattering gravel into the boys' faces. It was never going to do them much damage, but at least both of them jerked further away from me.

At that moment, as though on cue, Sean burst round the front wing of the Cherokee and came charging across the ground between us like an avenging angel. Dressed in black, face set, he was enough to strike terror into an enemy far more resolute than Nasir.

As it was, Nasir got off one wild shot before the FN mis-fed the next round and locked up solid. If he'd been halfway proficient he could have had the blockage cleared in moments and slotted Sean while he was still yards away.

As it was, he rattled fruitlessly at the jammed slide, threw a forlorn, fearful look to Roger, and bolted, taking the useless weapon with him. Roger was only a stride or two behind him.

They took off towards the area to the back of the gym. Sean came thundering past me and there was a deadly intent in his eyes as he followed. The boys were heading for the broken-down wire fencing behind the building. An easy escape onto open ground piled with the rubble of a demolished factory. If they made it that far, they'd be free and clear.

I hauled myself upright and, with more misgivings than I cared to count, I turned and gave chase.

I wanted to find out why Roger and Nasir were so keen on killing me, and if the look on his face was anything to go by, I needed to do that before Sean got his hands on either one of them.

Eleven

As I burst round the corner of the main gym building there was enough ambient light for me to see the boys separate. Sean's stride faltered, uncertain for once which to follow.

I was about to thank him for probably saving my life, but as he heard me closing he turned fast and made a snap decision. 'Go after Roger,' he rapped out. 'I'll take the other one.'

My words of thanks were swallowed quickly. 'Roger's *your* brother,' I argued, stubborn, as I reached him. 'You should go after him yourself.'

His face tightened. People didn't question Sean's orders, least of all me. 'The other kid may have managed to work out how to clear that pistol,' he said darkly as he started forward again, offering back over his shoulder. 'I can take care of myself.'

I opened my mouth to say, 'And I can't?' and then shut it again. Did I really want to persuade him to let me go chasing somebody who was fleeing, scared half to death, and armed?

Instead, I held my tongue as I set off in pursuit of Roger.

Sean's brother had made it through the tattered wire fence leaving a torn strip of T-shirt behind to mark his hasty passing. The pale cloth flapped feebly as it caught the light, like a pennant. I ducked through the spiked gap and followed, slithering precariously over the rubble under foot. In the darkness it was lethal.

Some months before, the demolition team had brought down the structure of the old factory building behind the gym and then knocked off – permanently, it seemed. In the intervening period the weeds had done their best to camouflage the ruins they'd left behind with tough-stemmed grasses that whipped against my legs as I ran.

Roger had a decent head start on me, but he wasn't exactly at his peak when it came to physical fitness. He was fading fast, and he knew it. I caught a glimpse of him, dodging clumsily out of sight behind one of the huge piles of broken bricks. He was stumbling as though exhausted and it galvanised me into an extra burst of speed.

That was probably what saved me.

Behind the bricks, I found Roger wrestling with a length of three-by-two that was tethered into the hard-packed ground by loops of rusty wire.

I came hying into view just as he managed to wrench it free, but he had no time to prepare his ambush. His head jerked, and he tried to wrench the timber up more quickly, but his reactions were badly off.

Hesitation would have been fatal, and I didn't have time to mess around. I shifted my direction slightly, locking my arm out straight to the side. I hit him from a flat run, just about where his collarbones met, putting the whole of my body-weight and momentum behind my clenched forearm.

Roger's feet literally flew up in front of him as the top half of his body was snapped back, like he'd just had a belt off the mains. All it lacked to complete the picture was a gentle wisp of smoke and a bad home perm.

It took him a while to think about getting up again and I admit I made no move to help. Instead, I thoughtfully toed the lump of wood so it was well out of his reach, and stood waiting for him to recover enough to take an active part in conversation.

I knew I should have felt guilty about the placing of that punch. I'd deliberately aimed a fraction high, which was malicious at best, and could have been very unhealthy if I'd got it wrong. Then I remembered his urgent commands to Nasir to shoot me, and faced him coolly unrepentant.

After a minute or so, Roger's breathing returned to some semblance of normality. He used one hand to push himself up into a sitting position, rubbing at his throat with the other and eyeing me warily. I made sure I was standing with my back to the lights.

'So, what's this all about, Roger?' I asked, surprised that I could put the question without rancour.

He shook his head. 'You wouldn't understand,' he said and, while his face was sour, there was the faintest trace of fear, like an underlying thread.

'Try me.'

He gave me a look that would have been taken off him if he'd tried to go into a nightclub wearing it, and remained pigheadedly silent.

I squatted so my eyes were on his level. He met my gaze cursorily, then slid his own away. 'I think it's *you* who doesn't understand the shit you're in, Rog,' I said lightly. 'In fact, you're in it so deep you need a snorkel.'

I was rewarded with a sneer.

'This isn't just aggravated burglary any more, Roger,' I said, speaking slowly and keeping my voice neutral. 'This is serious. You can't claim this was accidental, or it wasn't you. This is full-on premeditated attempted murder.'

I let that one settle for a moment. 'Attempted murder,' I repeated, pressing on without mercy, refusing to let myself weaken, 'is an adult crime, Rog, and you'll be dealt with in an adult court. Left to rot away your youth in an adult hell-hole.'

The fright jumped, full-fledged, in his eyes, in his face. 'I can't!' he cried, suddenly very much a child.

'Oh you can,' I said, 'and you will. You've gone way beyond the limits of teenage rebellion this time. What do you think O'Bryan's going to do about that?'

I glanced at him then, wanting to see how he was taking the information on board. He looked stricken. Tormented. I suppose I should have been pleased, but it wasn't much of a victory.

Roger opened his mouth to reply, but before he could speak we heard it, and it stopped both of us stone cold in our tracks.

A single gunshot.

The echo of it rolled over and round us, stark and un-compromising. I froze, straining for additional sounds, but there was nothing.

Silence.

There were no further shots fired. No angry protests. No agonised screams. No evidence of continued pursuit, either, which *could* have meant Nasir had simply missed.

Or it could have meant that Sean was dead.

My mouth dried instantly as my system shut down un-necessary functions, like the production of saliva. My heartrate had accelerated faster than a top fuel dragster. The shaft of panic that arrowed through me was quite dazzling in its intensity.

There was a time when I'd come damned close to praying for Sean Meyer's death. But not like this.

Oh no. If anyone was going to kill him, I'd wanted it to be me.

With half my brain numbed into insensibility by the picture my imagination had painted, I'm almost surprised it took Roger so long to take advantage.

I caught the faintest glimmer of colour and movement from the corner of my eye, then his lashing foot connected

122

hard with the underside of my chin and it was my turn to go pitching raggedly onto my backside among the brickwork.

By the time I'd laboured to my feet, I took one look at Roger's dim figure disappearing into the darkness on the other side of the site, and ruefully gave up any idea of the chase.

I put a hand up to my tender jaw, wriggling it experimentally a few times, but there was no permanent damage. Still, as an object lesson in what happens when you're stupid enough to take your eye off the ball, I suppose it could have been a lot worse.

When I got back to the gym, I found Sean leaning on the front wing of the Cherokee, waiting for me. He looked very much alive and kicking. I ran through a track-list of emotions about that, most of which I didn't care to put names to.

He straightened up as soon as he saw me, instantly alert like a cat, and lamentably unruffled by events. 'You OK?'

I bit back an angry retort about why should he care, and nodded. 'You?'

'Yeah.' He'd seen, of course, that I was alone and gave me a lopsided smile that suddenly took ten years off his harsh features. 'And Roger?' he asked.

'Long gone, I'm afraid,' I said shortly, half-heartedly batting some of the brickdust and extinguisher powder from my jogging pants. It was a losing battle. 'What about Nasir?'

'The other kid? Likewise,' he said wryly. 'He freed the blockage and his aim seemed to be getting better with practice. I came down strongly in favour of tactical retreat.'

I shrugged and walked past him, wanting to check on the external cabinet that housed the electricity meter, which was on the front of the building. Even without benefit of a torch I could clearly see that the cover was hanging off and the main circuit breaker had been thrown.

'They knew just where to look,' Sean commented quietly from behind me.

'Hardly surprising,' I pointed out, without turning round, 'seeing as how Nasir's an electrician.'

'Who was he, the other kid?'

'Nasir Gadatra. He's the son of my next-door neighbour,' I filled in. 'He and your baby brother seem to be big mates.'

Sean didn't answer, so I clicked the power on again and the fluorescent tubes inside the gym vibrated back into life. We went in to survey the damage. I was expecting it to be bad, and I wasn't destined to be disappointed.

The now-defunct extinguisher lay on its side on the floor at the epicentre of a sea of the pinkish white powder. The stuff had coated the carpet in the immediate area so thick you couldn't tell the original colour of the weave. It had blasted up onto the walls too, and layered round the machinery like dust in an old abandoned crypt.

We left trails of footprints as we moved into the main gym area. I noticed that the weight I'd chucked at the boys had splintered part of the wood panelling that Attila had used to line the lower half of the brick walls. I swore under my breath.

Sean bent and picked up the extinguisher. 'This your idea?' he asked.

'Yeah,' I admitted. 'It seemed like a good one at the time. No doubt I'll have to get the damn thing refilled.'

'I wouldn't bother,' Sean said, and something in his voice made me turn. He was staring at the cylinder in his hands. When I looked, I saw a big raw gouge out of the side, slicing through the paint like skin to the metal underneath. 'You were lucky, Charlie,' he said, voice sober. 'The round glanced off it rather than penetrated the steel. If this thing had gone up it would have taken your arms off.'

No, I thought, I had it on my shoulder at the time. It would have blown my damned head off instead . . .

I swallowed and didn't comment on that one. There wasn't a whole hell of a lot I could say. But my legs suddenly felt a lot less steady than they had done, before Sean had pointed it out.

I glanced round, pulling a face, distracting myself with the practical. 'I suppose I'd better call the police,' I said wearily.

'No.'

The denial was too instant, too emphatic. It stilled me, brought my head up. Sean put the extinguisher down, moved in. I had to fight the temptation not to back away from him. I remembered what had happened the last time I'd let him get too close, even after four years. God, he even smelt the same.

'I don't suppose you'd mind telling me why the hell I shouldn't?' I enquired, my voice low with resentment.

I had to tilt my head up to meet his eyes. Liquid black eyes, deep enough to drown in. 'He may be your kid brother, but he and his mate have just tried to kill me. That's not something you can just sweet-talk your way out of, you know.'

He sighed, hunching his shoulders. 'I realise that, Charlie, but I'd like some time to find out why.'

'I was hoping you'd be able to tell me that,' I said. 'Does Roger think *I* got him beaten up, is that it?' The last time I'd spoken with Nasir in the back garden he'd certainly seemed to think I was responsible, however indirectly.

Sean shook his head. 'He didn't say so, but he was in a pretty bad way when we got him home.' His face closed in for a moment, cold and hard at the memory. 'He says he doesn't remember much, and he certainly isn't aware that you tried to help him.'

'If I'd known who he was at the time,' I said bitterly, 'I might not have done.'

Sean cast me a searching gaze. 'Why? Because he hurt one of your neighbours?' he asked, still grim. 'Or because he's my brother?'

'Well now,' I said softly, 'there's a loaded question.'

I tired of the stare-out contest first, breaking away to do another sweep of the gym. 'Besides, it's out of my hands whether the police are involved or not. I'll have to call Attila about this, and then it'll be up to him.'

To my surprise, Sean broke into a smile. 'This place belongs to Attila, does it?' he said. 'Me and him go way back. I think I can persuade him to give me a few days to try and straighten things out.'

I shrugged and turned away. I suppose I shouldn't have been surprised that Sean was acting on his own motives, without any regard for me. Running true to form.

I moved to the phone on the counter and dialled Attila's home number. He agreed to come at once when I gave him the outlines of what had happened, then he asked to speak to Sean. I held the receiver out to him without speaking, and left them to their man-to-man chat while I went to shower and change out of my dirty clothes.

When I came back, in my bike leather jeans and the fresh shirt I always kept in my locker, Sean had finished the call, and was sitting on one of the cleaner benches, surveying the mess. 'Attila's on his way over to secure the place,' he told me. 'He says no police.'

'There's a surprise,' I said drily, plonking my helmet and jacket down on the counter.

Sean paused for a moment. 'I assume you got my message the other night, Charlie,' he said carefully. 'I meant what I said. We've unfinished business, you and I.'

'Oh, I think things are well finished between us, don't you, Sean?' I said, keeping my voice brisk. 'There's nothing more to be said or done. It was a mistake. A big mistake that cost me dear, and it's not one I intend making again.'

Sean regarded me sadly, his head on one side, suddenly looking older.

'I thought I knew you, Charlie,' he said quietly. 'I wasn't even close, was I?'

'Yeah, well, people change,' I bit back, fatigued. I was in no mood for some clever verbal fencing.

'I never would have believed you'd change so far, or so fast,' he said. 'What happened to make you so bitter?'

I stared. How could he ask that when he knew damn well what had gone on? What game was he playing now? He may not have started events rolling, but he'd sure as hell given them a push on their way down hill. Old resentment surfaced unexpectedly.

'What happened?' I struggled to keep my voice level. 'I got thrown out of training, Returned To Unit in disgrace, and muscled out of my career. What the hell do you think happened?'

'And you think I'm to blame for you being RTU'd?' My God, he even sounded affronted. 'You think that justifies you crying rape?'

Crying rape? Did he really think none of it happened? That I'd made the whole thing up? Suddenly I was tired of all this side-stepping, this careful dodging round the point without ever getting right down to it.

'Get out, Sean,' I said, quiet and flat, not meeting his eyes.

He stood up, moved to come past me, then changed his mind, whirling fast, angry, and catching hold of my upper arms. 'Talk to me, Charlie,' he demanded. 'I need answers from you and I can't deal with your silence.'

Instinctively, I brought my forearms up to break his grip. His hands slid off my shoulders, but his fingers stayed wrapped in my shirt, stretching it back away from my throat.

He stiffened abruptly, and I knew he'd seen the scar. That close he'd have to have been blind not to have noticed something that looked like an Ordnance Survey map of a railway line running halfway round the side of my neck.

'Christ. Jesus,' he whispered. 'What happened to you?' He reached out tentatively to touch it, as though it might have been a trick of the light.

I should have told him then that the scar was much more recent. That it had nothing to do with my getting thrown out of the army, but the fake sincerity in his voice choked my words.

I jerked back, shrugging his hands away, and pulled the shirt collar back into place. All the while I was blinking back the tears that were rising unbidden and unwelcome to my eyes. 'What the hell does it matter to you?' I growled. 'Just go.'

For a long time Sean just stood there, hands clenched tight by his sides. Then he turned on his heel, and walked out.

Physical pain would have been a relief at that point. The urge to smack my fist into something solid and unyielding, and to keep doing it, was uppermost in my mind. I barely resisted the temptation.

I admit I slept in the next morning. It wasn't until Friday started howling his protest downstairs in the living room that I finally hauled myself out of bed.

Feeling muzzy, I went down and let him out into the back garden, then headed for the shower. By the time he'd finished sniffing at tree trunks and doing whatever else it is that dogs do in gardens, I was dressed and much closer to being human again.

Friday seemed overjoyed when I got his lead out. It had been so late when I'd got back the night before, taking him out for a walk had been the last thing on my mind. Besides, with both Nasir and Roger still roaming around, I'd been more than a little nervous about wandering round at night in the open.

So, this morning I knew I owed Friday more than a quick turn around the block. I pulled on my jacket and gloves, and unlocked the front door, patting my pockets to check I'd got my keys. The dog pranced out onto the path almost skipping with delight. He did his best to sabotage my efforts to secure the door behind me, yanking the lead in my hands.

I took him the long way, crossing the waste ground and letting him nose around in the piles of rubble and fallen bricks that surrounded the derelict terrace of houses between the Lavender and Copthorne estates. But, as the dog dragged me along the home stretch of Kirby Street, I found that we hadn't been away nearly long enough.

There was a man walking down the short drive towards the police cruiser that was parked by the kerb. At first, I thought he must have been knocking at Pauline's door, but as I drew closer I realised he'd been calling on Mrs Gadatra instead. The man was in late middle-age, and his dark hair was longer than I recalled, worn brushed back from his face.

My feet slowed, despite Friday's insistent pulling. Was he here because of the gunfight at the gym last night? How had he pieced that one together so fast? For a moment I debated on making a tactical withdrawal before he noticed me.

I should have known I wouldn't be that lucky.

As if I'd spoken out loud, the man turned and then stilled, waiting for me to close the gap between us. Reluctantly, I complied.

I'd run in to Superintendent MacMillan before, and not in the happiest of circumstances. Only the winter before, I'd helped him stop a killer, but had damned near become another victim in the process. He hadn't liked my methods much, and the whole affair hadn't exactly endeared me to the man.

Which brought me round to a sudden realisation. MacMillan was too high-powered to be running round investigating unconfirmed reports of gunfire. He was strictly a murder and mayhem kind of bloke. So what was he doing outside my door on a Saturday morning?

'Charlie.' He greeted me now in that familiar clipped tone. 'I wouldn't have expected to see you living here.'

'Superintendent.' I nodded shortly in turn. 'It's temporary. I'm house-sitting for a friend.'

'I see,' MacMillan said. He glanced at Friday, then held out his hand for the dog to sniff. To my great disappointment the Ridgeback didn't sink his teeth into the proffered flesh up to the gum line. Instead, while the Superintendent rubbed him absently behind his ears, he stood quite happily with a soppy look of animal bliss on his face. I threw him a reproachful glance. Traitor.

'I suppose you noticed us calling on your neighbour,' the policeman went on casually. 'I'd like to have a word with you about her son, if you have a moment?'

'Of course,' I said. 'You'd better come in.' I unlocked the front door with my mind clicking over furiously. MacMillan was as canny as they came, and he had a sixth sense for lies. If I could avoid having to tell him any, then so much the better. *I know nothing,* I reminded myself. *Let him tell you everything.*

I nearly blew it almost as soon as we'd sat down on Pauline's flowery cotton loose covers. 'So, what's Nasir been up to?' I asked brightly.

'Why should you think he's been up to anything?' MacMillan asked with a slight frown. 'I know the lad had a record of juvenile delinquency, but from what I understand, he's been out of trouble for the last couple of years.'

'Oh,' I faltered, cursing inwardly. 'I just assumed that you weren't making a social call, and—'

'The boy's dead,' MacMillan told me bluntly, never taking his eyes off my face while he said it. Unless you play poker professionally, it's really hard to keep that sort of news from leaving its mark. I could feel my eyebrows lifting as my jaw fell.

'Dead?' I repeated stupidly. 'Dead — how?' *Let it be an accident*, I prayed. *Car crash, heart attack, fell in front of a train — anything would do except* . . .

'I'm afraid Nasir received a single gunshot wound to the chest some time late yesterday evening,' MacMillan informed me in his best official tone. 'It wasn't instantly fatal, but it would appear that he died as a result of it shortly afterwards, and I now find myself in the middle of a murder inquiry.'

Twelve

For a few moments I sat without speaking. Nasir was dead. I remembered that shot I'd heard while I was tackling Roger. Sean had told me Nasir had managed to clear the gun and so he'd given up the pursuit.

But what if Sean *had* caught up with Nas? When it came to hand-to-hand Sean was outstanding. Brutally effective. He wouldn't have hesitated for a second before taking down an armed opponent. Particularly an unskilled teenager, running scared, and with a jammed weapon.

What if he'd taken control of the gun and shot Nasir, leaving him dying before calmly returning to the gym to wait for me. He was certainly cold-blooded enough.

But why? It was a damned stupid way to try and protect his brother, if that was his motive. None of it made any sense.

I raised my head and found the Superintendent still watching me closely with the calm deliberation that made his company so uncomfortable. On the mantelpiece Pauline's dark wood-cased clock ticked loudly into the silence. All of a sudden my mouth was dry, and I had to swallow before I could speak.

'Where did it happen?' I asked, not stopping to think if the question was a logical one for a supposedly innocent party.

MacMillan gave no sign that I'd made a significant slip-up. 'He was found in a rubbish skip, near one of the old industrial estates in Heysham,' he said, matter-of-fact, as though he was describing a change in the weather.

'Heysham?' *Not on a piece of waste ground behind a gym in Lancaster, then.*

The wave of relief that washed over me brought light-headedness in its wake. 'Poor Mrs G,' I said, guilt following on like the next breaker onto the beach. My emotions must have been strung across my face like Times Square neon by this time. 'Do you have any ideas who was responsible?'

'We're working on several lines of inquiry,' he said automatically, but for the first time he looked a little awkward.

I caught the hesitation and was intrigued. 'Do I hear a "but" in there, Superintendent?'

MacMillan frowned for a moment, then leaned forwards in his chair, resting his elbows on his knees and straightening a cufflink while he considered what he was prepared to tell me.

Finally, he looked up. 'We're having a certain amount of trouble with our relationship with this neighbourhood,' he said at last. 'It's vital we clear this crime up quickly, and are seen to be doing so.'

I nodded.

'But, if we start carrying out thorough house-to-house inquiries we are in danger of being accused by community leaders of not looking beyond the Asian population for a culprit.' He sighed and dredged up a tired smile. 'It's a case of damned if we do, and twice damned if we don't.'

'I can understand that,' I said slowly, keeping noncommittal.

'Now I'm the one who's hearing a "but",' MacMillan said, his voice wry.

I glanced up, met the policeman's flat cool eyes with a micron-thin layer of composure. 'I don't really see what this has to do with me.'

The Superintendent paused again, sitting up and crossing his legs, paying particular attention to the crease in the fine material of his trousers. When he spoke it was as if he was picking each word with care. 'I need some eyes and ears on the ground, Charlie,' he said. 'I need to know everything about Nasir Gadatra's activities, legal or not. The sort of thing that people might not want to let slip to us.'

He ran a hand over his face, the first time I'd seen him let his frustration show. 'When something like this happens these people tend to close eyes, mouths and ranks. Then they accuse us of doing nothing. We can't win.'

For a while there was silence. Friday padded through from sloshing the contents of his water bowl over half the kitchen floor. He slyly dried his muzzle by wiping it across my knees while pretending to offer sympathetic support.

I scratched his head distractedly as my brain bounced on ahead. If Sean hadn't killed Nasir, then who had? I kept coming back to wondering why Roger had been so desperate for his friend to shoot me. What was driving the boy?

I tried to forecast the likely consequences of telling MacMillan about the attempted shooting. What would happen if I filled him in about Roger, and moving on logically from that, about Garton-Jones and his thugs? And what about Langford's involvement with Mr Ali? Where did they fit in to all this?

Sean was going to be livid if I involved his brother with the police again. Mind you, Attila probably wasn't going to be overjoyed to have his place dragged through the mud, either, and I needed my job. Perhaps it was better to be safe than sorry . . .

I shook my head slowly. 'I'm not sure if I can help you, Superintendent,' I said, managing to look him straight in the eye with amazing sincerity. 'Nasir had rather old-fashioned attitudes about the role of women that meant we didn't exactly see eye-to-eye,' I added truthfully. 'We never really hit it off, and he certainly never confided in me.'

MacMillan gave me a long stare that as good as told me he knew damned well I was holding out on him. It shouldn't have come as a surprise to him, though, because I'd done it before.

'If that's how you feel then perhaps I should be asking where *you* were last night?' he said, and even as I recognised the trace of humour in his voice, I had to struggle to bite back the panic.

'I was at work,' I managed shortly. 'The gym just behind the old bus garage.'

'Hm, maybe I'll check up on that,' he murmured and I cursed myself again.

Great. Just great. That's right, Fox, encourage MacMillan and his forensic team to go sniffing round at the gym. They wouldn't need a microscope to discover bullets embedded all over the damned place, which might even be a match to the same gun that eventually killed Nasir. I couldn't even be sure that Attila would have picked up all the empty brass shell casings. Oh, smart thinking, Fox.

'After all,' MacMillan continued now, 'you were an excellent shot, I understand. Marksman standard, if your military record is anything to go by.'

I felt my chest constrict so that I had to concentrate on breathing evenly. I had always thought that the army kept that kind of information strictly to themselves. 'That was a long time ago,' I said.

'Old habits, Charlie. Old habits,' he said, his tone almost light, so I didn't know if he was serious or not. 'I'm sure it's like riding a bicycle. You might become rusty, but you never forget.'

No, you didn't, and I hadn't. I could still remember what it was like to be on the ranges, concentrating on slowing my breathing and my heartbeat, gradually taking up the pressure on the trigger.

I could still remember feeling the kick of the butt in my shoulder, watching the holes explode through the wood and paper targets with nothing more on my mind than achieving a better aim, a closer grouping. Rifle or pistol, I had been as good with either. They'd drilled the ability to kill into me.

They'd done the same thing with Sean, only to a higher degree. A much higher degree. I suspected that I was primary school grade compared to his university graduate.

I looked up and found MacMillan studying me again. 'You said Nas was shot in the chest,' I said. 'Close range?'

He pursed his lips, but whether he was trying to recall the details, or trying to decide if he was going to let me have the information, I couldn't tell.

'I won't know precisely until I get the full post mortem report,' he said at last, 'but yes, preliminary indications are that his killer wasn't very far away when the shot was fired. Why?'

'Because if I'm as good with a weapon as you seem to think I am, and if I'd taken a dislike to the poor lad that was sudden and violent enough for me to want to kill him – oh, and if I'd also somehow managed to get hold of an illegal firearm,' I tossed at him, sarcastic and angry, 'I would have aimed for his head.

'And if for some reason I'd gone for a torso shot first,' I went on when he didn't respond, 'I would have followed it up with one round to the head once he was on the ground, just to be sure. Shooting him once in the chest and leaving him to maybe bleed to death smacks of an amateur.'

I stopped, appalled at myself. What was I trying to do, convince MacMillan that *I'd* killed Nasir? Oh, for God's sake . . .

To my surprise, the Superintendent hadn't jumped up to slap handcuffs on me. Nor was he laughing at my outburst, which was perhaps more worrying.

'You're assuming, of course,' he said seriously, 'that whoever killed the boy wanted him dead. That it wasn't an accident. If Nasir is as much of a reformed character as he appears to be these days, I wouldn't be surprised if it turns out to be a case of, "I didn't know it was a real gun, honest". Too many of these kids seem to live in a computer game world these days. It's cartoon violence to them. Unreal.'

'If that's the case, and it *was* accidental – one of his mates – then why leave him to die in a skip?'

He shrugged. 'Any number of reasons. Panic is at the top of my list. The problem is, Charlie,' he said, fixing me with that muddy-coloured gaze, 'that people don't trust us not to try and hang murder on them regardless. Forensic science is so sophisticated now, we can reconstruct a crime remarkably accurately from the minute evidence left at the scene. If someone swears the whole thing was an accident, the chances are that we can prove what they say. They shouldn't be afraid to come forward.'

His voice had become soft, almost gentle. *He thinks I know who did it, I realised, and I'm protecting them because I live here. Because I'm part of this community now, whether I like it or not.*

I kept my own gaze steady. 'I still can't help you, Superintendent,' I said.

He sighed, mouth thinning slightly as though he'd been expecting better things of me.

'OK, Charlie,' he said wearily, coming to his feet, 'but take my advice and don't go off doing any crusading on your own with this one. This whole estate is like a powder keg at the moment. One spark in the wrong place and they'll see the explosion in Carlisle.'

Rising, I said grimly, 'I know.'

MacMillan moved towards the hallway, saying casually as he went, 'I understand you're not teaching self defence any more.'

'No,' I agreed shortly, flicking the latch on the front door and pulling it open for him. The wood had swelled in the last lot of rain, so it stuck to the frame and rattled the door furniture when I jerked it loose. 'I haven't really got back into it.'

He paused on the threshold to look down at me. 'You should,' he said. 'Don't let what happened stop you, Charlie, it wasn't your fault. You did what was – necessary under the circumstances.'

I didn't try to hide my surprise at his words. Not at what he'd said, but the fact that he'd said them at all.

I didn't give him an answer, partly because I didn't have one to give. Logic agreed with the Superintendent, but emotion told me something different altogether.

As he reached the path, he paused and turned back to me, his last question halting me just before I'd got the door safely closed behind him. 'Oh, by the way, what happened to your hands?'

I glanced down at them on reflex. They were still looking pretty scabbed up where I'd hit the road bailing out of the Grand Cherokee. 'Friday,' I improvised quickly. 'He spotted a cat the other morning and pulled me right over. Doesn't know his own strength, the daft dog.' My voice sounded nervous and babbling, even to me.

MacMillan nodded with a quizzical half-smile which told me he didn't believe a word of that, either, but found trying to decipher my reason for lying probably more illuminating than a straight answer. Turning on his heel without further comment, he strode up the drive towards his patiently waiting colleague.

I shut the door and leaned my back against it. If I was going to face MacMillan again without getting myself arrested, I was going to have to learn how to lie a lot more convincingly.

Either that, or I was going to have to find out some answers. And soon.

An hour later I was knocking on another front door, in another street not dissimilar to the one I'd just left. The same neglected brick and pebbledashed houses. The same scruffy fleet of broken-down cars, and overgrown, rubbish-strewn gardens. The scenery may have looked largely identical, but the atmosphere was something different all together.

Unlike Lavender Gardens, there were no coloured faces on the Copthorne estate. Maybe there had been, once, but there's only so many petrol bombs through your letterbox you can smother before you take the hint and get out.

I may not have been Asian, but I stood out like a sore thumb on Copthorne nevertheless. It had only taken minutes before my presence on the estate was registered.

A group of grubby-looking kids playing football in the middle of the road spotted me first. They'd been using a handily parked Astra van as a goal, but by the looks of the dents in the side of it, their keeper wasn't up to much. As I walked by the whole group of them abandoned their game and froze, like a bunch of meerkats.

As I moved deeper into the estate there was always someone conveniently loitering to keep an apparently casual eye on my movements. If I hadn't been expecting it, it might have seemed natural, but I knew that the bush telegraph system on Copthorne made any high-grade military communications network look like a couple of tin cans joined with string.

The residents of Lavender Gardens, if they were serious about setting up their own Neighbourhood React, could have learned a lot from the smooth co-ordination evident on Copthorne, but they would have practically needed an armoured personnel carrier to observe it first hand.

The only thing was, the Copthorne inhabitants weren't keeping such a close eye on me because they thought I was a potential burglar, car thief, or vandal. They were more worried that I might be from Social Services, or the police.

I made sure that I didn't appear to be taking too much interest in the houses. I just kept my head down and kept walking like I knew exactly where I was going, that I had every right to be there.

I breathed a little easier when I finally opened the rotting gate and walked along the short lichen-covered concrete path leading to the mid-terrace house where a scan of the local phone book told me Sean's mother lived.

I'd no idea when I moved to Lancaster that's where Sean was originally from. In the time he and I had been together, he'd never told me much about his family. I'd certainly never been taken home to meet them.

We'd been to see mine, though. Spent a weekend at my parents' place in Cheshire. The contrast between their ivy-clad Georgian house, with its circular gravel drive and immaculate formal garden was sharp with the run-down property in front of me. Still, it made me wonder what he'd really thought of me, that he hadn't wanted me to see it.

Not that the weekend with my parents had been anything of a success. My mother hadn't known what to make of the self-contained, quiet soldier I'd presented her with. As for my father, well maybe they were too alike to have ever really got on.

He'd accurately read Sean's background, and made sure the younger man was subtly aware of the gulf between us. Even so, did Sean really think I would have looked down my nose at his own family home?

Now, there was a long enough pause before anyone answered the front door for me to begin planning an organised retreat. Then the curtain was pulled to one side in the front bay window, and a couple of small heads peered at me over the sill.

I smiled and waved, and the heads bobbed out of sight. It still didn't mean there was an adult in. There were more latchkey toddlers on Copthorne than you could shake a shoplifted box of rusks at.

Then, to my relief, there came the sound of bolts being drawn on the other side of the door. I struggled to martial my thoughts and realised, too late, that I'd no clear idea what I was going to say to Mrs Meyer.

I needn't have worried.

When the faded front door was pulled open, it was Madeleine who stood on the other side. The tall, dark-haired girl was wearing jeans and a pale green shirt, and looked like she'd just been modelling them for *Vogue*. There was remarkably little surprise registering on her smooth pale face.

'Hi,' she said. 'You must be Charlie. Sean said you might call round. He's not here at the moment, but do come on in.'

Thirteen

Madeleine stepped to one side and ushered me, unresisting, into the hallway.

It was small and cluttered, with a row of china ornaments on a shelf over the radiator, and a jumble of dirty child-size trainers piled in a heap on the floor. As Madeleine shut the door behind me two kids holding plastic water pistols came galloping down the stairs and disappeared through a side door, carrying on a running battle as they went.

Madeleine ignored them, leading me through into a tiny living room. It was made all the smaller by the presence of a huge three-piece suite with heavy wooden feet. There were three more kids arranged around the TV set, which had a games console plugged into it. The animated picture was frozen just at the moment some scaly double-headed monster with chainsaws for arms was having its head exploded in a dungeon.

It made me remember the Superintendent's words about the meaning of life and death to kids today. I began to think he might not be so far off the mark with his theory. If only I could be sure that Sean wasn't involved.

As soon as Madeleine reappeared, the kids started clamouring for her to continue their game. She favoured them with an indulgent smile. 'Do you mind?' she said to me. 'Only we're right up at Level Five. They'll never forgive me if I back out now.'

I shook my head, still a little bewildered by my reception, and she dropped onto her stomach on the floor with the kids. Almost straight away, her thumbs were stabbing agilely at the buttons on one of the hand controllers. Four pairs of eyes were suddenly transfixed on the screen.

I stood for a moment or two, unsure what to do other than wait, when the living room door swung open again and a small wiry woman with untidy grey hair dashed in.

'Ah, I thought I heard the front door,' she said, 'but I was just rolling out some pastry. Excuse me not shaking hands, won't you, dear.' She held up hands that were floured to the elbows. 'Now, would you like a nice cup of tea?'

'Thank you,' I said faintly. Madeleine gave me a quick grin over her shoulder and I followed the older woman as she bustled out to the kitchen.

That room, like the rest of the house I'd seen so far, was cluttered, but spotlessly clean. I leaned against a cupboard and watched as Mrs Meyer shot water into the kettle, clicked it on, plucked the teapot from its stand, and brought down two mugs from hooks on the wall. It took me a few moments to realise that there wasn't any particular reason for her to be hurrying.

'So, you know Maddie, do you?' she asked pleasantly, scooping loose tea into the pot from a tin that once contained Bassett's Liquorice Allsorts. She flicked me a brief bright glance. It was disconcerting to be staring into Sean's ebony eyes set deep in a lined face.

'Er, no, not really. I used to know Sean – a few years ago,' I said cautiously, watching as she grabbed her rolling pin and began vigorously flattening a dusty circle of pastry on the kitchen table. 'I was wanting to see him about his brother.'

'Oh, that boy,' she said, but gently, with affection. She dunked a hand into an open bag of flour and flumped more of it onto the table. 'He's caused me some troubles,' she added, smiling again, 'but if Roger grows out of it like Sean, I'll count myself blessed.'

'You have a daughter as well, don't you?' I asked, making conversation.

Just for a second, her busy hands stilled, then they were off again, as though the flag was down and the clock was against her. 'Yes, yes I do,' she said, distractedly. 'My Ursula's not living at home any more. Oh, now, there's that kettle.' She turned and sloshed the boiling water into the teapot so recklessly I feared she'd scald herself, but most of the liquid went where it was aimed.

'We've had a bit of a falling out,' she went on with un-expected candour when the teapot lid was safely rammed on and a rabbit-shaped cosy in place over the top.

Another quick smile, then she lowered her voice. 'Between you and me, she's gone and got herself into trouble. Won't tell us who the father is. Sean's been to see her, but he said she wouldn't tell him anything either. I was hoping Maddie might be able to get through to her. She's good at that, bless her, but no such luck.'

Sean's mother seemed so keen to impart information that I couldn't resist a little delicate pumping. 'Madeleine – er, Maddie – seems very nice,' I ventured.

The ploy, lame as it was, worked. Mrs Meyer plonked milk into the mugs, then poured the tea through a plastic strainer, handing mine across with a smile of satisfaction creating a new set of creases on her face.

'Yes, she is, isn't she? Between you and me, I keep hoping she and Sean will name the day,' she said happily. 'There now, I've surprised you. But, it's two years they've been courting. That's time enough to see if you're suited, don't you think?

Besides, I keep telling them I want some grandchildren while I'm still young enough to cope with them.'

'You'll never be too old to cope with kids, Mrs M,' Madeleine said from the doorway. 'Oh good, is there any more tea in that pot? I'm dying for a cuppa.'

'Did you win?' I asked, taking a sip of my own tea and discovering it surprisingly thick and strong, with the hard smack of tannin following on.

'Of course,' Madeleine grinned, helping herself to a mug from the wall. She looked very much at home, not having to wait politely for service, like a guest. Or an outsider. I tried to work out why that should bother me so much.

'I'll never understand those space invader games if I live to be a hundred,' Mrs Meyer put in, deftly peeling up the now wafer-thin pastry and flopping it over a ready-greased pie dish.

'They're easy,' Madeleine shrugged. 'You'd soon pick it up if you put your mind to it.' She leaned over the kitchen table as she passed and filched a cherry from the bowl waiting to fill the pie.

'Go on, out of my kitchen, you.' Mrs Meyer batted affectionately at her hand, but didn't look in the least offended, despite the words. 'You can have some when it's done, and not before. You're as bad as the children.'

Madeleine just laughed. 'Come on, Charlie,' she said. 'Let's drink our tea in the back garden. It's the only place we'll get some peace.'

Just then, the two kids who'd been shooting water pistols at each other now reappeared at similar speed, this time duelling with plastic lightsabers and copious verbal sound effects.

Madeleine rolled her eyes as she grabbed a jacket and led the way out through the back door. It opened onto a small neat garden that was mainly gravel and flagging.

There were a couple of benches set against the hedge furthest from the house, under a crab apple tree, and it was there we sat. It was surprisingly tranquil. The only concession to Copthorne's reputation was the fact that every movable object was chained or concreted to the ground.

Madeleine sighed heavily and slumped down, rubbing her eyes with a weary hand. 'Those damned whiny kids,' she said with quiet feeling, digging in her jacket pockets. The search eventually produced a crumpled pack of Marlboro and a Zippo lighter. 'Mrs M ends up sitting for half the neighbourhood, I think. Thank God for electronic pacifiers.'

She offered a cigarette, which I declined with a shake of my head. Madeleine stuck one between her lips and lit it with the air of someone who isn't allowed to smoke in the house, and has been indoors too long. When the initial buzz of nicotine had hit her system she turned, more relaxed, and eyed me curiously.

'You're not at all like I was expecting,' she said.

Her words made my heart jump, but I waited silently for her to continue. What had Sean told her about me?

'Don't get me wrong,' she hurried on when I didn't speak. 'Sean hasn't told me much, but you know how it is, you build up a picture more from what he *doesn't* say.'

Well, there was certainly a lot to be left unsaid about my relationship with Sean Meyer, but the idea that I'd been discussed in whispers in a semi-darkened bedroom somewhere made my stomach turn over.

I ignored it and buried my nose into the mug of tea, which was still stinking hot. I felt the liquid burning my throat all the way down and was perversely glad.

In between drags on her cigarette Madeleine took a gulp from her own mug and started again on a different tack. You couldn't fault the girl for effort. 'That was quite an exit you made the other night,' she said.

'Yeah, well, Sean and I didn't exactly part on the best of terms,' I said wearily. 'I wasn't particularly anxious to bump into him again.'

'You should go easier on him.' There was just a hint of censure in her quiet tone.

I felt my shoulders stiffen involuntarily. 'Excuse me?' I managed, my own voice low with anger. 'And just what do you know about it, Madeleine?'

Even she had the grace to look a little squashed. 'Hey, don't get me wrong,' she said again, turning towards me and speaking quickly. 'OK, so they threw you off your course. And I know it must have been tough on you, getting kicked out of the army just because you and he had a thing going, but at least they didn't try and kill you.'

That's what you think. It was my turn to feel the world pause under me. 'What do you mean?'

She drew a final breath through the filter tip, and dropped the cigarette butt on the ground, grinding it out. 'After you left they posted him again, and kept posting him. One shitty hell-hole after another. They were hoping he'd do the decent thing and get himself blown up, or shot, but Sean doesn't play by the rules like that. He kept coming back. Fortunately, when he realised what the bastards were trying to do, he got out before they succeeded. I know you think you've had it rough, Charlie, but he's had it tough, too.'

I watched the genuine anger sketch across her perfectly put together features, and tried not to look for some devious ulterior motive. I had to ask, anyway. 'Why are you telling me this?'

She took a moment to tamp down the emotion, draining her mug of tea before replying. 'Just so you'll understand,' she said at last. 'Beyond anything else, Sean admired and respected you, you know? He never expected you to fail, never mind that you'd take him down with you. That was the biggest blow for him. Finding out this girl he practically idolised had clay feet.'

I'd been intending to wait around until Sean returned home, but after Madeleine's soft-spoken attack I knew I had to get out of there, fast.

How dare Sean give anyone the impression that I'd had an easy time of it. Did he think I'd somehow brought it on myself? I remembered his words at the gym and suddenly it seemed more likely that he thought I'd made it all up. Or had he just conveniently forgotten to mention that part to Madeleine.

Besides, what Sean didn't know was that they had indeed tried to kill me. OK, so it wasn't quite the same as being sent on a suicide mission, but at the time it had seemed just as certain, and as terrifying.

Madeleine tried to get me to stay, seemed upset at my poor reaction. How did she expect me to respond to something like that, for God's sake?

I walked out of the estate under the same subtle surveillance that I'd entered it, and crossed the derelict area marking the boundaries without looking up, past the rows of abandoned, boarded-up houses that marked the centre of No Man's Land.

It was only when I'd gone a street or two into Lavender Gardens that my instincts coughed loudly enough to finally attract my attention.

By that time, of course, it was far too late to do much about it.

There was a gang of six Asian boys surrounding me, early teens by the look of them. Four in front, and two already circling behind. They moved suddenly out of gaps and appeared round pieces of broken fencing, approaching me with determination and purpose. I recognised only one of them, the boy with the dyed blond hair.

I took a good look around me, and realised with mounting unease that I was well trapped in a secluded alley with tumble-down garaging down one side. It was almost identical to the sort of place where Roger had been beaten up by Garton-Jones's men. Somehow, I doubted Sean and Madeleine would come galloping to my rescue this time.

For a while nobody moved, and I took my time assessing the situation, but my escape routes were blocked. Outwardly, I did my best to stay calm, even as I was inwardly cursing my own stupidity.

Automatically, I focused on the blond-haired leader. Close to, he was a few years younger than I'd thought. He'd managed to scrape enough facial fluff together to cultivate a bit of an artistic beard and moustache combo, and was probably the eldest of the bunch. That said, he was still only just old enough to legally buy cigarettes, and they'd probably make him show ID to do that.

'What you doin' here, *white girl*?' he asked, so softly his voice was almost a hiss. I caught the trace of a lisp under his words as he made a feature of a speech impediment he couldn't hide.

'I'm just passing through,' I said as calmly as I could.

'You come from Copthorne,' one of the others put in, sneering, and spat at my feet.

I glanced down to where the splatter of phlegm had landed. 'I'm not from Copthorne,' I said, looking away. 'I'm living here. Kirby Street.'

The blond stepped forwards, trying to face me off. 'Oh we know where you *live*,' he breathed, 'but we know you've just been over on Copthorne. Seeing your fascist mates.'

'You shouldn't pigeonhole someone because of the colour of their skin,' I pointed out mildly.

That provoked angry movement from a couple of the others. The leader stilled them with an impatient gesture. 'You think we won't lay a finger on a white girl,' he said, lip curled. 'Well, *some* of us aren't fussy. But then, you know all about that, don't you?'

He gave me a shove, hands against my chest. I allowed my body to roll with it, half expecting the next sharp push that came to my back. They formed a loose circle round me and I allowed them to jostle me backwards and forwards, like a party game. Trying to take them all on was stupid. I was far better to just keep calm and hope they didn't have the nerve to really put the boot in.

Still, it was difficult to stay relaxed in the face of such provocation.

The next time I was shoved at the blond-haired boy, I stumbled deliberately, falling against his bony chest to the jeers of the others. He gave a wolfish grin and put his arms round my waist, grabbing roughly at my backside with his left hand. Most of my good intentions dissipated right about then.

If you're going to do it, make it quick, I reminded myself. It was something I'd always drummed into my self-defence students. Once you'd decided to act, put your heart and soul into it. No holding back.

Just when I'd tensed myself to act, the decision on precisely what I was going to do was suddenly and unexpectedly taken away from me.

A forearm as thick as a child's thigh wrapped itself round the blond boy's neck from somewhere behind him, and he was yanked backwards. I didn't get a chance to identify the big man attached to the rest of the arm before I too was grabbed.

The rest of the gang scattered in enough different directions to foil effective pursuit. There only seemed to be one other man, in any case. I didn't recognise any of them until the black bomber jackets and short cropped haircuts finally registered.

My old mate Mr Drummond had the Asian boy by the back of his collar and had screwed one arm up behind his back with brutal efficiency, slamming him face first into the nearest piece of fencing.

I twisted my head and saw it was Harlow who had hold of me. I tensed, expecting similar treatment, but he contented himself with a pit bull grip on the back of my jacket.

Garton-Jones's faithful sidekick, West, came into my field of vision. His jaw was set rigid and there were veins standing out on his temples. I waited, half hoping he'd have an embolism, but this wasn't destined to be my lucky day.

'Well, well,' he said to the boy after a moment or two, his voice almost a snarl. 'Want to tell me what the fuck's going on here, then, sonny?'

The Asian boy gave him a sullen glare and said nothing. His gang had completely disappeared. So much for loyalty among thieves.

'What about you?' He swung in my direction, lips stretching into a mirthless grin as he got a clear look at my face. 'Well now, Miss Fox isn't it?'

'Mr West,' I greeted him, voice flat. 'I'm surprised to see you here.'

He moved in, stuck his face into mine in a gesture he could only have learned from his boss. He had breath like warm camel dung. 'Well, you'd better get used to it. It was a nice try you made to get rid of us, lady, but we're back now, and *this* time we're here for good.'

For a moment, my mind was too blank to be diplomatic. 'What do you mean, you're here for good? The Residents' Committee threw you lot out.'

'Yeah well,' he said, smoothing a hand over the stubble of his haircut, 'after recent "events" shall we say, they just couldn't wait to *beg* us to come back.'

I stilled, suddenly cold at the rich satisfaction in his voice.

Now, *there* was a twist I hadn't given much thought to. If Garton-Jones was as obsessed with the idea of keeping his claws into Lavender Gardens as he'd seemed that night, was he mad enough to kill to achieve his aims? And what *were* they, in any case?

'By the looks of it,' West went on now, 'we turned up just in time. Proper seventh cavalry, we are,' he mocked. 'So, are you going to tell me just what the game is here?'

I took a brief look at the Asian boy. Only half of his face was visible. The rest of it was wedged up tight against the fence where Drummond was crushing him, but I didn't need to see it to read the fear in every tense line of his body.

I remembered what Garton-Jones's men had done to Roger, and found with a sickly taste in the back of my mouth that I couldn't stomach having another beating on my conscience.

After all, Nasir had blamed me for getting Roger worked over, and then the pair of them had come looking for me with a gun. No way did I want to be seen to be siding with the Streetwise thugs. Not if I was going to stay in one piece until Pauline returned. Even if that meant letting go of my anger. Now wasn't the time to let it out.

I twisted myself out of Harlow's grasp, giving him a dark look as I straightened my jacket. 'There *is* no game,' I said sourly. 'I was just teaching the boys here a bit of self-defence.'

'What?' West spluttered his disbelief, incredulity lighting up his face. His gaze shifted from my face, to the boy's, and back again. 'You have to be jerkin' my chain.'

I stood my ground, even though the explanation had sounded just as unlikely to my own ears. Still, sometimes the ones that seem the most unlikely are the most fitting. Plus that was the best I could come up with in the time allowed.

'Of course I'm not,' I snapped. 'Since when did Garton-Jones introduce rules about that. It's like being back at school.'

West moved round until he was in the boy's line of vision. 'What's your name?'

'Jav,' the boy supplied in a voice breathless with his discomfort. 'Tell him to let go – he's breaking my arm, man!'

West nodded and, with great reluctance, Drummond slackened his grip on the boy and let him disengage his face from the rough wooden planking. There were spots of blood on Jav's cheek where splinters had gouged their way in. He sidled stiffly out of Drummond's reach, rubbing at his over-stretched shoulder and eyeing all of us with wary distrust.

'Well, sonny? I suppose you're going to back her up on this cock-and-bull story. Is that how it happened?' West's voice dripped with raw contempt.

Jav carried on staring at me for a moment longer, then peeled his gaze away, dismissive, as though I wasn't worth the effort. 'Of course not,' he said arrogantly.

My breath stopped.

West flashed me a savage look, then turned back to him. 'Go on,' he said grimly.

'Of course that wasn't how it happened,' the boy went on, growing in confidence. '*We* were teaching *her* how to defend herself. After all, she's only a girl.'

He'd gone too far. West's head ducked and his expression soured. He reached out and grabbed Jav by the back of his neck, digging his stubby fingers into the skin until his knuckles turned white as he dragged the boy up close. 'Don't piss me about, sonny,' he growled.

Jav swallowed, the fright jumping again in his eyes, but his nerve held. 'It's the truth,' he protested.

West's eyes narrowed as he thrust the boy away from him. He searched our faces for the first sign of a crack. We both kept them deadpan.

'All right,' he said at last to Jav, scepticism clear. He jerked his head. 'Get out of here. Go on!' he added, when the boy didn't move. He took a quick menacing stride towards him. It was enough.

Jav ran.

When he'd disappeared, West turned back to me. 'I suppose you realise that I don't believe a single word of that shit you've been shovelling.'

I shrugged. 'You're the expert,' I said, offhand. 'That's your prerogative.'

He ignored the dig, such as it was. 'So, what really went down back there?' he challenged. 'Don't tell me – they tried to jump you, right?'

'We were practising self-defence,' I said, stubborn, setting my teeth.

He let out his breath in a long hiss. 'You people make me sick,' he muttered. 'You let these young thugs walk all over you and you don't have the bottle to stand up for yourself just one time, do you?' He shook his head disbelievingly. 'You just have to say the word, and we'll take care of the problem for you. That's why we're here.'

'Are you really, though?' I murmured. 'So, who said the word when these two beat Roger Meyer half to death, hm?'

'We didn't need anyone to say the word over Meyer,' West bit out. 'He was caught, red-handed, remember?'

'That still doesn't justify what you did to him.' I cast a glance at Harlow and Drummond. They returned it with every appearance of a clean conscience.

'He half-kills an old man, and now you're feeling *sorry* for him?' West made an open-handed gesture of frustration, rolling his eyes. He groaned. 'God preserve us from yet another bleeding-heart liberal.'

'No, I don't feel sorry for him, but I don't believe Roger was directly responsible, and I think there's a lot more going on there than we realise.' I tried throwing that one into the mix, and was surprised by the end result.

'You mean with the Gadatra kid?' West chucked back at me straight away. He stepped in, grinning that nasty little grin of his again. 'Could well be, but *he* got what he deserved, now didn't he?'

How had the news of that one travelled so fast? I could feel my face stiffening with surprise, and fought to keep my expression even.

They made to leave, with West unable to resist a final jibe. 'I thought you had a bit more about you, but looks like I was wrong,' he told me scornfully. 'If you ever dig down deep enough to find the courage to point the finger at these scum, we'll be right in there, taking care of them for you, and cheap at the price.'

He looked me up and down, slow and insulting, and his lip curled. 'Yeah, and there'll be snowballs in hell.'

Fourteen

I don't remember getting back to Pauline's. My legs were on autopilot. It wasn't until I caught the faintest rustle in the hedge by the front door that I clicked out of it and lurched round, fast.

'Come out of there,' I snapped, 'or I'll drag you out.'

After a few moments the foliage parted to reveal a tearful Aqueel in the hollowed-out section at the bottom that seemed to be one of his favourite hiding places. He faced me with his bottom lip out defiantly, even if it wobbled.

My shoulders slumped. So that was what I was down to — frightening little kids and letting the real bullies get away.

'I'm sorry, Aqueel,' I said wearily. 'I didn't know it was you, and you made me jump.'

Aqueel raised a tremulous smile that didn't even have enough wattage to light up the rest of his face. His eyes looked bruised, sunken into dark-smudged sockets and red-rimmed from weeping. He must have been crying non-stop ever since MacMillan's fateful visit. Was it only this morning? It seemed like weeks ago.

'Hello, Charlie,' he greeted me, his voice lifeless and wooden as a bit-part actor in a daytime soap. 'And how are you today?'

'I'm fine, Aqueel,' I said carefully. 'What about you?'

'Oh, I'm very well, thank you,' he returned formally. He must have seen the sympathy in my face, maybe even pity, because he climbed jerkily to his feet. 'Please excuse me, but I must go and look after my mother, and my sister.'

With that he turned, stiff-backed, and stumbled back towards the front door, suddenly the man of the house at eight years old and doing his best to take it on the chin. My heart went out to him.

Inside Pauline's, Friday registered his usual delight at my reappearance. Eventually I bribed him into calm good behaviour with half a dry biscuit. His lanky tail wagged so frenetically at the prospect of even such a motley present that it made the whole of his hard-packed body wriggle.

God, isn't life simple when you're a dog? Cats and street thugs, bad. Trees and biscuits, good. And you know just who your friends are. Sometimes I envied him.

I was halfway through making a snack for lunch when the phone rang. I picked it up warily, in case it was Sean, even though I wasn't sure if he had Pauline's number.

'Hello, Charlotte,' said my mother's voice, characterised by its usual brittle brightness.

'Oh, hi,' I said, relief injecting more warmth into my voice than she was used to.

'Er, well,' she said, sounding pleased. 'Er, yes, I was just getting back to you about your young burglar, darling,' she went on. 'I've been talking to some of my colleagues about it.'

'Oh yes,' I said, with a pang of guilt. 'Actually, I think things have moved on a bit since we last spoke.'

'In what way?' she said, still pleasant, just curious.

'Well, it turns out that Roger is Sean Meyer's younger brother,' I explained. 'You remember Sean, I assume?'

The silence went on for so long I thought the line had gone dead.

'Mother? Are you still there?'

'Yes, yes, I'm still here,' she said faintly. There was a pause, then she went on more strongly, in a rush, 'Oh Charlotte, you're not thinking of getting involved with him again, are you?' Her tone was starting to rise. 'You can't, darling. You mustn't!'

She didn't quite say, 'I forbid it!', but it was there, all the same.

'I have no intention of getting involved with Sean again,' I said, surprised by her vehemence. 'I've hardly spoken to him, and when I have, it's been about his brother.' Well, that was mostly the truth, at any rate.

'He's dangerous,' my mother burst out. 'Look what he did to you last time!'

'That was hardly down to Sean,' I said, shocked to find myself defending him. 'He wasn't even there when it happened. They posted him.'

And kept posting him, Madeleine had said. It suddenly dawned on me that maybe Sean hadn't abandoned me after all. Perhaps he hadn't refused to come back and speak up for me at the court martial. Perhaps he hadn't even known that I was on trial . . .

I was so busy getting my head round the idea that I hardly noticed my mother making hasty excuses to get off the line. After she'd gone, I spent a little while staring rather stupidly at the telephone, and wondering how on earth I was going to find out the truth about the role Sean had really played in my getting chucked out of the army.

Later that evening, by way of contrast, I rode the Suzuki north from Lancaster and out past Caton village to Jacob and Clare's for supper as I'd promised. Not that it took much arm-twisting. Jacob is a superb cook and it seemed to have been a long time since I'd enjoyed a relaxed evening with my friends.

Once we'd finished eating we moved through from the farmhouse-style kitchen to their comfortable living room with its blazing log fire. It was then that I gently reminded Clare about her inquiries into Mr Ali and Langford.

She sighed, but more because she'd just curled up on the sofa with their terrier, Beezer, on her lap than anything else. She turfed the dog onto the floor and obligingly went to retrieve what she'd managed to dig out.

Mr Ali, it transpired, wasn't just a property developer and builder, he was also one of the biggest private landlords in the area. And the majority of the rental housing he owned was slap bang in the middle of Lavender Gardens, with some of it even spreading across into Copthorne.

'I'd like to bet that the residents *there* don't know who owns the roof over their heads,' I said.

'Mm, but it's unlikely they'll ever find out,' Clare agreed. 'He looks after them all through a separate letting agency, and that in turn is owned by another subsidiary company. It's quite a paper trail. It would be quite difficult to find anything out if you were just a tenant.'

'It might explain the connection between Ali and this vigilante bloke you were talking about, though,' Jacob said as he came limping in with a tray of cups and a full pot of coffee.

'What, you mean he's got a vested interest in wanting to clean up the estate?

'It makes sense, I suppose,' I said, shaking the pieces together in my head to see if they fitted any better now.

Jacob nodded as he pressed the plunger in the lid of the cafetière down slowly.

'It does,' Clare put in, 'until you look at the guy he's chosen to do his dirty work for him. Harvey Langford isn't anybody's idea of an altruist.'

'*Harvey?*' I asked with a chuckle. If I'd had to guess, we would have been there for some time.

Clare nodded seriously. 'He's got form as long as your arm, mainly for putting the boot in. He's particularly noted for racially-motivated stuff.' She leafed through various clippings. 'Going back a few years he used to belong to a local neo-nazi organisation, until they apparently beat up a young Asian lad, and then set him on fire.' She grimaced her distaste. 'Then the police clamped down on them pretty hard and the thing broke up. According to my crime desk pal, they arrested a few people, including Langford, but nobody was talking, and they couldn't prove it.'

'Well, that explains the secrecy I suppose,' Jacob said. 'If I was Ali, and Langford was the only bloke I could find to do the job for me, I wouldn't want to shout about our association, either.'

'You could be right,' I said. I picked up one or two of the pages Clare had laid out on the low table in front of the sofa. 'I don't suppose there's anything in there about him being involved with firearms, is there?'

'No, I don't think so,' Clare said. She sat back and eyed me warily as she sipped her coffee. 'Why, Charlie, what aren't you telling us about all this?'

I sighed, and told them all about Roger and Nasir's gun-toting visit to the gym, and then MacMillan's arrival with the news of Nasir's murder. Well, nearly all. Somehow I didn't feel ready to talk to anyone about Sean, so I left him out of the tale.

They listened in silence, then Clare said determinedly, 'I'll find out what I can on Monday. I'll come round and let you know after work, shall I?'

I thought of the restless atmosphere on the estate and shook my head. 'No,' I said quickly. 'I'll give you a call. Things are very uneasy on Lavender Gardens at the moment, especially if you're not a resident. I think it would be best if you stayed well out of the way.'

Clare nodded and bent to clear away the papers. Over her head, Jacob had sent me a brief, grateful glance. I smiled back, trying to reassure him that whatever other demands I might place on our friendship, putting Clare anywhere near any possible risk was not going to be one of them.

Sunday morning, seeing as I wasn't in at the gym, I made a desultory stab at the housework, throwing Friday out into the back garden while I ran the vacuum over his discarded fur. He was losing it at such a rate I was amazed the dog wasn't completely bald.

The noise of the hoover meant I almost missed the phone ringing. I made a grab for it at the last minute, out of breath. 'Yes? Hello?'

I almost expected it to be Clare, even though reason told me she probably wouldn't be able to get back to me until she was back in at work the following day.

'Charlie?' I recognised the voice immediately, but even so, he added, 'It's Sean.'

My first reaction was to drop the phone back on its cradle like it had suddenly gone live. I shook myself, tried to relax.

'Hello, Sean.' I tried for a light tone, but couldn't bring it off. 'What do you want?'

I heard a sigh at the other end of the line.

'I'm sorry I missed you when you came round yesterday,' he said, voice careful. 'I was getting a new front screen put in the jeep.'

I remembered the way the glass had crazed in response to Nasir's wild shot. 'That's OK,' I said, 'I had an interesting chat with Madeleine.'

'Yeah, she said.' Another pause. 'Look, we need to meet,' he hurried on. 'Roger's vanished, and I want to get to the bottom of what the hell the other night was all about. Can I come round and see you?'

'I don't think that would be a good idea.'

He let his breath out quickly and I could hear the frustration in his voice. 'Come on, Charlie. So we've got history together. Bad history. Well, I'm sorry about that, but nothing I can say right now is going to make it all *un*-happen. Deal with it and let's move on.'

I waited half a beat to check he'd finished. 'That wasn't what I meant,' I said mildly. 'Garton-Jones and his mob are back on the estate. They seemed particularly anxious to get their hands on you last time. I don't think absence will have made their hearts grow any fonder, do you?'

'Oh. No, you're right,' he said in a wry tone. 'To be honest, I want to stay put in case Roger shows up, and I don't want to cause trouble for you, either. Can you get over here again?'

I thought of Jav and his gang. 'It's starting to get a bit dicey going anywhere on foot,' I said. Copthorne, though, was no better. 'And I'm a bit reluctant to bring the bike.'

'You'll be fine.' Sean gave a short, mirthless laugh. 'It seems my reputation with the local bad lads somewhat exceeds me.' His voice was full of self-derision. 'Nobody will dare lay a finger on you if you're coming here.'

'OK,' I said slowly, temporarily unable to think of another excuse. 'Oh—' I opened my mouth to ask him about Nasir, then shut it again.

'What?'

'Nothing,' I said shortly. 'I'll see you as soon as I can,' and I put the phone down before he had chance to insist on an answer.

If Sean *didn't* know about Nasir's murder, his reaction would be telling. And if he *was* the one responsible, it might be even more so. Either way, when I told him the news, I wanted to be in a position where I could see his face.

The Suzuki was barely warm by the time I pulled up behind the dark blue Grand Cherokee outside Mrs Meyer's house.

Despite Sean's reassuring words, I was still aware of being watched on my way into the estate. Eyes followed me all the way up the path, and as I knocked on the door.

This time, it was answered quickly. Sean was dressed in jeans and a jumper, both black. Still, it made a change from either camouflage or khaki from head to toe.

He looked uncharacteristically uneasy as he stood back and waved me into the hall. It seemed much smaller than it had done the last time I was there.

'Go through,' he instructed, and I walked into the cramped living room ahead of him. Madeleine was sitting on the arm of one of the big squashy chairs, and she gave me a tentative smile of greeting. Mrs Meyer was bending down with a teapot to pour a cup for someone sitting on the sofa. It wasn't until she straightened up and moved aside that I saw who it was.

The sight of Eric O'Bryan gave me a jolt I hadn't been expecting, but I wasn't the only one who was surprised.

His hands gave an abrupt nervous twitch. The cup of tea chattered on its saucer, slopping half the contents over the rim. Most of it landed on his shoes, but the rest hit the carpet. He began stuttering apologies immediately, and Madeleine jumped up to fetch a cloth.

'Oh, don't worry yourself,' Mrs Meyer said placidly. 'There's been far worse than a drop of tea spilt on that carpet, I can tell you. I may not care for the pattern overmuch, but it does hide the stains, you have to give it that.' She brightened as she turned to bustle out and caught sight of me. 'Oh, hello again, dear. Would you like a nice cup of tea?'

I smiled and said yes please. Sean flashed me a momentary glance from under his eyebrows that could almost have been a warning.

I returned the gaze flatly. Gone were the days when he could pull rank on me. It didn't work that way any more. If I thought the Community Juvenile Officer could give me answers, I wasn't going to hold my tongue.

'Charlie,' O'Bryan said shakily when he'd recovered something of his composure. 'You're the last person I was expecting to meet here.'

I gave him a tight little smile. 'Yeah, you too. And on a Sunday.'

'Ah well, needs must,' O'Bryan said now. He sat perched on the edge of the sofa, knees primly together. His eyes flicked apprehensively over the group of us. 'You didn't mention before that you knew Roger's family,' he went on. There was a hint of reproach in his quiet voice, as though I'd played a cruel joke on him.

'I didn't realise that I did,' I said. 'Sean and I used to know each other. I'd never met his family.' I tried hard just to make it a flat statement, but I must have added something.

O'Bryan glanced at me, trying to read the undercurrents. 'Oh, I see,' he said, when clearly he did not. 'Well, I assume at least this means you're not still going to oppose Roger's caution, then?'

Sean reacted to that one, rounding on me, glowering. 'You were going to?'

'Of course.' I stood my ground. 'Roger did his best to help kill an old man, who happens to be one of my neighbours. What did you expect me to do?'

O'Bryan cleared his throat. 'Well, ah, if you've changed your mind that's good news, anyway,' he said cautiously, interrupting our mutual glowering match.

Sweat had broken out on his forehead. I could see a bead of it making an unsteady bobsleigh run down his temple. I realised that his discomfort came not from a dislike of such emotionally charged scenes, but from fear. He was afraid of Sean.

I suppose I couldn't really blame him for that.

'So then, Mr O'Bryan, if he's going to get another caution, that's the end of the matter, isn't it?' Mrs Meyer's voice was puzzled, but hopeful.

The man shook his head. 'Unfortunately, as I was saying before Charlie arrived, Roger should have checked in with the police this morning, and he didn't, which is going to get him into very hot water unless I can straighten things out pretty quickly. I really need to get my hands on him.'

'You're not the only one,' I muttered.

Sean shot me a dark look, which I ignored.

'Why wouldn't he have checked in?' It was Madeleine who spoke. Partly, I reckoned, to stop open hostilities breaking out, and partly because she was fishing. I saw the quick glance she exchanged with Sean, and realised that she knew all about the shooting at the gym on Friday night. I had to admire her tactics, if nothing else.

'He's probably scared stiff, and in hiding, don't you think, Mr O'Bryan?' I put in.

O'Bryan looked nervous at being put on the spot again. 'Er, why's that? Hiding from what?'

'Hiding from whatever, or whoever, shot his friend, Nasir Gadatra dead.' I watched Sean's face while I dropped that particular little bombshell. Not that it did me a lot of good. His expression hardened like a mask. If I'd been expecting a leap of guilt, I was sadly disappointed.

The news was met in a silence that stretched like bubble gum.

'Look,' O'Bryan said quickly after a few moments, 'all this doesn't change the fact that we need to find the boy. If anything, it just makes it more important that we do. I want to keep him out of prison as much as you do, but it's imperative that we find him. You must tell him that by absconding like this he's just making things ten times worse for himself.'

He got to his feet and Mrs Meyer, sensing the interview was over, thanked him gravely for coming to see them.

He gave her a weak smile as he shook her hand. 'That's my job.' He pushed his glasses up onto his forehead while he pinched the tension out of his nose like I'd seen him do the first time I'd met him.

We all moved outside onto the pavement to see him off, standing in a semicircle facing him. O'Bryan unlocked the door of a pale green Cavalier which was parked behind the Grand Cherokee. I hadn't noticed it when I tucked the Suzuki between the two.

'No MG today?' I asked him.

He smiled, almost relaxing. 'No, it turned out it was just the cable that had gone on this, so I didn't need a complete new clutch. The MG's more fun though.'

Suddenly, his face stiffened as though his heart had just given out. His eyes focused over my shoulder, beyond where Madeleine, Sean, and I were standing. His mouth dropped open in shock.

We all turned on a reflex. All saw roughly at the same time the figure who'd just stepped round the back of the Cherokee and come to a sudden halt at the sight in front of him.

'Roger!' Sean yelled. 'What the hell d'you think you're doing?'

Roger took one look at the assembled group of us. Recognition flashed across his face, and I saw a naked fear there. Then he turned tail and ran.

'Roger,' O'Bryan shouted. 'Give it up, boy. You can't hide forever!' There was genuine anguish in his tone.

Sean was already sprinting across the road after his brother, a head-down flat run. Roger panicked as he heard the steps behind him. He broke stride to stoop and grab a half-brick from the far gutter, slinging it at the figure chasing him. It was debatable if he even realised who it was.

Sean dodged out of the missile's way. Any of the rest of us would have been flattened.

'Don't just stand there,' he shouted back over his shoulder. 'Get after him.'

His words galvanised the rest of us into action. O'Bryan jumped into his car, fired it up and wheelspun away towards the end of the road, trying to head Roger off. Instead, the boy darted into one of the narrow ginnels that characterised both the estates. Sean went after him.

Madeleine and I broke into a run at about the same time, heading in a different direction to O'Bryan, so we'd got the exits covered whichever way Roger swerved.

'Why the hell's he running?' Madeleine gasped as we sprinted along the cracked pavement.

I didn't reply, saving my breath, but I remembered Roger's desperation that Nasir should shoot me. His outraged anguish when the other boy had failed to do so. His sudden flight now raised more questions than it answered.

Were we chasing someone who might be a frightened witness?

Or a brutal murderer?

Fifteen

Madeleine and I reached the next corner together, rounded it, and kept on running. We got level with a galvanised steel railing that partially divided the gap between two houses. It was the other end of the ginnel into which Roger had dived, but when we looked there was no sign of either brother in the narrow passageway.

We'd so been expecting to see one or the other, that our stride faltered as though by prior agreement. We dropped back into little more than a trot, looking round at the myriad of different openings and possible exits that Roger could have taken.

'What now?' Madeleine asked, panting.

'It's traditional that we split up, I suppose.'

She managed a grin. 'I'd hate to break with tradition,' she said. She waved an arm at the choice of directions. 'Any preferences?'

I shook my head, and she disappeared off towards the nearest ginnel. I couldn't find it in me to like Madeleine as much as I probably could have done, under different circumstances. But on the other hand, I couldn't bring myself to really dislike her, either.

I headed the opposite way, jogging to conserve my energy. Sean was built like a sprinter, and he'd always been fast, but it looked like his younger brother had the edge on him. I knew I didn't stand a chance of catching them unless they'd slowed down first. There didn't seem any point in going at it like an idiot.

I reached another corner, tossed a mental coin over which way to turn, and pressed on. By the time I'd made another three or four such arbitrary decisions, winding deeper into the estate with every one, the uneasy feeling grew that I wasn't ever going to find my way out again.

Even by Copthorne standards, the streets I was moving into looked shabby, and run down. The cars parked by the weed-encrusted kerbs were rusting and half dismantled. I doubt they could have rustled up a valid tax disc between the lot of them. One had the entire front end missing, including the engine, leaving the inner wings and chassis poking up like a cannibalised jawbone.

'What are you doing here, Fox?' said a sudden voice. It was close enough behind me to make me start, and the tone was sneering. 'Bit outside your territory, isn't it?'

Memory clicked. 'I go where I'm needed.' I didn't need to turn round to identify the speaker, but I did so now anyway. 'Hello Langford,' I said quietly.

He had popped up out of nowhere and was leaning against a gatepost a few feet behind me, grinning. The vigilante was wearing jeans and a heavy check shirt, which was the first time I'd seen him without his camouflage gear. He didn't look any smaller, or less menacing, even in his civvies.

'You're a real thrill-seeker, aren't you, Fox?' he said. 'Coming down here, wandering around in *my* territory, after that lucky punch you landed. Aren't you scared I'll hold a grudge?' He moved closer as he spoke, hands flexing by his sides.

'Enough people know where I am to make me feel safe,' I said, trying to stay calm and hoping that it was true.

Langford considered that one for a moment. I don't know if the bush telegraph had told him who I'd been visiting on Copthorne, but if so, Sean was right about his reputation warding off evil.

It was enough to make Langford back off doing anything physical, at any rate. 'Anyone causes me grief, I take care of them,' he said meaningfully, emphasising the point with a stabbing finger. 'You just remember that, Fox.'

I ignored the irritating digit. 'Like you offered to take care of Nasir Gadatra, you mean?' I let that one settle on him for a moment, then added, 'You certainly found one of his "areas of weakness", didn't you, Harvey? Breathing, was it?'

He stiffened, but whether it was having his own words thrown back at him, or because I'd used his Christian name, I couldn't tell. He decided, for the moment anyway, to let my over-familiarity ride.

'He was an interfering little git, and he got what was coming to him,' he said, but this time there was less conviction in his tone. He must have heard it, and went for bluster. 'You ought to remember that, too, Fox. What happens to the nosy ones.'

I knew I ought to stop there. We were alone, in Langford's province, and pushing him like this was a stupid, dangerous game to play, but I'd come too far to let the opportunity slip now. 'He was nosy, was he, just like that Asian kid a few years back?' I reminded him, my voice cool and deliberate. 'The one you set fire to?'

Langford straightened up, head on one side, and studied me through narrowed lids. 'You want to be careful, making unfounded accusations like that,' he said at last. 'It might get you into big trouble.'

'I don't think it's going to get *me* into trouble, but did Mr Ali know all about your National Front connections when you and he worked out your nice cosy little deal?'

Langford was standing close enough so that I could actually see him start to sweat. 'Of course,' he said now, but he was lying. His association with Mr Ali gave him not just money, but influence, and Langford liked his power plays. He pulled a crumpled cigarette pack out of his shirt pocket, and lit one of the contents while I eyed him in silence.

'OK, Fox,' he said tightly, letting out the first gush of smoke, 'how much do you want?'

I was surprised, and tried not to show it. 'I don't want your money, Langford, I want information. Give me a bigger fish than you, and I might not post a file full of your old newspaper clippings to Mr Ali.' Or improve my relationship with Superintendent MacMillan by dumping you straight into his lap, I added silently.

He nodded. 'Like who's really behind most of the crime round Lavindra Gardens, you mean?'

I hadn't been expecting that one, either. 'It would be a start,' I agreed.

He regarded me through the haze of smoke again. 'If I get you that – and I'm not saying I can, mind,' he added quickly, 'you'll lay off Ali?'

'You've got my word on it.'

His smile was a twisted parody containing no trace of humour. 'And I'm supposed to trust that?'

'You don't have much of a choice.' I knew as soon as I'd spoken that it was a bad idea to provoke him too far. There was a dark glitter in his eyes that sent a spark of fear through me.

He snuffed out the end of the cigarette with a forefinger and thumb, then advanced a step. 'I could always just make sure you're not in any fit state to talk to anyone,' he said, sly.

'You can try it if you like,' said a cold voice from the other side of the narrow street, 'but I wouldn't recommend it.'

We turned to see Sean step off the far kerb, and cross the road towards us. He had that familiar head-down stance, moving with deceptive speed. I don't know how long he'd been there. Neither of us had noticed his arrival.

Sean came to a halt just behind my shoulder, which was an interesting stand to take, and I was grateful for it. He was offering me back-up, rather than just taking over as though I couldn't handle Langford by myself. I threw him a brief, searching glance, then turned back to the man in front of me.

The vigilante suddenly seemed less solid by comparison. He took in Sean's quiet easy movements, the suggestion of hard-packed muscle, and recognised the underlying steel. For a few moments the two of them stared each other out, before Langford gave in.

He straightened up again, like a tomcat puffing up its fur when faced with a larger, fiercer rival. 'You'll be hearing from me,' he promised sourly, then turned and stamped away.

Sean put a hand on my shoulder, but when I turned to face him, I found him watching Langford's retreat with a frown. He brought his attention back to me with an effort. 'Are you OK?'

'Yeah, thanks,' I said, feeling slightly limp and light-headed. 'No sign of Roger?'

Sean shook his head. 'My dear brother seems to have developed quite a talent for the rapid disappearing act,' he said drily. 'I thought he was heading this way, but I lost him, and I don't know the area like I used to.' He still sounded distracted, eyes drifting over my shoulder in the direction Langford had taken. 'I'm sure I know that face,' he muttered, almost to himself.

'What, Langford's?' I asked. It shouldn't have come as a shock. After all, the two of them did use to live only a few streets away from each other.

'That's Harvey Langford?' Sean demanded. He whirled round, took a few strides, but the street was empty. 'Goddamn it, of *course*! How do you know him?'

I shrugged, reluctant to answer his sharp questions, even though he'd just come to my rescue. Again. It was starting to become a bad habit. 'He's leading the vigilante mob round here,' I said, grudgingly. 'They were there the night Fariman was stabbed.'

A bleakness crept over Sean's features that went so deep it seemed to freeze the skin to his bones as any animation faded. 'He's the one you stopped from beating up Roger?' he asked, although he didn't really need a reply. Under his breath he added, 'Next time we meet I think it's probably time Mr Langford and I had a quiet chat.'

I shivered at the ice lacing his tone. For the first time, when I thought of Langford, I could almost feel sorry for the man.

By the time we got back to Mrs Meyer's place, O'Bryan and Madeleine were waiting for us by the front gate. The expressions on their faces told us all we needed to know. They hadn't found Roger either.

We went inside, with O'Bryan wringing his hands and clucking anxiously about trying to keep the boy out of trouble, to the point where even Sean's mother was trying to comfort him.

There wasn't much more I could do, so I grabbed my gear and made my exit while I had the chance. Sean came out with me.

He watched silently while I unlocked the bike, hands dug deep into the pockets of his jeans. I didn't look at him while I went through the routine of turning the fuel tap on, and kicking the Suzuki into life, but having his eyes on me was making my neck itch. Before I could ram my helmet on, he touched my arm.

'We still haven't had that talk, have we, Charlie?' he said.

'No,' I agreed shortly, and couldn't help a certain feeling of relief at the fact.

'We need to,' he said. 'Now I've got your current number I'll call you tomorrow. Perhaps we could have a drink or something later on in the week?' He sounded hesitant, uncertain even.

Surprised, I felt my eyes slide to the living room window behind him. I could see Madeleine standing there, watching the pair of us through the glass. I cocked an eyebrow. 'Is that a good idea?'

He smiled, rueful, and knew what I'd seen without having to turn round himself. 'She trusts me,' he said. 'And it *is* just a drink.'

But I don't trust you, my mind shouted. *And more than that, I don't trust myself.*

'OK,' my mouth formed the word without consulting my brain first. I jammed my Arai lid on quickly, just in case it was thinking of saying anything else, and nudged the bike into gear.

I set off along the street with more gusto than the cold engine would have liked. When I reached the end I stopped at the junction, scanning my mirrors automatically, and found that Sean was still standing on the pavement where I'd left him, staring after me.

I spent the early part of the evening back at Pauline's watching some mindless film on the TV, with Friday stretched out on the sofa next to me. He snored gently with his head in my lap, limbs twitching to the dance of some doggy dream. I stroked the silky ears absently while my brain zigzagged backwards and forwards fruitlessly over the subject of Sean Meyer.

Our affair proper had only lasted a matter of a few months before he was sent overseas, even though there seemed to have been a long slow build-up to it.

To begin with I hadn't even liked Sean much, but I wasn't expecting to. Even among the other army instructors he had the reputation of being a real bastard. Right from the start he'd pushed me harder than I'd thought was fair, seeming to go out of his way to expose my weaknesses.

He told me later, while we were in bed as I remember it, that he was trying to hide just how hard and how fast he'd fallen for me.

Against my will, I'd found him physically attractive from the outset, but that wasn't so hard to resist when I'd convinced myself that he was mentally and emotionally such a cold fish. I'd got my first inkling that I was wrong during the Resistance to Interrogation training about halfway through the course.

The idea of the R-to-I exercise was to avoid capture, but they knew we'd all be hunted down, sooner or later. And when we were, then we had to withstand a prolonged interrogation that was as frighteningly realistic as they could make it. Another unit was tasked with interrogating us, and it was a matter of pride that they broke us before the time allowed was up.

It had been tough. Along with another batch of trainees I'd been stripped and beaten, humiliated, deprived of sleep, fed white noise until my teeth ached from it, and left blindfolded and handcuffed for hours at a time in the most painful positions they could devise. And the questions, the same things over and over, screaming abuse to push you to the edge.

It was after more than twenty hours or so of this that I'd heard one of the observers who monitored us all during the exercise come into the room where they'd been holding me, to check I still had circulation in my bound hands and feet. 'Don't worry, Charlie, you're doing fine,' a familiar voice had whispered in my ear. 'Only another two hours to go. Don't give up now. You've nearly made it.'

His was the first face that greeted me when they took the sack off my head at the end of the exercise. Despite the state I was in, he'd seen from my face that I was OK, and he'd smiled. It had dazzled me.

Starting a relationship with him had been an act of madness. For both of us. We knew it would cost us our careers if anyone found out, but we couldn't help ourselves. It was a strange but wonderful time, fearful and ecstatic, all bound up together. And then Sean had been posted.

It was a sudden posting, unexpected, and unwelcome. Looking back with a cool mind, I tried to work out if the top brass had suspected us, even then, and that was why they'd chosen Sean for that particular job. He hadn't said where he was going, and I'd known better than to ask, but the prospect of being apart from him for some unknown period of time had terrified me.

I was right to be scared. A week later, on the way back to camp from one of the local pubs, I'd encountered a group of my fellow trainees who were just drunk enough to be dangerous, and my whole world had come crashing down around my ears. Sean wasn't there to save me that time. In the aftermath I tried to get messages through to him, but I never received any response to my increasingly frantic calls.

At my lowest ebb, it wasn't hard to convince myself he'd abandoned me. That my first impression of him had been the right one.

I never saw him again until he and Madeleine had swooped into that alleyway to pluck me and Roger out of the dirt. Even then, it seemed his first instinct was to reject me. Too much had happened. How could I even begin to trust him now?

I sat up, aware of a dull ache in my temples. The light had faded, the film had ended, and some inane game show was playing out to squawks of canned laughter.

The dog jerked awake at my movement. He scrambled off the sofa, shook himself so vigorously that his ears flapped together, and padded through into the kitchen.

I heaved myself to my feet. My head was muzzy, as though packed with cotton wool. Perhaps I just needed some fresh air. 'Come on, Friday,' I called, collecting his lead, 'walk time.'

It was bitterly cold outside, with the hint of frost in the gathering night, so I decided to give the Ridgeback little more than a quick turn round the block. He didn't seem too upset by the lack of distance. We were out for such a short time that I realised afterwards they must have been watching the house, and waiting for their opportunity.

As soon as I unlocked the front door again and pushed it open, I knew there was something wrong. The draught that met me could only mean the back door was open and the cold air was suddenly being sucked through the intervening rooms like a wind tunnel. I knew full well I'd locked it before we'd gone out.

Friday got as far as the hallway, then went from semi-dormant to almost rabid instantaneously, like a shape-shifter. He gave a strangled whimper and bolted through my legs heading for the kitchen.

I ran after him, not bothering with the lights, but by the time I arrived, he'd already got the situation under control.

There was a figure hunched up on top of Pauline's draining board, trying desperately to keep his legs out of range of Friday's snapping jaws. The deep growls the dog was giving out were enough to bring the hairs up on the back of my neck. In the darkness they swelled until they were out of all proportion to his real size.

Much as I was reluctant to shatter my unwanted visitor's illusions about the mammoth hound that had him cornered, I reached out and flicked on the kitchen light.

'Well, well,' I said, surprised. 'Would it be pointless to ask what the fuck you're doing in here?'

Jav, the blond-haired Asian teenager, lifted his feet out of the sink and glared at me. His expensive white trainers were now smeared with a film of scummy washing-up water. He seemed more upset about that than the prospect of being ripped limb from limb by an increasingly agitated dog.

Then the boy reached up onto a shelf above him and grabbed hold of one of Pauline's ornamental teapots. He held it over Friday's head and glanced at me questioningly. 'Either you call him off, or I crack his skull,' he said, his lisp more pronounced than I'd remembered.

I clicked my fingers and Friday moved grudgingly to my side. I complied more because I knew how attached Pauline was to her pottery, rather than any fears for the Ridgeback's safety.

'So,' I said, 'what do you want, Jav?' I didn't bother to ask how he'd got in. Lock-picking was a compulsory pre-school subject round this area.

He swung his legs over the side of the kitchen unit and let his feet drip onto the lino. 'I came to warn you,' he said sullenly, 'but I can't be *seen* warning you, right?'

'Why do I need warning?'

'Because you've been seen with the wrong people, lady.' He saw the scepticism in my face and hopped down from the draining board with an elaborate shrug that was only slightly spoiled by the faint squelch he made as his feet hit the floor. 'It's your neck, not mine,' he said, and took a step towards the back door.

'Wait,' I said. He halted but more, I suspect, because Friday had started growling again. 'OK, let's start again. Excuse my natural cynicism, but what exactly are you warning me about?'

'Like I said, you've been seen hanging around with the fascists, and that don't do your rep round here no good at all.'

The communication system was amazing. I'd had a brief chat with Langford that afternoon on Copthorne, and by early evening the gangs on Lavender Gardens had got to hear about it and sent the boys round. Well, the boy, anyway. 'I hardly think that one conversation counts as associating with fascists, Jav.'

'Oh yeah?' he threw back at me, stung by the obvious amusement in my tone. 'What do you call going round to his house, then, and protecting his kid brother when that piece of shit's tried to kill one of us?'

I could feel my eyes growing wider. 'Whoa, whoa,' I said quickly. 'You're not talking about Langford?'

'Course not,' Jav said contemptuously. 'Sean Meyer, that's who. He was up to his neck with that National Front lot before this area got too hot for him and then he bailed. Army, I heard.'

The information hung over me like a dark, wet cloud just before the thunder starts. I could hear it building up in the distance. I glanced at the boy, found him watching me, nervous, wary. 'What else have you heard?'

He shrugged again. 'That Meyer hated Nas not just for leading his precious brother into trouble, but because he was a damned Paki,' he spat the word out. 'And now Nas is dead. Shot dead,' he emphasised meaningfully. 'It don't take a genius to work out that Army Boy's got to be involved somewhere along the line.'

No, it didn't. That was the trouble.

'Why are you telling me this?' I asked, suddenly tired.

'For your own good,' he said, looking disgusted with himself. He took another few steps, reaching the doorway before he turned back, shuffling his feet. 'You didn't rat on me to that bastard West,' he said, looking embarrassed, and defiant. 'I owed you. Now we're even. OK?'

I nodded. 'But Jav,' I added grimly, making him pause. 'You

179

ever break in here again, and next time I won't call the dog off. *OK?*'

He nodded, face grave, then disappeared out into the - darkness of the back garden. He left me with a barrage of unanswered questions that meant a long and largely sleepless night.

I got a few of them answered the next morning, but that didn't make me feel any better, on the whole. I was due in at the gym at ten, but I hit town just after nine o'clock and was soon rolling into the car park of the *Defender* on Meeting House Lane.

Clare was already at her desk in the busy accounts office when the disapproving woman from reception showed me through. My friend looked up with a ready smile that faded when she saw my face.

She swept a batch of files off the chair next to her desk and patted the cushion. 'Come, sit, and tell me all about it,' she said. She was wearing a brown suit that would have been frumpy on me, but looked like a catwalk special on Clare's willowy frame. She studied me with worry lines between her eyebrows. 'Spill it, Charlie, you look like death.'

'Thanks,' I said, dredging up a smile from some recess. She suggested coffee. I agreed, even though I'd had the dubious pleasure of the paper's office coffee machine before. Her brief absence gave me a chance to marshal my tattered thoughts.

'There you go,' she said, plonking down a plastic cup full of a sludgy dark grey liquid in front of me. 'Now, come on, what's happened?'

I filled her in on the weekend's events, mentioning Sean's name for the first time, but only as Roger's older brother. 'The thing is,' I said, 'I need to check what Jav's told me about him. You said after that attack on the Asian boy a few years ago they arrested some of the National Front group. Were there any names mentioned other than Langford's?'

Clare leafed through the papers on her desk. 'I'll check,' she said. 'You're lucky. I haven't had time to put the files away again yet.'

She handed over the clipping and I realised that I hadn't bothered to look at it myself when I'd gone round to Jacob and Clare's place. I hadn't needed to, because she'd read the highlights out to me.

If I had, then Sean Meyer's name would have leapt out at me like it was printed in dayglo ink.

My heart stuttered, then froze as I read on. Sean had been arrested, along with a number of other group members including Langford, on suspicion of the crime. I looked up at Clare unable to keep the grief out of my face. 'What happened to them?'

'Like I said, they were all released because of lack of evidence. Are you OK?' she went on, in a rush. 'You've gone really white.'

'What? Oh, don't worry – I missed breakfast,' I muttered, which was nearly the truth. I stood up. I needed to get out of there, to find some space to think.

'Before you go,' Clare said, looking doubtful, 'you wanted to know more about Nasir Gadatra's death. I asked my pal on the crime desk about it first thing, but it'll keep if you'd rather.'

I shook my head, trying to clear it. 'No, no, let's hear it now,' I said. I scraped another smile from my emergency stash. Supplies were starting to run pretty thin.

'Well, according to the post mortem report – and you mustn't breathe a word of this, Charlie, or you'll get me lynched – he was shot with a nine millimetre handgun fired from a distance of around fifteen feet. They recovered the bullet, so if the gun turns up they'll be able to do a ballistics match on it, but they still don't know where he was shot. Until they do, they're struggling to—'

'What do you mean "where he was shot"?' I broke in. 'I thought he was hit in the chest?'

She rolled her eyes. 'Well, yes, but that's not what I meant. There wasn't enough blood found around the body for him to have been shot where he was discovered, in the rubbish skip, so they reckon he must have been shot elsewhere, then dumped there when he was already dead, or pretty close to it. Charlie, are you *sure* you're OK? You're swaying.'

Sixteen

Despite his promise, Sean didn't call me on Monday. I'm ashamed to admit that I stayed up late, pretending to watch a mind-bendingly tedious film, just in case. Still, the delay gave me some time to work out what I was going to do about his invitation, when it came.

The strategy I'd worked out was going to take some nerve, but I'd been running scared from the spectre of the man for over four years. It was time to confront my demons.

It wasn't until Tuesday afternoon, just after five, that the phone at the gym rang. By chance, I was standing nearer to the counter than Attila, so I was the one who picked it up, without the faintest stirring of alarm to warn me.

'Hi, it's me,' Sean's voice said, assuming that I'd automatically know who. It nettled me that he was right. 'Sorry, I know I said I'd ring yesterday, but we've had another panic on.'

I put my irritation on hold. 'What's happened?'

'First my brother does a runner, now my sister Ursula's disappeared.'

'Disappeared?' I repeated. Where did *that* fit in?

'Yeah, she was staying at a friend's flat, but she hasn't been there since late last week. Nobody's seen her. I suppose Mum told you she's pregnant? That doesn't help.'

He sighed, sounding tired even at the other end of a phone line. For a moment I thought he was going to postpone our date indefinitely. After I'd spent all day Monday screwing up my courage to face him, I felt oddly let down.

'Look,' he said, 'I know it's short notice, but are you free later tonight? Can we meet?'

My mouth opened, but no words came out straight away. I had to shut it and start again. 'Er, yes OK,' I said, and suggested that he pick me up from the gym when I clocked off at eight. 'I'll need to change, but we could stop in at the flat.'

'No problem,' he said. 'I'll see you at eight.'

I put the phone down with my heart suddenly clonking against my ribs. Of all the bad ideas I'd ever had, why did I get the feeling that trying to play Sean Meyer on a line like a marlin could well turn out to be the worst of them?

He strolled into the gym only a few minutes after eight o'clock, wearing a gorgeous long black leather coat. Some of the lads were in catching a late workout, including Wayne, who favoured Sean with a slight nod. That kind of quiet acknowledgement of old ties. It had never occurred to me that the two might know each other.

The others gave the new arrival a wary appraisal, but there was an air of calculated violence about Sean that held their tongues. They took in the width of his shoulders, and the cool, flat gaze, and showed more restraint than I would have given them credit for.

Attila greeted him with a big grin, and a friendly slap on the back that would have had most other men reeling. Sean rode the abuse easily enough, then turned to me. 'Hello Charlie, you all set?'

I nodded. 'I'll pick the bike up later,' I said to Attila as I shrugged my way into my own somewhat more battered leather jacket, and followed Sean to the door.

The Grand Cherokee was parked outside. It felt weird to climb into it without having been beaten up or shot at first.

'Do you mind if we stop for a moment on the way?' he said as we set off round the one-way system. 'I need a cashpoint machine.'

'No problem.'

He pulled over on one of the quiet city centre streets without having to ask where the nearest branch of his bank could be found. For someone who'd been away from Lancaster for so long, he still seemed to know his way around.

'I won't be long,' he said as he slid down onto the pavement. 'Feel free to fly the radio.'

I watched him disappear across the road and past a row of shops, the coat flapping round his legs as he walked with that long easy stride. I gritted my teeth and reminded myself to focus on the facts. It had been easier to hate Sean without having him in front of me.

I reached for the stereo in the centre of the dashboard, but as I pulled my hands out of my jacket pockets, my sleeve caught on something and I heard the dull metallic thunk of my keys dropping down the side of my seat.

I muttered under my breath as I stuffed my hand into the narrow gap between the seat bolster and the central transmission tunnel. The keys dropped away out of sight under the seat itself.

'Damn it.' I undid my seatbelt, leaning forwards until the dashboard made my neck crick, reaching blindly underneath me. All I could feel was carpet.

I shifted off the seat until I was almost crouching in the footwell. I glanced up, hoping that Sean wouldn't return and catch me making a contortionist fool of myself, but he was nowhere to be seen.

The move gave me another couple of inches and this time my groping fingers touched something cold and hard. Metal.

I tried to push it aside, heard the clink of it brushing against my keys, then my hand suddenly stilled.

Very slowly, carefully, I managed to work my forefinger and thumb onto the object, gripped it, and pulled it out onto the rubber floor mat. The hooked-up keys came with it, but they were suddenly of minor interest.

I whispered, 'Oh shit.'

It was a gun.

In the gloom of the footwell, it gleamed dully, a blue-black semiautomatic. Hesitantly, I picked it up, weighing the cold heaviness of it in my hand, smelling the sheen of gun-oil like some half-remembered brand of scent.

Just for a moment my imagination moulded it into the FN that Nasir had used that night at the gym, but then sense kicked in, and I realised this was different. There was no hammer at the back of the slide and that jogged distant memory banks. A Glock, Austrian-made.

What the hell was Sean doing with a handgun under the front seat of his car?

Numbly, I operated the release for the magazine. It dropped smoothly into my hand. The first snub-nosed round was clearly visible wedged up against the top lip of the mag. When I thumbed it out into my palm, the next one sprang up to take its place. Standard full-metal-jacket ammunition, definitely not a blank.

Suddenly, my carefully worked-out plan of pumping Sean gently for information over the course of the evening shattered around me. I'd been trying not to acknowledge the possibility that he could be in this much deeper than he seemed. Now it was drowning me.

'Oh Jesus, Sean,' I muttered. 'What the hell are you up to?'

Sean! I flicked my gaze up again, but still he was out of sight. Quickly, I rammed the round back into place, feeling the resistance. The spring at the base of the magazine must have been wholly compressed. A full clip.

I slotted the magazine back into the pistol grip and pushed it home firmly with the flat of my hand. It seemed like a hell of a long time since I'd handled firearms, but the drills drummed into us on the ranges meant it was done on a reflex, even under the shadowed streetlight. I actually had to stop myself snicking back the slide to chamber the first round.

I looked up again and this time a dark figure rounded the corner by the row of shops. I grabbed my keys and slid back up into my seat. Instinct made me shove the Glock into my inside pocket, hoping the bulk of it wouldn't pull the jacket noticeably out of line.

Sean opened the jeep door and climbed into the driver's seat. I blinked as the interior light came on, tried to act calm and casual.

He reached for the ignition key, then paused. 'Are you OK?' he asked.

'Yeah,' I said, smiling, lying through my teeth. 'I'm fine.'

Sean drove down onto St George's Quay as though he knew the way. I waited for him to ask for precise directions, because my place is above a cheap carpet wholesalers, and doesn't follow any numbering pattern recognisable in the modern world, but he pulled up right outside. I felt a cold finger of suspicion trip down my spine.

How did he know where I lived? He couldn't have been following me, because I'd hardly been back to the flat since Pauline had gone away, and that was before Sean turned up on the estate. Or was it?

When he switched off the engine I opened my door and forced another smile. 'Come on up, if you like,' I said. 'This won't take long.' *I hope . . .*

He followed me up the wooden staircase to the first

landing, and waited for me to unlock my front door. I flicked on the lights as we moved inside.

'This is quite a place you've got here,' Sean said, looking round as he moved further into the living room.

While his back was towards me, I pulled the Glock quietly out of my jacket pocket, bringing it up level with my right hand even as I worked the slide with my left. My movements were a little jerkier than I would have liked, but it was an old rhythm. One I hadn't danced to for years.

As Sean caught what must have been to him the familiar sound of the mech working, he stiffened, then started to turn round very, very slowly. All the while he sensibly kept his hands where I could see them, fingers outspread.

Finally, when he was staring narrow-eyed into the muzzle of his own gun, he said calmly, 'Well, Charlie, I don't suppose you'd like to tell me what this is all about?'

I ignored him, concentrating on keeping the sights of the Glock steady and lined up on a point about two inches down from his Adam's apple. 'On your knees first, Sean,' I said, and my voice was cold. 'You know the drill. Hands linked behind your head, feet crossed at the ankles.'

I almost missed the look of surprise that passed over his features. It was chased on by anger that left just a trace of bitterness behind. 'You really don't trust me at all, do you?' he murmured, not moving.

'Come on, Sean,' I said, shifting to a standard double-handed grip. 'You always got the better of me when we went hand-to-hand. I'd like you on your knees if we're going to talk.' When still he hesitated, I added drily, 'Even this far out of practice I can slot you from here without thinking about it, and I don't have any curious neighbours, so make your mind up.'

I don't suppose either of us believed for a moment that I was actually going to shoot him dead in my own living room, but I kept my face just neutral enough for there to be a sliver of doubt.

He allowed himself a half-smile that lapsed into a grimace, then he finally complied, playing the game. He laced his fingers together behind his neck once he was down. 'I take it that *is* my Glock, by the way?'

I nodded. 'Under a car seat is really not the best place to keep a loaded handgun, you know. Anyone could come across it, and then where would you be?'

He smiled again, rueful this time. 'Ah, well, I only put it there when I picked you up this evening,' he admitted. He had the grace to look a touch sheepish. 'Since that trouble at Attila's I've been carrying it tucked into the back of my belt, but I didn't want to risk you finding it there.'

I raised an eyebrow at that, battled with a smile and only just beat it. 'And just what would I be doing investigating any part of your trousers on a first date?' I demanded. 'Taking a little for granted there, aren't you, Sean? Have you forgotten the lovely Madeleine so quickly?'

'Hardly our first date, now is it, Charlie?' he said softly. 'We go back a long way.'

I didn't want to think about that one. It brought back too many old memories. Some of them I was so very tempted to refresh. 'And Madeleine?' I prompted.

'Ah yes, the lovely Madeleine,' he said with a certain amount of dark relish, then grinned suddenly. 'Not jealous, are you, by any chance?'

'I don't have the right to be jealous,' I pointed out levelly, 'But by the looks of it she does. If that's how you treat your women these days, I don't want to get involved.'

He nearly flinched. The smile blinked out like an extinguished light. 'Madeleine is camouflage,' he said bluntly. 'On the rare occasions I come home my mother loves to matchmake. Madeleine works for me, and when I need her

189

she's happy to keep the heat off my back. She's living with a West Indian chef who's six-foot five and would gut me like a trout if I laid a finger on her. There's nothing sexual going on between us, and there never has been. OK?'

I thought for a moment he was going to declare that he never mixed business with pleasure. If so, I could have called him an outright liar without fear of contradiction. Perhaps that was why he didn't bother.

I swallowed. 'You wanted to talk, Sean, so let's talk,' I tried instead. 'Nasir Gadatra. Remember him at the gym with your baby brother? You go after him across that waste ground and next thing I know his body's turned up dumped in a skip in Heysham, shot dead with a nine millimetre semiautomatic. Like this one.'

Sean nearly laughed out loud. 'You don't seriously think *I* killed him, do you?' He sobered fast when he saw my face. 'My God, you do,' he added. 'So *that's* what this is all about.'

'Not entirely,' I said coolly, 'but I'd be happy to hear your side of the story.'

'I told you,' he said, speaking clearly and slowly, as though repeating something for the tenth time, 'he cleared the blockage and took a shot at me, so I let him go. Why would I want him dead?'

'You tell me.'

He shrugged, not an easy motion when your elbows are bent up level with your ears. 'Look, you don't really need to keep me on my knees like this do you, Charlie?' he pleaded, giving me a disarmingly boyish grin. 'I'm hardly likely to try anything sitting quietly on your sofa, am I? Not if you're still half as good with one of those things as I remember.'

After a moment's hesitation, I nodded warily to his request, tensing as he came to his feet with a lithe ease that belied the awkwardness of the position I'd put him into.

I had a nasty feeling that I'd just somehow tipped the

balance into Sean's favour, played into his hands, but he merely strolled over to my sofa and sat down, keeping his hands in plain view. 'That's better,' he said, looking more relaxed than he had any right to. 'You were saying?'

'Nasir Gadatra,' I repeated. 'You didn't like him, did you, Sean? Why was that?'

He shrugged again. 'I didn't really know him,' he said, side-stepping the point. 'Providing he didn't try to mess Ursula around, or slide out of his obligations, then I'd no real objections to—'

'He what?' I demanded, cutting him short. 'Now wait a minute. *Nasir* was the father of your sister's kid?'

Sean looked at me almost blankly. 'Of course, didn't you know? You don't think I'd kill my own would-be brother-in-law, do you?'

'Not even if he was a damned Paki?' I taunted, aiming for provocation.

It worked. Sean's head came up, and there was a flush along his cheekbones that could have been brought there by anger, or it could have been shame. 'Now whatever gives you the idea that something like that would matter to me?' he queried, his voice dangerously soft.

I disregarded the warning bells and pushed on recklessly. 'There can't be many former National Front members who would exactly welcome an Asian into the family to dilute their pure Anglo-Saxon blood.'

'National Front? Me? You're joking,' he bit out. 'Anyway, on my mother's side I'm Irish, and on my father's I'm German. You've got your facts well screwed there, sweetheart.' The endearment sounded like a threat.

'Yeah? So you deny that you've ever had any connections to any right-wing organisations? That you were arrested as a member of a neo-nazi group for a racially motivated attack?' Go on, Sean, I thought bitterly, deny it. Tell me how wrong I am. Tell me I can trust you. *Just don't expect me to believe it.*

He paused and took a breath, then leaned forwards, resting his forearms on his knees. 'No,' he said, sounding suddenly tired, 'I don't deny it. When I was a kid, not that much older than Roger is now, I mixed with a bad crowd. They just happened to be involved with the National Front, but that wasn't their main attraction, and I was never actually a paid-up member. Yeah, they pulled me in for the attack on that Asian kid. My God, you should have seen the pictures. They burned off half his face. It sickened me, convinced me I had to get out. I cut loose, started afresh, joined up.' He glanced up, met my gaze and held it constant.

I don't know what it was that made me realise that I believed him utterly. Maybe it was the fact that he'd never lied to my face, not directly. Maybe there was some part of me that was still clinging to the hope that, whatever else he was capable of, he couldn't do that. I didn't want to believe him, but I just couldn't help it.

Without speaking, I moved to sit opposite, facing him across my coffee table. Slowly, carefully, I thumbed the magazine out of the Glock and placed them down together on the table top, then sat back, leaving them between us.

Sean's shoulders dropped a fraction. He'd played it so cool I hadn't recognised the tension in him. He linked his fingers together and sat with his chin propped on them, just looking at me. I kept my face expressionless.

'Colonel Parris was a fool to let you go,' he said at last. 'You were perfect for Special Forces.'

I said nothing, managing to convey polite enquiry in the lift of an eyebrow.

'If anyone else had been pointing that at me,' he went on, gesturing to the Glock, 'I might not have taken it so seriously, but you were one of the best shots with a pistol I've ever come across, Charlie. Cool-headed. Deadly.'

'There were plenty who were just as good.' I shrugged off the compliment, feeling gauche.

He shook his head. 'A lot of people had a reasonable ability to aim,' he said. 'That doesn't mean they'd got the stomach to pull the trigger for real. Not like you, Charlie, you had what it took. Still do, at a guess.'

'Thanks,' I said, tartly. 'I'm not sure it's very flattering to be told you've got all the makings of a cold-blooded killer.'

'Not quite. A sniper, more like. A soldier. With the nerve to kill when necessary, that's true, but under the right circumstances. For the right cause.'

If only you knew, I thought, and the pain of it seared like fire. 'Like a terrorist?' I shot back. 'Or an assassin?'

He sighed and made no reply, reaching for the Glock and snapping it back together with practised ease.

'I suppose you do know that carrying one of those things is illegal these days?' I pointed out mildly, watching the unconscious skill in his deft movements.

'In my line of work, they're often a useful, if not essential bit of kit,' he said, cheerfully unrepentant. 'Besides, I have contacts with the security services, and they allow me some leeway.'

'And what *is* your line of work, Sean?' I said, feeling a sudden chill seep through my bones.

He smiled unexpectedly, transforming his severe facial structure. 'I don't kill people, if that's what you're afraid of. Not even a damned Paki who gets my sister pregnant,' he said, mocking me gently as he tucked the gun away out of sight. 'In fact, if I'd known Nas was in danger I probably could have helped him. I'm in close protection now, Charlie. After I left the army, I became a bodyguard.'

That one threw me and I didn't trouble to hide the fact. 'Do your family know what you do?' I asked.

193

He paused, frowning as he considered the question. 'No, they don't,' he said eventually. 'They know I work in security, but I've always tried to make it sound boring – like it involves sending night-watchmen round building sites. They don't know I do personal stuff. No-one round here does. Only you.'

I filed away the possible significance of that for reflection at a later date. Standing, I said, 'If we're not going out for that drink, would you like some coffee?'

Sean smiled again. 'OK.'

He followed me as I moved through to the kitchen and dug out the ingredients. I hadn't stocked up for a while, but fortunately I had a pack of long-life milk in the bottom of a cupboard. Sean leaned in the doorway and watched me spoon instant coffee granules into two mugs.

'It's come to something when you feel you can't get the truth out of me without a gun to my head,' he said quietly.

I glanced up at him as I flicked on the kettle, kept my voice dispassionate. 'Old wounds take a long time to heal.'

'Yeah, well.' He raked a hand through his hair, looking tired again. 'Maybe you should have thought of that before you went shooting from the lip and told everyone about us—'

'Hang on, before *I* told anyone?' I spun round, slamming the milk down hard enough to slop some of the contents over the side of the carton. '*I* didn't say a word. I thought it was you.'

'Me?' He looked genuinely astonished. I saw the anger building in the bunching of his shoulders. 'OK, let's backtrack for a moment here, shall we?' he said tightly. 'When I took up that last posting everything was fine, yeah? I was out of touch for what, three weeks? Then I try to contact you and I'm told you're on leave. *Permanently* on leave. It went on for months. I even rang your damned parents, not that I expected them to be helpful. And what was I told? Charlotte doesn't want to speak to you again. Ever.' The bitterness welled up in his words, overflowed. 'What the hell was I supposed to think?'

I wanted to stop him going on. To tell him he'd been wrong. To reach out to him, but I couldn't seem to move. He threw me a single, dark unfathomable look, then went on.

'So, next thing I know I'm being hauled into the local company commander's office and told I'm up on a charge for screwing one of my trainees. They told me you had failed the course, but when they'd RTU'd you, you'd started screaming about slapping them with a suit for sexual harassment against me, if not actual rape. I was told there'd been a court martial, and you were out, but not before you'd brought me down with you.'

'I didn't,' I whispered, stricken. 'Sean, I swear that's not how it happened.'

'So, what did?' he threw back.

I swallowed, unwilling to tell him what had really gone on that dark, and miserable night. I opted for half-truth instead, and hoped that would be enough. 'I–I was attacked,' I said at last, 'the week after you left. A group of them jumped me and I was pretty badly beat up. That's why I was on leave.'

That much at least was true. The secret of a believable lie was to stick as closely as possible to reality. There was less opportunity to stumble.

Donalson, Hackett, Morton, and Clay. The names went round and round again. I shut them out.

'There *was* a court martial,' I went on, 'but it went against me. They said I'd provoked them, made it out to be my fault. I tried to get hold of you, to speak up for me as one of my instructors, nothing more than that, but you never returned any of my calls. So,' I shrugged my shoulders, 'I was out.'

'I never got any messages. They kept me moving around a lot, out of regular contact. I never knew you'd called me.' He shook his head, then looked up at me intensely. 'And you let it rest there?' he demanded. 'After what they did to you?'

For a moment my breath stopped, fearing he'd tumbled to it. Then I saw his eyes shift to my throat, understanding dawning, laced with compassion. I knew I should have told him he was jumping to the wrong conclusions about that, but I was too much of a coward.

'No, I didn't. I wish I had.' The kettle boiled and clicked off, giving me the chance to turn away, fuss with pouring boiling water into the mugs, stirring them. 'I went for a civil action against them. That was when it all came out about us. I don't know who told them, but it certainly wasn't me.'

'You never told *anyone*?' he demanded. 'What about those two other girls on the course? What were their names? Woolley and Lewis. You all seemed to get on OK. You're sure you never had any heart-to-heart girlie chats with them?'

I shook my head, not insulted by the question. 'We were never that close, so yes, I'm sure,' I said.

In fact, Woolley, Lewis and I had never really liked each other. We knew we were in the minority, as women training for the job we hoped to do, and that we had to stick together. But, at the same time the three of us were in direct competition with each other. I knew without undue conceit that I'd been a better soldier. They knew it too, and they hadn't liked me for it.

Woolley in particular had been struggling to keep up. She was supposed to speak up in my favour at the trial, but her carefully neutral testimony about my general behaviour had a damning effect. Afterwards, she'd left the courtroom without talking to me, unable even to meet my eyes.

I learned later that although Lewis failed to complete the course, Woolley passed it and went on to active service. In my more bitter moments I wondered if that was her reward for sinking me.

'However it came out about us,' I said, 'I lost the case because of it. I went from model soldier to—' I broke off, aware of how close I'd come to letting too much slip. 'Well, I'm sure you can guess.'

'That's why you disappeared, changed your name?'

I nodded. In the army I'd been Foxcroft. In an effort to escape the hounding of the press afterwards, I'd shortened it to Fox. It had seemed like a good way to disappear, and it had worked.

'I did try to find you, you know, but I kept coming up empty. When I realised it was you the other night I had my people working round the clock to find out where you were. I couldn't believe it when they told me about this place. I never dreamed you'd ended up so close to home.'

I gave him a rueful smile. 'If I'd known how close to *your* home it was, I probably would have gone somewhere else,' I admitted, holding his coffee out to him.

He stepped forwards, eyes fired. I froze while he peeled the mug out of my nerveless fingers and plonked it back on the worktop, grabbing hold of my upper arms. 'I didn't betray you, Charlie,' he said fiercely. 'You have to believe that.'

'I-I do,' I said unsteadily, mildly surprised to discover that it was the truth. 'I didn't, for a long time, but I do now. They screwed us both over, didn't they Sean? Madeleine told me they did their damnedest to get you killed afterwards.'

'Yeah, well,' he relaxed his fingers, took a breath, 'it wasn't the easiest of times, but I survived.' He picked up his coffee mug with a steady hand, took a sip and regarded me over the rim. 'It seems we both have that knack.'

Seventeen

I lurched awake the next morning from a night's sleep fractured by dreams of anger and betrayal, pain and death. I sat up abruptly on a raft of tangled bedclothes, and shivered at the rapid cooling effect of the sweat on my goosebumped skin.

It was a long time since I'd been hit by the nightmares, to the point where I even thought they'd gone away completely. I should have known my luck wasn't that good.

They always followed the same pattern. I went through the rape again and again, unable to change a word of the dialogue, or a moment of the action. This time around events took place in a public arena, and they'd sold tickets. My parents were in the front row, eating popcorn and cracking jokes with my commanding officer. Woolley and Lewis were chatting together a couple of rows further back.

I could no longer clearly remember the faces of the four men who'd attacked me. They'd faded into that area of the subconscious that hides trauma from your waking mind. I had a hazy knowledge that Morton was short and wiry, and Clay had been built like a Challenger tank, but beyond that, they all blurred into one.

This time, though, there had been an unpleasant variation to the dream. This time, the quartet all had the same, familiar face.

Sean's face.

I swung my legs over the side of the soft mattress, and stayed there for a while, gripping the edge, head bent, trying to catch my breath. When my heartbeat had slowed to something approaching a normal level, I looked up slowly, and found myself staring into my own haunted face in the mirror on Pauline's wardrobe door.

I looked terrible. My eyes were sunk into shadowed sockets, my hair lank, and my skin had the waxy tinge of long-term sickness. I tried a smile, but somewhere along the line my nerves fumbled the message and it warped into a grimace.

Somehow, it all came back down to Sean Meyer. Much as I hated to admit it, my mother was right. I just couldn't afford to get involved with him again.

I might believe Sean now, that he'd been just as much a victim in the whole mess as I had, but there was too much pain and too much bitterness surrounding both of us to try and recapture a happier time. The very fact that I'd been so convinced he was capable of such a gross act of betrayal had destroyed whatever fragile bond of trust had been growing between us.

What we'd had was dead and buried. I'd done my grieving. It was time to finally lay the ghosts, and move on.

Downstairs, I gave Friday his food and left him shovelling his bowl round the kitchen floor. I made a coffee and stood for a while, cradling the mug and staring out into the back garden without seeing much of it at all.

The dream still disturbed me. I recognised the need for closure, and that I wasn't going to get it until some lingering questions had been answered.

On impulse, I went back through to the living room, and picked up the telephone, dialling a number I'd known off by heart since I was a child.

A man's voice answered, calm, cool. My father.

'Hello,' I said, warily. 'I was hoping to speak to my mother. Is she there?'

There was the slightest pause. 'I'm afraid she's not here at the moment,' he said, but somewhere beyond him, I swear I heard a door closing. 'Can I help you at all?'

I took a deep breath. 'Why didn't you tell me that Sean Meyer had tried to contact me after – after I left the army?'

'Ah,' my father said, almost on a sigh. 'So, you know about that.' He didn't even have the grace to sound embarrassed.

'Yes, I know about that,' I snapped. 'Tell me, were you *ever* planning to tell me? Or were you just hoping I'd never find out?'

'Find out what exactly, Charlotte?' For the first time he let the irritation creep into his detached tone. 'Find out what excuses Meyer had managed to dream up for what he did?'

'They weren't excuses,' I argued. 'He didn't know. They posted him.' I was sure of my ground now, but I didn't like the defensive note in my voice, even so.

'If you're happy to believe that then, of course, that's your choice,' he said, indifferent. 'Your mother and I discussed it at the time, and we decided that it was better that you didn't know. It was too late to affect the outcome of the case, and it would only have served to distress you further.'

I felt temper rise in my throat like bile. '*You* decided,' I said bitterly. 'What right did you have to make that sort of choice for me?' *Didn't you realise the effect it would have*?

'We had every right, Charlotte,' he said, in the same tone he would have used to rebuke one of his junior doctors for some badly handled diagnosis. 'You were under our protection, and in no fit state to make your own decisions. You would rather have known everything that was being said about you? That we'd reported every phone call, showed you every lie the papers printed? You wouldn't have thanked us for it. Then or now.'

I tripped up a little over the word 'lie'. It was the first time he'd let his neutrality slip and actually seemed to come down on my side. My God, he might be human after all.

I've no doubts at all that my father was an excellent surgeon, his obvious success notwithstanding. He had that arrogance, that total belief that he was doing the right thing, making the right decision. You listened to him and you knew that the hand holding the scalpel would not slip at the vital moment.

'We shielded you as much as we could,' he went on now, almost coldly. 'If you will take some advice, Charlotte, you won't go raking it over again now. It won't do anyone any good to open up old wounds again. Least of all yourself.'

'*Somebody* betrayed us,' I said, stubborn. 'Even if *I* was prepared to let it go, don't think for a moment that Sean is.' And I put the phone down without giving either of us the chance to say goodbye.

Getting out of Lavender Gardens that morning proved difficult. A gang of kids had set light to a stolen Citroën BX, which was blocking one of the main roads out of the estate.

The fire brigade were already on the scene by the time I arrived, running out hoses to deal with the wreckage. On the far side of the burning barricade, a young crowd had gathered. The firemen looked nervous as they worked, as though they weren't sure if the real danger came from the flames, or the mob.

I saw a flash of blond hair among the dark heads of the crowd, and recognised Jav. He clocked the Suzuki and went very still, but from that distance I couldn't read the expression on his face.

I had a nasty feeling that, if I'd been closer, I would have seen triumph there.

I called in on Clare at the *Defender* again on my way to the gym. By the time I got to work, Attila was already in, and the place was buzzing, so I didn't have much chance to mull over the information she'd given me until later that afternoon.

Things went completely dead after lunch, as they usually did. Attila and I were taking advantage of the total lack of clientele to shift some of the benches around when Madeleine walked through the door, immaculately dressed as always.

'Hi, Charlie,' she said guardedly, but treated my boss to a sunny smile that had him preening his muscles. I introduced her as a friend of Sean's, and left it at that. If Sean wanted Attila to know the real score he could tell the man himself.

Attila came over all good manners and suggested coffee, which Madeleine accepted with enough enthusiasm to send him scuttling for the kettle in the office.

When he'd gone Madeleine looked about her with un-disguised curiosity. 'So, this is where you work,' she said. I couldn't tell from her voice if she was impressed or horrified. Like I said, Attila didn't go much for frills. I looked round, but what had, before, seemed businesslike and uncluttered, now looked spartan and shabby.

I shrugged, and finished moving a pile of loose weights across to the bench's new position. When I straightened up, I found Madeleine was watching me closely. 'I understand you teach self-defence,' she said.

'I used to,' I said shortly. 'I don't any more.'

'Why not?'

For a few moments I considered the question. 'I was injured last winter,' I said at last. It sounded so innocuous, like I'd fallen down a set of steps, or come off the bike. 'Attila offered me this job while I was recuperating, and I never got back into it.'

She nodded, seeming to accept that watered-down explanation. 'I've done a few courses myself,' she said now. 'Tell me, what do you recommend for defences against someone with a knife?'

I looked up sharply, wondering if she thought she was being clever, but her face was without particular guile. My eyes slid past her to one of the mirrors on the wall behind her head, checking my reflection to see if the scar was on view above the collar of my polo shirt. It wasn't.

I checked Madeleine's face again. 'What do I recommend?' I said, keeping my voice level with an effort. 'That you run away. As fast as you possibly can. And you keep running.'

She frowned, and looked about to ask some more, but Attila returned at that moment with three cups of coffee bunched around a single fist, and the moment was lost. I was never so glad of the interruption.

'Excuse me a moment,' I muttered, and escaped to the ladies'. Once I was there I closed the door and leaned back against it, with my eyes shut.

Madeleine didn't know what had happened, I told myself. She couldn't do. I was just being paranoid. Over-sensitive. Wasn't I?

I opened my eyes, stepped up to the mirror, and stretched the collar of my shirt to one side. The scar wasn't old enough to have faded much. They'd warned me that it would always be visible, and they'd offered further surgery as an alternative, but with only dubious chances of success. In the end, I'd decided to leave it well alone.

After all, it was a sharp reminder to me that I should follow my own teachings more closely. That I should run instead of standing to fight. Next time I was faced with a lunatic wielding a knife, maybe I'd do just that.

Next time.

Someone tripped down my spine wearing icy boots. I
shivered, took a deep breath like a submerging swimmer, and
straightened my collar again. A normal-looking girl stared
back out of the mirror, giving no hint to what lay beneath the
surface. I turned away before I was tempted to try and look
much deeper, and walked back into the gym.

Madeleine glanced up at me as I moved back across the
floor, but before she could say much the door went again to
herald Sean's arrival.

He flashed a quick grin in Madeleine's direction, then
turned his attention on my boss. 'Hi, Attila,' he said. 'Can I
steal your lovely assistant away from her work for a little
while?'

'For sure,' Attila said. He stood up with a ripple of muscle
under his T-shirt, and looked from one of us to the other as if
reassessing the relationship between the three of us. 'But first
you can help me move another of these benches, yes?'

Sean rolled his eyes, but pitched in without any real
complaint, taking off his jacket and pushing up the sleeves of
his vee-necked shirt. He didn't have Attila's sheer bulk, but he
didn't seem to find the weight a problem, either.

Looking back with an even mind, it had been that
economy of movement, that air of total competence, which
had all been part and parcel of Sean's attraction. I don't think
I'd ever seen him fumble.

When they'd finished he moved over to Madeleine,
touched her shoulder in a way I might once have found
intimate. Now it simply seemed one of friendship, concern.

For her part, Madeleine reached up to kiss him, but Sean
stopped her.

'It's OK, Madeleine,' he said, and his tone was wry. 'You
don't have to put on a show in front of Charlie. She knows
the score.'

For a moment the other girl allowed herself a scowl of pure wounded feminine pride, then the full import of his words dug in, and her eyes widened.

'You told her?' The disbelief was plain. 'But, I thought—'

Sean shrugged it aside. 'She had a gun to my head,' he said, without the barest flicker of a smile in my direction. 'What can I say?'

Both Attila and Madeleine stared at him, hoping for some indication that he was joking. After a couple of seconds Madeleine gave up waiting, and started digging in her shoulder bag. I wondered what exactly he'd told her about our confrontation in the flat.

'I've been running a background check on Nasir Gadatra, as you asked,' she said, businesslike, retrieving a spiral-bound shorthand notebook and flipping it open. 'He certainly had an interesting past. At one time there was a whole string of arrests for vandalism, burglary, stealing from cars, even assault. O'Bryan had to bail him out on numerous occasions. It seems that when his father died he went right off at the deep end. It was only when it looked seriously like he was going to get put away that he got his act together.'

She checked her notes again. 'For the last few years he's kept his nose clean, and there hasn't been a sniff of trouble. He got the job working as a trainee electrician for Mr Ali and did his qualifications at night school. He paid his way towards the rent on his mother's house, like a good boy. He was a member of a local snooker club, and he had a standing order to a gym as well. Sorry, Attila, not this one.' She shot a quick smile to the German and came out with a name I'd only vaguely heard of.

Attila grunted. 'I know it. A poseurs' place,' he said, dismissive. 'No decent equipment. No decent staff.'

Madeleine grinned at him, but before he could add anything further, the phone on the counter started ringing. Attila went to answer it.

When he'd gone we sat down on the benches, Sean hunched forwards with his elbows on his knees, fingers linked. He nodded to Madeleine to continue.

'The only real oddity I could find is that although he paid his motorbike insurance in instalments, he did it in cash,' she went on. 'He used to go into a local broker every month with the money.'

'Bike insurance?' I queried. 'I didn't know he *had* a bike.'

'According to the DVLA computer – and don't ask, by the way – he's been the proud owner of a new Honda CBR 600 sports bike practically ever since he passed his test.'

'How on earth did an eighteen-year-old sparky, who's apparently firmly on the straight and narrow, afford a CBR?' Sean wondered aloud. 'The insurance company must have been totally hammering him for it.'

'They were,' Madeleine said, and listed premiums that should have made Nasir's hair stand on end.

'How the hell did he afford that?' I demanded.

'Good question,' Madeleine said, casting me a quick smile as though trying to make up for the earlier animosity between us. 'His wages didn't cover it, that's for certain.'

'So,' Sean said, frowning, 'he had to be getting the extra cash from somewhere. Any clues?'

'None, sorry. I'll keep looking,' she said. 'I suppose we can't rule out the possibility that he was on the fiddle somewhere at work. Snaffling stuff away off the site he was on, maybe. What d'you reckon?'

Her words jogged my memory towards the conversation I'd overheard on that building site in Heysham. 'What if he'd found out that Langford was working for Mr Ali, and threatened to spill the beans. He could have been doing a bit of blackmail,' I suggested.

Sean was frowning again. 'Could be. I suppose that brings his boss into the frame, but don't forget that Nasir had been paying out this extra cash for a while. Why would Ali wait until now to get rid of him? And surely on a building site they could have conjured up some likely-looking "accident"? Besides, who was Nasir threatening to tell, and was it really worth killing him over?'

We fell into a glum silence, pondering over the variables and not managing to make them slot together in any sort of order.

'What about you, boss, any sign of Ursula?' Madeleine asked.

Sean shook his head. 'Nothing yet. I'll keep on it, though. There's only so many people she could have gone to.'

'Is there any point in talking to that Community Juvenile bloke, O'Bryan, to see if he knows anything either about Nasir or your sister?' I offered. 'He seems to be the one with his finger on the pulse as far as extra-curricular activities go.'

'I don't see why not,' Madeleine said. 'We know Nasir's been in a lot of trouble in the past, and O'Bryan would be the man who'd have the details. If Nas's been up to anything recently it might even give us an idea where he was getting his money. What d'you think?'

He nodded. 'OK,' he said slowly, then turned back to me. 'Have you had a chance to find out any more from your friend on the paper?'

'A little,' I said. 'They've fixed Nasir's time of death to around three hours after we last saw him, and they reckon he was practically dead before he was moved.'

Sean rose, began pacing restlessly. 'OK,' he said, 'so let's take some jumps in the dark here, shall we? Nasir comes and takes a pot-shot at you, Charlie, under duress, or so it would seem. He and Rog run away, and within a few hours Nasir's been shot and left for dead. Question: why?'

'Was he shot because he tried to kill Charlie, you mean?' Madeleine supplied. 'Or because he failed?'

'Exactly,' Sean said, turning to me. 'Which brings it down to this – why does somebody want you dead?'

I swallowed. It was a question I hadn't wanted to give much thought to. 'I don't know,' I said. 'O'Bryan did warn me I'd become a target for the kids who've been doing these robberies if I stuck my neck out. It could have been that.' It sounded unlikely, even as I said it.

'What about this Garton-Jones character?' Madeleine said. 'From what I saw of him at that Residents' Committee meeting he's a nasty piece of work, and he didn't like being thrown off the estate. Disposing of you would have been a good way of killing two birds with one stone, as it were. He gets rid of his opposition, and frightens people enough to want him back at the same time.'

'And when that failed he took second best, you mean, and shot the messenger instead?' Sean pondered. 'I don't know. It's all a bit extreme, and Garton-Jones strikes me as the sort of guy who'd have wanted Charlie to know who was behind it, and why, before the hit.'

Attila finished his phone call and replaced the receiver. Sean and Madeleine seemed to take this as their cue to leave, and I walked out to the car park with them.

'What about Langford?' I asked. 'I don't suppose you've had a chance for your little chat yet?'

Sean shook his head and gave me a half-smile as he unlocked the Cherokee's doors. 'He seems to be keeping a pretty low profile at the moment, but I suppose that's hardly surprising after he tipped you off about my neo-nazi past.'

I glanced at him, puzzled. 'But he didn't,' I said slowly. 'It was Jav who told me about it first. Then I confirmed it through the archives at the paper.'

Sean stopped, turned. 'Jav?' he demanded. 'Young lad, peroxide hair?'

'That's him. Why, d'you know him?'

He nodded, thoughtful. 'Yeah, he went to the local college with Ursula. He was interested in her at one time, but Nasir supplanted him. I don't think he took it very well.'

I digested the information for a moment. 'Hang on, if Jav knew about Nas and Ursula, why did he tell me all that stuff about you hating Nasir? He must have known you didn't have a problem with it.'

'Maybe he was jealous that she turned him down,' Madeleine suggested. 'Maybe he wanted to cause trouble for the family by way of revenge.'

Sean glanced at me, his expression troubled. 'Or maybe someone else just put him up to it.'

'Like who?'

'We come back to Langford again,' I said. 'He certainly would have known about your past connections.'

'Yes, but so would anyone who had access to a newspaper library,' Madeleine argued.

'Well, there's one way to find out,' Sean said, climbing into the Cherokee and sticking the keys into the ignition. 'I'll ask Harvey Langford. You ask Jav.'

'Yeah, great,' I muttered under my breath, stepping back as they slammed the doors and the V8 fired into life. 'All I've got to do now is find him.'

Eighteen

Two days later, Pauline came home. I had mixed feelings about it, on the whole. Of course, I was delighted to see her back safe, but with the situation on Lavender Gardens worsening, it might have been better if she'd stayed away.

The police had implemented a Zero Tolerance policy on the estate. Their uniformed presence was high, but it wasn't providing the calming effect they'd been hoping for.

Inevitably, it seemed to be the teenagers who were bearing the brunt of the draconian measures. Between the boys in blue and Garton-Jones's mob, they were getting it from all sides, and the temperature was rising. I was uneasy about leaving the house with only Friday in residence to go and meet Pauline from her flight.

All the kids were keeping their heads down, including Jav, who seemed to have gone to ground. I hadn't even caught sight of the Asian boy since Sean, Madeleine and I had our meeting at Attila's place, never mind caught hold of him.

Now, sitting in traffic on the M61, I had time to let my mind wander in circles, mentally cursing the lack of hard information I had to go on.

Still, at least I didn't have to slum it getting down to Manchester. Jacob said he had some parts to collect from a dealer friend of his in the area, and he'd kindly agreed to combine the trip with an airport run. Pauline hadn't mastered the art of travelling light, and the cavernous rear load bay of Jacob's battered old Range Rover was filled to bursting by the time we'd crammed all her cases in.

I took the back seat and let Pauline ride up front. She settled into the worn leather upholstery with an air of satisfaction. 'This is a proper way to travel. It beats a smelly old taxi any day,' she announced. 'You should try sitting in one of those airline seats for hours. The feller next to me was all elbows and a weak bladder. Up and down every five minutes. I swear I didn't get a wink of sleep all the way back. I've no idea what day it is, even.'

It wasn't long before she worked the conversation round to the situation at home. Then I spent the rest of the journey being bombarded with questions about Fariman's state of health, Mrs Gadatra's state of mind, and Lavender Gardens' state of readiness.

When I told her about the new policing policy, she snorted. 'Daft buggers, they're going to make things ten times worse.' She twisted over her shoulder to look at me. 'I hope you told them, Charlie.'

'Unfortunately, the local chief constable doesn't consult me before he decides these things,' I said drily.

'Well, what about that policeman feller who used to come calling when you were ill last winter?' she demanded. 'MacMillan, wasn't it?'

'He came to see me twice,' I pointed out. And I hadn't exactly been welcoming. His overwhelming disapproval of the actions that had led to my temporary incapacity had been too plain to be ignored, however much he seemed to have softened down his attitude since.

Wisely, perhaps, Pauline didn't pursue that one any further. We managed to get into Lavender Gardens unmolested, although we attracted close scrutiny from Garton-Jones's heavies as we went past. They'd already checked out Jacob when he turned up to collect me earlier.

As I should have expected, Friday went totally ballistic at his owner's return, bouncing round the living room like a puppy and letting out ear-splitting yelps. The Ridgeback had that crafty look in his eye which said he knew full well this was one occasion when he could get away with total disobedience, and he was damn well going to make the most of it.

Our efforts to shut him up had Jacob grinning. He made his excuses and left quickly once we'd unloaded Pauline's cases. I supposed I couldn't blame him for not wanting to leave a Range Rover too long unattended anywhere on Lavender Gardens at the moment. It didn't matter that it was fifteen years old, and the body was slowly taking on an interesting mottled two-tone colour scheme as the rust encroached on the cream paintwork.

In the midst of all this havoc, it would have been easy to miss the sound of the phone ringing. Pauline dragged her frenzied dog off into the kitchen and closed the door behind her, leaving me to pick up the receiver.

'Charlie!' It was a woman's voice on the line that I didn't immediately recognise, the tones made echoing by the distortion of a mobile phone. 'Where on earth have you been? I've found him!'

'Madeleine?' It took me a moment to catch up. 'Who have you found? Roger?'

'No, more's the pity,' she said. 'Jav. He's inside at the moment, but I don't know how long he's going to stay there.'

'Inside where?'

'That gym that Nasir went to, remember? I found out he was also on the membership list and I've been keeping an eye on the place to see if he turned up. He arrived about an hour ago. I'm in the car park. Do you want me to go in and talk to him?'

I bit my lip, glanced at my watch. 'No, stay put. I'll be with you in ten minutes and we'll go in together. That way he's less opportunity to try and lie about what he told me. OK?'

'OK,' she said, and rang off.

I turned to find Pauline in the doorway with a resigned look on her face. 'I won't ask what you're mixed up in now,' she said.

'I'm sorry, Pauline.' I shrugged helplessly. 'I didn't go looking for trouble.'

'You don't have to go looking, dear – it comes and finds you,' she said, then gave me a quick grin. 'Go on, girl, don't look so mortified. Get off with you if it's so important. Just don't think you can fob me off indefinitely. I'm going to want to know what you've been up to before too long, in all its gory detail!'

If only you knew, I thought.

When I turned into the car park of the gym Madeleine had mentioned and pulled up alongside the Grand Cherokee, she climbed out as soon as I'd brought the bike to a halt.

'Jav's still in there,' she said, by way of greeting. 'Let's just hope he can give us some answers.'

I nodded as I dumped my helmet and gloves onto the passenger seat. She blipped the door locks and we walked across the mainly deserted car park towards the squat pale blue building that was the health club.

Nobody was manning the reception desk as we pushed open the main doors, and we didn't give them chance to be slow on the uptake. Instead, we carried on straight through a second set of glass doors into the gym proper, then paused to look about us.

It wasn't difficult to spot Jav. Apart from the blond teenager, the place was deserted. He was working on a set of barbell bench presses at the far side of the room, and his technique was poor enough to make me wince.

He didn't look round when we walked in, too busy concentrating on locking his arms out against a weight that must have been ten kilos too heavy for him. I nodded silently to Madeleine, and we moved quickly over to stand on either side of him.

He twitched as we came into his line of sight, one elbow buckling. If Madeleine and I hadn't grabbed hold of the bar he would have been in trouble.

Mind you, he was in trouble anyway. We pushed down at both ends until it was driving onto his chest, pinning him to the bench.

I shook my head sadly. 'One thing I always say to people when they start training, Jav, is never to do bench presses without someone to spot for them,' I said, my voice bland. 'If we hadn't come along then you might have had a nasty accident.'

'Get it off me!' He writhed under the bar, but the combination of the two of us pressing on top of it, and the fact he'd overloaded it to begin with, was enough to hold him.

Madeleine tutted. 'Now now, Jav, don't get stroppy,' she said. 'We just want a little chat.'

He kept struggling, but it was a lost cause, and it didn't take too long before even he realised the fact. Then he stilled and asked sullenly, 'What do you want?'

'That's better,' I said. 'I want to know who put you up to coming round and priming me up with all that bullshit about Sean Meyer.'

'I don't know what you mean,' Jav spat, his lisp conspicuous. He gasped as Madeleine and I leaned a bit further onto the bar.

'Yes you do, Jav,' Madeleine said. 'Somebody gave you the

information, patted you on the head and sent you off in Charlie's direction, and you did as you were told like a good little boy, didn't you?'

I took in the mulish look on Jav's face and gave her a harsh glance. And I thought she was good with children. Ah well, too late now.

'What are people going to think when they find out you've been tipping off the police?' I tried a different tack.

Jav's expression didn't change much, but at least he said, 'They won't think anything, because it wasn't me. *I* don't talk to the filth,' he panted, no doubt making a sly dig at MacMillan's interest in me.

'Well, somebody's been talking to them, Jav, trying to drop Sean in it, and it doesn't take a genius to work out that you're the common element here,' Madeleine pressed. 'So, who primed you?'

There was a flash of movement on the other side of the glass doors. A couple of figures dressed in pale blue polo shirts, and moving hurriedly.

I saw from Madeleine's face that she'd seen them, too. Knew that our time was running out fast.

'So, come on, Jav,' she tried one last time, 'who was it?' and before I could stop her, she added sharply, 'Was it Langford?'

I held back an inward curse, as the doors to the gym flew open, and two large members of staff hustled in.

'Oy,' one of them shouted, 'what the hell d'you two think you're doing!'

We ignored them for a second longer, holding the bar down on Jav's chest. 'Yes, all right, yes!' he cried. 'It was that bastard Langford, all right? Now let me go!'

We complied with his request abruptly, but left him to shift the bar himself. For a few moments he just lay there, dragging air into his constricted lungs. One of the staff grabbed the barbell to lift it off the boy. I noted in passing that Attila had been right about the quality of the staff here. His technique wasn't much to speak of, either.

The other man snatched at my arm, started to try and drag me across the floor towards the exit.

Big mistake.

I broke his grip in an automatic reflex action, twisting his hand back to reverse our positions. Getting out of wrist holds had been part of Lesson One on my self-defence courses. I could do it in my sleep.

The man swore and struggled, but I had his wrist joint, elbow and shoulder all under considerable tension. I could have held that lock all day with one hand, and there wasn't a damn thing he could have done about it.

Jav was on his feet by this time, rubbing his chest and glaring at us. The other staff man had jerked the barbell back onto its stand and was eyeing up Madeleine, clearly wondering if she was dangerous, too.

'It's OK,' I said, 'we're leaving now. There's no need for the strong-arm tactics.' I met Jav's eyes and held them for a long moment. 'But God help you if you've lied to us, Jav.'

I let go of my captive with enough of a shove to send him sprawling, giving us space for a dignified retreat. At the doorway I glanced back at Jav, and saw the fear there. Stark, it was in the lines of his body, behind his eyes.

But somehow I knew that it wasn't me he was afraid of.

'Look, I'm sorry, I panicked,' Madeleine said later. 'I saw those two coming for us, and I just wanted to get an answer out of him quickly.' She turned away from the window and shrugged with a rueful smile. 'I guess I just wasn't thinking straight.'

Sean put down his coffee cup, moved over to put his hands on her shoulders, and smiled back at her. 'It's OK,' he said lightly. 'We'll work round it.'

We were in the living room at my flat, which had seemed like the only safe neutral territory to meet up with Sean after our abortive interrogation of Jav.

Apart from telling Madeleine to follow me I hadn't said a word to her since we left the health club. I couldn't believe she'd given Jav such an easy escape route, and I didn't trust myself not to tell her so in short, pithy sentences. I should have realised that Sean would take a line of less resistance.

Watching the two of them together now I wondered, briefly, what it was about some women that made men so desperate to hold the nasty world at bay for them. Whatever it was, I knew I didn't have it.

'So, what happens now?' I asked, breaking in more abruptly than I'd intended. 'Have you had any luck tracking down Langford?'

Sean let his hands fall away and shook his head. 'He's dropped right out of sight,' he said.

'Is there any chance Jav might have been telling the truth?' Madeleine asked now, with some hesitation.

'Doubtful,' I said shortly.

'But possible, nevertheless,' Sean said. The look he directed towards me lasted only half a second, but it was enough for me to read the warning.

'We still need more information about him.' He sighed, passed a hand across his eyes, and leaned against the wall by the window. He had that focused quality I'd seen in him before. Whenever we'd been out in the field, even just during training, Sean switched into a different mode, pared-down, alert.

'Madeleine, would you go and see O'Bryan?' he said now. 'See what you can wheedle out of him about Nasir's background, and quiz him about Harvey Langford while you're at it.'

I opened my mouth to argue, then shut it again. Sean had always had the knack of inspiring his troops. The way the other girl reacted, so pathetically grateful at being given the responsibility, took the wind right out of my sails.

'What would you like me to do?' I asked instead.

'If you've nothing more pressing, I've got a couple of leads on where to find Ursula,' he said casually. 'I'd like you to come with me.'

I nodded, downed the rest my coffee in a gulp and collected the empty mugs together. By the time I'd dumped them in the kitchen sink and gathered my leather jacket, Madeleine had already used her mobile phone to check that Eric O'Bryan was available, and willing to see her.

'He's in his office all afternoon,' she said brightly when I returned to the living room.

We moved out of the flat, and I followed the two of them down the wooden stairs to the street where the Grand Cherokee was parked next to the kerb.

We took the back streets into Lancaster, winding up through the Marsh estate, before dropping Madeleine off near the Castle prison. It was easy enough for her to make her way down from there through the pedestrianised shopping centre to O'Bryan's office.

She left us cheerfully enough, with a purposeful stride. Sean watched her cross the road in front of us and set off along the far pavement.

'You should go easier on her,' he said as we nosed back out into traffic.

Surprised, I twisted in my seat to face him. 'Funny,' I said drily. 'That's almost exactly what she said to me about you.'

He glanced at me then, nearly smiled, but not quite, and when he spoke his voice bordered on the chilly. 'Not everyone's had the training you have, Charlie,' he said. 'Not everyone can stay so together under pressure. Madeleine's speciality is electronic security and surveillance, and she's very, very good at it. She's not a field agent, and never has been. I won't have her confidence dented because she made a human mistake in circumstances way outside her usual remit.'

'I'm not a field agent either,' I said, stung by the hinted rebuke. The lights changed and we moved forwards into the flow. 'You seem to forget, *sergeant*, that I've been out of the army now for longer than I was ever in.'

'Speaking of which,' he said, 'I've been doing some digging.'

My heart was suddenly thumping in my chest. 'And?'

He let the Cherokee freewheel down the hill past the new bus station, changing lanes to head for Morecambe and keeping his eyes on the road, so it was difficult to tell what he was thinking.

'There was a phone call,' he said at last. 'Just after the court martial, apparently. Female. She rang the guard room at camp wanting to speak to me. When they told her I wasn't available she said to pass on a message. Said I shouldn't have let it happen to you. Said to tell me not to be so cruel as to keep ignoring your calls. That if I still felt anything for you at all I should get in touch.'

My skin shimmied. 'Oh shit,' I murmured. 'They didn't exactly need anyone to draw them a diagram after that, did they?'

'No,' he said, voice neutral, 'I dare say they didn't.'

The traffic slowed where it merged from two lanes into one along the opposite side of the river from my flat. I stared out of the window at the jagged pale blue supports for the new Millennium footbridge that spanned the water, but I didn't take in a line of it.

'So, any ideas who it was?' I asked after a while.

'That we *don't* know,' Sean said. 'The call came in on an outside line, but that's as much as my contact could tell me. Why, who do you suspect?'

I shrugged. 'It's difficult to tell without hearing the voice whether it was malicious or genuine. The words sound concerned for my welfare, but that could just be a clever way of disguising the intent.'

I swallowed, alarmed to discover I was close to tears. I was damned if I was going to cry in front of Sean. Instead, I managed with surprising calm, 'That call couldn't have done my cause more harm than it did at the time.'

'I suppose it could have been someone connected with one of the men involved,' Sean said. 'A put-up job to stir it for you. You didn't tell me Hackett was one of them, by the way,' he added. 'He always struck me as a nasty piece of work.'

My neck and shoulders seized instantly, and I could hear the thunder of my own pulse inside my ears. Fear was like a stone in my stomach. *Oh God, what else had he found out?*

'I still wouldn't rule out Lewis and Woolley as candidates either,' he went on, as though not noticing my reaction. 'It wasn't much of a secret that they didn't like you, I'm afraid. You were in a different league, and it showed.'

'If I'd known where it was going to lead, I would have happily moved to the back of the class,' I said, trying not to let the bitterness creep out.

'No you wouldn't,' Sean said straight away. He flicked his eyes across at me dispassionately. 'I know how your mind works, Charlie. You want to win, or you don't want to play.' He managed a smile that mocked himself as much as me. 'In that respect, we're very much alike.'

'Is that why you quit?'

'Not really,' he said. 'In the end I found that I just enjoy breathing.'

Nineteen

We didn't speak again until we'd travelled through Morecambe and were heading further out towards Heysham. Sean had three locations to try, and we drew a total blank on the first two.

'If this one is a wash-out, we're back to square one,' Sean said as we pulled up outside the last address. He peered out through the windscreen at the grim-looking three-storey flat complex in front of us. 'Ah well, let's get this over with. I have a feeling if we're up there for too long the wheels will have gone by the time we get back.'

We left the Cherokee parked on the broken-up tarmac, and headed across the rubbish-strewn grass to the outside staircase at one end of the block. We took the stairs to the top floor in silence, stepping over the soggy detritus scattered over each exposed half-landing on the way up.

The flat we were after was in the centre of the row. Sean knocked on the shabby front door while I tried not to listen to the full-scale screaming match going on in the next flat along.

Eventually the door was opened by a girl not yet completely out of her teens, with a baby balanced on her right hip. She had a lank blonde ponytail, and the remains of a hare lip. At the sight of Sean her eyes widened and her mouth formed into a soundless oh.

She tried to slam the door shut on us, but Sean had his shoulder against it before she had half a chance. The flimsy hardboard rebounded off him and he kept right on coming, as unstoppable as a truck, and about as compassionate. The girl retreated backwards down the tiny hallway, clutching at the child.

I stepped across the threshold after them, closing the door firmly behind me.

'You can't come barging in here like this, Sean,' the girl protested, her voice high with panic.

'Give it up, Leanne,' Sean said now. His voice was tired rather than angry, which somehow made it all the more threatening. 'You know why we're here. Where is she?'

'I don't know what you mean,' Leanne snapped. The baby took its cue from her. Its little face crumpled around the dummy in its mouth, then it turned a healthy shade of puce, and started screeching.

Leanne jiggled the child by way of comfort. It didn't seem to help much. She lowered her voice, but it lost none of its venom. 'Get out before I call the cops.'

Sean laughed, and it wasn't a happy sound. 'Go ahead,' he invited. He stepped to the phone on the hall table, lifted the receiver and held it out to her. 'Your phone was cut off six months ago. You could always try a letter.'

'It's OK, Leanne, you may as well let him in,' said a dull voice from the sitting room doorway. 'Once he sets his mind to something there's not much can stop my brother.'

Sean turned to face her. 'Hello Ursula,' he said quietly.

Leanne tried to smother the baby's cries against the stained shoulder of her T-shirt, then whisked the infant off into the kitchen. The thin plywood door she slammed behind her did little to muffle its wailing.

'You'd better come through,' Ursula said. 'Don't take it out on Leanne, she's only trying to help.'

Sean's sister led us into the cramped living room and sank down into the single armchair by the gas fire. He sat on one end of the sofa nearest to her, and was so close their knees almost touched. I stayed on my feet, trying not to look like I was hovering.

Roger didn't look like either of them, but Ursula was almost as tall as Sean, with thick dark hair cut short and feathered in to her pale face. The facial structure was the same, high wide cheekbones and a good jawline. Arresting, rather than conventionally pretty.

'Mum's worried about you,' Sean said gently. 'You should get in touch with her, at least. Let her know you're all right.'

'But I'm not, am I?' Ursula said. She sat up, and for the first time I could see the curve of her belly beneath the baggy jumper she wore. Four, possibly five months gone, if I was any judge.

She looked her brother in the eye and demanded bitterly, 'What do you want me to say to her, Sean? "Hi, Mum, I'm pregnant to an eighteen-year-old Paki, but don't worry, there's not going to be any mixed marriage, because he's just been shot dead." How do I tell her that?'

It was a fine defiant speech, only let down by the way her chin trembled at the end of it.

'She already knows,' Sean said, keeping his tone quiet and measured. 'And what she doesn't know, she's guessed. Anything you tell her now isn't going to be as bad as her sitting at home worrying about where you are, and what's happening to you. Mum doesn't give a stuff who the father is, not really. You should know that.'

He reached for her hands, took them in both of his, smoothing his thumbs over her bones. 'This is her first grandchild, for God's sake. It could well be the only one she ever gets. Don't take that away from her.'

Ursula sat motionless for a moment, then jerked her hands out of his grasp, but only to wipe them quickly across her rapidly filling eyes. Sean waited half a beat, then folded her into his arms and held her there, listening to the sobbing.

Our eyes met over the top of his sister's head. It was strange to watch him offering such tender comfort with his body, while his face was so utterly cold.

I continued to stand and say nothing. There was nothing I could say.

It was a little while before Ursula moved again. She sat up, dug down a sleeve for a handkerchief, blew her nose and got herself together. She threw Sean a shaky smile. Not much of one, but better than nothing.

'So, do I tell Mum you'll come home and let her fuss over you?' he asked.

'I can't,' she said, anxious again. 'I–I don't think it's safe for me to be where anyone can find me at the moment.'

To his credit, Sean didn't point out that we'd traced her here without vast effort. Instead he said, 'Why? Why isn't it safe at home?'

She shrugged. 'Nas was – he was scared. Last week, he told me to get out and find somewhere safe to stay for a while. Told me not to go home until he said it was OK. He didn't say what was wrong, and now he's dead.' She looked up at him with overflowing eyes. 'And *I'm* too scared to go back.'

Sean stood up. 'I've got friends down south,' he said. 'We'll get you right out of here until this is all sorted out. Go pack your stuff.'

She sniffed again, nodded. 'OK,' she said, sounding subdued, but eager, all at the same time. She made it as far as the doorway before Sean called her back.

'Just one thing,' he said. He always did know when to apply pressure. He'd been so good at that in the army. 'Where was Nas getting his money from?'

Ursula's expression flashed over from gratitude to mistrust. 'I don't know,' she said carefully.

'Don't lie to me,' Sean said, his voice even. 'Was he back up to his old tricks again?'

'No!' she denied instantly, but couldn't meet his gaze. 'He knew if he got caught again he'd get put away for it, not just juvenile detention centres, the real deal this time, so he kept out of the action. He, well, he was doing a bit of scouting, that's all. Passing on names, you know?'

'Who to?'

'I don't know,' she repeated, and this time it had the ring of truth about it. 'He didn't say, and I didn't ask. I didn't want to know.' She paused, memories hitting her like a bad dream. 'He just wanted the best for the baby,' she said. 'He was so pleased about it,' and her face started to dissolve again. She stumbled out of the room and across the hall, wrenching the door shut behind her as she went through it.

We started after her, but Leanne appeared out of the kitchen at that point. She was minus the baby, which was manacled into a high chair behind her, and trying to chip its way to freedom with a plastic spoon. Leanne stood with her hands on her hips, as though daring Sean to follow his sister into her bedroom.

He eyed the closed door for a moment, then turned that intense gaze onto Leanne instead. 'Has Roger been here, too?' he demanded.

Leanne tried to stand her ground, but quailed rapidly. 'Yes, but we haven't seen him since—' she glanced at the door and lowered her voice. 'Since the night Nas was killed. Roger came to tell her he was dead.'

'When?'

She thought for a moment. 'Late, close to midnight, I think. I'd been having trouble with the little one. She's teething. I was still up with her.' She glanced back at the child, who was now attempting to redecorate the kitchen in something pale green and pureed out of the dish in front of her, and letting out shrieks of delight.

'Roger was in a right state,' Leanne went on. 'Covered in dirt, and crying like a little kid. Kept saying he was sorry over and over. Crazy with it, you know? Scary really. I've got some leftover diazepam in the cabinet. I tried to give him some to take the edge off it, but he just chucked it back at me and took off.'

'Did you go after him?' Sean asked, tense.

'What, at that time of night, round here?' Leanne's voice was scornful. 'No I did not! Besides, by that time I'd got enough on my hands coping with Ursula. She was frantic.'

The bedroom door opened then, and Ursula came out again, carrying a small canvas bag. We waited while she hugged Leanne, and promised to be in touch, then she allowed Sean to shepherd her out of the front door and along the open walkway to the stairs.

We were down to the second floor before we heard the motorbike arriving. I registered the sound of a big four-stroke out of habit and, glancing over the slatted balcony rail on my way past, I saw the black and yellow Honda CBR 600 come wheeling off the street into the parking area below us.

By the next half-landing, the rider had the side stand down, and the engine cut. The bike was too big for him, and although he was wearing a nice Shoei helmet, he had on just a denim jacket, and no gloves. I often wonder what makes these lads go out and buy machines that will do one-fifty plus, without bothering to get the proper gear to go with it.

As we turned onto the final half-landing, Sean suddenly stopped dead. I pulled up short and followed his gaze. The

CBR rider had removed his helmet, and was walking across the grass towards the stairwell, with his face clearly visible.

This time, Sean didn't make the mistake of yelling his brother's name. He didn't bother with the rest of the stairs, either. He just put both hands on the railing, and vaulted straight over it, coat flying. Ursula let out a strangled cry as he dropped out of sight.

Roger had frozen at her cry. It was only when Sean started heading for him at speed that he sprang into action.

He panicked completely then. He threw the helmet he was carrying at Sean, who swiped it to one side without breaking stride, as though it had no substance. The expensive lid smacked onto the rough ground of the parking area, bounced a couple of times, and finally rolled into the gutter, the gelcoat cracked and useless.

Roger managed to get to the Honda first, but fumbled getting the key into the ignition. I almost thought Sean had him, when the boy managed to get his thumb on the starter and the motor fired up. He snatched the Honda off its stand and kicked it clumsily into gear with the throttle already halfway open.

The effect was electric. The rear wheel ripped free of the road surface, spinning wildly, and churning up clouds of grey smoke as the transmission tried its best to bring the bike's substantial horsepower into play.

Sean leapt clear as the rear end started to crab towards him. Finally, it dug in and bit, launching the Honda forwards with a lethal shimmy. Roger must have gone fifty yards in the blink of an eye, before he backed off the throttle enough to stay upright.

It was only a momentary ebb, then he was viciously back on the power. He laid down a haze of rubber right to the end of the street.

I headed straight for the Cherokee, practically towing Ursula along behind me. By the time I got her there Sean already had the doors unlocked and was in the driver's seat. I bundled her into the back with a short instruction for her to buckle up, and jumped for the front seat just as Sean twisted the key and slammed the gear lever into reverse.

He set off out of the small car park and into the road with a squeal of protest from the tyres, and another from his sister.

'Sean,' I said, loud over the howl of the engine. 'He's on a CBR, with a head start. We don't stand a hope in hell of catching him in this.'

'I know.' Sean's face was grim as he accelerated down the narrow street, swerving the jeep into a gap between the parked cars to miss an oncoming delivery van by less than I'd like to think about. 'But I've got to try.'

In fact, his pursuit lasted longer than I would have expected. Roger made a frenetic series of turns through the back streets. He was riding increasingly wildly, showing an obvious lack of skill and familiarity with the sheer bulk of the Honda.

The boy tried to go far too fast into one junction, locked the rear wheel at the last moment, and couldn't make the turn in. He over-shot, cannoning off a parked car on the far side of the road.

Ursula let out a short scream, and I held my breath, waiting for the crash. He wasn't even wearing a helmet now, so it was probably going to be messy, and it was definitely going to hurt, but the accident never happened. Just when I thought he'd lost it altogether, Roger somehow managed to cling on to control.

How in the name of hell, I wondered as Sean sent the Grand Cherokee thundering after his brother, did a fourteen-year-old get his hands on a sub-superbike?

The answer didn't so much form inside my head, as it just

arrived, fully grown, as though it had always been there. I twisted in my seat to face Ursula.

'Is that Nasir's bike he's on?' I demanded.

She looked at me as though I'd gone out of my mind.

'What are you talking about?' she said, distracted, trying to see over her brother's shoulder. 'Nas doesn't *have* a motorbike.'

I turned back, catching Sean's eye as I did so. 'Remember the reg number,' he said, 'I'll get Madeleine to check it.'

But we both knew instinctively whose name would be spat out as the registered keeper when Madeleine finessed the DVLA computer.

I realised briefly that Nasir's age should have meant that the CBR's power output had been restricted down to 33bhp for him to legally ride it. It soon became pretty obvious that it wasn't.

Now, Roger kept on riding as though his life depended on it. At first, I thought he was just fleeing in a blind panic, but it soon became apparent there was method to his seemingly chaotic flips and turns.

'He's heading for the escape road,' Sean said tightly as he drifted the four-by-four through another corner. 'We won't catch him if he makes it that far.'

The escape road out of Heysham wasn't dual carriageway, but it was so wide that it might as well have been. Roger would be able to give the CBR its head and that would be it.

'What are you suggesting?' I demanded sharply, 'that you run him off the road before he gets there?'

Sean's hands clenched on the wheel, and he said nothing, but I didn't like the sound of his thoughts.

In the end, we didn't get the chance for drastic action. Sean hit congestion on the approach to a roundabout, and Roger nipped away from us up the inside of an artic, coming within a hair's breadth of putting himself under the rear wheels of the trailer in the process.

Then he was away, throwing the power on in great hand-fuls, rocketing straight down the white line. As soon as we were clear of the roundabout Sean swung out to overtake the truck, but the driver had clearly decided we were lunatics. He did his best to make his rig even wider and longer. It seemed to take a painfully extended few seconds before Sean managed to carve past him. We could still just about see the Honda up ahead.

Sean planted the accelerator, and the jeep squatted down and ran under us. It had pace that amazed me for such a big, unwieldy vehicle, but with the best will in the world it wasn't built for sheer speed.

Besides, the escape road was raised above the marshy farm land around it, dreadfully exposed to the wind as I well knew from the bike. As we hit a hundred miles an hour a savage gust whipped under the body, almost seeming to lift the Grand Cherokee right off the surface of the road.

We strayed over the white line as Sean fought with the steering. The inoffensive Peugeot coming the other way locked all its wheels up as the driver desperately attempted to avoid a head-on.

Blenched white, Sean managed to rescue that one, and still he kept his foot hard in.

Finally, it was Ursula, bracing herself into a corner of the back seat, whose nerve broke. 'Stop, Sean, please! You're going to kill us all,' she cried. 'Why are you chasing him like this? What's he running from?'

It was a good question. After only a moment's hesitation, with a muttered curse, Sean lifted off the throttle. We coasted down to a more legal speed while we watched the Honda's rear numberplate grow ever smaller in the distance.

He didn't answer Ursula's question, but he caught my eye again, and the bleakness was back in his features. I knew then that he'd reached the same terrible conclusion as I had, back there listening to Leanne recounting her story in that dingy hallway.

I couldn't get around the fact there was no way Roger should have known that Nasir had been killed at midnight on the night the two of them had attacked me at the gym. According to the official line, Nas's body wasn't discovered until the following morning.

Which begged the question, how did Roger know his friend was dead? And for what, exactly, was he so sorry?

Sean dropped me off at my flat on St George's Quay, helped a subdued Ursula into the front passenger seat, and left with a tight-lipped smile. I retrieved the Suzuki and headed back to Pauline's, feeling guilty at having abandoned her so completely on her first day home.

I should have known it wasn't over yet. When I turned in to the end of Kirby Street the first thing I saw was the dark blue Vauxhall police car sitting right outside Pauline's house.

It was an unmarked, but it had that official look to it, nevertheless, and the usual giveaway of no dealer stickers in the rear window. There was a single occupant, sitting in the driver's seat. I saw him duck his head when he heard the Suzuki's distinctive two-stroke exhaust note, checking me out in the door mirror. I glanced in as I wheeled past, but didn't recognise the face, and wasn't inclined to wait for an introduction.

Someone else must have recognised the vehicle for what it was, too. There was an ugly dent in the Vauxhall's front wing, extending halfway across the bonnet, and the windscreen was cracked. The damage had to be very recent, if the complete lack of rust on the exposed metal was anything to go by. I wondered if they'd collected it on the way in.

I rolled straight down the side of the house to the back without stopping, putting the bike away in the shed and then letting myself in through the kitchen door. I paused, and heard voices from the living room. Pauline's, and a man's deeper, slightly clipped tones. With a sinking heart, I pushed open the door.

'Ah, Charlie, there you are, dear,' Pauline said. 'We were just waiting for you to get back. Look who's come to see you.'

MacMillan was sitting on Pauline's sofa, drinking tea with the lady of the house, and looking very much at home. She'd even brought out one of her best ornamental teapots in honour of the occasion.

Friday, some guard dog, was lying at the policeman's feet with his head across one polished shoe. I took a certain amount of dark satisfaction to note that at least he'd slobbered over it.

'Hello Superintendent,' I said, instantly cautious, dumping my helmet and gloves on the back of a chair. 'What can I do for you?'

MacMillan took one look at me and sighed. He put his cup and saucer down carefully on the side table next to him and sat forwards.

The movement jerked Friday out of sleep. The dog clambered to his feet, ambling off into the kitchen.

Pauline's bright eyes flicked backwards and forwards between the two of us like we were playing a tactical game of tennis.

After a moment or two she stood up. 'I think I'll just freshen up this pot,' she said. 'If you'll excuse me?'

When she'd followed Friday into the kitchen, and pulled the door to – but not all the way shut, I noticed – behind her, I raised my eyebrow in MacMillan's direction.

'Well?' I stuffed my hands into the pockets of my jeans. 'What do you want?'

The Superintendent shot a cuff, straightened up one of his cufflinks. He regarded me carefully for a moment, and then he dropped it on me.

'I want you to tell me all about Sean Meyer,' he said.

I felt the involuntary stiffening of my spine, like it had just been scaled by a fast-moving frost. 'Well, what you're going to get,' I said, managing to keep my voice level, 'is me telling you to go to hell.'

He raised an eyebrow at that. 'I wasn't referring to your past – association with him,' he said, choosing his words with care. 'I'm talking about now. The last few weeks.'

I knew I should relax, come off the defensive, but I couldn't help it. I just glared at him.

After a few moments the Superintendent sighed. 'Look, Charlie, I'm not your enemy,' he said, spreading his hands. 'When are you going to start trusting me?'

Probably never. I didn't speak the words out loud, but judging by his face I might as well have done. 'Why are you suddenly so interested in Sean?'

'Because the boy we arrested for his part in the assault on one of your neighbours was Meyer's younger brother, Roger, as I'm sure you're aware,' he pointed out mildly. 'Because it would appear that Nasir Gadatra was a known associate of Roger, and was possibly the one who was leading him into trouble. And because Nasir is now dead.'

'And you think Sean killed him?' I asked. It wasn't such a leap in the dark, I suppose. I'd jumped to much the same conclusion myself. Still, I had to try my best. 'That's a bit of a long shot, isn't it? Metaphorically speaking, of course.'

'Not really. There are certain people in the local community who *are* prepared to talk to us,' he said coyly, 'and the information we've received strongly suggests Meyer's involvement in the killing.'

I digested that one in silence. It would seem that whoever had put Jav up to dishing the dirt to me about Sean now had a more ambitious agenda. I wondered briefly if Langford really could be behind it all. If only Madeleine hadn't put it to Jav like that. If only we could be sure . . .

I glanced up at the Superintendent, swallowed, and said, 'Sean can't have been involved, because the night Nasir was shot, he was with me.'

I saw the look on his face and added quickly, 'I was at the gym working late and he called in to see me there, that's all, but we had a break-in and I had to call the boss out. And before you ask, no we didn't ring the police – it was just kids breaking windows – but Attila did call a glazier, so they should have some record, if you want to check.'

MacMillan sighed again, and took his time considering before he spoke. 'Are you quite sure you want to give the man an alibi, Charlie?' he said gently at last, and there was almost a hint of sadness in his tone. 'I've seen your army record, and the trial transcripts, as a matter of fact. I would have thought if anyone wanted to see Meyer taken down it would be you.'

How the hell did he know that? I tried not to flinch, riding out what must have been a best guess. Oh he was clever, all right, dropping in supposition and presenting it as fact. 'Life is never simple,' I said.

His face shuttered down, as though he'd given me my chance, and I'd blown it. He stood up, just as Pauline made a timely reappearance with her refilled teapot. He said his polite goodbyes, then moved to the front door. I followed him into the hallway, partly just to make sure he went.

MacMillan got as far as turning the handle, then paused on the doorstep. 'Once we've got hold of Meyer you will, of course, be required to come in and make a sworn statement to confirm the story you've just told me,' he said. I thought I caught the barest hint of a smile, but it could have been a trick of the light. 'I'll give you until then to change your mind, at least.'

I watched his back as he walked down the short driveway

and climbed into the passenger seat of the Vauxhall, but he didn't look back.

Pauline was still in the living room when I got back there.

'Can I use your phone?' I asked quickly. Now she was home I felt out of order just helping myself.

She waved me towards the receiver and I snatched it up, dialling Madeleine's mobile number. When she answered I jumped straight in without wasting time on niceties.

'Madeleine! Where are you? Is Sean back yet?'

'No,' she said, 'he's just brought Ursula home and now he's gone out again. Do you want to know what I found out from O'Bryan about Nasir and—?'

'Later,' I interrupted. 'Can you get hold of Sean?'

'What? Oh – er, yes,' she said, somewhat blankly. 'Charlie, what's happened?'

'I've just had the police round. They're looking for Sean. They've had a tip-off and they think he did it. Tell him to ditch the Cherokee and stay out of sight.'

'I'll tell him, but you know Sean,' she said, and her voice was rueful.

'Tell him anyway,' I said, and put the phone down.

I turned to find Pauline still standing with the teapot poised. She put it down and fixed me with a determined eye.

'I won't ask if you're all right, because I can see you're not. Sit down, dear, and have a cup of tea,' she said, feinting right before catching me with a killer left. 'Then you can tell me all about it.'

Twenty

With the benefit of hindsight, I think I would rather have gone ten rounds with MacMillan and a couple of his heftiest sidekicks, than have to sit through half an hour of the third degree from Pauline.

'If you know the man who murdered poor Mrs Gadatra's lad, don't you think it's your duty to tell the police where to find him, not help him evade capture?' she said now, grimly.

'Sean didn't kill Nasir,' I said, and I could feel my chin coming out, stubborn.

We'd moved through to the kitchen and faced each other across the width of the room, me leaning with my back to the sink. There seemed to be a lot more than a brief expanse of lino between us.

'And you're quite sure of that?' she asked.

'Yes.'

Pauline planted her hands firmly on her hips, unwilling to unbend, not quite yet. 'How so?'

'Because I know who did,' I said. 'Well,' I corrected almost right away, 'I *think* I know.' I saw the steely look on the other woman's face, and knew I wasn't going to be able to carry on hedging for much longer, so I added, with some reluctance, 'I think it was Roger – Sean's younger brother.'

Pauline frowned. Whatever she'd been expecting, I don't think that was it. 'Roger?' she murmured. The frown grew deeper, cutting a vee between her eyebrows. 'But he's round next door all the time,' she said. 'He's one of Nasir's friends. Why would Roger want to kill him?'

'That's what we're trying to find out,' I said gently.

'It's all very well you going off crusading, Charlie, but look where it got you last time,' she warned, and I resisted the sudden urge to hang my head and shuffle my feet. 'If Roger's the one who did it, then working out *why* he did it is beside the point. Mr MacMillan's a smart man in my book. He'll get to the bottom of it. Leave it to him.'

'It's not that simple,' I said. I sighed, hovered over telling her the whole story, and plumped for the edited highlights. 'Earlier, on the night Nasir was killed, he and Roger turned up at Attila's place with a gun and tried to shoot me.'

'Good grief,' Pauline said faintly. 'I knew you weren't telling me everything. Why on earth did they try and do that?'

'I don't really know, which is part of the problem, but I think it's something to do with the trouble on the estates.'

'In what way?'

'I don't know that, either. One minute O'Bryan's telling me I'll become a target if I try and help the residents control the crime themselves instead of calling in Garton-Jones's bunch of thugs, and the next I'm being shot at.'

I shrugged, aware of a grinding weariness creeping through my bones. 'Nasir himself certainly knew there was something up,' I continued. 'According to his girlfriend – who just happens to be Sean and Roger's sister, by the way – he was frightened enough of something, or someone, to tell her to find some place safe to stay and keep out of sight. I don't want to believe it was Roger who killed him, but everything's pointing in that direction.'

'Well, I still think you should turn the whole business over to MacMillan and let him sort it out,' Pauline said. She gave me a considering glance. 'But you're not going to do that, are you?'

I shook my head. 'I can't,' I said. 'There's too much else going on in the background. Someone's prepping Sean as the sacrificial lamb. I can't just back out now and leave him to swing for it.'

'And what about his brother?' Pauline asked grimly.

I tried not to think about Sean, about his loyalty to his family. I turned away from it, closed my mind to the possibilities. 'If Roger *is* the one who killed Nasir,' I said, 'regardless of who was behind him, I'll make sure MacMillan gets him, don't you worry.'

She nodded, seemed satisfied by that reply. Still, I felt uncomfortable giving it to her. Not when I wasn't entirely sure if I was telling her the truth or not.

I went home that night, to a flat that felt unlived in and neglected. I was welcomed by another complaining note from my landlord, threatening seven shades of hell to pay if I didn't get him a new key cut. I made a half-hearted note to myself to get it done on Monday, and went to bed.

I was due in at the gym the next morning. I'd told Attila I'd work the weekend to make up for sloping off so much during the past week. I was feeling pretty guilty about it, if you must know. Particularly when he'd been good enough to give me the job in the first place.

The morning arrived lit by sunshine so bright it made me squint when I threw open the shutters. That clear, winter light that carries nothing in the way of warmth, but lets you see for miles.

I drank my first coffee of the day braving the chill, staring out over the river, and listening to the rumble of the trains that ran high across the water over Carlisle Bridge.

In my heart, I knew what that note from my landlord meant. I'd known when I moved in to the flat that I could be asked to leave at short notice. It was the reason the rent was so cheap for the size of the place.

For the last eighteen months I'd watched the redevelopment of St George's Quay creep nearer and nearer. And I'd buried my head and tried not to notice that my home was slowly turning from a damp-walled landlord's liability, into something with desirable investment potential.

Despite the trains, and the traffic on the far side of the river, it was strangely peaceful. I was going to be more than sad to see the back of it.

I was going to be desolate.

With a sigh, I turned away from my view, elbowing the shutters closed behind me. I dumped my empty coffee cup into the sink, and reminded myself that now I was back, shopping was high on the list of priorities.

I might even go mad, do a major raid on the nearby Sainsbury's, and treat myself to a taxi for the ride home. One of the problems of not owning a form of four-wheeled transport is the lack of carrying capacity.

Anyway, before I could give too much serious thought to going shopping, first I was going to have to work to earn the money to pay for it. I glanced at my watch, shrugged into my jacket, and jogged down the wooden stairs to the street, kicking the Suzuki into life.

The RGV liked the cool air rushing into its twin carbs and it ran with a sense of real enjoyment that made it feel like a skittish horse. Perhaps that similarity was part of why I'd taken to motorbiking so readily.

It didn't take long to get to Attila's place, and I chained the bike up in the car park. 'If I'd had you with me yesterday, Roger never would have got away,' I murmured, giving it a regretful pat on its rump.

Surprisingly, for a Saturday morning, it started off quiet. In fact, I took the opportunity to get my own workout in before the rush I knew was going to happen. I nearly managed it undisturbed.

It wasn't until I was on my last set of incline sit-ups that the main door went to signify the first customer of the day. I rushed the last three reps, rather than stop halfway through a set.

When I was done I dragged myself upright, breathless, feeling a sliver of perspiration slide down between my shoulder-blades. I turned to discover Eric O'Bryan leaning against one of the stationary bikes and cleaning his spectacles on a dark blue cotton handkerchief.

The Community Juvenile Officer was once again wearing his grey anorak, this time with a pair of cavalry twill trousers and sensible brown brogues visible below. He was sweating, too, just one of these men who perspires as part of breathing, and not as a sign of physical exertion.

'Hello Charlie,' he said cheerily, smiling. 'Sorry to interrupt you.'

'You haven't,' I said, 'I was just finishing up, anyway.' I stood up and reached for a towel, ostensibly to mop the sweat from my face, but actually to drape round my neck.

I was wearing a stretch sports top that left the scar across my throat much too visible for my liking. Abruptly, I felt too naked, too exposed. It seemed to shout to the world that there was a time I'd been stupid, and vulnerable, and had so nearly paid the ultimate price for it. I found it easier all round if I just covered up.

O'Bryan had seen it, though. As he came over to me his eyes were riveted on the towel, as though hoping for another grisly glimpse of what lay underneath it. I observed with a certain sense of detachment that his eyes strayed to pause at another, smaller scar across my bicep. Finally, as he caught himself staring, they darted up to my face. He found me watching him and slid his gaze away altogether, guilty.

I moved over to the counter area, and pulled on my sweatshirt. He seemed to relax a little once he no longer had to be careful what part of me he could look at.

'So, Mr O'Bryan,' I said briskly, 'something tells me you aren't here to take out a new membership. What can I do for you?'

He looked round hesitantly before speaking, and when he did, he seemed to be choosing his words carefully, like he was picking his way across a muddy field in his Sunday best shoes. I was unkindly reminded of a cheap imitation of MacMillan.

'I had Sean Meyer's young lady, Madeleine, in to see me yesterday asking certain questions about Nasir Gadatra, and also about one Harvey Langford,' he said, circumspect. 'I don't suppose you might know what that was all about, would you?'

'Maybe you should be asking her that,' I said.

O'Bryan sighed. 'I tried,' he said, 'but she's a charming girl who's rather good at stonewalling you totally and smiling sweetly while she's doing it.'

He smiled, rueful. I could just imagine Madeleine cajoling information out of him. He stood as much chance as a chocolate fireguard.

'Yes,' I said, keeping my face straight, 'I suppose she is.'

O'Bryan continued to look hopeful for a few moments longer, then the smile faded as he realised that I was pretty good at stonewalling, too. Even if I didn't quite possess Madeleine's allure while I was at it.

'I don't suppose you've managed to catch sight of Roger recently?' he asked instead.

'He hasn't shown up at home since you were there,' I said, which was true, technically speaking.

O'Bryan seemed to recognise that evasion for what it was.

He pushed his glasses up onto his forehead to pinch the bridge of his nose. Then he said, earnest, 'Look, Charlie, I'll level with you. I'm very worried about the lad. Going AWOL will land him in very hot water, but I'm afraid he may also be mixed up in some way with what's happened to Nasir. Has he said anything about that?'

'I told you, we haven't spoken to him,' I said, thinking that vanishing back view on the Honda didn't count as conversation.

'Of course.' O'Bryan's shoulders slumped. 'I just thought you might – ah, well,' he said, suddenly sounding tired. He turned away, sank down onto the nearest bench.

Then he glanced up and met my eyes, and the fussy little man receded for a moment. 'It's just, you see—' he stopped, started again. 'I'm not sure I can save him this time.'

The words sent a prickle of apprehension through me. If O'Bryan didn't know for certain what Roger might have done, then he strongly suspected.

I tried for a casual tone. 'What if you're right,' I said. 'What if Roger's involved in something pretty serious. What would happen to him?'

He paused for a moment without speaking, pursing his lips. 'Well, that would depend on exactly what it is that he's done,' he said at last. 'At one time just the fact that he was a minor would have been enough to ensure that he could get away with murder, but—'

He saw the tic that I couldn't prevent from skating across my features and stopped short. 'Oh dear God,' he murmured, 'you don't think—?'

'Unfortunately, we're beginning to, yes,' I agreed.

I didn't need to elaborate any further than that. O'Bryan got to his feet as though the bench was suddenly too hot to sit on. He paced away briefly, then turned back. 'Roger and Nasir were the best of friends,' he said, but there was no real heat in his protest. 'What reason do you have for thinking he could have done such a thing?'

'Roger knew Nasir was dead hours before his body was officially discovered,' I said, not going into the details. 'And he's now been seen going round on Nasir's bike.'

'I don't believe it,' O'Bryan said, resuming his pacing as he spoke quietly more to himself than to me. 'I *can't* believe it. They'll throw away the key this time. Oh, you stupid lad, Roger!'

'It may have been an accidental shooting,' I put in, and had to stop myself adding that the gun was in poor condition, and liable to jam, which always increased the probability of an unintentional discharge. Nothing had made the army range instructors more nervous.

Besides, that would also maybe explain Roger turning up on Ursula's doorstep saying how sorry he was . . .

On the other hand, it could have been done in a flash of temper. I recalled, starkly, Roger's reaction to Nasir's seeming inability to execute me in cold blood.

'She's got to die, tonight,' he'd screamed. *'Don't you know what's going to happen? Don't you care?'*

I swallowed, and took a leap of faith. 'Much as I know Sean doesn't want to believe it, either,' I said. 'We think Roger's to blame for Nasir's death.'

O'Bryan shook his head. 'Oh no, I'm to blame,' he said, and his tone was bleak. His glasses caught the light as he looked up at me, blanking out his eyes. 'There must have been some sign I missed, been *something* I could have done to have prevented this tragedy. And he's got Nasir's bike you say? A Honda 600, wasn't it?'

'Yeah, we saw him on it yesterday,' I admitted. 'So, where do we go from here?'

O'Bryan gave another shrug, letting his hands fall back to his sides as though he'd lost nerve control over them. 'There isn't anywhere *to* go, apart from prison,' he said. He regarded me gravely. 'Even at his age, Roger will go down for this, for a long time. You do realise that, don't you?'

Now it was my turn to feel the weight of the world dragging at my shoulders. 'I suppose so,' I said.

A big part of me knew that Roger should get what was coming to him, just as I knew I should do whatever I could to help bring him in. But, there was another part, smaller yes, but no less loud and insistent, that squirmed and twisted at the thought. At what the boy's capture and conviction would do to Sean, to his mother, and to Ursula and her unborn child.

Besides, Roger hadn't set out to kill me on his own account, I was sure of that. There was still someone else out there, a shadowy figure lurking in the background. One who'd set the boys on their way with a loaded gun. One who'd whispered in MacMillan's ear that Sean was a murderer. I needed to find out who that was.

What was *going to happen if you didn't kill me, Roger?* I wondered. *Who was putting so much pressure on you to do it?*

'So,' O'Bryan said now, nudging at a wisp of fraying carpet with his toe, 'what do you plan to do next?'

A sudden thought occurred to me, and with it, a course of action. 'Find Harvey Langford,' I said.

O'Bryan looked surprised. 'Why would that help Roger?'

'Because the last time I saw Langford he told me he knew who was behind the crimewave on Lavender Gardens,' I said. 'Or if he didn't know, he could find out.'

'And you think he'd be prepared to tell *you* that?'

I gave him a cynical smile. 'Let's just say I know certain things that good old Harvey definitely does not want broadcasting.'

'Ah, I see,' O'Bryan said, looking clearly mystified. 'Well, that information would be worth knowing, I suppose. I just don't see how that's going to help the boy.'

'Roger isn't in this alone,' I said, my voice grim. 'It's only fair that he shouldn't go to prison alone, don't you think?'

After O'Bryan had gone, folding himself into his MG and disappearing out into the flow of traffic, I determined how best to make good on my promise to find Harvey Langford.

I recognised that if Langford didn't want to be found, it wasn't going to be easy. I knew Sean had been after him since our run-in on Copthorne, but without success. He'd even spent the previous Thursday afternoon hanging around near the building site, but the vigilante hadn't shown.

I flipped through the Yellow Pages until I found Mr Ali's building firm, and rang the office number. A starchy-voiced woman answered, and took my request to speak to her boss with a certain amount of disdain.

'Ai'm afraid Mr Ali is very busy this morning,' she said. 'He left strict instructions that he wasn't to be disturbed.'

'Tell him it's Charlie Fox,' I said. 'Tell him that I want to speak to him about his business dealings with Harvey Langford. I'm sure he'll find time to speak to me then.'

I waited while she relayed the message, listening to a first-year rendition of *Greensleeves* scratch through two verses.

'Ai'm sorry, Miss Fox, but ai'm afraid Mr Ali is still unable to take your call,' the woman said when she came back on the line, and this time the sneer was all but evident in her voice. 'However, he has asked me to inform you that he has no "business dealings" with anyone of that name. If you'd like to arrange an appointment, then ai'd advise that you approach in writing. Goodbye.'

She'd put the receiver down before I had chance to say anything else, leaving me spluttering into an empty tele-phone. I hung up my end slowly, trying to work out exactly what this new development meant. Then I spent the rest of the day quietly simmering over Mr Ali's barefaced ability to lie.

By the time I got home later that evening, I was in the mood to give half an hour of serious pain to the punchbag in the corner of my living room.

As it turned out, I almost got an interesting substitute.

I saw the hunched figure waiting under a streetlight as I trundled down St George's Quay, and I kept a wary eye on him as I slowed to turn off the road. Even through the restriction of my helmet, I saw him drop and grind out his cigarette butt, moving forwards to meet me.

I couldn't fail to recognise Jav's peroxide hair, despite the shift from the sodium lights overhead. How the hell had he known where I lived? I toed the bike's side stand down and dismounted quickly, unsure of my reception from the boy. After all, the last time we'd met, Madeleine and I had been lightly crushing his chest with a barbell.

I needn't have worried, though. He paused a dozen or so feet away from me, waited until I'd dragged off my helmet and gloves before venturing any nearer. He watched me wheel the bike onto its patch of hard standing with narrow-eyed distrust.

It was only when he'd moved closer that I saw he didn't have a choice about the way he was looking at me.

'Nice black eye,' I said, by way of greeting, as I threaded the roller-chain through the Suzuki's back wheel and swinging arm.

He shrugged, wrapping his arms around his chest. He was wearing a thin jumper which did little to keep out the bitter chill that nightfall had brought with it, and he was shivering. For a moment we just faced each other in silence, but I was in no mood for games.

'Whatever it is, Jav,' I said shortly, shifting to unfold the cover over the Suzuki and not looking at him, 'it must be important that you've been hanging around here waiting for me, so why don't you just spit it out?'

'I might have some information for you,' he said at last, cagey.

'Yeah?' I said. 'Well, I'm not sure just how reliable your information is, Jav, if you know what I mean?'

He shrugged again, started to turn away. 'OK, lady, but you're the one who's been looking to get your hands on Langford. If you've changed your mind that's fine by—'

Before he'd finished I'd got his back slammed into the brickwork and a forearm across his throat. I pressed my face towards his. 'Do not,' I said, speaking slowly and clearly, 'mess me about, Jav. If you genuinely know where Langford is, then tell me now, otherwise get out of here before I do something you'll regret.'

He swallowed, which is not easy when someone's elbow is jammed up against your windpipe. 'OK, OK,' he managed. 'Ease up and I'll tell you.'

I released my grip and backed off a step. He rubbed at his neck. 'And I thought you'd be easier to tackle without that bloody dog,' he muttered.

'Friday's as dangerous as a stuffed pyjama case compared to me,' I said grimly. 'Now talk.'

'Langford,' he said. 'You want him. I know where to find him.'

'Where?'

He hesitated. 'Look, this didn't come from me, all right?'

I sighed, passed a hand across my eyes. 'Just tell me where he is, Jav.'

'OK, OK. You know that new industrial estate that's going up out near Heysham?'

A creeping sense of recognition came over me. 'The one Mr Ali's firm is building?'

'That's it,' he nodded, almost eager. 'He's camping out in there.' He saw my next question forming, and held his hands up. 'I don't know where, exactly, just that he's somewhere on the site.'

I paused for a moment, considering. I still didn't think I could trust Jav. It was a damned sight too convenient, for one thing, but I couldn't afford to ignore the tip-off, either. 'Why the handy hint, Jav? What's in it for you?'

'It's time the bastard got what's coming to him,' he said, touching a hand to his face and favouring me with a tight little smile.

He started to move away, turned back after a few paces. 'If you want to catch him, you'd better hurry,' he said. 'Rumour is that Langford's planning on doing a moonlight flit – *real* soon.'

Despite Jav's warning I took the stairs up to the flat slowly, lost in furious thought. Was he on the level this time, or was this just another set-up?

I unlocked the front door, flicked on the lights, and headed for the phone. I didn't hesitate over dialling Mrs Meyer's number, and asking for Sean.

As I waited for him to come on the line, I reflected that one thing was for certain. If this was for real, then I was going to need help I could rely on to confront Langford.

And if it was a trap, there was no-one I'd rather have covering my back than Sean.

Twenty-one

Sean picked me up twenty minutes later from outside the flat, in a dark metallic red Nissan Patrol that struck me as more of a truck than a car.

'I thought I'd better ditch the Cherokee after your warning,' he said when I commented on the change of vehicle. 'Madeleine's taken it — and Ursula — back down south. She'll swap it for one of the pool cars and be back tomorrow.'

After I'd called Sean I'd changed out of my leathers into black jeans and a dark fleece. He was dressed for night work, too. Neither of us mentioned that we were going on a jaunt that was probably going to include illegal breaking and entering, but it was there, all the same.

As we rolled along the quay and joined the flow of traffic on Cable Street I glanced round at the interior of the Patrol. There must be some money in close protection, I realised idly. It was just as plush as Sean's last motor, with dark grey leather upholstery throughout. And cavernous.

'I don't suppose I can use you as a taxi service the next time I go shopping, can I?' I said, only half joking.

'Why, are you looking to buy wholesale?' he said, and I caught the flash of his teeth.

'Well, you certainly don't have any trouble with carrying capacity in this,' I said, 'You should try shopping on the bike, when all you've got is a rucksack and a tank bag.'

As the words came out, something shifted inside my head, like turning the focusing rings on a pair of binoculars to bring a blurred image up pin sharp.

Carrying capacity.

Sean, concentrating on avoiding being cut up by a couple of young lads in a wildly-driven Vauxhall Nova, didn't spot the change that came over me straight away.

'What?' he demanded a moment later, but I couldn't immediately voice what had come into my mind. 'What is it?'

'He couldn't have moved him,' I blurted out, almost fearing that if I didn't say something quickly I'd lose my grip on the whole idea.

'What? Who couldn't? Charlie, you're not making any sense.'

I shook my head, trying to clear it. 'Roger,' I started again. 'Don't you see? The police have said that Nasir wasn't shot where he was dumped, so he had to've been carried there. If all Roger had was the bike, *he* couldn't have moved the body. Particularly not if Nasir wasn't even dead at the time. There's no way he could have done it.'

Sean didn't speak right away, and for a second I thought he hadn't followed my line of reasoning. It wasn't until I caught sight of his hands, gripping tight to the steering wheel until the knuckles stood out through the skin, that I understood.

'Don't get too excited.' I hated having to put a dampener on his hopes, but I had to do it. 'It doesn't mean Roger didn't shoot him,' I went on, but gently. 'It just means he wasn't alone when he did it.'

Sean unclenched his fingers slowly. His features were shaded so that there was no discernible difference between pupil and iris. His eyes just looked totally black. The single word that came out was thick with anger.

'Langford?'

I met his gaze without flinching, but couldn't give him the reassurance he was after. 'I don't know,' I said truthfully, 'it doesn't really fit, but somebody's trying very hard to point us in that direction.'

'Well,' Sean said, 'let's not disappoint them, shall we?'

We drove the rest of the way out to Heysham without further conversation. At my suggestion, Sean passed the open entrance to the site, and pulled into the same neglected industrial estate where I'd hidden the Suzuki on my previous visit.

Fortunately, whoever was occupying the units that weren't standing empty there didn't believe in working late. A quiet circuit of the place found no lights showing under the rollershutter doors of any of them.

He nosed the Patrol to a halt under the shadow of a building, and cut the engine. Without artificial lighting, the brightness of the full moon was revealed, bathing the concrete in silver splendour. For a moment we sat there in a heavy silence. Then Sean leaned over and flipped open the glovebox lid.

Inside was the Glock semiautomatic, with a spare clip tucked in behind it.

Sean picked the gun up, slipped the magazine out and checked it anyway, almost a ritual, although he must have known it was full and ready to go.

He slotted the mag back into the pistol grip, pushed it home with his palm, just as I'd done when I'd found the Glock under the seat of the Cherokee. But this time, he pinched back the slide. I heard the twin snap of the first round loading, and shivered.

Sean shoved the gun into the back of his belt, under his

jacket. The extra magazine went into his jacket pocket. He looked across at me.

'Don't worry, I'm not going to use this unless I have to, otherwise I'm definitely going to have the cops on my tail,' he said quietly, 'but if Jav's telling us the truth, and Langford *is* here, and he *is* behind all this, he could turn nasty when he's cornered. Are you ready for this?'

I shrugged, trying to act casual despite the adrenalin pulse. 'As I'll ever be,' I said, reaching for the door handle.

But as I made to get out Sean put his hand on my arm. 'I'm sorry you've been dragged into this, Charlie,' he said, 'but I'm glad you're here.'

I nodded, swallowed. 'You can thank me later,' I said, throwing him a quick, hard smile. 'Let's just get this done.'

Not surprisingly, perhaps, nobody had tidied up between the units since I'd last passed that way. The loose slats in the wooden fence were still hanging loosely by their rusty nail.

Once on the other side, the moon clearly highlighted the stretch of mud in front of us. I followed Sean across the expanse of it, slithering behind him while he picked his way without seeming to miss a step. It was a relief to get on to the compacted hard-core.

We carefully circled the Portakabins where Mr Ali had his site office, but each of them was secured with bolts and padlocks. There was no way Langford could be hiding out inside, unless he was content to be locked in every night when the site closed down.

We moved on.

Then Sean jogged my arm, and pointed to the partially-completed office building itself. At one corner of the top floor, we could make out the glow of a light.

We edged closer, hugging the shadows, acutely aware that our possible enemy had the advantage of superior elevation.

All the time, we kept one eye on the window above us, but there was no change in the light to suggest movement.

The building had a lot of glass which, in my opinion, was an open invitation to the local kids to throw stones. The windows made us feel vulnerable, as though we were under surveillance from every angle.

We had to search three sides of the block before we found a way in. There were fire doors on every side, but when I gave the handle of one an experimental tug, it pulled open without difficulty. Several layers of gaffer tape held the latch compressed. We moved through, easing the door quietly closed behind us.

Inside, the office block was a darkened tangle of unfinished pipework and dangling wires. Although the floors were in, it seemed that most of the internal walls had yet to be completed, and we skirted carefully round piles of thermalite blocks stacked up on yards of plastic sheeting. I wondered briefly if the wires were live, and how anybody managed to work in such a minefield.

There were two staircases leading to the upper floors, at opposite corners of the building. Sean nodded to the nearest one, and we made our way cautiously up it to the top.

The effort of keeping up with his quietly economical movements made sweat break out along my hairline. My mouth was as dry as my palms were damp. At that precise moment, if I'd had more faith in my own intuition, I would have turned and run. It was screaming at me.

The top floor was closer to completion than those below it, but not by much. It seemed that the centre of the office was going to be an open-plan layout on this level, with separate cubicles around the outside edges.

The building work had reached the stage where the side walls of the cubicles were up, but not the ends. The unfinished walls stuck out like breakwaters along a beach. We used the cover they provided to work our way closer towards the corner office until we could make out the reflected glow of a lamp bouncing off the tinted glass of the windows and the pale plasterboard ceiling.

Then Sean stopped abruptly, and I stiffened behind him as I heard the murmur of voices. It was only when a burst of music replaced them that I realised we were listening to a radio.

Sean caught my eye, and I read his meaning, wondering if he could hear my heartbeat. It was loud enough to be deafening me.

We reached the final wall that separated us from the last room. Sean paused for a moment, as if gathering himself, then we both stepped round it, into the light.

And froze.

Langford had made a comfortable nest for himself in that end office. A military surplus sleeping bag lay rumpled on a piece of camping foam against one wall. The lamp we'd seen, and the radio, were next to an overflowing ashtray on a paint-encrusted table to one side, together with a chipped mug that was striped down the outside with trails of old coffee.

To go with the table there was a single wooden chair, which was now lying on its side in the middle of the floor.

Langford's corpse was still tied to it.

We didn't bother checking for a pulse. It was difficult to see how anyone could have lost the amount of blood that was pooled around his fallen body and have survived the experience.

It spread outwards around the vigilante's torso, still liquid, but congealing so that it had the consistency of syrup. The smell of it turned my stomach. Langford's head rested in the lake of blood. It stained his temple and matted in his short hair. His nose and mouth were caked with it.

We didn't have to wonder how he'd died. The knife was still embedded in his chest, leaving only the camouflage-coloured plastic handle showing. The blade had been inserted somewhere between his sixth and seventh ribs on the left-hand side, slanted slightly upwards, and driven home with a vengeance.

Langford's eyes were open, rigid, frightened. Incredulous, even. He'd never thought it was going to happen. Hadn't believed that he was destined to die this way.

Sean crouched by the body and regarded it for a long time without any emotion showing.

'They were aiming for his heart,' he said at last. 'Looks like they missed.'

He was right. The wound was too low, or the angle was too shallow for that. Instead, Langford must have suffocated slowly as his lungs flooded with his own blood. It would not, I judged, have been an easy way to die.

The heart is a small organ, all things considered, barely five inches by three, and not easy to hit. Our weapons handling instructors had always advised us to pick another target, if we had the chance. Like the throat.

My own scar prickled in nervous sympathy. I stepped round the body on the pretence of examining the rest of his hide-away, but it was more so I didn't have to keep looking at the knife, and at the dead man's eyes.

I was careful to keep my feet out of the spilt blood. I noticed, with a detached eye for detail, that his hands had been bound behind him with wicked thin cord. He'd fought against the restraint, which had cut deep into the flesh of his wrists.

I was making a conscious effort to breathe through my mouth, so I didn't gag from the sickly stench of the blood. Instead, I could almost taste it, and I'm not sure which was worse.

I glanced away, took in the contents of the table instead, the coffee cup and the ashtray. It was only then that I noticed what was wrong about that cup. There was a wisp of steam still rising from it. I passed my fingers over the rim, felt the faint warmth, and then the implications started to roll in.

I turned to find that Sean had leaned over and touched the backs of his fingers to the dead man's cheek, almost a parody of affection. He stood up fast then, tense.

'Come on,' he said, 'we've got to get out of here – now!'

'The coffee's still warm,' I told him.

But Sean was already on the move. He turned back as he reached the far wall of the office, and nodded towards Langford. 'I know,' he said, grim. 'So's the body.'

We set off across the office floor with much less regard for stealth than we'd exercised on the way in. I reckon we made about one-third distance. Then the gloom of the interior shattered in a flare of light and deafening sound.

I heard the sound of the shot change abruptly as it swerved off one of the partially-completed walls. It must have hit part of the wooden framework, rather than the blocks.

I dropped instantly, diving behind the nearest pile of thermalite blocks and thankful of the solid cover. Sean, I saw, was already down, making a mockery of my reflex time. He'd been forced further away from me, and was only just sheltered by a low wall of plasterboard off-cuts. He was trying to ease a look over the top of them.

I kept my own head well down. It was getting to the stage where I'd had enough experience of being shot at to recognise the fact without needing visual confirmation.

Sean didn't even manage to get his head up to clear his eye-line before the second shot discharged. I don't know what it hit. One of the block walls to our right, by the sound of it, and sizzled off harmlessly into the darkness.

Breathing hard, Sean delicately tried to alter his position.

'Charlie,' he whispered, 'can you pinpoint him?'

I screwed round, keeping low, and peeped cautiously over

my protective stack of blocks, expecting the blaze and the thunder of another shot. None came. I glanced back to Sean, shook my head.

'Keep looking.'

I'd just time to cram my fingers into my ears before he risked another exposure. It helped stop them ringing as we were treated to a third deafening concussion.

The shooter was getting his eye in with practice. This time the bullet hit close to Sean's head, scouring across one of the sheets of plasterboard and disintegrating part of it into a puff of white chalk. He ducked back fast, swearing under his breath.

I blinked a few times, trying to clear my vision, but the four dazzling outward streaks of the muzzle flash in the low light seemed permanently burned across my eyes. I shut them, but it didn't help much.

'He's in the stairwell, I think,' I told Sean quietly.

'In that case,' he murmured, 'you'd better take this.'

I opened my eyes again to find the Glock was out in his hand, and he was offering it to me. Before I'd a chance to argue, he threw it across the gap that separated us. I caught it automatically, closed my hands round the pistol grip, and slipped my right index finger onto the trigger.

And, suddenly, I was back in the killing house on camp. Back inside the skin of the girl who'd trained to be a soldier. Back up against the system that hadn't wanted me there, didn't believe I had what it took to succeed. Back with the observers waiting for every hesitation, and mistake.

I swung my arms over the top of the blocks, holding the gun straight out in front of me, and snapped off two quick shots in the direction of the stairwell.

I dropped back into cover almost, it seemed, before the empty shell cases had finished bouncing onto the chipboard.

As my ears cleared, I thought I heard movement, the clatter of feet, but by the time my hearing had recovered enough to be sure, the noise had faded. I glanced across at Sean, still keeping low.

'D'you think he's still there?' I whispered.

'I don't know.' He slithered round again, grabbed a piece of plasterboard in front of him and rattled it enticingly, but there was no further response. 'I think you might have scared him off.'

'I damned well hope so,' I said, shaky. 'It would have been enough to scare me.'

I left my protective stack of blocks reluctantly, tiptoed round the obstacles between me and the stairwell, keeping the gun up and ready. Nobody shot at me on the way there. I rushed the last few metres, hit the wall and waited a beat, listening, before I swung my body round it, breathing hard.

The stairwell was empty.

I crossed to the window, stared down through the glass at the unfinished site below. At first there was no sign of anyone running away, then I caught a silvered flash of movement, right over by the road. It was brief, disappearing quickly behind one of the earth movers, but it had to be our man.

As I watched, I realised that the very character of the moonlight was changing, from silver to blue.

Flashing blue.

Oh shit.

I spun round, to find Sean at the doorway behind me. 'Come on!' I shouted. I was compensating for the ringing in my ears, speaking too loudly. I lowered the volume and went on. 'It's the police – we've got to get out of here, right now!'

I was on the first step before I realised Sean wasn't hard on my heels. That he was still in the doorway, leaning against the wall. I stopped, and found myself invaded by a swift, stark fear.

Shoving the Glock into my pocket, I moved back to him. He started forwards then, belatedly, but as he reached the top of the stairs, he staggered, and almost fell.

I grabbed him on reflex, recoiling as my hands came away slick with blood.

'Christ! Where are you hit?' I flipped him round, braced him against the handrail, and yanked open his coat with numbed fingers.

'Left shoulder,' he muttered through gritted teeth. 'That first one ricocheted and got me. Don't worry. It's not bad.'

Not bad. Oh God . . .

His words seemed to convince himself as much as me. He went first down the stairs, moving faster than I'd feared he might. I kept a wary eye on his back as we stumbled across the lower floor, and burst out through the fire door.

The moon, which had proved so useful to light our way into the site, now seemed like a curse. We had to take the long way back towards the gap in the fence, moving from one piece of cover to the next, in bursts. As we ducked behind a big Cat digger I could just see the pair of squad cars that had pulled up close by the entrance. The lights flashed in and out of sync as the patrolmen talked together in undertones.

We waited, tense, until they'd picked up torches and moved in towards the office building drawn, as we'd been, by the light in the top corner. I tried to remember if we'd shut the fire door as we came through it, but my recall failed me.

'We haven't got long before they find him,' I muttered.

Sean was pale as death. He swayed, eyes closed, and I pushed him back against the digger's panelwork with the flat of my hand, fighting down the sudden flare of panic.

'Sean!' I said roughly. 'Stay with me, sergeant!'

His eyes opened slowly. For a moment he looked at me without seeing me, only bringing himself back on track with a visible effort. 'Giving me orders now are you, private?'

'You better believe it,' I bit out. 'Can you make it to the truck?'

He nodded briefly and, with a last check to make sure the cops had their attention focused firmly on the building, we set off again.

Once we were on the mud, the going proved harder. Where Sean had seemed so nimble before, now he moved heavy and slow. It seemed to take forever to cross the last few metres. My back had never felt so exposed.

The gap in the fence had shrunk since we came in, and getting through it to where the Nissan waited was a painful struggle. I had to loop Sean's arm over my shoulder and half-drag, half-carry him the rest of the way.

As we reached the Patrol, Sean dug in his pockets and handed me the keys. 'You'll have to drive,' he said tiredly.

I took them without argument. After all, we had enough of a job to heave Sean up into the passenger seat. There was no way he could have got behind the wheel.

Once I'd hauled myself into the driver's side, I had to stop for a moment to catch my breath. I found I was almost sobbing for air and my hands were shaking. I could hardly see for the sweat running into my eyes.

Something hard was digging into my hip, and I yanked the Glock out of my pocket, staring at it stupidly, as though seeing it for the first time. I shook my head, trying to clear the fog that seemed to have settled down over my brain.

Come on, come on! Get with the programme, Fox!

I twisted the key in the ignition, dumped the handbrake, and selected reverse on the auto gearbox. I'd forgotten to cover the brake as I did so, and the Patrol jerked backwards as the transmission engaged. I nearly put the damn thing into the wall of one of the units, and by the look of the construction, the building would have come off worse.

Sean moaned at the rough movement, but I had little time for finesse.

Finally, I managed to get myself together enough to switch

on the headlights and roll out of the estate. Christ, I hadn't driven anything with four wheels since I'd left the army. At least the Patrol had a bit more sophistication than the old Land Rovers I'd been in then.

I tried hard to make our departure look casual. I made sure I turned the opposite way to the site when I came out of the industrial estate, trundled off down the narrow lane as though this was a perfectly normal occurrence, that I had every right to be there.

All the time I was straining to hear the first wail of the sirens.

I glanced at the Glock, which lay where I'd dropped it on the dashboard, grabbed it and stuffed it quickly into my door pocket. The last thing I wanted now was to be caught fleeing the scene of a murder, with a wounded fugitive, and a smoking gun. . .

I drove without a clear destination in mind, just knowing that I needed to put distance between us and Langford's body. I had to concentrate hard on keeping the Patrol positioned on the narrow road. From the high driving seat, the vehicle seemed fantastically wide.

I glanced across at Sean. He'd slumped sideways with his head resting on the window, and his eyes were closed again. I wanted to check him over there and then, find out how bad the wound was.

Eventually, when I'd driven for ten minutes or so, my nerve failed me. I spotted a gateway and nudged the Patrol into it. Sean's eyes fluttered open as he felt us come to a stop.

I groped around until I found the interior light, flicked it on, and twisted in my seat to face him. It took an effort to keep my hands steady as I opened his coat, following the liquid trail, and ripped his shirt up the side seam.

Underneath, swimming in blood, the bullet had left a puckered entry hole in the skin just below the point of his left shoulder. Bright and raging, it seemed so small to be the cause of so much oozing fluid.

I tilted him forwards gently, lifted the shirt at the back, running my hands tentatively over his goosebumped skin. I was feeling for the exploded exit, but couldn't find it. I'd been hoping for a flesh wound, but the bullet was still in there.

I pulled my fleece off over my head, dragged the T-shirt I had on underneath out of my jeans and yanked that off, too. Sean wasn't in any state to admire my underwear, and I didn't give him much chance to, quickly shrugging my way back into the fleece. I used the T-shirt to wad against his shoulder, trying to stem the flow with fingers that felt abruptly fat and clumsy.

'You never could keep your hands off me, Charlie,' Sean said, his voice blurred. He tried a laugh, but something went wrong on the way out and it became no more than a gasp. He was staring at me without focus again, his exhaustion total, and I realised how much it had taken out of him to stay operational until now.

Operational. Jesus, the people who trained me would have been proud that I fell back instinctively on their evasive terminology. Operational. It meant alive and conscious. Sean becoming non-operational, on the other hand, was something I didn't want to think about right now.

I leaned him back into his seat. 'Sean, listen to me.' I was mildly surprised to find my voice came out relatively calm and clear. 'The round's still there, and I don't know where it is. I have to get you to a hospital.'

'No!' His response was stark, immediate. 'No hospitals,' he reiterated, struggling to get the words out. Struggling harder not to plead with me. 'When they've found that blood bath back there, the first place they'll come looking for us is the local hospitals. You know what'll happen then, don't you, Charlie?'

I tried hard not to let him get to me. 'You can't help your brother if you're dead,' I told him brutally.

He managed a weak half-smile that looked as though it was ripped out of him by something with claws. 'I can't help him if I'm in a prison cell, either.'

I said nothing for a few moments, not meeting his eyes, then let go of his coat and sat back in my seat, annoyed. With Sean. With myself. It was as though he was deliberately trying to kill himself and it was eating away at me to have to watch him do it.

'Dammit, Sean, you need a doctor,' I said at last, my voice low with anger.

'If you can find me one, Charlie, who won't go running to the police, I'll see him,' he said, and I knew by the stubborn set of his mouth there wasn't going to be any shifting him on this one.

'It's all going to be academic if we don't stop you bleeding,' I threw at him, wanting to hurt him as much as he was hurting me. 'I could always just let you pass out, and then cart you off to the nearest A&E anyway.'

I saw the flinch he tried not to let show, and my temper deflated like a slow-punctured tyre.

I sighed. 'OK, OK, we'll deal with this,' I said. 'But first, we've got to get you some place safe. Some place out of the way, where the police aren't going to find us.'

Twenty-two

I took Sean to Jacob and Clare's. Under pressure, it was the only place I could think of that was secluded enough to hide him.

Besides, Jacob's work means he has a tendency to be highly security conscious. As well as a sophisticated alarm system, a couple of sensors hidden on the driveway link direct to a buzzer in the house. At least we would have fair warning of unexpected visitors.

When I rumbled the Patrol to a jerky standstill on their moss-covered forecourt, the whole place looked dark and quiet, lying as it did under the shadow of the trees, but I knew Jacob would be watching the strange vehicle warily from somewhere. I cut the engine, suddenly aware of a fatigue so overwhelming it made me want to weep. I twisted in my seat.

'Sean?'

For a moment there was silence and all manner of nasty scenarios slithered past my eyes, but then I heard the quiet rustle of clothing as he moved.

'Yeah.' His voice was clogged and raspy. 'I'm still with it.'

I climbed out and, once they'd seen my face, both Jacob and Clare came hurrying out of the front door. The orange glow of the hall light flooded out after them, and threw elongated shadows onto the stone sets.

'My God, Charlie, what the hell's happened?' Jacob demanded, limping forwards as I yanked the passenger door open and Sean's bloodied figure all but fell out into my arms.

'He's been shot and he needs help,' I said bluntly, staggering under the weight. I caught their instant withdrawal, their hesitation, and swung to face them.

'I know I'm pushing my luck coming here, but I didn't know where else to take him,' I said, speaking fast and low. 'If you want me to go, tell me now, but make your minds up quick, before he bleeds to death.'

That broke them out of it. Jacob came forwards to help me then. If he hadn't, I never would have got Sean into the house.

Clare went ahead, fluttering anxiously, holding doors open for us and shooing the dogs out of the way. They were taking far too much interest in the state of the new arrival for my liking.

By general consensus, we put him in the kitchen, where at least the blood he was losing could be mopped off the flagged floor. We propped him gently against the kitchen table and Jacob supported him there while I carefully peeled his coat away from the wound.

Underneath it, my makeshift dressing was drenched scarlet. In the strong light it seemed that the front half of his jacket was stained wet with it. It scared me, the amount he was losing. He couldn't hope to sustain it.

I took one look at Jacob's troubled face, and realised he knew it, too.

I clenched my teeth with the effort it took not to cry. *You are not going to die on me, Sean . . .*

Clare came bustling in then with a big First Aid kit. We broke the seal and found decent-sized sterile dressings inside. I'm not sure they were much more effective than my T-shirt, but at least they looked the part.

Jacob moved away, filled the kettle and shoved it to boil on top of the Aga. Clare had gone again, reappearing with a bundle of ragged towels. 'They're only old,' she said, pale but determined, 'but they've been washed.'

I nodded gratefully to her, suddenly fiercely proud of my friends. The way they'd taken us in without asking awkward questions. Like who was this guy? And why would anyone want to be shooting at him?

All the time I kept up pressure on the site of the wound, leaning into him, the only way to curb the bleeding. It finally seemed to be slowing up, and at least it gave me the excuse to watch him for a few moments.

Even through the pain and the anger, the times when I'd hated Sean as violently as I'd loved him, I'd never forgotten the beauty of him.

'Sean.' His eyes flickered open at my soft call. There were grim circles round them, shadows etched in deep. 'We need to get to that wound, clean it up,' I said. 'Are you up to this?'

He nodded once, and eased himself upright. I helped him with the coat, but left as much of his tattered shirt in place as I could. Despite the warmth of the kitchen, he still felt chilled.

'Get him onto the table,' Jacob suggested.

We laid him down flat then, bunching the coat under his head. Clare unfolded some of the towels and laid them over Sean's torso and legs, trying to keep him warm.

Once the kettle had begun to hum, we ferried hot water in bowls to mop the worst of the blood away. He could still move his fingers, but the front of his shoulder had started to swell, and he didn't seem to be able to lift his arm much.

At length, I stepped back. 'It's no good, Sean,' I said, dropping another ruined towel into the bowl at my feet. 'That bullet's going to have to come out, and the sooner the better.'

He lifted his head cautiously, body tight with the pain, but his voice seemed detached. 'Then you'll have to do it,' he said.

'You're joking!' I snapped. 'What? Douse you down with whisky and go rooting about in there with a knife and fork? What happened? You in a hurry to die now, soldier?'

He let his head drop back. 'What other option is there?' he asked, sounding unbearably tired.

'Let me make a phone call,' I said, throwing a glance as much to Jacob for his permission as to Sean. 'Then we'll see.'

When neither man made any dissent, I moved over to the phone and dialled a number that I didn't have to look up. While the line rang out at the other end I tried not to pray for the right person to answer. He did.

I didn't bother with much of a preliminary, and didn't mention any names, just gave him the bald facts. I asked for his help. It wasn't easy, but I'd been driven that far before and had come out lucky.

There was what seemed like a long period of silence on the other end of the line. A careful and measured consideration. Not of the possibilities of treating the patient, but of the morality of helping me at all. And all the time I stood there watching Sean across the other side of my friends' kitchen, and fighting the misery.

'Look,' I said at length, turning away and trying to keep the suppressed rage out of my voice. 'If you're not prepared to come and do this yourself, at least tell me what to expect when I go in there, because one way or another, that bullet's got to come out of him tonight.' I took a shaky breath, then added, 'I just think he'll have a better chance of surviving if you do it.'

'All right, Charlotte,' said my father, 'I'll come. Keep him warm. Keep him awake if you can, and keep trying to control the bleeding. I'll need some things, but I should be with you in less than two hours.'

I gave him directions, started to thank him, but I was already speaking into a dead line.

267

I turned back to Sean as I put the receiver back on its cradle. 'Help's on the way. Just you keep breathing until it gets here or my name's going to be lower than shit.'

It was not much of a joke and, correspondingly, it raised not much of a smile, but under the circumstances it was the best any of us could muster.

'Thank you, Charlie,' Sean said quietly.

I swallowed. I couldn't cope with him when he was being anything other than a cold and clinical bastard. 'Don't thank me,' I said bluntly. 'We're nowhere *near* out of this yet.'

Even though we were expecting it, the squawk of the drive alarm made me jump. I looked at my watch, and saw that it was precisely an hour and forty minutes since my phone call. Nevertheless, Clare quickly drew the kitchen curtains and we waited, tensed like deer, while Jacob went to the door.

When he returned a few moments later, my father was behind him.

My father strode immediately to his patient, only pausing to favour me with one brief reproving glance as he came in. He was dressed as though for a Sunday lunchtime stroll to the village pub, in dark green corduroy trousers and a wool check shirt.

Only the stiff tan leather bag didn't quite fit. The case he'd always carried, first as a doctor, then as a surgeon, for more than thirty years. When he put that down on one of the kitchen chairs it landed with a solid thump that was unnerving.

He unfolded a pair of expensive gold-framed glasses from his inside jacket pocket, and pulled on latex gloves, moving with a deceptively slow kind of haste. As though he was aware that an outright rush would have caused panic.

'What's his name?' he asked quietly as he slotted a stethoscope round his neck and pulled an inflatable cuff out of his bag.

'Sean,' I said.

For a moment he frowned, then the memory and the realisation hit almost at the same time, flashing over like a sparking match.

He shot a quick glance at Sean's supine figure, but this time it wasn't the concerned gaze of doctor to patient, but something darker, and more impenetrable. He waited until the flame had flared and died before trusting himself to speak again.

'All right, Sean,' he said, more loudly, 'I'm just going to check your blood pressure.' By the time he'd done so, he was frowning again. For a moment the only sound in the room was the hiss of air escaping from the cuff as he deflated it.

'How is it?' I demanded, recognising the twin dents between his eyebrows as he peeled the stethoscope out of his ears.

'Only a little low, all things considered, but he's young and fit, and they're the worst,' my father said, speaking over the top of Sean like he'd suddenly gone deaf. 'They maintain pressure on you right up to the point where they crash, and then they can go in seconds.'

He glanced around at the bloodied towels. 'You seem to have done a fair job of stopping the bleeding, but I'd like to get some fluids into him, just to be on the safe side, I think.'

He moved me aside almost with impatience and, having been relieved of my immediate responsibility, I felt the energy and the strength slowly seep out of me. I leaned numbly against the nearest wall, limbs heavy, so that it was Clare who ended up holding Sean's hand as my father slipped the cannula into his distended vein and taped it down.

He plugged a bag of clear liquid into the line and suspended it from the Welsh dresser to one side, seemingly unfazed by the need to improvise.

'What are you giving him?' I asked.

He flicked me a brief glance. 'Hartmann's solution,' he said shortly. 'Something to keep his blood vessels inflated and his pressure up.'

I dredged my memory. 'Saline? Don't you think he needs something more than that?'

'It's a little better than straight saline, and I'm afraid I didn't have the time or the access to whole blood, even if I'd had a match for him,' he said, irritated. 'This will do quite well, Charlotte. Don't interfere.'

I opened my mouth, then shut it again. He was already pulling out more bottles from the magic bag, moving neatly, with precision. He used the cannula to deliver morphine, and plenty of it, although with an almost cheerful warning that even with an anti-emetic added it would probably make Sean vomit.

Even so, I watched the kinks flatten out of Sean's spine as the opiate hit his bloodstream, releasing the pressure, gliding him down.

'All right, young man, now let's have a look at you,' my father said as he bent over the wound, his voice cool as though this sort of thing happened all the time.

He lifted the dressing and inspected the front of Sean's shoulder for a few moments, gently manipulating the skin around the entry site. Although his hands moved quietly, their touch sure and delicate like a concert pianist, Sean grimaced, trying not to wince.

My father gave him a hard stare over the top of his glasses. 'This is not a trial by ordeal,' he said, his tone vaguely acerbic. 'I'm sure it's all very heroic to stay so silent in the face of what must be considerable discomfort, but if you don't tell me where the pain is greatest, I'm not going to learn where that bullet lies. I'm not a vet who can work by grunts and squeaks alone. Do you understand me?'

'Yes sir,' Sean said, his face bone-white.

He resumed his inspection, but only briefly. 'All right, I think I've found it. It's sitting in the belly of the deltoid muscle, not too deep.'

He glanced at Jacob and Clare. 'Normally, I'd prefer to do an exploratory under a general anaesthetic,' he said, adding with grim humour, 'I don't suppose either of you two happens to be a trained anaesthetist, by any chance? No, ah well, I had to ask.'

Instead, he injected lignocaine close to the wound and we waited a few minutes for the local anaesthetic to take effect. It was like being at the dentist, being sent out into the waiting room to read old copies of the *Reader's Digest* until your mouth has gone numb enough not to notice the drill.

While we were waiting he dug into the bag again and laid out more equipment in a precise line on a piece of sterile cloth. A pack of forceps, stainless steel kidney-shaped dishes, black suture, and thin curved needles, like the unsheathed claws of a small but lethal cat.

'The adrenalin with the anaesthetic should help to stop the bleeding when I've completed the extraction,' my father said to Jacob, nodding to his array of tools, 'but you'll need to be ready with that swab anyway, just in case.'

He seemed to be ignoring me. I doubt I would have been much use as a scrub nurse, anyway. I didn't want to watch as he pulled back the skin round the entry site and slid the tips of the forceps into the wound, but I found I couldn't tear my eyes away. It seemed so barbaric.

Even Sean turned his head, preferring to stare into Clare's fearful face as she sat on the other side of the table, still clutching his fingers. The knuckles of both their entwined hands had turned white.

The look of concentration on my father's face as he probed the wound was profound. The time ticked by, but he refused to be hurried, making absolutely sure he had a firm grip on

271

the bullet before he attempted to withdraw it along the same track it had followed on the way in.

When the squat, misshapen round finally emerged in a fresh welter of blood, he dropped it with a clang into the waiting dish that Jacob held out for him. The five of us let out our breath in a collective gush at its successful delivery.

My father dealt with the cleaning out and closing up process with an efficiency born of long practice, leaving a neat line of stitches as the only evidence of his invasion. Then he stood back and nodded once, as if pleased with his own handiwork.

While he taped a dressing in place over the stitches I picked the bloodied bullet out of the dish and turned it round in my fingers. The copper outer jacket of the slug had compressed to less than half its original length, mushrooming slightly. It was deformed from the initial contact with whatever had deflected its path, sent it spinning into Sean's body.

I glanced up, found Sean watching me, and held the bullet up so he could see it. 'It's a nine millimetre,' I said, and the significance of that wasn't lost on him.

It rang no bells with my father, though. He unhooked the now-empty bag of saline and withdrew the cannula. 'Perhaps there's somewhere a little more comfortable where we can move the patient to rest?' he asked Jacob.

Jacob suggested the living room, where there was a fire burning and the sofa was large enough to sleep on. Clare jumped up again and went in search of spare pillows and bedding. Between the rest of us we managed to get Sean on his feet and half-walk, half-carry him the short distance to the living room.

'He's had enough morphine to keep him quiet tonight,' my father said, 'but you'll need to watch him fairly carefully. I'd like to think I've cleaned the wound out completely, but there's always the chance that any clothing debris pulled into it will lead to infection. I'll leave you a course of antibiotics, but if he starts showing any signs, you're going to have to get him to a hospital, whatever the consequences. Do you understand me?'

It was my turn to say, stiffly, 'Yes sir.'

Clare offered to sit with Sean for a while and Jacob, recognising that there were things that needed to be said, went to keep her company, quietly closing the door behind him.

My father moved back through to the kitchen, peeling off his gloves as he went. When I followed he was scrubbing his hands thoroughly at the butler's sink. I watched him without speaking until he was done.

'So, Charlotte, are you going to tell me what happened?' he said carefully then, wiping his hands on a towel with vigorous efficiency.

'It's a long story,' I said wearily.

There was a pause as he waited for me to continue. I didn't.

He turned. 'Did *you* shoot him?'

I couldn't work out if I should be flattered or affronted by the question. 'If I had done, he'd be dead,' I said, matter of fact, without bravado. 'No, I didn't shoot him.'

He raised a dubious eyebrow at that. 'Really? I would have thought Sean Meyer was a prime candidate for it.'

'Why?'

He made an impatient gesture. 'He ruined you, Charlotte, in more ways than one,' he said. It should have sounded ridiculously old-fashioned, but from him somehow it didn't. What did surprise me was the vehemence in his tone.

'I never knew you cared,' I said lightly.

His face tightened at that, the only outward display. 'Of course we cared – and still care – about you. Your mother and I had to stand by and watch you go through the torments of hell twice over because of that man.'

'I knew having a fling with Sean when he was my instructor was against the rules, and it was stupid, with hindsight, but it was my choice,' I argued. 'But it wasn't his fault that I was attacked. He wasn't even on camp when it happened.'

'Has it never occurred to you that perhaps the very reason you were singled out as a victim by the men who raped you,' my father demanded now, 'was because they found out about your relationship with Meyer?'

I tried not to flinch. He may have seen it anyway, because his voice softened slightly. 'I know you weren't allowed to say much about it, but you were doing well at your course, weren't you? Better than most of the men you were training alongside, as I recall.'

'The marks I scored were on my own merits,' I said, suddenly defensive. Sean had been famously tough as an instructor, and not just on me. They said that if he didn't lose a few trainees from every intake on medical grounds, he was a disappointed man.

He had seemed to know instinctively where everyone's own personal breaking point lay, just so he could drive you up to and beyond it.

'I'm not suggesting for a moment that you received any sort of preferential treatment,' my father commented. He folded the towel neatly, put it on the draining board. 'But what better salve to their wounded egos than to imagine that it wasn't talent drawing you ahead, but good old-fashioned sex? And what better way for them to reassert their male superiority than the somewhat violent method they chose?'

I shook my head. 'Sean didn't betray me,' I said, 'but then, you already knew that, didn't you?'

He'd been gathering the soiled equipment he'd used, stowing it into his bag, and his momentary stillness told me what I needed to know. The last vital piece of the jigsaw dropped into place, and the picture suddenly became painfully, blindingly clear.

'After I was — after it happened,' I said, annoyed at the way I faltered, 'it was my mother who rang camp asking for Sean, wasn't it? Who else would have wanted to accuse him of letting harm come to me, of not standing up for me at the court martial? But he'd been posted before any of it happened and he didn't know.'

I met his eyes steadily, and pressed on. 'Whoever she spoke to put two and two together. It was only afterwards that she must have realised what she'd done, when they paraded the information at the civil trial. That's why she didn't support my appeal, isn't it? In case it all came out that she'd been disloyal to her own daughter.'

It was a long speech, and it was greeted by a wary silence. My father sank down onto the kitchen chair next to him, suddenly looking every year of his age, defeated.

He sighed, heavily, before he went on. 'Yes,' he said quietly, 'I know. She went through hell wanting to confess, but your relationship was so bad by that time that she didn't see it would help. I persuaded her not to tell you.' He looked up at me, as though resigned to accusations, and bitter rhetoric. 'What do you propose to do now, Charlotte?'

I shrugged. 'Nothing,' I said, tired myself, like we'd been physically sparring. 'What would it solve? It wouldn't make me feel any better to confront her now, and it certainly wouldn't do her any good. What's the point?'

He nodded a little at that, turning it over in his mind. 'But it doesn't explain why Meyer didn't come forwards and speak up for you afterwards. At the time you felt that the amount of detail exposed could only have come from him. That pressure had been brought to bear from a higher authority and he'd capitulated in order to preserve his own career.'

'It wouldn't have been so difficult for them to piece it

together, not once they knew what they were looking for,' I said. 'Besides, like I said, they posted him. Sean didn't know what happened to me, nobody saw fit to tell him, and he still doesn't know.' I pinned my father with the same kind of hard stare he so often used himself, keeping my chin up. 'I want to keep it that way.'

'Why?' There was no anger in the question, only curiosity.

'For the same reason I won't say anything to my mother,' I said, my voice neutral. 'It wouldn't do anyone any good now to open up old wounds. They didn't give Sean an easy time of it afterwards, either, and for a while he blamed me for that without knowing why. I think I'm beginning to earn his respect again. I don't want that to change to pity.'

My father nodded again. 'That's very – noble – of you,' he said. He stood, straightened up, and the authority he'd always carried was back, and the arrogance.

He snapped the catches shut on his bag, lifted it, and moved towards the door. 'I know you think we've treated you poorly over this, Charlotte,' he said, with the faintest trace of a smile playing round his mouth, 'but looking at the way you've turned out your mother and I must have done something right, somewhere along the line while you were growing up, don't you think?'

Twenty-three

I took over watching duty from Jacob and Clare at around two the following morning, and they went gratefully upstairs to bed. I wasn't bargaining on getting much sleep myself, too aware of every unconscious shift and murmur that Sean made.

At least, as my father had said, he'd had enough morphine to allow him to get some rest. He seemed so much younger when he was asleep, so much more vulnerable. I never thought I'd see him with his guard down so completely.

I sat in one of the armchairs to one side of the fireplace and watched him with my chin resting on my hand. The fire was warm, the crackle and dance of the flames soothing.

Eventually, they got to me.

The next thing I knew Clare was gently shaking my shoulder. Weak grey daylight was trickling in through the open curtains, and there was the splattery drum of rain against the outside of the glass. She offered coffee in a whisper.

I nodded thankfully, trying to roll the crick out of my neck and, with a last glance at Sean's sleeping form, I followed her through to the kitchen. He didn't seem to have moved an inch since last night. I'd no worries that he was suddenly going to go walkabout now.

'I checked him before I woke you,' Clare said as she bustled round the kitchen. 'He doesn't seem feverish or anything.' She plonked a freshly-brewed mug of strong coffee in front of me at the table.

'Is Jacob still asleep?'

'Oh yes.' She smiled. 'He does late nights, and he does early mornings, but not both together. I thought I'd better give him a bit longer to come round or he'll be grouchy all day.'

'Clare, I'm very grateful to you, you know – to both of you,' I said awkwardly, in a rush, 'for all you did last night. I had no right to ask you, really. Especially not after—'

'Don't worry about it,' she said, cutting me off as she slid into a seat opposite. She flashed a quick grin. 'Tell me everything that's going on and I'll consider it a debt paid.'

I told her as much as I could, about Jav's tip-off, our visit to the building site, and stumbling over Langford's body. She made shocked exclamations of surprise, and then demanded answers I just didn't have about who was responsible, and why.

I gave her the bare bones of our escape, too, aware again of just how big a chance I'd taken, what a difficult position I'd put my friends into, by bringing Sean here.

Clare digested the information in silence for a moment, then said, 'Is Sean the one who hurt you? I mean, you've never said, but somehow I always knew there must have been someone.'

I was taken aback by the question, but tried not to show it. 'Yes, well no, but he was all part of it.' I shrugged. 'Sort of. It's a long story.'

Clare nodded and sipped her coffee. 'I could tell there was something when you brought him in here last night. I mean, I know more than anyone how far out on a limb you'll go for your friends, Charlie. If it wasn't for you, I'd be dead,' she said, and her face was grave. 'But this was something more. You had this air of—' She flapped a hand while she searched for the right words. 'Controlled panic. That's the closest I can get to describing it. Are you still in love with him?'

Her eyes slid away over my shoulder and I thought she'd embarrassed herself with the question. Then I caught the suggestion of a movement behind me. When I turned it was to find Sean in the kitchen doorway, leaning heavily on the frame.

He was still wearing last night's jeans which had dried blood sheening the left thigh, but no shirt. The square of white dressing was still taped efficiently to his shoulder. I skimmed my eyes over him as he came further into the room. He was holding himself awkwardly and was still pale, but his eyes were clear, and his gait was steady.

Clare jumped up, a faint flush lighting her cheekbones and the tips of her ears. 'I'll make fresh coffee,' she muttered.

Sean treated her to one of his brighter smiles. 'I didn't have a chance to thank you last night,' he said, 'for offering me sanctuary.'

I suppressed a grumpy sigh as I formally introduced them. Sean clasped her proffered hand with enough deliberation to refresh the blush that was still lingering round Clare's features. I took one look and knew she was smitten.

She hurriedly refilled the polished copper kettle on the top of the Aga and then, mumbling something about seeing if Jacob was up, she all but ran out of the room. The pair of us were left alone together in a silence that was deafening.

Sean eased himself into the chair my friend had just vacated. 'So, Charlie,' he said quietly, 'are you?'

'Am I what?'

'Still in love with me?' It was said lightly, without a hint of conceit. I saw the curve of his lips and for a moment I was tempted not to treat the question seriously, but then I took in the clenched fingers and decided against levity.

I rubbed a hand across my eyes. They felt full of grit. I was bone tired and my brain was functioning strictly on the lower levels. This was just not the time to trawl through ancient history.

Briefly, I leaned my face down towards the table top, resting my chin on my fist while I considered. 'No, I don't think so,' I said at last, seriously. 'What we had was a long time ago, Sean.' I raised my head to meet his eyes. 'Whether you intended to or not, you hurt me more than I ever could have imagined.'

As he started to speak I cut him off, keeping my voice admirably level. 'But, I got over it, I moved on. We're neither of us the same people we were then. It would be a mistake to try and go back.'

'So why the "controlled panic" last night?'

I scowled. 'Were you eavesdropping on the *whole* conversation?'

That killer smile again. 'No, just the important bits,' he said. 'Now answer the question.'

I pushed back my chair and got to my feet, suddenly too restless to sit. 'Because I've had someone die in my arms before and I didn't like it much,' I said brutally, turning back just so I could watch his face. 'Certainly not enough to want to repeat the experience if I could do a damn thing to prevent it.'

I was saved from having to elaborate much on that theme by the arrival of a bleary-eyed Jacob. He limped in, seemingly unaware of the combative silence between us.

The dogs were jostling round his ankles. Jacob didn't say a word until he'd fed them, made a fresh pot of coffee, and had taken his first mouthful. Then he sat back and studied us with far more alert attention. 'Ah, that's better,' he said. He nodded to Sean. 'How's the shoulder this morning?'

'Stiff and sore,' Sean said easily, 'but I'll live.'

'Muscle damage is nastier than broken bones, in my opinion,' Jacob said, adding with a rueful smile, 'I've had enough of both in my time to know.'

'I was lucky.'

Jacob treated me to one of his arresting smiles. 'Hm, she's a useful lady to know, is our Charlie.'

'So,' I broke in, trying not to squirm, 'where do we go from here?'

'Well, for a start I don't think it would be a good idea for Sean here to go anywhere for a day or two,' Jacob said straight away, pouring coffee into our mugs. 'You're welcome to stay here, lad, keep your head down, pick up a bit of strength.'

Sean looked taken aback by this unexpected hospitality. 'That's very decent of you,' he said.

Jacob waved away his thanks as he pushed the milk and sugar bowl towards us. 'It gives us a bit of time to try and work out what the hell's going on,' he said briskly. 'Clare's just filled me in on the details. Any ideas who might have wanted to put the knife into Harvey Langford – speaking literally *and* figuratively?'

'How long have you got?' I said, 'I'll make a list.'

Jacob grinned at me, and I went on, more seriously, 'Whoever killed him didn't just want Langford out of the way, though, they wanted us dead, too.'

Sean shook his head at that. 'I don't think so,' he said, 'In fact, the more I think about it, the more I realise they just wanted to keep us pinned down for long enough for the police to arrive.'

He shifted awkwardly in his seat, caught his breath, and waited for the biting pain to subside before he continued.

'I think finding that we were capable of shooting back at them put them off their stroke, ruined the plan. If our friendly shooter had wanted us dead he had more than enough chance to ambush us while we were inspecting the body. Anybody halfway competent could have slotted the pair of us while we were helpfully hanging around against the light. They wouldn't have waited until we were moving across that floor in the dark.'

The terrier, Beezer, finished wolfing down her food, trotted across the kitchen and jumped on Jacob's lap to see if there was anything interesting for dessert at table height. Jacob fondled her moth-eaten ears absently. 'Surely you don't think he was killed just as a means of getting the pair of you arrested? That seems a bit drastic.'

'Not necessarily,' Sean told him. 'After all, they've already made one attempt on Charlie's life, and the police have been tipped off that I was involved in Nasir's death. From their point of view, neither of those efforts have worked too well.'

'So,' I said, 'was Langford a victim, or just a pawn in somebody's game?'

Sean shrugged, raising just his right shoulder, and reached for his coffee. 'Search me. That day on Copthorne he offered to bring you information about who's behind the crimewave on the estates, didn't he? Next thing we know, he's dead. What does that tell you?'

It was my turn to shrug, helplessly. 'I don't know. Maybe we should be asking Mr Ali what he was doing letting Langford hide out on his site, and what exactly he was paying him to do. After all, Ali must have known he was there.'

Clare walked in just as I was speaking. 'Is that Mr Ali the builder?' she asked, looking surprised. 'You remember I told you he owns great chunks of Copthorne and Lavender? Apparently there are big discussions going about redeveloping the whole of that area. Lots of Euro money up for grabs and lottery funding, according to the people at work. If it all goes ahead Mr Ali's not only going to make money on the property as the values and the rents go up, but his firm's also right in the running for quite a chunk of the renovation work as well.'

Suddenly a whole rake of ideas started to firm up like shapes appearing out of the fog on a motorway. 'How certain is all this?' I demanded.

Clare frowned. 'Well, from what I understand, if the crime rate carries on rising like it has been doing, it's getting more certain all the time. Why, Charlie, what is it?'

I sat back in my chair and a long chill settled over me. 'We've been looking at this all wrong,' I said slowly. 'Ali wasn't paying Langford to keep the estates quiet. He was paying him to stir them up . . .'

I recounted the snatch of conversation I'd overheard between the two men the night I'd first trailed Langford to the building site as it came drifting back to me. 'That's why Ali was so worried in case anyone found out about his arrangement with Langford,' I finished. 'Langford got well out of hand the night Fariman was injured, and Ali was shit-scared that if they knew about it people would blame him. They would have done, too. He'd have been lynched.'

There was silence as everyone turned the idea over. 'I think you might just be on to something there,' Jacob said after a while. 'But, that still doesn't bring us any nearer to knowing who killed your man Harvey.'

Sean sighed. He'd turned paler during the time we'd been talking, started to slump a little more in his chair. 'I suppose at least we know that Jav was definitely lying to you,' he said. Even speech seemed an effort. 'He must have known he was setting us up for something last night, even if he didn't know what.'

'Yeah,' I agreed grimly. 'I think he's my first port of call – *if* I can find him.'

The phone started to ring then, and Jacob looked round for the cordless handset. When he couldn't spot it right away, he shoved the terrier onto the floor and left the room in search of it, muttering.

Clare took advantage of his departure to fuss anxiously round Sean. 'I've made up the spare bed. You'll be more comfortable there than on the sofa,' she said. 'You look all in.'

'I've felt better,' Sean admitted, which I thought was probably understatement on a global scale. 'I could do with making a couple of phone calls myself, though, if that would be OK?' He glanced at me. 'I need to let Madeleine know I'm all right. She'll be fretting.'

I couldn't suppress a twitch of amusement. 'I don't know what your Ma will make of you abandoning your fiancée to spend the evening with me, and then not coming home all night,' I said, finishing the last of my coffee. 'She's waiting for you two to name the day.'

Clare looked blank at the exchange, and I'd just begun to explain the complicated relationship between Sean, Madeleine, and Sean's mother, when Jacob reappeared looking troubled.

'Didn't you mention that Roger had been seen blatting around the place on a CBR 600?' he asked, and got his answer from the frozen expression on Sean's face.

'Why?' he said sharply. 'What's happened?'

'Well now, we don't know for certain,' Jacob said. He was trying to be soothing, but his voice gave him away. 'That was a mate of mine on the phone, does a bit of dealing in modern stuff out towards High Bentham. The police have dumped a bike in his yard this morning, a black and yellow CBR. They pulled it out of a ditch and he reckons it looks like it's been run off the road. Got car paint on the fairing and blood on the tank, but no sign of the rider. It's a local bike, from the plate, and he wondered if I might know whose it was. I said no.'

Sean looked stricken. 'I need to see it,' he said. He staggered upright, almost toppled. Both Clare and I put a hand out to steady him, but he waved us away angrily. 'I can manage.'

'Sean, don't be a prat,' I said mildly. 'You can't just bounce straight back into the thick of it, not after what you've been through.'

'I'll run him out there after lunch,' Jacob interrupted smoothly. 'You go and see if you can lay your hands on this Jav character, Charlie.'

'Are you going to be OK by yourself?' Sean wanted to know.

'Don't worry,' I said, 'I know just the back-up I can call on.' I glanced down at my rumpled clothes. 'But first, I think I'm going to go home for a shower and some clean gear. Am I actually insured to drive your truck?'

'It's a company vehicle,' Sean said. 'Anyone who works for me is covered.'

'Right,' I said. 'I'll consider myself hired.'

Despite my apparently cavalier attitude, I drove the Patrol back to Lancaster very slowly and very carefully. It seemed to lean alarmingly round corners, and the bonnet, with great chrome bull bars, went on for miles. By the time I pulled up outside the flat my neck was cranked tight and I had the beginnings of a growling headache spreading up from it like a stain.

I let myself in and headed straight for the shower, stripping off as I went. It wasn't until I'd emerged from a long stint under stinging needles of hot water, towel-dried my hair and put on fresh clothes, that I thought to check my answering machine.

There was only one message, but it was enough to have me grabbing the keys to the Nissan and running for the door.

'Charlie, it's Mrs Gadatra,' said a woman's wavering, frightened voice from the tape. 'It's about Pauline. She's been attacked in the street. I think you'd better come.'

★

Getting in to Lavender Gardens proved easier said than done. For a start there were a pair of panda cars parked at a slant across the entrance road. One of the uniforms flagged me down and walked up to the driver's window, head bent to the rain.

I sat paralysed for a second or two, suddenly realising that the Glock was still where I'd carelessly shoved it in my door pocket, and Sean's blood had dried to a sticky stain on the passenger seat. Thank God the leather upholstery was dark enough for it not to show too badly.

I pressed the down button for the electric window until there was a gap about eight inches deep. 'Morning, officer,' I called over the top of the glass, aiming for puzzled cheeriness. 'What's the problem?'

He ignored my greeting. He looked wet, cold, and the kind of tired you get from having had your nerves stretched constantly for hours at a time.

'Have you got business on the estate?' he asked, looking at the Patrol's nearly-new registration. 'Only they're chucking rocks at anything that moves in there.'

I thought of Sean's insurance, which had already paid out for a new windscreen in the Grand Cherokee. It wasn't my problem. 'I need to get to Kirby Street,' I said, stubborn.

He shrugged dismissively. 'Well, you've been warned,' he said, and turned away.

In fact, I got in without encountering any trouble. Kirby Street itself looked much the same as usual, apart from the shell of a burned-out Metro on the corner that nobody had yet got around to shifting. The council obviously hadn't sent the bin men in that week, either. Cat-torn bags of rubbish slumped across the pavement like couch potatoes.

As I pulled up outside Pauline's place and hurried down the short driveway, I was aware that a dozen pairs of hidden eyes had noted my arrival.

Friday went apoplectic when I banged on the front door. There was a long pause, then I saw the curtains flutter in the living room window. Finally, the lock was clicked back, and the door opened to reveal Mrs Gadatra, rather than Pauline herself.

'I'm sorry I didn't get your message until this morning,' I said as she motioned me into the hallway. 'How is she?'

Mrs Gadatra jerked her head through to the kitchen. 'Come and see for yourself,' she said.

Friday, banished to the living room, had subsided to anxious squeaks and whines. He came sidling up to me as though he knew something was seriously awry. I skimmed my hand over the top of his broad skull as I went past, and was rewarded with a quick wet tongue across my wrist.

In the kitchen, Pauline was sitting at the end of the table, with Aqueel and Gin on either side of her. They seemed to be playing a lively game of snap. Taken aback for a moment, I halted in the doorway, and Pauline glanced up. It was only then that I got a good look at her face.

Whoever had hit her had caught her a belter across the right-hand side. The gauzy dressings taped over bits of her chin and forehead suddenly reminded me of Sean. The cheekbone itself had been left to the open air, and the scabs that had formed over the abrasions there were dark and ugly.

Pauline gave me a cautious, watery smile, as if not sure her mouth would stretch to it.

'What happened?' I demanded.

'Oh, it was just kids, you know, throwing stones,' she said vaguely.

Mrs Gadatra snorted in disgust. 'Kids! Stones!' she said, flinging her arms up and shaking her fists so that the bangles she wore on both wrists clashed and rattled. 'They threw a brick at her. A *brick*! It's a miracle she isn't dead. Who knows what they might have done after that if she hadn't had the dog with her.'

Pauline smiled again with remembered affection. 'Apparently he wouldn't even let the ambulancemen get near me for a while,' she said.

That, I reckoned silently, would have done Friday's mad dog reputation no harm at all. Both Aqueel and Gin looked mightily impressed by it as they carefully gathered the snap cards together.

'Why don't you come and stay at my place for a few days?' I suggested, perching on the corner of the table nearest to Pauline. 'Just while you recover. Let things settle down round here for a bit.'

'We can look after her perfectly well,' Mrs Gadatra said sharply, offended. 'Mr Garton-Jones will find the culprits, mark my words, even if the police don't seem to be doing anything.' She sniffed.

'I don't suppose you knew any of them?' I asked.

Pauline shook her head.

'It all happened so quickly,' she said sadly. 'I didn't see anybody.'

So much for finding out if Jav was mixed up in this, too. On impulse, though, I asked Mrs Gadatra if she knew the blond-haired Asian boy.

She pursed her lips for a moment. 'I don't think so,' she said. 'I may have seen him around the place, but—'

'Jav used to play snooker with my brother,' Aqueel piped up, concentrating on holding the box open so his sister could messily put the snap cards away into it. 'He's a very good player.'

His mother glared at him, and I realised that some subtle shift had taken place since I'd moved off the estate. I was an outsider again, and not really to be trusted with inside information about anyone, or anything.

I stood up, gave her a cool stare as I thanked Aqueel. 'I'll go and look for Jav there,' I told him. 'I have some questions that I think he may be able to answer.'

'Is there anything I can help you with, Charlie?' Aqueel asked, with a defiant look to his mother. Since his brother's death he'd grown up at an accelerated rate. And here he was, determined to show her that he was the head of the family now, his own man, and took orders from nobody.

'Thank you Aqueel,' I said again, smiling, but careful not to mock him. 'I don't think so, but if there is, you'll be the first to know.'

Since there seemed to be little I could do for Pauline that wasn't being done already, I left soon after.

The Patrol was still sitting by the kerb with, surprisingly perhaps, all its tyres, paint, and glass intact. I was just about to try and keep things that way by getting out of there when movement further along the street caught my eye.

A front door had opened, and a large suited figure had emerged. It didn't take a moment to recognise Mr Ali. I stilled, and for some reason that made him glance in my direction. Immediately, he began hurrying along the path to the road, and fumbling in a pocket for his car keys.

He was slow finding them, and I've found I can run quite fast when I'm given the right motivation. I'd reached him before he'd managed to get the door open, giving him little option but to speak to me.

'Ah, Charlie,' he said nervously, his strangely soprano voice strung fit to snap. 'How nice to see you again. I have just been visiting Fariman, you know. Thankfully, he is feeling much better.'

'How much better would he be feeling if he knew what you were really up to round here?'

'Up to? I don't know what you mean,' Ali squeaked. 'I have done nothing wrong.'

'No?' I said, advancing grimly and planting my hip against his car door, just in case he got any ideas. 'So you won't mind if people round here find out what you were paying Harvey Langford to do? Keeping the crime figures bad enough for you to make a killing when this whole area gets redeveloped. Do they know you own half their houses, too?'

'No, no!' If Ali's voice got any higher he'd be attracting passing bats. 'You've got it all wrong. Please! I must go now. I had nothing to do with—'

He broke off abruptly, eyes swivelling wildly as he realised he'd been about to deny something he hadn't been accused of yet.

'Nothing to do with what? With Langford's death?' I jumped straight in with a laugh that was gone before it had arrived. 'Oh come on, Ali, he couldn't have been hiding out at the site without you knowing about it and permitting it. Who was he afraid of?'

I don't know if Mr Ali was going to answer that one, because at that moment a mid-sized rock came whizzing past my ear and smashed into splintered fragments on the paving slabs a few feet away.

Twenty-four

Cursing, I instinctively ducked and spun round.

Mr Ali didn't need telling twice that this was a good time to make his getaway. He yanked open his car door, thumping it against my shoulder. The blow caught me off balance and sent me sprawling. He was into the driving seat with the engine fired and the gear lever shoved into first before I'd had time to recover. The tyres chirruped as he spun the wheels halfway along the street.

Once he'd gone I got to my feet warily, keeping low, as though the overflowing black bin liner next to me was going to provide decent cover. I couldn't see anyone nearby. After my somewhat frosty reception from Mrs Gadatra, I suppose being used for target practice was a logical progression, and I shouldn't have been surprised about it.

Or maybe someone else on Lavender Gardens had discovered Mr Ali's treachery. Maybe the rock had been aimed at him. Maybe, if he'd hung around longer, we might have had a chance to find out . . .

I waited, with the silence that came after Mr Ali's dramatic departure punching and kicking at me. Eventually, I realised it was a case of move now, or stay there all day. Besides anything else, something in the bin bag next to me smelt ripe enough to make my eyes water.

I weighed up the distance to the Patrol with my heart banging painfully against my ribs, but decided against making a run for it. It wasn't likely to make much difference and, in the end, it boiled down to trying to hold on to my dignity.

I nearly made it, too.

I suppose I can't have been more than half-a-dozen hopeful paces away from the Patrol. I had the keys out ready in my hand, thumb on the remote door lock button, when four bulky figures appeared from one of the ginnels to my right.

My stride faltered, and I stumbled to a halt.

'Miss Fox,' Ian Garton-Jones nodded as he closed in. 'I didn't expect to see you round here any more.'

I couldn't tell if he sounded disappointed or not.

He showed his teeth briefly as he stepped between me and the Nissan. Harlow and a man I didn't recognise moved to cut off a line of retreat. West took station behind his boss's shoulder, and leaned insolently on the Patrol's front wing with his arms folded.

I shrugged. 'I'm just visiting,' I said.

'Ah yes – Mrs Jamieson,' he said, and there was a certain amount of grim satisfaction in his voice. 'Well, we've had a little chat with her, and you won't be needed next time she goes away.'

Did his idea of a 'little chat' include thrown bricks, I wondered silently?

'Nice vehicle,' he went on, shifting to stare in through the Patrol's side window at the interior. He seemed to pause just a fraction too long with his gaze on that dull stain on the passenger seat. I shoved my hands into my pockets so he wouldn't see the clenching of my fingers.

Eventually he turned back to me. 'He lets you drive it around, does he?'

'Does who?'

'Sean Meyer,' Garton-Jones said. 'It *is* his vehicle, isn't it?' He watched me carefully for a reaction, then added in a sly tone, 'Maybe he just isn't feeling up to driving at the moment.'

He and his men exchanged nasty grins, the kind that sent a spasm of alarm rippling across my shoulder-blades. I fought not to let it show.

While Garton-Jones was talking, West had been casually nudging the mud flap behind the Nissan's front tyre with the toe of his boot. The earth that was caked there dropped out onto the tarmac in small clods.

Garton-Jones glanced down at them. 'Been off-roading, have we?' he asked and when I didn't answer he went on, 'Lots of good places for that round here, so I understand. You know – green lanes, bits of waste ground, *building sites . . .*'

The smile left his face as he said the last words, all pretence at good humour wiped away.

Jesus, had he killed Langford just to frame Sean? Jacob had dismissed that scenario as being too drastic, too unbelievable. I wondered if he would change his mind now.

But, if Garton-Jones *was* responsible, why give me what amounted to a confession? Unless they were going to make sure I wasn't in any fit state to repeat it.

I was almost surprised, then, when he stepped back from the door of the Patrol and let me open it. He moved in again quickly, though, getting right in my face. I prayed he wouldn't look down, otherwise he couldn't fail to miss the Glock in the door pocket.

'I'm a reasonable man, Miss Fox,' he said, in much the same tone that he'd once used to tell me he was a violent man, too. 'Grudges and feuds are all part of my business. Just tell Meyer to stay off my estate and this won't go any further. OK?'

Ah, so that *was it.*

I glared at him without making any moves he could possibly take as a sign of acquiescence. Eventually, he just grinned, the action accentuating the tightness of the skin over his death's head skull. He stepped back again with an arrogant wave of his hand, bored playing games with me.

I bit my tongue and did as I was invited. Resisting the urge to mow down the lot of them was a difficult one, particularly since I was probably in an ideal vehicle to do so.

Sometimes it's just heroic, the self-control I have.

Much to the obvious surprise of the policeman who'd warned me on the way into Lavender Gardens, I escaped from the estate without picking up any unexpected modifications to the Nissan's bodywork. I gave them a cheery wave as I weaved between the panda cars, but this time I didn't stop.

Instead, I headed back into Lancaster. I drove through town concentrating too much on the actual mechanics of driving to give a great deal of thought to the little confrontation I'd just had with Garton-Jones and his men. But it was there, all the same, niggling away in the background.

At least my driving seemed to be getting better with practice, and it was quite a revelation to suddenly have road presence. Other car drivers just didn't try and cut me up like they invariably did when I was on the Suzuki.

Ten minutes later I pulled up outside Attila's place and killed the engine. I sat for a few moments before getting out, trying to work out how I was going to phrase my request to my boss.

I had told Sean that I knew just the back-up I could call on before going to confront Jav, but now it came down to it I wasn't sure if I had any right to ask.

A loud knock on the side glass made me jump. Wayne was grinning at me through the window.

I opened the door with a hand on my chest. 'God, you frightened the life out of me!'

'Sorry girl,' the black man said, still grinning. He had his coat collar turned up against the steady beat of the rain. Gym bag in hand, he was just leaving from his workout. 'So, what's with the motor? You finally get fed up of that bike of yours, or did you just win the lottery?'

'Neither,' I said, jumping down from my seat onto the gravel. 'It's Sean's.'

'What did you do, shoot him for it?' Wayne asked quietly then, and I realised that I still hadn't shifted that damned gun out of the driver's door pocket. Wayne's eyes were riveted to it.

I sighed. 'No, but someone else did,' I said. I picked the Glock up and leaned over to shove it into the glovebox, slamming the lid. Then I shut the car door and rested my back against it.

Wayne seemed to snap out of it once the gun had disappeared from his view. He put a meaty hand on my shoulder, and when I looked up I found his face full of genuine concern.

'What's going on girl?' he asked, brow furrowed.

I jerked my head towards the gym door. 'Come inside,' I said, 'I've got to tell Attila all about it anyway and there's no point in saying it twice.'

The place was going through its usual early-afternoon lull when we walked in. Attila and Wayne were able to sit on a couple of the weights benches and listen to my story about Langford, Ali, Jav and Garton-Jones without an audience.

Very little expression showed on either man's face when I came to the part about finding Langford's body, and about Sean being hit.

I listened to my own voice calmly explaining it all as though I was going through a shopping list, and realised that it simply hadn't sunk in. When it did finally register, I was probably going to come apart at the seams. I knew I couldn't let that happen.

Not yet.

Now though, as I finished my tale, Wayne sat up straight and gave me a level stare.

'What d'you need girl?' he said. He grinned in Attila's direction. 'Want us to go round there and sort out this Garton-Jones bloke?'

'Not yet,' I said, throwing him a quick smile. 'I've got to make sure he was the one pulling Jav's strings. If he wasn't, then there's someone else involved in all this that I haven't even considered yet.'

'And you think you know where this Jav might be found?' Attila asked.

'Apparently he plays a lot of snooker. I know Nasir was a member of one of the local snooker clubs and they used to play together. All I have to do is find out which one.'

Attila stood up, muscles rippling under his T-shirt. He gestured towards the phone on the counter. 'Find out,' he said. 'I don't like people shooting up my place, and then shooting up my friends. Find out, and I'll help you put a stop to it.'

They were brave words from a man as intrinsically gentle as Attila. Under the surface he's a complete pacifist, with a tendency to go queasy at the sight of spilt blood. His own, particularly, but other people's would usually do the trick.

Wayne stood, also. 'I've nothing on this afternoon, girl,' he said casually. 'I'll give you a hand if you like.'

I paused for a moment, not in hesitation, but in surprise that these two men should offer their support without reserve. Eventually, I nodded.

'Thank you,' I said simply. As I headed for the phone I was aware of the sharp prickle of unshed tears in my throat.

★

I tried Sean first, at Jacob and Clare's. Clare answered the call, and told me the boys weren't back yet.

'Jacob rang in about twenty minutes ago,' she told me. 'It's Nasir's bike all right, and they were going to go out to the scene before they come home, so they might be a while, I'm afraid.'

'Never mind,' I said. 'There's someone else I can try.'

Ringing Madeleine wasn't easy, and I wasn't quite sure what I was going to say to Sean's mother, if she picked up the receiver instead. In the event, I didn't recognise the little voice who answered the phone.

'Hello, hello?'

'Hello,' I said carefully. 'Who's that?'

'I'm Tara,' the voice said proudly, 'and I'm nearly five.'

Slowly, clearly, I asked for Madeleine, then listened as the handset was dropped on the floor and a minute or so of shouting and giggling went on in the background. I was just about to ring off when Madeleine came on the line, sounding out of breath.

'Charlie!' she said sharply, cutting off my greeting. 'Sean rang me earlier. How is he?'

'He's OK,' I said, cautious at her abrupt tone. 'He and Jacob have gone out to look for the bike Roger was on, but—'

'What?' Madeleine bit out. She lowered her voice as if wary of eavesdroppers and went on in a savage whisper. 'You've let him go gallivanting around when he's just been *shot*? He should be in hospital, for Christ's sake! What were you thinking?'

I felt my own temper flare and climb steadily. I made sure Wayne and Attila were far enough away not to be able to overhear my end of the conversation. They weren't. Attila had drafted him in to relocate one of the far stacks of dumb-bells.

'Just back it off will you, Madeleine?' I snapped. 'Don't you think that getting him to a hospital wasn't my first priority? I tried. He wouldn't go. So I got him out of there before the police grabbed him, and I got one of the best surgeons in the country to come and sort him out. What more did you want me to do?'

There was a long silence as both of us struggled to find some means of diffusing the situation, of backing down.

Neither of us succeeded.

Eventually, necessity intervened. 'Anyway, I need some information,' I said stiffly. 'Where was that snooker club you said Nasir was a member of?'

'Why?'

'Because I think that's where we might find Jav.'

There was another tense pause. 'Where are you now?' she demanded.

I let my breath out slowly through my nose, but none of my irritation went with it. 'What does that matter? Just tell me the name of the place, Madeleine.'

At that moment, Wayne accidentally let one of the dumb-bells slip. The clatter it made when it hit the thinly-carpeted wooden flooring was loud, and distinctive.

'You're at the gym, aren't you?' Madeleine guessed, and took my lack of reply as confirmation. 'I'll tell you when I get there. I'll be with you in less than ten minutes.'

'Madeleine, you are not coming with us,' I warned. *Not this time*, I added silently, but I should have saved my breath. She wasn't listening.

'I'm on my way, Charlie,' she tossed back at me, mulish. 'Deal with it.'

I started to argue, forcefully and with expletives, but that was a waste of time, too.

'Aah, that's a *naughty* word,' Tara's voice said on the other end of the line. 'I'm telling!'

★

In fact, Madeleine *didn't* tell me where the snooker club was when she arrived. She must have worked it out on the way over that as soon as she did I'd leave her behind.

When we heard her pull up the three of us went outside, Attila locking up behind him. We found her still behind the wheel of another Grand Cherokee, bottle green and right-hand drive this time.

'Hop in,' she said. 'I'll take you there. It's easier than explaining.'

The boys went for the back seat, leaving me up front with Madeleine. Wayne grinned at my attempts not to grind my teeth too obviously.

My enamel was in particular danger of disintegration when I realised exactly where we were going. Explaining where the snooker club was would have taken her about ten seconds, because it was the one down near the new bus station, over the top of a café. I could have put my finger on it right away, given half a chance.

She pulled up and switched the engine off, but before she could get out I put a hand on her arm.

'We play this one my way,' I said firmly. 'Don't tell him anything. No names. If we frighten him he'll just tell us crap to make us go away. So, we reason with him,' I went on, jerking my head in the direction of the rear seat, 'with these two looking menacing in the background, just in case. OK?'

She nodded. Reluctantly, but she nodded.

'Don't worry about me,' she said.

I should have known.

With me leading, and Madeleine close on my heels, the four of us pushed through the single shabby door which was the only part of the snooker club at ground level.

The doorway led straight to a narrow staircase up to the first floor, then opened out into a huge room, dimly lit, with eight full-size tables lined up down the centre. I wondered for a moment if the floor had been reinforced to take the weight.

Jav and a couple of his mates were playing at one of the tables at the far end. As soon as they recognised us, they started to scatter.

One of them tried to make a dash for the door past Wayne, who grabbed him with one huge hand, twisting the cue the boy had been about to use as a weapon out of his grasp with disdainful ease, and slamming him against the edge of the nearest table.

'You may as well let him go,' I called across, nodding to where we had Jav cornered. 'This is the one we want.'

Madeleine, meanwhile, had walked right up to our quarry.

'Hi Jav, remember me?' she said brightly, then brought her knee up sharply between his legs.

Jav reeled back, gasping, and bumped against the nearest wall. He slid down it to the floor as all the strength leached out of his limbs. Tears sprang to his eyes. Wayne and Attila shifted their feet in unconscious male sympathy.

I grabbed Madeleine's arm, spun her round.

'This was not how we agreed to do this,' I said in a low growl.

'It wasn't how *you* agreed to do it,' she threw back, eyes fired, 'I never got to have *my* say, did I Charlie?'

When I didn't immediately answer she stepped forwards again and dug her fingers into Jav's hair to wrench his head up. His face looked more puffy and bruised than it had done when he'd collared me outside the flat, only the night before.

It seemed a lifetime ago.

'This bastard set you and Sean up,' Madeleine went on, voice rising. 'Sean took a bullet in the shoulder because of this little shit, and you want me to *reason* with him?'

I stared at her blankly for a moment as she dropped her

hold on Jav's hair and stalked round me, then I caught the faintest glimmer in her eye.

I shrugged. If you can't beat 'em, join 'em. 'Well, we've a hole dug if we need to use it, Mad,' I said, keeping my voice artfully casual, 'but you ice him too fast and we won't find out what we need to know.'

Jav's eyes swivelled between Madeleine and me, and back again. He looked beyond us, but Wayne and Attila, bless them, just stood a few feet away like a two-man roadblock, their faces devoid of expression.

I watched as it finally dawned on him that there was no escape. Whatever threats had been made to him, they were nothing in his mind compared to the danger he was facing now.

Madeleine smiled nastily. 'Oh, he'll talk,' she said, and somehow managed to inject just a trace of insanity into her voice, a slightly unbalanced singsong note. 'It may take a while, but he'll talk. They always talk in the end.'

I shrugged again, flicked my eyes dispassionately over Jav's huddled figure. 'Sorry Jav,' I said, sounding genuinely regretful. 'You had your chance.'

I started to move away.

Madeleine took one step closer to him. That was all it took. Jav scrunched himself into a ball and started wailing.

'OK, OK,' he yelled. 'I'll tell you! Just keep that crazy bitch away from me!'

I jerked my head to the boys and they moved forwards like they'd been practising for a synchronised display. They dug a hand under Jav's armpits and lifted him clear off the floor. I swept the loose snooker balls on the table top out of the way and they dumped him on his back in the middle of the green baize.

I glanced round the rest of the room. There seemed to be more people than there had been when we arrived. I kept a wary eye on them, but for the moment they didn't seem prepared to do more than watch.

Madeleine leaned over Jav, turning the blue ball over in her hand, and then clenching her fingers round it. 'D'you think I should leave him with his teeth?' she asked.

Jav tried to struggle upright, but Attila put one hand in the middle of his chest and pushed him down hard against the slate. The boy took one look at the German's impassive face and stayed down.

I moved round into his line of sight on the other side of the table. 'OK Jav,' I said. 'Talk. Who set us up?'

He twisted his head from one to the other. 'It was them security men,' he said, fright making his words vibrate with sibilance, 'you know, the ones on the estate. They wanted you out of the way before they grabbed Roger Meyer.'

'They've got him?'

He nodded. 'Yeah, not for long, though. Lavender's about to go up in flames. They goin' to torch them derelict houses, the ones between the estates. When they do, Roger'll be in one of them.'

'When?' Madeleine snapped at him.

His eyes rolled, showing all the whites. 'I don't know. Soon.'

'How come you know all this?' I asked, wary in case he was still lying to us.

'They got me to scope out a place for them. Told me to find one with a cellar, somewhere they could stash him.'

'We better get over there right now,' Madeleine said.

Jav shook his head. 'He won't be there yet. They don't want to risk anyone finding him before the place goes up.'

'Why are they doing this?' I wanted to know. 'They're supposed to be protecting the estate. What's in it for them?'

Despite his fear, Jav looked scornful. 'It's big business, lady,' he hissed. 'You didn't think it was random, did you – the crime round here?'

'So who's behind it?' Madeleine pressed, but even with her looming over him, Jav couldn't, or wouldn't, tell.

'Langford knew, though, didn't he?' I said quietly. 'Is that why he took a knife in the chest?'

Fresh dread bloomed on Jav's features. You could smell the fear in him as he began to struggle afresh.

I knew we weren't going to get anything further out of him. Besides, the crowd was growing. They still didn't try and intervene, but there was a burgeoning air of menace about them, nonetheless.

I touched Madeleine's arm. 'It's time to go,' I said.

Wayne and Attila let go of the Asian boy and left him still lying there as we all moved towards the stairs. The onlookers took in the solid width of the German's shoulders, and the mean look the black man had contrived onto his normally cheery face, and carefully gave us room to depart.

Once we made it out at street level, I let my breath out slowly, and turned to find Attila frowning, but Madeleine and Wayne exchanging big grins.

'That,' I said tiredly, 'was not exactly how I wanted to play this, Madeleine.'

She shrugged. 'It worked, didn't it?' she said, defiant and completely unrepentant. 'We found out what we needed to know.'

'Yeah,' I said, my voice grim as I recalled the sea of watchful faces, 'but so did everybody else.'

Twenty-five

I thanked Attila and Wayne again for their help when we dropped them off back at the gym, then I retrieved the Patrol, and Madeleine followed me up to Caton.

The rain was still falling, glazing on the windscreen in the oncoming headlights. The day had already started to weaken into evening, the light levels dropping fast. God, I hate the winter.

The boys had returned by the time we arrived at Jacob and Clare's. Sean was sitting propped in one of the kitchen chairs, very much at home, with his left arm in a very professional-looking sling, and Beezer asleep on his lap.

Jacob had broken out a bottle of wine, which I wasn't sure was a wise move, in view of the amount of morphine Sean had had over the last twenty-four hours, but it wasn't up to me to tell him that. In any case, Madeleine jumped straight down that track as soon as we walked in, so I was glad I hadn't opened my mouth.

'So tell me what happened with Jav,' Sean interrupted the other girl's flow, calmly stroking the terrier's ears.

Madeleine stopped talking abruptly, realised that she was onto a loser if she pursued things any further, and let it lie.

Clare smiled at her sympathetically. I got the impression she'd already voiced her objections before we'd arrived, and had met with the same outright disregard.

Clare was bustling round making us all some food, a giant native American sweetcorn soup, reinforced with celery and onions. Madeleine was overcome with enough of an attack of good manners to lend a hand.

Weariness was settling down over me like a leaden fog. I can function on around four hours' sleep a night if I work up to it, but it's not a combination that works well with high levels of stress.

I dropped into a chair opposite Jacob and Sean, and helped myself to a glass of the dark, almost metallic red. I gave them the bare facts about what had happened that morning, trying to mask the annoyance I'd felt at Madeleine's actions. It wasn't easy.

Sean grinned at my carefully worded account, but his amusement faded when we got to the substance of what Jav had told us.

'So, how do we find out when Roger's likely to be moved into one of the houses?' he wondered.

'Do you even know where he'll be?' Jacob put in.

I nodded as I sipped my wine, twirling the short fat stem of the glass in my fingers. 'I think so,' I said. 'Most of the houses were built in the fifties, but there's half a street of stone Victorian stuff left, right in the middle of No Man's Land. They're the only ones old enough to have cellars.'

'That should narrow the search down a bit,' Sean said, frowning in concentration. He eased his shoulder in its sling, flexing his hand. Would he be ready, if it came to a fight?

'As for when,' I said, 'I thought I'd see about moving back in with Pauline for a few days so I can keep an eye out from there. I'd be happier being with her at the moment, in any case. Did I tell you someone threw a brick at her?'

This, of course, was news to Jacob and Clare, and the time between then and the arrival of the food was largely taken up with recounting my last visit to Lavender Gardens.

'That dog of hers is worth its weight in gold,' Jacob said. 'You don't think she'd ever want to part with him, do you?'

I remembered at this point that I also hadn't told Sean about my latest run-in with Garton-Jones. He listened in silence to the sly hints the security man had dropped about him, his face giving nothing away.

'I really will have to do something about that man,' he said at last, and the calm in his voice was chilling.

We none of us talked much once the food was in front of us, and I realised just how hungry I was. The Succotash was so thick you could have eaten it with a fork rather than a spoon. There was Caesar salad, too. We mopped up everything with chunks of fresh bread torn rather than sliced from a crusty loaf.

Afterwards I think it was Clare who suggested we listen to the local radio station, to see if there was anything mentioned on the early evening news about Langford's murder. There wasn't, but what we did hear had us abandoning the dirty crockery where it lay, and heading for the door.

'Police aren't naming the Asian teenager whose badly beaten body was thrown from a moving car in the Lavender Gardens area of the city earlier today,' the announcer said, 'but he's known to be local to the area. His condition is described as critical. Police officials are calling for calm, but gangs of youths are already forming between there and the neighbouring Copthorne estate.

'Reports are coming in that missiles and some petrol bombs have been thrown, although as yet there are no confirmed injuries. The exact situation is unknown as even fire and ambulance crews are having difficulty gaining access. Police are advising everyone to stay clear of the area until matters have been brought under control . . . '

Out on the forecourt, it was Madeleine who commandeered the keys to the Patrol, and I surrendered them without argument. At least the rain had eased, but the air was heavy with the promise that more was on its way.

'We'll come, too,' Clare said, making for their Range Rover.

'No!'

All of them stopped, turned to look at me as I voiced my dissent. I registered uncomfortably that my tone had been just a touch too vehement, and a tad too loud.

Sean stepped in front of me, searched my set face and didn't find the answers he was looking for written there.

'No,' I repeated, more reasonably this time. 'There's no need for them to come with us.'

'Why not, Charlie?' he murmured. 'We might be glad of their help.'

I shook my head. 'They've done enough,' I said, dogged. 'More than enough. I won't have you risking their safety.'

Jacob appeared at my elbow. 'It's all right, Charlie,' he said gently. 'We know what we're getting into this time, and we want to do what we can.' He put his arm round my shoulders. 'You don't have to keep protecting us forever.'

'I know that,' I said, swallowing, and wished that I believed it, too.

Jacob seemed to take that as agreement. He released me with a reassuring squeeze, and he and Clare climbed into the Range Rover. The rest of us piled into the Patrol, with me in the back seat. Madeleine led the way, our headlights bouncing wildly in tune to the rutted drive.

It wasn't until we'd almost reached the edge of town that I realised how quiet she'd gone since we'd heard the news report.

'It's my fault, isn't it?' she asked finally, not taking her eyes off the road ahead.

Sean, busy in the process of squirming out of his sling, twisted in his seat to face her. 'What is?'

'Well, that was Jav, wasn't it, who was beaten and dumped?' She flicked her gaze briefly to mine in the rear-view mirror. 'Did you know something like this was going to happen?' she wanted to know. 'That was why you wanted to handle things more quietly this morning, wasn't it? I didn't realise . . . '

Her voice trailed off and for a few moments there was no more noise inside the cabin than the roar of the Patrol's tyres, and the rumble of the engine. It was a measure of her error, I thought, that even Sean hadn't leapt straight to her defence.

'I don't think it would have made any difference however we'd tackled him,' I said slowly, almost surprised to find myself giving her a way out.

My thought processes creaked laboriously into action. 'We know that Garton-Jones doesn't like leaving loose ends, or witnesses. I think this was probably what he had in mind all along. It's so neat, isn't it? He needed the right trigger to grenade the estate, and this way he not only achieves that, but he also gets rid of Jav now his usefulness is exhausted.'

Madeleine stopped as the set of traffic lights across Parliament Street turned red against us. 'But why did they want to cause a riot in the first place?'

'I don't think they did, not originally,' I said. 'I think it just mushroomed until all they could do was go with the flow.' I remembered that conversation – more like a confrontation, really – I'd had with Nasir over the garden fence.

'*Violence – that's all you people understand!*' he'd spat. '*Well, I hope you're happy now with the trouble you've caused, spying on us. You and your fascist bully boys! But you make the most of it while it lasts, because I swear to you that we won't lie down and be beaten for much longer!*'

I repeated his words to Sean and Madeleine now. 'The only thing I can't understand is why he thought I was tied in with Garton-Jones in the first place,' I said.

'Maybe it was just because you both arrived on the estate at more or less the same time,' Sean suggested. 'Who knows how their minds were working.'

'But if that's the case, then the gangs may well hold you partly responsible for Nasir, and for what's happened to Jav,' Madeleine pointed out with apprehension clear in her voice. 'Getting in there to get to Roger is going to be that much more difficult.'

Sean gave us both a tired smile that didn't quite make it to his eyes. 'I never thought it was going to be easy,' he said.

Once we'd got over Greyhound Bridge we realised that the orange glow we could see in the distance didn't come from the streetlights. Smoke and flames billowed up into the darkened sky, scattering burning embers which were caught and carried by the wind.

'Oh God,' Madeleine said, 'it's started already.'

'Either that,' I muttered, 'or Heysham Power Station's finally done a Chernobyl.'

A fire engine came screaming past us then. Madeleine stuck two wheels into the gutter as he overtook, giving him room. A police Sherpa was close behind, with the riot shield flipped up above the windscreen like a visor.

We slowed to a crawl by the entrance to Lavender Gardens. Where the panda cars had been parked earlier in the day was now a crush of different police vehicles. The Sherpa pulled up in the midst of them and began to disgorge men in full protective gear, carrying four-foot clear polycarbonate shields.

A dark blue horsebox was ignoring the double-yellow lines on the main road, under the streetlights, but I don't think the driver was likely to get a ticket. The ramp was down and four big well-muscled police horses were being hurriedly led out. They had riot gear on, too.

Madeleine was abruptly waved on by one of the fluoro-jacketed coppers directing traffic.

'Move it on,' he shouted. 'Now!'

Madeleine wound down her window. 'What's happened to the residents?' she demanded. It would have taken a more determined man to have ignored her.

The copper jerked his head. 'The ones that aren't still in there are down at the Black Lion,' he said, grudgingly. 'Now get this thing shifted!'

We moved away, heading for the pub where I'd attended the Residents' Committee meeting. This time, though, there'd be no Langford sneering at me from a corner of the bar.

Most of the residents of Lavender Gardens seemed to be crowded together in the car park outside the pub. They milled around with the kind of shell-shocked lethargy that over-whelms disaster victims the world over.

We pulled up by the entrance, and Jacob slotted the Range Rover in behind us. We all jumped down onto the tarmac.

As soon as I was out, I'd started moving. 'Look for Pauline,' I called back.

'But what about Roger?' Madeleine asked.

I turned briefly. 'If we're going to have to go in there we only want to do it once,' I said. 'If Pauline hasn't got out yet, we may as well get two for the price of one, don't you think?'

Nobody argued and we pressed on. It wasn't easy to pick out one specific person in the darkened mass, but eventually it was the flash of the white dressings on Pauline's face that led me to her. That and Friday standing rigidly at her feet.

When I got closer I discovered that Pauline was also holding Mrs Gadatra's youngest, Gin, wrapped in a blanket and fast asleep. Mrs Gadatra herself was sitting on part of the low car park wall a few feet away, her arms wrapped round her body, weeping loudly.

Aqueel was standing stiff and scared next to his mother, with one hand clutching at her shoulder. He was staring at her as if she'd suddenly grown another head. I called his name, and the look of utter relief that passed across his features when he recognised a friendly face was heartbreaking.

Pauline threw a shaky smile towards us as we approached. She was dry-eyed, but very pink around the lids to show what that was costing her.

'They burned the houses,' she said, trying unsuccessfully to stop her chin from wobbling. 'We only just got out in what we're standing up in.'

The simple statement sent Mrs Gadatra off into a fresh spasm of grief. Her words were partially obscured by the frenzied chop of the police helicopter as it swung low over-head, heading back towards the estate. The searchlight mounted under the front stabbed into the darkness.

'You can't stay here,' Clare said with a decisive edge. 'Come on, Pauline and you, too, Mrs G. You can all come back to the house with us.'

When there were signs of objection from both women, Clare went straight for the emotional jugular. 'You can't leave the children standing around all night in this cold,' she said briskly. 'Besides, it feels like it's going to pour down again at any minute.'

Mention of the impending weather seemed to be the deciding factor. Mrs Gadatra and Pauline allowed themselves to be shepherded towards the Range Rover then. Madeleine had taken Gin from Pauline. The little girl had woken up as soon as she was moved, but she made no protest.

Clare dug in the glovebox and produced a tatty bag of chocolate limes, her emergency stash. Aqueel and Gin accepted this offering with some fervour, a symbol of normality in an otherwise blown-apart world.

'If we're going to leave, I should tell that nice young girl from the social services,' Mrs Gadatra said, fussing. 'They came round and took names, to try and find us temporary shelter,' she explained. 'I will tell her they can give our place to some other poor family. Aqueel, look after your sister.'

Jacob and Clare said they'd go with her. The three of them hurried off through the crowd, and were soon gone from sight in the crush.

Pauline was standing staring back in the direction of Lavender Gardens, hugging her thin cardigan around her shivering body. Friday was glued to her leg. Sean retrieved a rug out of the back of the Patrol and draped it round Pauline's shoulders, ignoring the warning growl from the dog.

'I don't suppose you've seen anything of Garton-Jones and his men since this all kicked off?' Sean asked her quietly.

Pauline shook her head. 'I understand they're still in there, though, doing what they can,' she said. She glanced across at me. 'I know you didn't think much to Ian – I didn't, for that matter – but if it wasn't for him, we probably wouldn't have got out of there at all.'

Sean was looking at her, surprised. 'Didn't you know?' he said. 'Good old Ian Garton-Jones is up to his non-existent bull neck in this whole thing.'

Pauline's confusion and disbelief were plain. 'But that's ridiculous,' she said faintly. 'He's here to protect us.'

Sean tried to let her down gently, but there wasn't an easy glide path open to him. 'He was on to a winner either way, Mrs Jamieson,' he said. 'You were all paying him to keep the estate clear of crime, but we now think he was probably behind the crimewave in the first place. Drumming up business.'

'Oh no, it was Mr O'Bryan who was doing that.'

We all of us froze, then turned very slowly to stare at Aqueel, sitting swinging his heels on the sill of the Range Rover. It was like our heads were suddenly made of steel and he had just become an eight-year-old electromagnet.

The boy himself appeared not to notice the sudden attention his words had gained. The clear cellophane sweet wrapping had ripped, and he was carefully making sure it was all peeled away before he gave the sticky lime to his sister.

It was only when Sean crouched alongside him, brought his eyes down to Aqueel's level, that the boy tore his gaze away from his task.

'Aqueel, this is important,' he said gently. 'Are you sure you mean Mr O'Bryan?'

Aqueel regarded him gravely while he chewed the remainder of his own sweet, mindful of his manners. We held our collective breath until he'd swallowed. Then he said, 'Oh yes. My brother told me. Mr O'Bryan was trying to make Nasir do things for him that were wrong, stealing things for him.' His big liquid-dark eyes rested on each of us, serious. 'Nasir didn't want to do that any more. He was going to be a daddy.'

'Was that why you damaged Mr O'Bryan's car?' I asked, thinking of the group of kids I'd seen running away from the Mercedes.

Aqueel looked a bit sheepish. 'We found some things in the boot that had been stolen. Nasir was very pleased. He said he was going to show them to Mr O'Bryan. He said they would make Mr O'Bryan stop bothering him, and leave Ursula alone. I like her,' he admitted shyly, 'She's pretty.'

But Nasir's amateur attempts at blackmail hadn't stopped O'Bryan, I realised with a growing sense of horror, they'd made things ten times worse.

They'd upped the stakes to murder.

I hadn't considered for a moment that O'Bryan was a player in all this. In fact, I was the one who'd tipped him off at the beginning that Nasir had been making vague threats that day at Fariman and Shahida's house.

Cold all over, I shut my eyes for a moment, unable to believe how stupid, how gullible I'd been. It wasn't a surprise now that the CBR had been run off the road and Roger grabbed. After all, I'd told O'Bryan exactly what to look for.

Whatever else he was, the man was efficient. O'Bryan must have set Garton-Jones on the trail of the Honda as soon as he'd walked out of the gym after our last meeting.

Sean was staring at me with the same dismay reflected on his face. 'That's why Roger ran from us at the house,' he murmured. 'It wasn't us he was scared of at all, it was O'Bryan.'

'And it would explain why Nasir thought I was involved,' I said, 'if he knew O'Bryan had been to see me.'

'So why was the man trying to get Roger off with a caution for injuring Fariman?' Madeleine wanted to know.

'The reason Roger and the others were in Fariman's shed in the first place was because O'Bryan had sent them there to rob the place,' Sean told her. His mouth twisted into a mocking smile. 'He was just looking after his own, wasn't he?'

'Where is he now, your brother?' Pauline asked.

Sean jerked his head towards the estate, just as a traffic car came howling past. 'They've dumped him somewhere in the middle of that lot and they're going to make damned sure he burns,' he said bitterly.

Mrs Gadatra hurried up at that point saying she was good to go. We began squeezing them all into the Range Rover, piling up children on the back seat.

'We'll put Friday in the back,' Jacob said, but Pauline shook her head.

'He's staying,' she said. She handed me his lead. 'I think you might need him.'

I opened my mouth to object, but she held up a finger.

'Friday's a good guard dog,' she said, 'but he's a better tracker, and Rhodesian Ridgebacks were originally bred to fight lions. Take him.'

She glanced in Sean's direction and lowered her voice. 'I know you told me your young man didn't have anything to do with Nasir's death, dear,' she added, troubled, 'and you're probably right, but I'd watch him now, if I were you. He's got blood in his eyes.'

I turned to skim mine over Sean where he stood talking quickly to Madeleine by the Patrol.

'Don't worry,' I said, dragging up a smile. 'I'll keep a close eye on him. And on Friday, too.'

She gave us both a quick hug, although I didn't try and lick her face by way of a thank you, then she turned and trotted back to the Range Rover. I watched the four-by-four rumble out of the car park with a sense of relief that they, at least, were out of harm's way.

The road outside was a mass of vehicles with flashing lights. More police cars arrived in the Black Lion car park, but I didn't pay much attention to them.

Instead, I walked back over to the Nissan with Friday, who had now transferred his attention firmly to me, treading on my feet all the way. His eyes were anxiously fixed on my face as if looking for some sign that I was going to abandon him, too. I scratched the back of his neck by way of reassurance, and he butted against my legs.

Madeleine glanced at me, her face fearful as her eyes slid to her boss. Sean had moved away to stand near the front of the Patrol and from the back his body was stiff with rage. At his sides, his hands spasmed briefly, once, as though he could already feel his fingers tightening round O'Bryan's neck.

'Out of the mouths of babes, eh?' he said, not turning round as I closed in. 'That little lad knew, all the time, and we never

315

thought to ask him. He could have told us all about O'Bryan right at the start. Dammit!'

'Sean,' I said quietly. 'Don't do it. Leave O'Bryan alone.'

He still spoke without meeting my eyes. 'Give me one good reason why I shouldn't kill him?' he said, and it was his conversational tone that scared me most, as though he was discussing washing the car.

'Have you ever killed anyone, Sean?' I asked. He turned then, and as he started to make an impatient gesture I added quickly, 'No, I mean really, actually killed someone? Deliberately? Face to face?'

There was a long pause, and I realised I wasn't going to get an answer. I pressed on doggedly, anyway.

'If you haven't then you have no idea what it will do to you,' I said, my voice low with feeling. 'What it will take away from you. Even if you managed to get away with it, the consequences will stay with you forever. Think about that, Sean. You're not in the army any more.'

He offered a half-smile that gave up trying almost before it formed. 'And here was I thinking you were going to give me a lecture about the moral rights and wrongs of it.'

I shook my head. 'There was a time when I'd have been first in the queue to help you plan the hit,' I said. 'The man's a shit of the lowest order and he probably deserves to die, but not at your hands, Sean. Not if I can help it.'

'What really happened to you, Charlie?' he asked, and must have seen my face close up. He held up his hand. 'OK, OK, you don't want to tell me, and I think I can understand that, but one day I hope you'll feel you can trust me enough to tell me about it, because that sounds like the voice of experience talking.'

With that, he moved past me, and for a moment I didn't follow him. I did trust Sean, I realised, but I didn't think I'd ever be ready to bare my soul to him.

I didn't much like looking in there myself.

'So,' Madeleine said, pale and nervous, 'what do we do now?'

'We have to get to Roger – if he isn't dead already,' Sean said. 'We'll worry about how to deal with everything else later—'

'I would say,' said a measured voice behind us, 'that you've got far more important things to worry about right now.'

We spun round, to find Superintendent MacMillan and a pair of uniforms large enough to have been Streetwise men themselves were looming behind us.

'Charlie,' MacMillan nodded sharply in my direction, then turned that flat gaze onto Sean's suddenly tense figure. 'And you must be Sean Meyer, whom I've heard so much about. Well, much as I hate to break up the party, I'm afraid you're under arrest.'

Twenty-six

Just for a moment there was silence. Not that any of the people who thronged the car park stopped talking or crying. Not that the distant sirens stopped blaring. But for the six of us there was utter silence, nonetheless.

It was Sean who broke it.

'What's the charge?' he said, with that slight lift of his chin I knew so well. The one that issued a challenge you'd be foolish to ignore.

'Murder.'

'Whose murder?'

'Harvey Langford's – for now,' MacMillan said, composed, 'but I'm sure we can add to that later, if need be.'

One of the coppers standing behind him reached for his cuffs, shook them loose, and took a step towards Sean.

Without clearly recalling doing it, I found I'd shifted my feet halfway into a stance. When I looked, I found we all had. Even the Superintendent looked poised and Friday was standing motionless but alert.

Sean turned his head slightly, stared straight into the approaching policeman's eyes. 'Come near me with those now, and I'll break both your arms,' he said. His voice was light, pleasant, but I'd never heard anyone mean a threat more.

He looked back to the Superintendent. 'Give me until tomorrow morning,' he said, 'and I'll turn myself in.'

'What happens tomorrow morning?'

'By then I'll either have found you the real killer, or my brother will be dead,' Sean said evenly. 'Either way, it won't matter much any more.'

The copper with the cuffs took another step. His mate unhooked the baton from his belt. Madeleine and I closed in on either side of Sean, and I slipped Friday's lead.

The Ridgeback moved smoothly in front of us, showing every incisor in his considerable array and making a noise in his chest like the continuous droning of a light aircraft engine. It was enough to stop all three policemen in their tracks.

I took advantage of the breathing space. 'Don't you want to know what's going on round here?' I asked MacMillan quickly, trying to keep the note of desperation out of my voice. 'Don't you want to find out not just who really did kill Langford, but *why* he died? Don't you want to know who's been organising the crimewave, masterminding the burglaries, fencing the gear?'

The Superintendent tore his eyes away from the dog's teeth.

'What makes you think that we don't know already?'

'Because if you could prove it you wouldn't be here, going through the motions of arresting a man you *know* isn't the one you really want.'

MacMillan eyed me without speaking for a long moment. I could almost hear the gears in that calculating mind engaging. I don't know what conclusions he came to, but maybe he remembered back to another time when we hadn't trusted each other, and someone had died because of it.

'Come on, MacMillan,' I said, unable to stand the waiting any longer. 'I got you the proof you needed last time. Don't do this again.'

Eventually, he sighed and his hand went out, stilling the advance of his men. 'OK,' he said cautiously. 'Tell me what you know and maybe we can talk about this. Just don't let me down, Charlie, or we'll both swing for it.'

I acknowledged the enormity of the concession he'd just made. 'So,' I said, 'you don't have anything solid to go on, then?'

'Nothing that would stand up in court, no,' he admitted at last.

The balanced shifted. I felt the tension began to unwind out of my shoulders. I glanced at the others, but their faces didn't give me any encouragement to collaborate with the enemy. 'We think the person who's been running the burglary ring on the local estates is your Community Juvenile man, Eric O'Bryan,' I began.

'Why?' MacMillan rapped out, but there was no real surprise there.

'Because he's got the perfect access to all the local teenage criminals,' I said. 'We think he and Garton-Jones's mob have had a deal going where O'Bryan revs up the crime rate, and then takes a cut when the private security men are called in.'

'You think, or you know?' MacMillan asked sharply now. 'We've suspected the same for a while. O'Bryan's got expensive tastes in classic cars that he couldn't finance from his official earnings, but he's been clever, and it's been extremely difficult to prove it. He tells a good story about buying them as wrecks and doing them up himself, and witnesses have been singularly reluctant to come forward.'

'Your proof's in there,' Sean said tightly, indicating Lavender Gardens. 'O'Bryan's arranged for my brother to be killed in there tonight, because of what he knows. Unless you get to him first.'

'Where?' MacMillan asked.

I told him about the derelict houses with cellars, omitting to mention how we'd obtained the information.

Once he'd pinpointed the exact location, MacMillan gave a frustrated grimace and shook his head. 'We can't do it,' he said.

'What the fuck do you mean, you can't do it?' Sean flared. 'We're talking about saving the life of a fourteen-year-old boy. Don't you give a damn about that?'

'Yes, but there's no way I can get my men in there,' the Superintendent said, keeping his own anger in check. 'It's the middle of a war zone, the way the gangs are fighting. They'll treat it as an invasion. I haven't got the manpower to cope as it is. The best we can do at the moment is contain the trouble within the estates. Let them slug it out and pick up the pieces afterwards.'

He cocked an eye upwards. 'The only thing you can do now is pray for rain. Nothing quells a riot like a good downpour.'

'So let us go in and get him,' I said urgently. 'If you can't, then for God's sake let us do it.'

MacMillan's gaze was even as he considered the implications and the consequences. 'No,' he said. 'I don't want your deaths on my conscience, Charlie. I can't allow it.'

Sean gave him a thin smile. 'What makes you think you're going to get the opportunity to stop us?'

And suddenly we were back to a stand-off again, half a beat away from violence.

It was Madeleine who spoke then. 'Look, Superintendent,' she said, calm and reasonable as though breaking up squabbling children, 'you've just said you haven't got men to waste. Why waste these two trying to arrest us?'

MacMillan did his best to hold back a smile, but it escaped across the corner of his mouth, even so. He glanced back at me, and in that brief connection I saw the struggle, the tightrope he was walking between the result he so badly wanted to obtain, and utter, bleak disaster. He sighed again, more heavily this time, and gave in.

'What do you need?' he said.

Beside me, I felt Sean loosen. 'Body armour would be good,' he said. 'It'll have to be covert stuff, though, or they'll think we're with your lot.' He cracked a tired smile of his own. 'And I wouldn't say no to a couple of MP5s.'

MacMillan threw him an old-fashioned look. 'Body armour I can manage,' he said grimly. 'Firearms are quite another matter.'

I thought of the Glock, still in the glovebox of the Patrol.

'We'll manage,' I said.

MacMillan jerked his head back towards one of the Sherpa vans on the other side of the car park. 'Come on,' he said. 'We'll get you kitted out.' As we started to follow him across the wet tarmac, he added, 'Are you sure you realise the dangers of what you're doing?'

Sean paused at that, met the Superintendent's eyes and said simply, 'I realise the dangers of doing nothing. Roger's my little brother. What else can I do?'

In the back of the Sherpa was a pile of spare body armour like thin black nylon life jackets. MacMillan's sidekicks started sorting through it and dragging out appropriate sizes for the three of us.

Sean looked at the one he was handed, clearly unimpressed. 'Where are the plates?' he demanded.

MacMillan favoured him with a pointed stare. 'This is all I can supply at short notice,' he said. 'Take it or leave it.'

'What plates?' Madeleine wanted to know, as Sean helped her strap on her vest.

'Thick ceramic plates that fit into these pockets on the front and back,' he explained. 'As they are, these wouldn't stop anything heavy.'

Madeleine looked down at the vest as she shrugged her jumper back over the top of it. 'You mean that without them they're not bullet-proof?' she asked faintly.

Sean gave her a savage grin. 'Nothing's ever bullet-proof,' he said. 'It's just bullet-*resistant*. It's like a rain jacket. Even if it's supposed to be waterproof, if you stand out in the rain for long enough, you *will* get wet.'

There was a short, pregnant silence.

'Thank you,' I said tartly, 'That's very reassuring . . . '

We quickly discovered, though, that Sean couldn't stand having the straps of the armour anywhere near his injured shoulder. Trying to work round the wound just exacerbated the problem.

Eventually, he gave it up, threw the armour back on the pile in frustration. 'I'll just have to risk it,' he said, sweat standing out on his forehead. 'But I'll take a spare one for Roger. The smallest you've got.'

MacMillan had eyed him in stony silence while he struggled. 'I won't ask what happened to that shoulder,' he said quietly, 'but you're going to have to give me the full story tomorrow. And it had better be good.'

Twenty minutes later, we climbed into the Nissan and Madeleine cranked up the engine. A thin drizzle had started to fall. MacMillan put his head in through the open window.

'I'll try and pull my men back from the area so you don't get any interference,' he said. 'I can't warn them you're on your way. We think half this lot are listening in on police scanners and I don't want to tip anyone off.'

'Thank you,' Sean said, and meant it.

MacMillan nodded shortly, rapped his hand on the top of the door briskly as he stepped back. 'Don't forget,' he warned, in more like his old clipped tone, waving a finger. 'I want both you and your brother in my office tomorrow morning. First thing.'

'Don't worry,' Sean said. 'If we make it, we'll be there.'

★

Getting into the estate without first tangling with the police lines was the easy part. MacMillan had opened up a small gap for us in the perimeter, and we shot through it without stopping.

To begin with, the outward demeanour of Lavender looked normal. Quiet, maybe, but normal. Except for the total lack of population. The first houses we passed were unnervingly still, as if the empty properties were watching us blankly under the streetlights. There didn't even seem to be any cats.

Madeleine made another turn. This time there was more evidence of haste, and fear. Windows had been left open, letting the net curtains behind them flutter at the end of their tethers, as though they were trying to get away, too. The odd front door was ajar. The Patrol's headlights picked out a child's red plastic pedal tractor, lying on its side in the gutter.

We nearly got as far as Kirby Street, when we turned a corner to find the road completely blocked from one hedge to another by a pair of burning vehicles. One of them had once been a police patrol car. The road was covered in debris, a pavement tree lay uprooted, and a road sign had been pulled up and bent double, its concrete footing still attached.

Madeleine braked to a halt about twenty metres away just as the tyres burst on one of the cars. They went off like pistol shots, echoing from the brickwork on either side of us, making us jump.

'What do we do now?' she asked, shaky but holding. 'Is there another way round?'

'We'll look,' Sean said. I gestured to the glovebox. He reached in and came out with the Glock, which he checked briefly and shoved into the back of his belt. 'Stay here and keep the motor running,' he told Madeleine. 'If there's any sign of trouble fall back two streets and we'll meet you there.'

She nodded whitely and I jumped out with him, slamming the door on an indignant Friday. The stench of the smoke instantly clogged my nostrils. I held my breath as we slipped into the nearest ginnel.

The raucous noise grew louder as we approached the next street, and our pace slowed to a cautious tiptoe in the darkness. It was impossible to see what was under your feet, in any case. I stayed a pace or so behind Sean, my eyes constantly straining to cover the ground behind us.

At the end of the ginnel we crouched low to the fence and peered around the corner of it.

A white kid who couldn't have been more than twelve ran out of the nearest house doorway and down the short path away from our position, with a flat square box clutched to his chest that was probably a video recorder.

He was followed by a blonde-haired girl, perhaps a year or so younger. In one hand she was carrying a ghetto-blaster, running so the plug bounced along on the end of its lead behind her like a toy dog. In the other she had a cordless electric drill.

The next person out of the house was older, but that still didn't mean he was out of his teens. He came out walking backwards, emptying the last of a green plastic fuel can over the hall carpet as he emerged. Once the can was empty he threw it aside, pulled a box of matches out of his pocket, and struck one.

As we watched, he flicked the match into the house and darted back out of reach of the blaze that clawed instantly at the doorway. The fire seemed to burst into the world fully grown by the accelerated nature of its birth, and ravenous.

The older boy grabbed his fuel can, but was no more than four strides down the path when something small, dark, and blurred came raining out of the sky. We heard the sound effects of impact, a crack, a grunt, then falling.

'He's been hit,' I whispered, starting to rise.

Sean grabbed my arm and yanked me back against the fencing, still far stronger than I'd ever be. I rebounded as I hit. It knocked the breath out of me.

'Keep down,' he hissed.

Seconds later, I picked up the sound of running feet. A group of Asian boys pounded into view, armed with lengths of timber and baseball bats. One of them even carried what looked like a sword. They pounced on the one who'd fallen, dragging his lifeless form out into the street so the pack could get at him.

They were onto him like jackals then, thrashing and tearing. I tried for my feet again, but as suddenly as it had started, the beating stopped. They abandoned their attack with a few last, heartfelt kicks and retreated. The firestarter was left washed up on the pavement behind them, bleeding into the gutter.

It only took a moment before the reason for the rapid withdrawal became apparent, even from our screened location.

A line of well-drilled bodies pressed forwards, hiding behind makeshift shields and plastic dustbin lids. Despite the cast of the streetlights, I could see they were all white, teenage at best.

Behind them, another wave were lighting Molotovs and throwing them casually towards the enemy. Those without a cigarette lighter were lobbing bricks or bottles instead. The cacophony was unbelievable. It was a devastating barrage to endure, and the Asian gangs fell back in disarray in the face of it.

The newcomers advanced until they'd moved over and round the firestarter, paused for a moment, then backed away. When the piece of pavement where he'd been lying re-appeared, he'd been gathered up and taken from it as though he'd never existed.

I glanced at Sean, found his eyes narrowed. He jerked his head to indicate we should leave, and I followed him silently back down the ginnel.

Madeleine was still waiting for us beside the burning police car. We didn't speak again until we'd climbed into the Patrol.

'What the hell was going on back there?' I demanded, fighting off Friday's ecstatic reaction to our safe return.

'A very pro operation,' Sean said, twisting in his seat. 'They're clearing everything of value, burning the evidence, and carrying out their wounded. It's slick, you have to give them that.'

'You mean the whole thing's been planned?' Madeleine asked when he'd quickly run through what we'd just seen. The disbelief was plain in her voice. 'I can't believe O'Bryan would engineer a riot just so they could rob a few houses.'

'But it's not just a few,' I said, catching on. 'It's the whole estate, if they can get away with it. This isn't just a battle, it's a campaign.'

'We need to tell MacMillan what's going on in here,' Madeleine said, reaching for her mobile phone.

We didn't have a direct number for the Superintendent, so the best we could do was dial the main police station in town. Half the population must have been doing the same, because we consistently failed to get a connection.

After half a dozen tries, we gave up. 'MacMillan's got a helicopter up there,' Sean said. 'He probably doesn't need us to tell him what's happening. We've got more important things to focus on, and we're probably going to have to take the long way round now, so let's move.'

Even being circumspect, we caught a by-blow of the violence. Turning a corner we almost ran down a small gang of Asian boys who were trying to mount an untidy rearguard action against the interlopers. Both sides reacted immediately to our arrival, turning their missiles onto the Patrol as though by prior agreement.

Madeleine let out a shriek as a petrol bomb shattered on the front bull bars, blocking our forward view in a sheet of flame. Without needing to be told, she slammed the Nissan into reverse and shot backwards. She managed to largely ignore the lump of rockery stone that cartwheeled across the corner of the bonnet, striking the paint to the bone.

Suddenly, we seemed to be surrounded by running figures on all sides. A feral face appeared outside the side window opposite me, making me gasp. Friday hurled himself towards it, all teeth and hackles, and the face dropped away. There were slobber marks left behind on the glass, but I couldn't tell who'd made them.

Before, the Patrol had made me feel enclosed, protected, but now it was a small steel trap, airless and contracting. My heart seemed to be trying to trampoline its way out of my chest. I bore down hard on the sheer panic that gripped my gut. If they caught us there wasn't any line of dustbin lid-wielding comrades to come and rescue us. They would hack us to pieces.

Madeleine kept going backwards for several hundred metres with her foot hard down, ignoring the screaming protests of the twin differentials. She steered with one hand, looking back over her shoulder as she swerved wildly down the obstacle-strewn street, jolting over debris and detritus.

I didn't see anyone standing in our way, but if they were Madeleine didn't alter course to avoid them. It was best not to look. I expected the tyres to burst at any moment, send us slithering out of control, but somehow they held.

'OK, OK,' Sean shouted. 'We're clear.'

She lifted her foot off the accelerator jerkily. In the low gear the engine braking effect was sharp and severe, throwing us back in our seats. The dog half-fell into my lap, and wasn't careful which bits of me he trampled on to regain his footing.

Once we'd stopped, Madeleine slumped forwards over the wheel, her whole body shuddering. Sean reached out, stroked her hair. She sat up quickly then, scrubbing at her eyes with an angry fist. 'I'm sorry,' she said, forcing out a tight, bright smile. 'I'm letting you down.'

'You're not,' he said, firm, but gentle. 'You're doing great, Mad. Don't give up on us now.'

She flicked her eyes in my direction, as though expecting to see scorn, but I didn't have any to give her. Although she'd had a terrifying situation thrown at her, she hadn't frozen. You couldn't ask for more than that from anyone.

'Courage isn't about not being scared,' I said. 'It's about overcoming it.'

She looked surprised for a moment, then nodded and squared her shoulders.

'OK,' she said, back on level ground. 'I'm OK. Let's go.'

We detoured round the trouble-spot through one of the kiddies' playgrounds, sideswiping a slide in the darkness and splintering the fragile glass fibre. I pushed away the pang of guilt.

The short cut brought us out close to our target, on the far side of Kirby Street and further out towards the darkened No Man's Land between the estates. The lights of Copthorne blazed in the near distance.

Sean eyed the black outlines of the last remaining line of terraced houses in the centre with relief.

'At least they haven't torched them yet,' he said.

The row in front of our destination had long since collapsed. The slate had gone to thieves, the glass to vandals. Then the rain had picked away at the mortar between the rubble-filled stone walls until, at last, the houses had simply tumbled into their own cellars.

The weeds and the brambles had whipped up to hold what was left fast to the ground, as if they were afraid it would be taken from them, if they let go.

We couldn't get right up to the front of the row where we suspected Roger had been stashed. Madeleine nosed the Patrol to a careful halt as close as she could among the fallen masonry and dead timber, and cut the engine.

We all climbed out, feeling the bite of the night air. Sean handed Madeleine the body armour we'd brought for Roger, and picked up a big Maglite.

Friday jumped down and lifted his head, blinking as he sampled the breeze, as if overwhelmed by the barrage of scents that assaulted him. He circled aimlessly round the Patrol, seeming interested in everything. Pauline had said he was a good tracker, but it was difficult to know if he was onto something.

The fronts of the houses had been boarded up with sheets of de-laminating plywood, and although we walked quickly down the row with the torch, none of them looked to have been recently disturbed.

'We'll try the back,' Sean said. 'We'll be here all night if we have to fight our way into every one from this side.'

The rear of the houses could be reached down what had once been an alleyway, with cobbles underfoot, and a gully drain down the centre. The mirror-image row that would have backed onto it was no more than a disconnected pile of stones.

The gates leading to the tiny back yards had mostly disintegrated, or were dangling by the rusted remnants of their hinges. One dislodged completely and clattered to the floor as we brushed past.

The back doors had been made of sterner stuff than the gates, but they'd been kicked in instead. Inside, the houses were very dark and reeked with a pungent blend of old urine like a neglected public lavatory. The beam of the torch picked out empty two-litre bottles of cheap cider, scrunched-up crisp packets, and blackened shards of silver foil. I didn't see the needles, but I tried to curb Friday's explorations with a hand slipped through his collar, just in case.

The Ridgeback didn't show any signs of involvement until the fourth house along. As we stepped through the doorway he suddenly went rigid, and jerked forwards out of my grasp.

He shot through the kitchen. We followed at a slightly slower pace, trying not to break our necks in the gloom by tripping over rotting furniture too shabby even for the house clearance gannets to cart away.

In the living room we found Friday scrabbling at the base of a mattress that was leaning up against the wall by the stairs.

I clicked my fingers and the dog reluctantly pulled back. Between the three of us we dragged the mattress into the centre of the room and dropped it onto the boards, raising musty clouds of dust that spiralled and spun in the beam of the torch.

Behind it, the door leading to the cellar had been secured with a shiny new galvanised bolt and padlock.

Sean gave the door an experimental nudge, but the house dated from the 1890s, back when they built them strong. I tapped him on the arm and handed him my Swiss Army knife. The Philips screwdriver attachment was already unfolded.

'You always were the prepared one, Charlie,' he said with a grin that I heard in his voice rather than saw. 'I think you must have been a Boy Scout in a previous life.'

'Didn't you know?' I said, laconic. 'I'm a member of the Anti-Woggle League.'

Madeleine shone the Maglite onto the door. It didn't take Sean long to undo the two screws which held the catch onto the outer frame. The door swung outwards with the bolt and padlock still attached, without us having to bother forcing them. Sean gave me back the knife and took the torch from Madeleine.

Its narrow beam revealed a small dank stairwell that seemed to disappear much further than it should do in order to descend just one level into the cellar.

Something brown and furred scuttled across one of the lower treads and paused to stare red-eyed up into the flashlight, unconcerned. It was the size of a small rabbit, igniting a dread I hadn't experienced since childhood. Friday growled deep in his throat, and Madeleine groaned.

'You stay here,' Sean told her. 'I don't like the idea of all of us being down there, anyway, just in case.'

She nodded gratefully, and I was forced to swallow my own fear, starting nervously down the stairs as though I was expecting the damned thing to leap out at me at any moment. All the hairs on my arms had stood bolt upright like I'd had a static charge.

'Are you OK?' Sean asked.

I forced a smile, managed through gritted teeth, 'If there's once thing I can't stand, it's fucking rats.'

Sean glanced at me, and when he spoke his voice was dry as the desert. 'So don't fuck them,' he said.

Friday wasn't in the mood to miss out on the action, particularly with the prospect of an interesting snack in the offing. He was destined to be disappointed. The rat scarpered as soon as he put his first foot on the stairs, disappearing into a hole in the stonework from which it failed to re-emerge.

Sean edged downwards with more circumspection, holding the torch at shoulder height, just behind the bulb so he could use the other end as a club. Once we reached the rough floor we both stood silent for a few moments, scanning the corners of the cramped room.

The cellar was little more than ten feet square, the walls

covered with crumbling plaster which had slipped to reveal large areas of mouldy stone underneath.

Sean cast about with the light, but the search pattern revealed the cellar to be almost empty, apart from the junk. Piled against the far wall were great stacks of mildewed newspapers, wilted slabs of cardboard, and rags, all mixed up together. It smelt of corruption, and festering decay.

For a minute we thought it was a false alarm, and I felt the sharp, sour tang of disappointment. Then Friday gave up inspecting the hole where the rat had made its exit, and came over to give us the benefit of his sensitive nostrils.

He padded casually across the uneven cobbles and thrust his face straight into the dross until he was buried up to the ears, like he'd put his head under water.

The result sent us both reeling back in shocked amazement.

The pile of rubbish exploded upwards and outwards with a wailing cry. A small, stinking apparition launched itself from the dregs and lunged for the gap between us and the freedom of the stairs.

Twenty-seven

For a moment I was totally stunned, made too stupid by it to act, but Sean snagged his foot under a shin as it rushed past him, sending the figure sprawling.

'For fuck's sake, boy,' Sean roared, shining the torch on him. 'Just for once in your life will you stop running away from me?'

Roger had been scrabbling away on his hands and knees and it took him a couple of seconds to register the sound of his brother's voice. His desperation subsided, but the wariness didn't leave him.

'We're not with O'Bryan in this, Roger,' I said quickly, moving forwards. 'We've never been with him.'

Roger recognised me and suddenly it was like something cracked open inside him. The tears overflowed to drip down his cheeks, leaving clear tracks through the dirt.

'I didn't want to do it,' he said, desperate, anguished. 'We had to. He made us.'

'We know, kid,' Sean knelt by the side of him, put his arms round the boy's shoulders and hugged him fiercely. 'We know all about O'Bryan.'

'He said, if we didn't k-kill Charlie, he'd make sure Ursula went to p-prison,' Roger went on, the words spilling out of him in gulps, even though his face was buried in Sean's chest, and his voice was muffled. I had to bend closer to hear what he was saying.

'He said they'd give her a rough time inside. He said—' he broke off as a fresh breaker of tears rolled over and smashed, 'that he'd make sure she l–lost the baby.'

His thin shoulders shook as he wept for what seemed like a long time. Sean had let the end of the torch dip, so that the beam hit the cellar wall, but in the light reflected back I could see the sorrow in his face, and the anger.

I touched his shoulder, feeling like an unwelcome intruder into their grief.

'We need to move,' I said.

He was still for a moment, then he nodded, gently levering Roger back so he could look into his face.

'Are you ready to get out of here, kid?'

The boy nodded mutely, the fight gone out of him. I led the way up the cellar steps to find that Madeleine was using her Zippo to light the stubs of some old candles she'd found. She gave Roger a big smile, and a hug too, which was pretty brave of her considering how rancid he smelt.

We used the flickering light to strip off the kid's ragged sweatshirt so we could put him into the body armour we'd brought for him. Roger let us undress him, pliant, like a doll.

He barely made a sound as his sleeve was peeled away and the top of a big scab from a deep abrasion on his forearm came with it. The wound was maybe a couple of days old. It hadn't been treated, and had started to heal, after a fashion, into the material.

'How did this happen?' Sean asked him.

Roger stared at his arm as if he'd never seen it before. 'Oh. That,' he said slowly. He shrugged. 'They knocked me off the bike.' His voice was disconnected, as though he was reporting a dull incident that had happened to someone else.

335

Sean tightened the velcro straps on the body armour without trusting himself to speak. He fed Roger's head and arms back into his sweatshirt, trying to keep the oozing arm away from the sleeve.

We were about to move out when the sound of shouting and the clatter of movement outside had us all freezing in our tracks. Sean tiptoed to the back door and disappeared briefly and silently into the yard. He was back a few moments later.

'Is that O'Bryan's lot?' I demanded in an urgent whisper.

'Not unless he's learned to speak Gujarati,' he said. 'They're just kids, but I'm not prepared to risk getting into a confrontation. We'll hold tight until they've gone.'

Madeleine produced half a bar of chocolate – from where I'm not entirely sure – and handed it over to Roger. The boy tore at the wrapping and devoured it like he hadn't eaten for days. The sugar hit seemed to put some animation back into him, some life back behind his eyes.

'What happened to Nasir, Rog?' Sean asked him then.

'O'Bryan shot him,' Roger said tonelessly, licking his fingers when he was done, and the inside of the wrapper, too. 'We had to go back and report. You know – after.' His eyes skated over me briefly, then fell away. 'Nas said he'd talk to Mr O'Bryan, but I was scared. He'd tried to talk to him before, when Aqueel took—'

He broke off again, aware that he'd said too much, but Sean nodded encouragingly. 'We know all about Aqueel and the others breaking into O'Bryan's car. What did he take?'

'I'm not sure. Nas never showed it to me. He just said he knew it had come from one of the robberies. Said he could use it to get us off the hook, but Mr O'Bryan just laughed at him and said he knew Nas'd been about to make trouble because *she'd* told him.'

He waved a hand in my direction. There was an accusing note in his voice that I couldn't deny. After all, I had indeed told O'Bryan about that, too, the first day he'd come to see me.

Guilt walked cold fingers into my chest cavity and clutched at my heart. Again, I remembered Nasir's outburst that day in the back garden, and realised now why he'd been so vehement.

Roger shrugged and went on. 'Anyway, Mr O'Bryan said he couldn't prove anything. And if Nas did try to stir it he'd make sure we all went down. That's when he started getting nasty about Ursula.'

'So what happened this time, when Nasir went to talk to O'Bryan after the shooting?'

Roger swallowed, as though the chocolate he'd wolfed was now making him sick. 'Mr O'Bryan's got this barn on the road out to Glasson where he keeps his classic cars. He told Nas to meet him there. I went with him, but Nas told me to wait outside. He was cool with it, you know, thought he could reason with him, get us another chance.'

Another chance.

My God, I thought. They were going to have *another* go at killing me. As if that first time at the gym wasn't enough.

'What went wrong?' Sean asked, and I opened my mouth to say, 'They missed,' when I realised we were at cross-purposes. I closed it again, and let Roger go on with his story.

'They were ages in there,' he said now, shivering so hard that Sean slipped out of his jacket and put it onto the boy. He had to turn the sleeves up three times before his fingers showed at the end of them. 'I wanted to know what they were saying, so I found a little window, round the back, and I looked in. I couldn't really hear, but Mr O'Bryan was ranting at him, I could tell. Then he just grabbed the gun off Nas and shot him with it.'

His eyes had lost immediate focus, seeing again in his mind's eye the argument, and the shooting. He must have seen it over and over, bound up in the torment of knowing that nothing he did or said could call it back, or cancel it out, or change the outcome. I'd been locked in a similar little cul-de-sac of hell myself, and I could recognise the signs.

'Nas went down screaming,' Roger whispered. 'Even through the glass and the walls I could hear him. And Mr O'Bryan just stood there, and watched him lying on the ground, writhing and screaming.'

He turned his face up to Sean's, and the candlelight showed that he was crying again. 'And then Nas didn't scream any more. And I ran away. I didn't help him. I didn't even *try*!'

'There wasn't anything you could have done, Rog,' Sean told him quietly. 'If you'd tried, he would have killed you, too.'

Roger wiped his nose on the back of his hand, nodded, but it was a desultory kind of nod. The kind that carries no real conviction. I could see it being a long time before he was going to be able to look in the mirror and not see the face of a coward staring back at him. Some people never managed that leap, never made it back.

Friday had started to pace and whine, making eyes towards the way out as if he was the one wearing a wristwatch. Taking the hint, we checked the back alley and found it was clear. Madeleine snuffed out the candles and we headed for the door.

We'd just gone through it and out into the back yard when the thump and crack of a tremendous explosion rippled through the air like someone had let off a giant petrol bomb in the next street.

Which, in a sense, they had.

We looked upwards, seeing a tongue of flame licking at the clouds over the rooftops of the houses, close by, and heard the patter of fallout on the slates. Some of it landed too close for comfort.

'What the hell was that?' Madeleine demanded.

I glanced at Sean. 'At a guess?' I said. 'That was the No Claims Bonus on your motor insurance.'

Sean turned, grabbing Roger's shoulders. 'Get out into the rubble and hide,' he told him. 'Don't come out until I come and get you. Understand?'

Roger looked about to argue, as stubborn as his brother, but Sean didn't have the time or the patience for a long and involved dialogue. 'You're a vital witness, Rog,' he said. 'If they get hold of you they'll kill you and all this will have been for nothing. Go on, get out of here!'

This time Roger did as he was told. We already knew he'd have made a world-class sprinter, given the opportunity. If the way he scaled the nearest pile of shifting stones was anything to go by, he hadn't lost much of his form.

The rest of us walked round the end of the buildings, carefully skirted the rubble, and were faced with the conflagration that had once been Sean's Nissan. He gave it a single, regretful glance, and moved on.

'Well, well, if it isn't Miss Fox,' said a cool voice from the shadows, and three figures stepped forwards into the pagan circle of light from the fire.

Somehow, I knew who they were before I saw their faces clearly.

West was in the centre, with Harlow and Drummond flanking him. Garton-Jones's men. They advanced with an arrogant confidence that only faltered slightly when they saw the dog.

Friday had started to growl as soon as he'd heard West's voice, pulling his lips back to emphasise his teeth. Even his neck seemed thicker, his collar going tight around the engorged muscles.

'If you've come to burn the boy, you're too late,' Sean said. 'He's gone.'

'He won't get far,' West said, almost lazily. He looked at the burning Patrol with the satisfaction of someone admiring their own handiwork. 'After all, your transport seems to be out of action. I don't think the RAC will be able to fix that by the side of the road, will they?'

As if at some unspoken signal, Harlow and Drummond started towards us then, closing in on Madeleine and me. Sean had said that Madeleine wasn't a field agent, hadn't had the training, but I just had time to see her let out a dreadful cry and charge forwards to meet Harlow head on. Then my attention was lost in my own problems.

Drummond launched in with a crafty look on his face. We'd crossed swords before and he'd made the mistake of not taking me seriously. This time, his face said, he was more than ready for anything I might throw at him.

Well, almost anything.

'Friday!' I yelled, pointing at Drummond. 'Get him!'

I wasn't sure if Pauline had ever included an attack trigger word in the canine training classes she'd attended with the Ridgeback, but I needn't have worried that Friday wouldn't get the right idea.

The dog streaked across the ground between us, his toenails digging up clods as he tore at the earth to gain extra purchase, head low and shoulders hunched.

Drummond hesitated for a moment too long before he started to twist away. With a devious look in his eye, Friday bounded the last few strides, reached up, and with great deliberation clamped his jaws around the fly of the man's jeans. It was like hearing the lock snapping shut on a prison door and knowing that, without the key, you're going to have to use Semtex or a gas-axe to get it open again.

Drummond instantly started squealing and battering at Friday's head and body, although without noticeable effect. The dog just tucked his ears back flat and shut his eyes. His skull was so thick he might as well have been wearing a crash helmet.

Then the pair of them overbalanced, and once the man was on the ground, I knew the Ridgeback had the upper hand. I had no qualms about leaving the two of them scuffling while I went to help Madeleine.

I ran past Sean and West to get to her. The two men were circling each other with their hackles up. Both were on guard, moving with that easy grace that suggested training, and skill. Even injured, I was still confident that Sean could take him.

I kept running.

Harlow had managed to land a couple of hefty punches on the dark-haired girl by the time I reached them, and seemed to be enjoying himself.

I threw myself onto his back in a move Friday would have been proud of, lacing one arm tight round his throat, and the other over his eyes. He just managed to get an elbow back before Madeleine took a run at him and brought her knee up hard. It seemed to be something of her trademark.

I swear I felt two lumps come up into his throat before I let go. I just had time to dismount as the man folded, gasping.

Madeleine and I both turned then to find Sean and West trading blows. Sean was taller and heavier than the other man, and he'd been taught by the nastiest people in the business, but he was still weak from the wound and the blood loss, and it was clear he was already tiring.

Even so, he'd scored a few hits, and for a moment I thought he'd done enough to disorientate West. The smaller man's aim was off. His punches seemed to be consistently missing Sean's ducked chin, deflecting off to the side.

Then I saw the determination in his eyes, and the cunning.

My legs had carried me a couple of steps, my mouth opening to shout a warning, when West finally got lucky and landed the blow he'd been planning all along.

He hit Sean, hard, just under the point of his left shoulder.

West didn't bother to keep his guard up after that. He already knew it was a punch that would finish the fight.

Sean went backwards silently, unable to spare the breath even to cry out. He twisted and fell, his whole body shuddering. His eyes were open, but there was only shock in them, and his breathing was quick and shallow. The blood started to well up, passing through the layers of dressing, tracking across the front of his shirt. It glistened in the firelight.

West gave him a savage smile, and moved in for the kill.

A wheaten blur suddenly shot past me and dived into the fray. Friday, bored with the game of ravaging at Drummond, had spotted a new target. His blood was up. His tribal instinct, so long contained beneath the veneer of domestication, had been let loose, and there was no stopping it now.

By the time I saw the knife in West's hand, it was too late. The dog had already started its run, muscles meshing smoothly under the skin as he powered forwards with a single-minded purpose.

I yelled Friday's name, but he didn't hear me. Or if he did, he was too far beyond control to listen and obey.

I saw West's lips stretch back in a parody of the dog's grimace as Friday attacked. The man took a couple of quick steps backwards, and for a moment I thought he meant to retreat, but it was just a bluff. He held his left arm out as he started to turn, a red flag that Friday couldn't resist.

'Friday!' I shouted desperately. 'No! Leave him!'

The Ridgeback gathered himself and leapt with perfect co-ordination and timing, clamping his jaws round the man's exposed forearm just as he reached the crest of his jump. The sheer momentum should have carried West right off his feet.

As it was, the man allowed himself to be spun about, pivoting on his toes to keep his balance. His right arm swung round towards the dog's body, the blade flashing in the dull light.

I'll never forget the scream that Friday gave out as the knife went in. It was horrible, and oddly human. I don't think I've ever heard a noise like it, and I pray that I never will again.

West stabbed him hard enough to sink the blade into the dog's flank right up to the hilt. Even so, Friday wouldn't give up his grip without a fight. He hung on bravely, taking two quick, nasty blows about the head before he let go at last and dropped, bleeding, to the stony ground.

I was moving forwards before the Ridgeback had hit the deck. Out of the corner of my eye I saw him struggling gamely to rise. This time it was Madeleine who called my name, told me to stop. Her voice was high with alarm.

I paid no more attention to her warnings than Friday had done to mine. I just had to hope that the end result wouldn't be the same.

West grinned as he jumped away from the dog, waving the knife that ran crimson with his blood in front of me. Seeking to taunt. All it did was brace my courage.

As I closed on him, he tried a couple of swift slashes to test my reflexes, didn't seem worried that they failed to connect. He was high on confidence, the conviction of his own invincibility running through him like fire.

He came at me with the knife held underarm, aiming to drive it upwards into my body, to slit me open from stomach to breastbone like a snared rabbit.

On the upstroke, I grabbed the top of his wrist tight with both hands outstretched, thumbs overlapping to form a vee. I made no attempt to wrestle the knife from his grasp, which would have been stupid, and probably lethal.

Instead I used the force of his own charge to swing his arm up and out to the side. Still holding his wrist I stepped inside it, underneath it, turning my back into West's body as I did so, as though we were partners in some deadly form of old-time dancing.

Our arms reached the top of their arc and gathered speed on the way down. I had control now, using his own size and weight against him. I tightened my fingers around his hand, then, still wrapped firmly in his own fist, I plunged the knife down and sank it into West's right leg at the top of his thigh.

I felt the blade go in, tugging and tearing. It glanced off the bone, then settled deep into flesh. West howled much less convincingly than Friday had done, and I was aware of a fierce blast of grim satisfaction. It left a dark and bitter taste in my mouth.

By the time I turned to face him, West was on the ground, writhing. Both hands were clamped round the handle of the knife, which was all I could see protruding from his leg. Blood was welling from the wound in gushing spurts like a burst water main coming up through clay.

Numbly, I left him there and stumbled over to kneel by Friday's body. The dog lifted his head as I reached him, and begged me with those big expressive eyes to make his pain go away. There was a trickle of blood coming out of his nose, and his sides rose and fell shallowly, as though he was afraid to breathe. The sight of him stung my eyes with tears.

Madeleine had helped Sean to his feet. He moved across, producing from the side pocket of his trousers the sling he'd discarded earlier. He thrust it into my hand as he came past.

'Here, stop the bleeding with this and watch he doesn't bite you,' he said. He still looked pale. 'You OK?'

I nodded, and he carried on, bending over West.

Loudly, with expletives, West was demanding a doctor, and an ambulance. He'd pulled out a grubby handkerchief from his pocket and was clumsily trying to knot that round his thigh. Sean eyed him coldly, and made no moves to help.

Then, after a few moments he reached down and took hold of the knife's greasy handle.

West's body jerked at the touch. 'No, no!' he shouted. 'Let them do it at the hospital. Don't move it. I'll bleed to death.'

Sean cocked an eyebrow at that less-than-convincing argument, and hauled the knife straight out of the wound with a vicious jerk. West bucked and twisted, swearing.

'You didn't think,' Sean demanded quietly, 'that I was going to leave you with a concealed weapon, did you, you sick fucker?'

West stopped thrashing about long enough to spit at him. Sean leaned closer, ignoring the splatter of phlegm that landed near his feet.

'Did you know that you can pick up virulent infections from dogs' blood?' he lied conversationally, then turned on his heel and walked away, with the polluted knife still dangling from his fingers.

Sean moved back to where Madeleine and I were trying to patch up Friday's wound. He held the knife out towards me without speaking, and for a moment I didn't understand what he was showing me.

It was just a knife. A combat knife with a long serrated blade and a camouflage-coloured plastic non-slip handle. Then I suddenly realised where I'd seen it before.

Well, maybe not *that* particular knife, but one very much like it.

In fact, I hadn't seen the blade. That had been buried deep in Harvey Langford's chest, but the rest was identical.

I didn't have time to react to the discovery, though, because it very quickly became apparent we weren't alone any more. That the burning Patrol had served as a beacon for trouble.

Madeleine and Sean turned a slow circle, staring out beyond the area lit by the flames. I came to my feet, also, aware of a tightening in my chest, a drumming in my ears.

Slowly, gradually, there came the slip and slither of feet approaching across the rubble from all sides until at last more than a dozen men took shape out of the darkness, and formed a semicircular perimeter in front of us.

A final figure appeared, and they parted to let him through. Ian Garton-Jones looked much as he had done at our last meeting, shaven-headed and dressed in black. There was one notable exception, however.

This time, he was carrying a double-barrelled shotgun, and he was pointing it unswervingly in our direction.

Twenty-eight

The shotgun was a twelve gauge Browning with stacked over-and-under barrels, a middle-of-the-range sportsman's gun. Garton-Jones probably used it for clays.

A brief picture of one of my old army weapons' handling instructors flashed into my mind at that point. There was nothing to beat a shotgun for house clearance, he'd said. In a confined space you hardly even had to aim. They were deadly.

On open ground, though, there was always a chance you could sprint out of effective range. Providing you were prepared to risk it that the gun hadn't been choked down too far, and the shooter's aim wasn't too accurate. With a normal spread pattern of the shot you'd probably escape serious injury at anything over thirty metres. Forty, to be on the safe side.

I glanced across at Sean, but he had that stubborn look about him that said he wasn't going to run away from this one, even if he got the opportunity. And besides, Friday wasn't in any state to sprint anywhere. There was no way I was going to abandon the Ridgeback to Garton-Jones's tender ministrations.

'Let that dog loose on me or any of my men,' he'd said, *'and I'll personally break its spine.'*

I stood my ground.

West squirmed round, recognised his boss, and started making a lot of noise. He pointed to the knife which was still in Sean's hand, screaming that we'd stabbed him, and exhorting Garton-Jones to shoot us.

Garton-Jones silenced him with a dark look, the play from the firelight emphasising the older man's deep eye sockets, making it difficult to read him. He jerked his head to one of his men, who approached warily and snatched the knife away from Sean.

The man trotted back across to Garton-Jones and handed it over. He studied the knife for a long time, turning the blood-smeared blade over so it caught the light.

'Look at it,' West shouted then. 'It's just the same as the one they used to kill that vigilante bloke.'

I half-turned in surprise at his words. Whatever tactic I'd been expecting from West, that certainly wasn't it. My eye caught Harlow and Drummond, both now back on their feet and trying to merge in with the other security men. They looked edgy, ill at ease.

Sean ignored them, pinning West with a contemptuous stare. 'And just why would I want to do a thing like that?' he demanded in a deadly quiet tone.

West tried to stand, but his leg wouldn't support him. He fell back heavily, addressing Garton-Jones rather than Sean.

'Like I told you, Langford knew Meyer was trying to take over the turf now he was back on Copthorne,' he said, the lies forcing the sweat out of his skin. 'He knew Meyer had killed the Gadatra boy for getting his brother into the shit. That's why they got rid of him.'

Sean took a step forwards then, intent. 'You miserable, lying little—'

'That's enough,' Garton-Jones rapped. He brought the barrels of the Browning up, just to hammer home his point. 'I think I'd like your hands where I can see them, all of you. Now – if you don't mind.'

Sean put his out by his sides. The left one wouldn't lift more than a few inches. The blood had reached as far as his hand, trickling down his wrist and dripping from his fingers. West must have blown my father's neat and careful stitches wide open. He was going to be livid.

At that moment we caught the sounds of shouting, breaking glass, and missiles being thrown. The riot was moving closer, only a few streets away now. The sky was lightening up all the time as more houses fell to the flames.

'I think we should continue this interesting discussion from a fallback position,' Garton-Jones said. He raised his voice. 'Let's move it out.'

'We're not going anywhere,' Sean said, between clenched teeth. 'My brother's still out there.'

Garton-Jones regarded him levelly. 'It wasn't optional, Mr Meyer,' he said. His cold stare shifted to me. 'Ladies first, I think.' He waved the shotgun briefly in my direction. 'Over here where I can keep an eye on you, Miss Fox, if you wouldn't mind.'

I glanced at Sean before I moved, caught the faintest flicker of his eyes, and understood instinctively what he was driving at. To follow Garton-Jones's orders, I kept out of his line of fire, and that meant crossing behind Sean.

In the middle of Sean's belt, tucked into the small of his back, lay the Glock. As I moved close behind him it took only the smallest of movements to reach out for the gun. My right hand closed round the butt, warmed to the touch from his body heat. I felt Sean breathe in, loosening the barrel to my grip.

Smoothly, I brought the gun out into view round his body. I didn't trust Garton-Jones's bulky clothing not to be hiding body armour of his own, so I took a bead dead centre on the exposed flesh of his neck, just below the ear.

Garton-Jones heard the precise, sharp double click of the first round snapping into the breech, and froze.

The barrels of the Browning were down and away from me by then. It would have taken him much too long to have brought them to bear. He turned his head slowly, blinked twice into the business end of the Glock's muzzle, ten feet from him, then almost seemed to relax. He turned his head back towards Sean.

'It would appear that your girlfriend's been watching too many bad movies, Mr Meyer,' he said, with a nasty grin.

Sean smiled back at him, harmless as a shark showing its teeth before the bite. 'My *girlfriend*, as you call her,' he said with calm deliberation, 'is ex-Special Forces. She's lethal. At that distance she could shoot your eyeball straight out from between the lids without even smudging your mascara.'

Just for a moment, Garton-Jones looked shaken, then he laughed. 'Nice try,' he said, 'but I'll bet she doesn't even know how to take the safety off,' and started to bring the shotgun up.

'Hold it!' I snapped. He halted on a reflex to the command, and once I'd got his attention, I aimed to keep it.

'This is a Glock 19 nine millimetre semiautomatic,' I said, speaking fast. 'There is no conventional safety catch; it's built into the trigger. As soon as I depressed the first stage of the trigger, the weapon became active. It's active now, and my finger's getting twitchy.' I paused, then added quietly, 'Don't think I can't or won't do this, if you leave me no other choice.'

I saw Garton-Jones register the utter conviction in my voice and start to waver. Watched as he weighed up the chance that I might be bluffing. Knew precisely the moment when he finally realised that I was not.

He carefully thumbed the safety back on and dropped the Browning into the mud at his feet. An amateur, with no respect for a decent gun. His hands went up as Sean's came down.

I heard Sean's breath hiss out, relief escaping like steam as he ducked to rescue the shotgun. He retrieved it, and moved back to my right. Madeleine took the knife, trying to hide her revulsion at the amount of blood that still covered it.

All the time, I kept the Glock level, kept the front sight up, pointing straight at Garton-Jones. And all the time, he kept his gaze locked on mine.

It took every ounce of sheer bloody-minded will I possessed to keep the gun steady, not to let my arm and hand tremble. I was damned if I was going to show him a sign of weakness and I silently thanked all those hours I spent at Attila's, working out.

'See,' West spat, disgusted by his boss's capitulation, 'I told you they killed the Asian lad. He was shot with a nine-mil, right?'

'Oh shut up, West, you're starting to bore me,' Sean snapped, swinging the Browning in his direction. It was enough to silence the other man.

I turned back to Garton-Jones, and played a hunch. 'I have no idea what's going on here,' I said, lowering the Glock, 'beside the fact that your man West is trying his guts out to persuade you that we're guilty of something we haven't done. Maybe you can shed some light on why that is.'

As if on cue, we all turned towards West. His eyes swivelled in panic and he started to hutch backwards, still clutching the now sodden handkerchief to his leg. 'She stabbed me,' he repeated, his voice almost a squawk, as if that answered the question.

'Yes, I did,' I admitted. I eyed Garton-Jones again. 'But if it's Sean's knife, as he's claiming, then how do you explain the fact that Friday's also been injured. Do you think we'd stab the dog ourselves? And how does West know what sort of knife was used to kill Harvey Langford? Unless he was there.'

I let that one settle on them for a few moments. Jav had pointed the finger firmly at the security men the last time we'd spoken to him, and he'd been too frightened to lie to us again. It wasn't his fault that we'd lumped them all together and automatically assumed he meant Garton-Jones, rather than West . . .

'But you were there, too,' Garton-Jones said now, and it was a statement.

Sean nodded. 'We were manoeuvred into being at the building site just after West killed him,' he said. 'He even took pot shots at us to try and keep us pinned down until the cops arrived.'

Garton-Jones looked at the blood on Sean's shirt. 'Is that what happened to the shoulder?'

'He got lucky.'

The security chief gave West a long considering stare, and it was impossible to guess from his impassive face what thoughts were passing through his mind.

'He told me it was all down to some long-running feud between you and Langford going back to your National Front days,' he said at last, curling his lip. 'He told me that Langford had winged you before you'd stuck him. Oh when fascists fall out.' He shrugged. 'I didn't care as long as you didn't bring it onto my estate.'

'So how did he know what kind of gun was used to kill Nasir?' I asked.

Garton-Jones seemed suddenly weary, barely able to look at his second-in-command. He sighed. 'He was responsible for that one, too, was he?'

'No! Ian, you can't believe these lying shits,' West said, pleading now. 'We've been working together for ten years. For God's sake, trust me on this.'

Madeleine, who'd gone back to tending Friday's wound, had been listening without taking part in the exchange. Now, she got to her feet and moved forwards. 'How did you find out about the contract on Lavender Gardens?' she asked.

Garton-Jones stared at her blankly for a moment, as though he couldn't see the relevance, then something connected. 'He put me onto it,' he said, waving a hand in West's direction, 'through a pal of his from the TA. He works for the Community Juvenile office. Chap called Eric O'Bryan. We pay him a commission for putting work our way.'

'O'Bryan's the one who's running the crime ring on the estates,' Madeleine said, breaking the news to him almost gently. 'O'Bryan's gang of kids crank the crime rate up until the residents are prepared to pay you to come in and sort it out for them. West and O'Bryan have been making money twice over from the scheme.'

'You can't believe this crap, Ian,' West broke in, but the desperation was clear in his voice. 'I wouldn't do something like that to you. You're my mate.'

'You're his fall guy,' Sean said clearly. 'His scapegoat. Once this riot's over, who d'you think they're going to blame for antagonising the Asian community, stirring it all up? West and O'Bryan will skip with the proceeds and you're going to be left carrying the can. Face it, you've been had.'

West made another failed attempt to rise. 'Ian, I—'

'Shut up, Mr West,' Garton-Jones said without turning his head. 'Don't dig your grave any deeper than it is already.'

I had the nasty feeling that he wasn't speaking meta-phorically.

West wasn't a fool, he'd seen the tide turning against him, knew when he was beaten. He sat back in the mud, looked at the blood on his hands and gave a high-pitched laugh. 'You won't be able to prove any of this,' he said. 'You won't make any of it stick.'

'You're forgetting my little brother,' Sean told him. 'He's a witness. You were trying to get rid of him tonight, and you've failed. It's over.'

If anything, that made West laugh louder. 'Of course it's not over,' he said scornfully. 'As soon as we saw the jeep and realised you were here we knew you'd probably have found the kid, got him out, so O'Bryan went looking for him while the rest of us kept you occupied. He's been out there, all this time.' Triumph made his voice a crow. 'Your brother's already dead.'

'You'd better hope not,' Sean told him, his voice icy. 'For your own sake.'

Garton-Jones jerked his head to some of his men, who moved forwards to grab hold of West, haul him to his feet. 'Get him out of here,' he said, his face twisting with distaste. 'And watch those two, as well,' he added, pointing to Harlow and Drummond, who'd been trying to slink back into the ranks.

He glanced again at Sean's shoulder. 'You look as though you need a medic, too.'

Sean shook his head. 'I'm OK,' he said. He looked pale, tired, but I knew it was useless to try and talk him out of his objective. 'If you've got transport, though, can you get Friday out of here? Get him sorted?'

'Of course,' Garton-Jones said, but when a couple of his men tried to approach him, the dog opened his eyes and did his best to snarl at them. Even battered and wounded, the Ridgeback presented a fearsome obstacle. They hesitated, and I couldn't say I blamed them for it.

'One of us is going to have to go with him,' I said, my voice hollow. I looked at Sean and Madeleine. There was no way I wanted to let Sean go out after O'Bryan alone, and I didn't want to let Madeleine go with him, either. It wasn't that I didn't believe the dark-haired girl could take care of herself, or of Sean. That wasn't what I was afraid of.

Pauline had been right. Sean was after blood, and if the chance came up I was afraid Madeleine wouldn't be able to stop him from taking it.

It was a fast downhill route, through anger to death. Coming back from the power and the thrill of it left you constantly unsure of yourself, like a newly sober alcoholic.

'Don't worry, Charlie, I'll go with Friday.'

I realised it was Madeleine who'd spoken. She bent down by the dog's head, talking to him and stroking his ears while two of Garton-Jones's men got a coat under him, using that as a sling. This time, the Ridgeback didn't protest, allowing them to pick him up, start to carry him away.

I put my hand on Madeleine's arm as she moved past me. 'It should be me,' I argued, stumbling to find the right words. 'He's my responsibility. I promised Pauline I'd—'

'Don't,' Madeleine interrupted, but kindly. 'I can take care of Friday. Sean needs you.' She lowered her voice. 'I've seen him change like this before – when he's working. He drops into another mode, another skin,' she said, almost sadly. 'You move just like he does, Charlie. You can't help it. Just watch his back for me, OK?'

She smiled at me quickly, and then she was gone, jogging nimbly over the rubble to catch up. I noted that the security men were taking a great deal more care with the dog than they were with West.

Garton-Jones watched them half-carrying, half-dragging his former lieutenant over the rough ground, then he turned back to Sean. 'This O'Bryan character,' he said. 'How dangerous is he?'

'We know he's killed once, and he probably still has the gun,' Sean told him.

'In that case, you'd best keep the shotgun,' Garton-Jones said. He eyed us both, subdued, diffident even, and it had nothing to do with the fact that Sean still had hold of the

Browning. 'Are you sure we can't help you search for the boy?'

'Positive,' Sean said. 'If Roger's managed to evade O'Bryan this long he'll run a mile if he sees your lot. He doesn't know you and West aren't in this together.'

Garton-Jones looked disappointed to be denied the chase, but he nodded.

'Thanks for the offer, anyway,' Sean said, sounding sincere. 'I appreciate it.'

They shook hands. It seemed an ironic gesture of civility, somehow, in view of the circumstances.

'You gave me a good runaround,' Garton-Jones told him, then added in my direction, 'and if I'd known how handy you were, young lady, I'd have offered you a job.'

Sean smiled at him. 'You'll have to get in the queue for that,' he said.

We stood and watched the last of Garton-Jones's men disappear into the shadows, moving quickly in a direction that took them away from the worst of the conflict.

It seemed to be getting nearer all the time. The sounds of it swelling like surf on a beach, relentless and profound. If we didn't find Roger soon, the gangs would do O'Bryan's work for him.

For a moment Sean didn't seem in any hurry to move off himself, and I thought that maybe he was more badly hurt by his altercation with West than he'd wanted to admit. He just stood, staring at the burning hulk of the Patrol, as though mesmerised by the wheel and twist of the fire.

'You do realise, Sean,' I said quietly, 'that even if O'Bryan's—' I broke off, unwilling to voice what was so clearly running through both our minds. I tried again. 'No matter what O'Bryan's done, you can't kill him.'

'If West's right, and Roger's dead,' Sean said evenly, 'he's got to pay for it, one way or another.'

'He will pay – in prison,' I said. 'They'll lock him up and throw away the key for what he's done here.'

But even as I spoke I knew that the courtrooms didn't always bring justice to the guilty. I could just see O'Bryan swivelling his way onto a lesser charge, overriding the evidence of a fourteen-year-old thief.

Particularly if that thief was no longer alive to give it in person.

Sean knew it, too. 'Even if he gets life,' he said. 'Life doesn't mean *life* any more, Charlie. With good behaviour and remission, he'll be back out sooner than you think.'

He glanced up at me then, and although the firelight crackled in his eyes, his face was very calm, as though he'd had a vision. 'I want more than that for him,' he said. 'I *need* more than that.'

'You can't have it, Sean,' I said, and the pain of denying him cut like glass. 'If you're thinking of trying, you know I'll have to stop you, don't you?'

Sean didn't answer right away. He carefully flexed the fingers of his left hand, finding they were still just about under his control. He broke the Browning and checked the cartridges, snapped it shut again.

'Well,' he said at last, cold, hard, almost a stranger, 'let's just hope it doesn't come to that.'

Twenty-nine

In the end, we didn't have to look far.

We'd commenced the best search pattern we could manage with just the two of us, moving in a zigzag layout across the waste ground, when a shout rang out.

'Hold it right there!' O'Bryan's voice rolled across the brickwork and echoed around us like gunfire.

We spun round fast, hearing the crunch of the broken-up masonry under our feet. Automatically, I brought the Glock up in a double-handed grip, heart revving.

O'Bryan was thirty metres away, edging out from behind the rubble with the FN nine millimetre he'd used to kill Nasir Gadatra gripped clear in his fist.

There was a half-heartbeat pause, then I straightened up slowly, letting the gun drop to my side. What was the point?

Thirty metres is a long shot with a handgun. Don't believe most of what you see in the movies. The greatest distance I'd fired over with a pistol on the army ranges had been fifteen metres, and most of the time it was half that.

Even so, I'd been good enough to have winged O'Bryan, despite the distance involved. It wasn't that which stayed my hand, and had Sean lowering the Browning defeatedly.

'Sensible people,' O'Bryan called, close to jeering.

He had Roger in front of him as a shield, holding the boy roughly by the collar of the coat Sean had put him into. If I'd been more familiar with the Glock, I might have risked it even at that range, but I just couldn't. Until this whole sorry business, I hadn't even picked up a gun in more than four years, for Christ's sake.

Roger looked white. There was a smear of blood across his cheekbone which stood out starkly in contrast. He seemed dazed, stumbling over the uneven ground, but at least he was still alive. I was suddenly aware of an overwhelming urge to keep him that way.

O'Bryan shook the boy, as though he was faking it, snapping his head back and forth. I could feel the rage building in the tensing of Sean's body beside me.

I growled his name under my breath, wasn't sure the warning had any real effect.

'Let's see those guns. Nice and slow,' O'Bryan ordered. 'Take the magazine out of the pistol, Charlie. That's it, good girl. No tricks, or the boy's dead.'

I complied with stiff fingers, thumbing the release and dropping the magazine into my hand with slow and deliberate movements. Only Sean knew the weapon was already cocked, the first round already lying snug in the breech.

I threw the magazine out sideways into the darkness, making a big show of it. But the gun itself I let fall much closer, so that it came to rest only a little way past Sean. I saw his eyes skim over it, and knew at once that he was aware of what I'd done.

O'Bryan made him break the shotgun and pick out the live cartridges, then send the weapon spinning into the rubble. It landed with a dull clatter, kicking up the dirt. Sean did as he was ordered with a rigidity born of a cold, icy anger, needle sharp.

When it was done O'Bryan smiled widely, the light from the fire behind us flaring on the lenses of his glasses. In his grey anorak and his sensible shoes he looked like everyone's idea of the friendly uncle, or the family vicar. How many people, I wondered, had trusted him. How many kids had he corrupted, and betrayed.

'Why?' I said. I didn't think about the question. It arrived already spoken. 'Why did you do all this?'

If anything, O'Bryan's smile grew wider. He tut-tutted. 'Oh Charlie, so naïve for one so cynical,' he said with mock sadness. 'Money, of course. I like money. It's not the be-all and end-all, but it certainly has a healthy cushioning effect against the harsher realities of life.'

'That's it?' I demanded, filled with a sense of anti-climax, of disbelief. 'You're not trying to tell me that a few nicked video recorders are really worth killing someone for?'

O'Bryan almost snorted. 'You really don't see the big picture, do you, Charlie? The annual turnover from the credit card haul alone is worth killing a dozen punk kids like Nasir Gadatra.'

'There must have been another way to make a decent living,' I said quietly.

'Oh, probably, but why go to all that trouble when I had the perfect means and opportunity handed to me on a plate? These kids are cheap, willing to learn if you give them the right motivation.' O'Bryan was still smiling as though this was all some big joke to him. 'Besides, I hate to see things go to waste, get put on the scrap-heap. I suppose that's why I like my classic cars so much.'

'And what do you think you've been doing to kids like Roger by getting them involved in your grand design, if not wasting their lives?' Sean said tightly.

O'Bryan's smile faded, as though he'd hoped we'd under-stand his vision, and was disappointed that we obviously did not.

'They were already well on the scrap-heap by the time they got as far as my office,' he said, sharply. 'They were never going to be useful members of society, but they did have certain – talents, in other directions.'

He paused, settled himself. 'All I did was tap into that latent talent and utilise their existing skills,' he said, as though he was expecting adulation. 'In return for that I gave them order, discipline, and a suitable financial reward. I gave them more stability than most of them ever got from their damned families! I care about these kids! Where were *you* when Roger needed you, hm?'

'So,' Sean bit out, 'where do we go from here?'

'We?' O'Bryan asked with a nasty grin. 'Oh, *we* don't go anywhere.'

Once he'd got the two of us disarmed, he'd urged Roger forwards, until we were only three or four metres apart.

I could see the sweat rolling down O'Bryan's temples. Realised that he was as hyped up with the thrill as with the fear. I'd seen that look before, and it terrified me.

In the split second before he moved, it came to me what he was going to do. I had no time to react, to do anything to intervene.

I could only stand beside Sean and watch, horrified, as O'Bryan shifted his grip so he had Roger held firmly across the throat with his forearm. He looked straight at Sean, and he smiled.

Then he shot his brother in the back at point-blank range.

Roger's body jerked with shock, limbs dancing. He gave a single hiccuping cough, then his eyes rolled upwards leaving only the whites showing, and he went down like a stone.

O'Bryan let go and allowed the boy to drop away from him without a glance, as though he was no more than a carelessly discarded cigarette wrapper. His eyes never left Sean's taut face, and an expression of savage glee never left his own.

Sean stood locked, immobile. Both of us stared at the slumped figure, desperately searching for some flicker of life. A trickle of breeze ruffled a lock of Roger's hair. Apart from that, there was nothing.

He'd landed half on his face, one hand stretched out towards us, the fingers curled in the dirt. The smell of cordite hung thick and bitter in the air. The hole in the back of Roger's jacket, surrounded by scorched powder burns from the cloaked muzzle flash, seemed a damning confirmation.

I glanced at Sean, but could read nothing from the bleakness of his features. Surely the vest should have been enough to save the boy. Did they work at such close distance without the extra plates he'd mentioned?

I looked back towards Roger, but still he hadn't moved.

'You bastard,' Sean whispered, giving me my answer. I turned my head numbly towards him, saw a cold death in his intentions, and was suddenly so afraid for him, what he might do, that it was like being dropped into a winter sea. 'I swear you'll burn in hell for that.'

'Very probably,' O'Bryan sneered. 'But I'll see you there first.'

The clock stopped. I turned my head back, so slowly it seemed, and watched with a mildly detached kind of interest as O'Bryan started to bring the gun up to fire.

My mind flashed ahead like a data-squirt down a modem line. One course of action came zinging back, almost blinding in its intensity. When I tried to analyse it afterwards it all seemed so cold-bloodedly simple, and so simply cold-blooded, that for a long time any thought of it made me shudder.

As O'Bryan's hand came up, my feet had already started to stir. I felt the sluggish transfer of my own weight from even spread, across onto my left leg. The rugged sole of my boot twisted a little until it gripped into the dirt. I used that purchase to launch my body sideways.

I could feel my heartbeat slamming out at an accelerated rate. Heard the thunder of it in my ears. The roar of my indrawn breath as it seared down into my lungs.

All the time, I kept my eyes locked on O'Bryan. Watched minutely as the hand holding the FN reached a level attitude. Was acutely aware of the whitening of the skin round his knuckles as he began to take up the pressure on the trigger.

I had no intention of getting to O'Bryan. He was too far away. I achieved my real objective though, completing my reckless leap in front of Sean, arms raised out by my sides as though in surrender.

As I did so, I could sense rather than see Sean start to move, as though I could hear the rasp of air as he used the cover I'd given him to dive for the Glock, with its single loaded round.

I don't think I'll ever be able to forget the expression that passed across O'Bryan's face at that point. Fleeting irritation, clearing rapidly as he recognised my intervention as a temporary one. One easily disposed of.

Then he shot me, twice, in the chest.

I saw the muzzle flash lance out as the first of the full-metal-jacket rounds launched from the end of the barrel at three hundred and sixty metres a second. Much too fast for the human ear to register the sound of the discharge. I was already reacting to the initial impact before anyone ever heard it.

I can't accurately describe what it's like to be shot while wearing body armour that isn't fitted with a ceramic plate.

Damned painful is the first thing.

Somehow, I'd expected to be punched backwards. Instead, my body just seemed to absorb the double shock internally, collapsing in on itself like a tower block going down under the delicately-placed charges of the demolition team.

I think I heard someone screaming as I fell.

I don't remember hitting the ground. I must have done

because the next thing I knew I was on my back with an inconvenient half-brick cricking my neck back. Breathing was difficult and hurt like hell. I was gulping in air in short, useless little pants like I'd just gone into labour.

To be honest, to begin with, I'd no idea how badly I'd been hit. I hadn't any past experience on which to base it. The whole of the front of my chest burned with a dead white heat. My eyesight started to buzz, graining my vision. All I could see was the heavens, cast orange from the distant sodium lights and the cloud-reflected looting fires along the next street.

Then another shot exploded into my awareness. It seemed so much louder than the first two, loud enough to make me twitch, which was, I discovered, altogether a deeply bad idea.

From a great distance, I became aware of the sounds of a scuffle. Someone was crying out, in pain and anger. There came the squelchy thuds and grunts of blows landing. The dull, muffled crack of a breaking bone, and a final shrill, whimpering cry.

I listened to the noises like they were the sound effects in a radio play. Half my mind was screaming at me to get up, to join in. The other half told me another minute's rest wasn't going to make much difference to the outcome one way or the other.

I started to slide into unconsciousness, the clamour growing further away, as insubstantial as the cries of seagulls circling a plough.

It was only as I slipped beneath the final layer that I heard the fourth and final gunshot.

By then I couldn't tell if it was real or imaginary. Whichever, it didn't seem dreadfully important any more. My vision was blackening at the edges like burning paper. The darkness rushed up to meet me and gratefully, like a coward, I gave in to it.

★

'Charlie! Come on, come back to me!'

Gradually I became aware that someone was shaking me. Why couldn't they just leave me alone? I was comfy where I was. Warm and dry.

They shook me again, more roughly this time, and I realised that actually I was freezing, and that damned brick was still under the back of my neck. To cap it all, I felt the first splashes of another burst of rain on my face. Just great.

I opened my eyes slowly and found Sean's face a few inches from my own. His nose was bloodied and there was a nasty cut over his right eye. It took me several seconds to register that the wetness I'd felt was caused by his tears, running freely down his cheeks and dripping onto me.

I reached up slowly, and wiped one of them away with a grimy thumb. I realised with a sense of small wonder that it was the first time I'd ever seen him cry.

'Christ. Jesus,' he managed at last. His voice cracked. 'Suppose he'd gone for a head shot!'

I gave him what passed for a shaky grin. 'He's not good enough, and he wanted to be sure,' I said, struggling to sit up.

The sudden stabbing pain in my chest made me gasp. I looked down and saw two small torn holes in the front of my sweatshirt, no bigger than the end of my finger. It was a sobering moment, but at least I didn't have a matching pair exiting out of the back.

O'Bryan's first hit had landed dead centre and, I discovered later, had cracked my sternum. He'd pulled his second, as people do when they're not used to, and not compensating for, the spent shell eject mech. That struck about three inches higher up and to my right, and left me with an exotically bruised cleavage, but did no lasting damage.

Sean met my eyes without speaking. As much as he could, one-handed, he helped me ease the sweatshirt off over my head. He yanked open the velcro straps to release the vest, peeling it away from my body. The inside of the chest section had two inch-deep indentations in the polycarbonate sheet, that corresponded exactly to the bruises I could already feel forming.

The vest itself was ripped and torn, the yellow kevlar inner showing through the holes. As Sean tossed it aside I thought I heard the metallic jingle of the stopped rounds rattling together somewhere in the lining. I made a whimsical mental note to retrieve them. Some souvenir.

Then I looked past him, and my heart lurched at the sight of two still figures lying near me on the ground.

'How's Roger?'

'He's OK,' Sean nodded towards the inert form of his brother. 'He fainted. He's probably bust a couple of ribs, but he'll be fine.'

I swallowed. 'And O'Bryan?'

'He's not so fine.' Sean gave an evil smile and for a moment I thought he'd given in to instinct, and to blind anger. 'Don't worry, he's not dead – he's just out cold,' he said.

The relief made me sag. 'What happened?'

'I managed to get to the Glock just before O'Bryan realised what I was doing. I think we must have fired at each other at almost exactly the same time.' He flashed me a quick grin. 'He missed. I didn't. Took a nice gouge out of his forearm.' He nodded towards his own injured shoulder. 'It levelled the playing field a bit.'

I shook my head, trying to clear it. 'But I heard another shot,' I said, puzzled.

Sean stood up then, seeming very dark and very dangerous. 'I said he wouldn't get away scot-free, Charlie,' he said. 'You just told me not to kill him. You didn't say I couldn't kneecap him.'

I had no sympathies for O'Bryan, but I winced at the thought of his shattered joint. 'Which leg?'

'The right,' Sean told me. He smiled again, a look of ultimate satanic satisfaction, of perfect revenge, but when he spoke his voice was completely calm and matter-of-fact.

'Even if he does get away with this, I'm afraid he'll have to sell those classic cars he's so fond of,' he said. 'Now he won't even be able to drive an automatic.'

Epilogue

The riot on the Lavender Gardens estate went on for two days and nights. By the time it subsided the estimate of the damage ran into millions. The police officers involved suffered numerous minor injuries. One unlucky constable lost an eye. The rioters themselves came off worse, on the whole, but there were no reported fatalities.

Later, they referred O'Bryan to an orthopaedic specialist for his shattered knee, but the man only confirmed Sean's field prognosis. The bullet, the specialist announced with no discernible irony, couldn't have done more damage if it had been carefully aimed.

Of course, O'Bryan had tried to claim that Sean had taken the FN away from him, wilfully breaking his arm in three places in the process, and had then deliberately shot him. By that time the jury weren't in any mind to listen.

The bullet Sean had fired from the FN entered O'Bryan's leg at an oblique angle, just above and to the inside of his patella, then exited again through the outside of his shin. En route it completely destroyed his knee joint beyond any hope of viable repair.

The best the surgeons could do was bolt the top and bottom of his leg solidly back together and leave it at that.

Even the prospect of an artificial joint was ruled out. Prison hospitals are little more than glorified health centres, and I gather that they aren't too well-equipped for that sort of procedure. Even if they thought he was worth the effort.

Besides, his now-permanent inability to operate an accelerator pedal was a bit of a moot point, anyway. The back of a prison sweat box was the only vehicle he was due to be climbing into for what was adding up to be a very long time.

MacMillan got O'Bryan cold for masterminding the local crimewave, and for Nasir's murder, thanks to the ballistics match on the FN nine millimetre Sean took away from him, and the evidence supplied by Roger.

They tried to rip the boy apart in court, of course, but Roger stubbornly refused to deviate from his statement. Besides, he had his brother sitting behind him every single day of the trial, to give him silent support, and I must admit I envied him that. In the end the jury was forced to believe the boy's dogged persistence.

And speaking of dogs, Madeleine managed, by luck or good judgement, to get Friday to the best vet in Lancaster. They reckon the Ridgeback will probably always carry a hind leg in cold weather, but it could have been so much worse.

It transpired that Mr Ali had skipped the country after our last encounter, but the police caught up with him at his holiday home in southern Spain. He was only too ready to come clean about his part in the build-up to the riot, and his involvement with Langford, and West.

The police were all set to arrest West for Langford's killing, but he seemed to have done a disappearing act. By some unspoken agreement, Madeleine, Sean and I conveniently omitted to mention our last sighting of the man.

And wherever Ian Garton-Jones has found to hide the body, it must be weighted down somewhere deep, because it still hasn't come to light. It gives me the odd passing qualm, the odd sleepless night, but it's no worse than my other nightmares.

I think I'll learn to live with it.

As for me, Sean offered me a job with his security firm. Quite a compliment, if rumours in the trade about the exclusivity of the outfit are to be believed, but I understand that the demand for female bodyguards generally far outstrips the supply.

Gender aside, he told me it takes a certain mindset to do what I'd done. To react coolly under that kind of intense pressure, and intentionally place yourself in the line of fire. He was really quite flattering about it.

Nevertheless, I turned him down.

You see, Sean thinks the reason I stepped in front of him was because I had complete faith in the stopping power of the body armour MacMillan had provided. But the truth is, having seen Roger go down with such apparent finality, I didn't really have the faintest idea if it was going to save me or not.

The implications of that one are not something I'm ready to think about just yet.

Sean gave me his business card, with his private line penned across the back. I've taped it to my phone so I don't lose it, and I probably look at it just about every day.

And who knows? One of these days, when I've worked out exactly what I still feel for him, I might even be able to make that call.

But I'm not holding my breath.